The Witch's Boy

Alex Beecroft

ISBN no: **978-1-84753-729-4**

The characters and events described in my books are fictitious. Any similarity to any person living or dead is merely coincidental.

All rights reserved. No parts of this publication may be reproduced, stored in a retrieval system, or transmitted, in any form or by any mean, electronic, mechanical, photocopying, recording or otherwise, without the prior permission of the copyright owner.

©Alex Beecroft

To Andrew, who believed in me more than I believed in myself. To my family, who are the best. To all my friends on the web who cheered me on in the writing process and celebrated with me when it was done. And to Black Hound, the immensely talented cover artist who designed this beautiful cover for love and marmalade. Thank you all!

Chapter 1

Chapter one

The door slammed open. Light blazed into the darkness as a massive, brown haired man strode into Oswy's cell. Scrambling to his feet, Oswy backed into the wall opposite, doing his best to look younger and more pitiful than his eleven years of age. It made no difference; within seconds he was pinned, an arm around his neck, one large hand clamped about both of his wrists. His heart hammered fiercely, and the humming started in his head, whining in counterpoint to his trembling.

Then the witch walked in, his blond hair tied back and his shirt sleeves rolled up. He carried a long thin knife and two large glass jars. To Oswy, hardly breathing now with fear, it seemed a shadow walked in with him, a shadow edged with bruise-colored fire.

"Hold the boy still," the witch said, his light voice barely audible to Oswy over the scaling notes of panic in his head. "I shall want the eyes and tongue first."

He came forward, the knife glimmering in his hand, his face full of anticipation. Oswy stopped breathing, stopped thinking, stood like a sparrow mesmerized by a snake, with his vision tinted red at the edges from the white noise of his fear, and the world stopping all around him, when suddenly the glass jars were wrenched from the witch's hand and smashed against the wall. Some unseen force lifted the pallet and blanket in the corner of the room and flung them in his face. He brushed them aside as though they had no more weight than a curtain, and smiled.

An invisible assailant hit the other man hard, splitting his lip. "Lord!" he cried, looking about himself wildly, his hand raised protectively before his mouth.

"Get out," said the witch, "Now." And the brown-haired man fled.

Something was screaming. Glass shards were flying in a lethal whirlwind around the room. Oswy started breathing again with a great sob of horror – this was almost worse than sudden death - backed into a corner and crouched there, cowering.

"Stop it!" he shouted, "Stop it!"

"You stop it. It is your doing."

"No it isn't!" wailed Oswy, frightened in a whole new way now, both body and soul. "It's not me!"

The witch paced calmly through the tempest of broken glass, the open door behind him turning his blond hair into a saint's halo. Nothing touched him. For a long moment, he stood looking down at Oswy, then he drew back his hand casually and slapped him hard across the face. One of his rings left a long red graze.

Oswy burst into tears. Around him, in the sudden hush, came the crash and tinkle of glass fragments falling to the ground. He buried his face in his hands and sobbed.

For a short eternity the witch-lord stood, studying him as he wept. Then, tentatively, he went down on his knees and pulled away the hand that covered the graze. "Why are you crying?" he asked, "I have hardly hurt you."

Wriggling further back into his corner, Oswy snatched his hand from the man's grasp – just the touch of it felt filthy in a way that had nothing to do with the good clean dirt he was accustomed to. If only he could squeeze himself through the mortar of the walls; turn himself into a cloud and float into the sky. If only he was a great warrior who could fight back. If only... If only the man would go away!

Eventually the witch got up again, dusted himself down as if fear could be as easily brushed off as dirt. "This was done to teach you two things," he said. "When we meet again I shall expect you to tell me what they were."

He stood a little longer, watching Oswy cry, then he turned silently and strode out.

Some time later the brown-haired man returned, carefully gathered up the broken glass into a ragged blanket and, when he had finished, came gently over to where Oswy crouched.

"I'm Leofwine. And you?"

"Oswy," it was difficult to get the breath out. He wanted them all to go away – the whole world to go away - so he could cry properly, on his own, in peace.

"Oswy?" Leofwine said, smiling, "'Glory of the heathen gods'? Yes, well that seems appropriate. Listen then, I'm sorry we frightened you, but my lord Sulien felt it was important to do so, and he has his reasons. He's gone off to Scricleah now, so there'll be no chance of accidentally meeting him, should

Chapter 1

you choose to come down to the kitchen. Why not come where it's warm, have something to eat?"

"Leave me alone."

"It does no good to mope," Leofwine frowned, straightening. "But I dare say I can spare you a few moments to recover your courage. Come down to the kitchen when you're done." He threw a contemplative, even sympathetic, look over his shoulder as he reached the door, but Oswy had the marks of the man's fingers going purple about his wrists and knew better than to trust this reversal into mildness.

When he had gone, Oswy huddled back into his itchy rags and gave himself up to misery, contemplating the open door with bitterness. They were so confident of his obedience, of their legal possession, that the open door was more of a symbol of slavery than any amount of chains. Inside or outside that door, there was still nowhere to go. His father had sold him to the witch for the price of a good milk-cow and one less mouth to feed. No amount of tears could wash away the memory.

"Come here, lad," his father had said. "We have a buyer for you."

"I don't want to go!"

Fear had been plain in his father's face, in his shaking voice; "We have to, son. You know why we have to. But that aside, you don't say no to this man."

Inside their shabby hut the air had been rank with the smell of fear – bitter and humiliating at once. His mother and sister had hidden behind a blanket in the smoke-loft in case the Holmr lord should be insulted at the sight of women, and without them he had felt defenseless, exposed. His brothers' gazes kept sliding away from him, to the hearth, where once he had lost his temper, and the cooking pots had burst apart. Ill-luck, they called him after that, and now the ill-luck had come home.

Against their squalor the witch-lord, with his poise and his fine clothes seemed almost godlike, deigning to haggle, his pleasant voice full of threat and amusement, playing with them.

Children grew up, in Oswy's village, with this man's name used as threat and blackmail against them. The rumors had been the climate of his infancy; the whispered hints, the stories the adults stopped telling when they saw him listening. He had never imagined the creature they spoke of could one day be sitting in his house, with a face carved and cold as a stone angel, and brown eyes which caught red glints from the fire, like a wolf's eyes in winter.

Oh he had expected to be sold, of course. He knew how bad the harvest had been, that this was the only way his family would all make it through to the spring. Dreams had even shown him his new place in a Lord's household - with two tunics, and bread to eat every day. He had been planning to work hard, be honest, to try and earn a little on the side so one day he could buy himself back. But those hopes died in him the moment he heard his buyer's name.

Yet the door *was* open. The door was open, he was unshackled, the witch had gone on an errand and his household was giving Oswy a moment to compose himself. *Why should I stay here,* he thought, suddenly, with a flare of astonishment and defiance. *Just to be cut up as ingredients for some witch's brew? Why should I?*

It was a heady thought. Was there anything out there that could be *worse* than belonging to Sulien FitzGuimar? Surely not. And therefore there was nothing to fear, other than staying here. Nodding to himself, fiercely, he wiped his eyes on the back of his hand, rearranging the dirt, and stood up.

The door made no sound as he pushed it further open. Pale sunshine lit the corridor outside, slanting in from arrow slits along the far wall. The autumn air carried the smells of water and smoke, the sound of starlings squabbling in the meadow beyond the moat, a bracing coolness.

An avid listener to tales, Oswy had followed the storytellers from village to village, learning the words. Now all the stories of heroes, who had escaped the dungeons of evil kings, came back to him, resting on his shoulders like an armor of strength. Straightening up, he began to walk quietly in search of the stairs.

A soft, muffled noise tugged at Oswy's curiosity, drawing him as surely as glitter draws crows. The door of a corner room was ajar, the sound stealing out - clearer now - identifiable as the labored breathing of someone trying very hard not to cry. Oswy edged closer, peered into the darkness.

It took a while for his eyes to adjust, but at last, dimly lit by the corridor's light, he made out a blond boy of about his own age sitting half naked in a chaos of knotted blankets and scattered clothes. He was lacing his shirt with hands that trembled. From a deep gash in his upper lip blood flowed splashing onto the white linen. He barely raised his head when Oswy came in.

Chapter 1

"What happened?"

The boy said nothing.

His abandoned tunic, which lay by the door, was Holmr style, embroidered and costly. Under the spreading bruises his skin was clean; there was no smell of him on the dusty air. But the yellow hair, the pallor, the shape of his face, were all Sceafn. After some thought Oswy concluded; *He's a Holmr Lord's bastard. Thrown away, now the legal heir has arrived. Half gentle, half wild. Rubbish, like me.*

"What happened to your lip?" he insisted.

The lad looked up with the angry snarl of a child who has been very badly hurt, but does not want anyone to know it, "What's it to you?"

"Hush, it's fine..." Oswy tried reassurance, in the voice he used to tame the stray dogs that whined around the door at home. He crouched down and offered a hand, which was ignored, "I've been crying too."

"I have not been crying!" the boy rounded on him with blazing eyes and clenched fists, his affronted dignity fierce and ridiculous, sharp but fragile as the broken glass. Still, Oswy knew better than to laugh.

He scuttled back a safe distance, "So what happened?"

Anger kept the boy bright for a moment longer, blazing like a spark. Then, like a spark, it went out and he slumped back against the wall, drained and surly. "He bit me."

"I'm escaping." With no idea what to reply to that and no desire to think about it long enough to form an idea, Oswy turned the pause with, he thought, impressive tact. "Come with me."

"It won't work," shifting position gingerly, the boy shook his head, "There's nowhere to go."

"I'm going home."

"Are you that much of a fool?" a hand went questing out, closed on blue linen hose. He pulled them on violently, without taking his challenging gaze from Oswy's face, "He will have killed them by now. Even if he has not, they'll be so terrified they bring you straight back."

"Oh," said Oswy blankly, and sat down by the edge of the pallet, some of the wind gone from his sails. The bastard was right of course, he could not go home.

"Noble or common," the boy thawed visibly as he realized he was not going to be mocked, "Everyone fears him. You'd get no help. And if you didn't tell them who you were running from - if you lied - when he came after you he would kill them. And that would be on your conscience for the rest of your life."

"We could go to the city," said Oswy after a moment's thought. "He'd never find us there – among so many people. We'd only have to work there for a year and a day, and we'd be free."

The boy glared at him, his fine dark eyes filled with misery and scorn beneath their long lashes. "That's very well for you, you're ugly. But I know what work they'd find for me in the City."

Even Oswy, who was no expert on such things, could see he was a very good looking boy. He did not exactly understand, but he knew enough to know he did not want to learn any more. "Church then," he said.

"They'd burn me."

"Why?" Oswy edged nearer. Dispiriting though the conversation was, it was nice to have company in this place – so full of threat and evil memories.

"Because I see things," said the boy, as if it should be obvious. "And I make things move."

"So do I." Competitiveness made the admission suddenly easier; "Make things move I mean."

"They'd burn you too then."

The knot that had unraveled in his chest when he made his decision to leave now began to tangle itself together again, catching at his throat, bringing back the threat of tears, and that was not something he was willing to indulge in front of this boy. "We could go to the forest."

"We'd get eaten by wolves or monsters," the little noble laughed bitterly, pressing his fingers to his lip and wincing at the sting, "Or caught by outlaws, which would be worse than the city. Or we'd starve. It's no good, we're stuck here."

Quickly, before the despair stuck and made his temporary courage desert him, Oswy got up. "I don't care. I'm going. At least I'm going to try. You can stay here with him if you like. I don't care."

He hurried to the door, but guilt and sympathy stopped him under the lintel, and he looked back at the misery on the boy's bloodstained face. "What will you do then?" he said, quietly.

Chapter 1

"Stay here," the lad replied, with an unexpected resolve which made him seem suddenly formidable. "Wait until he gets used to me... Then I'll kill him."

Oswy paused again, and admiration of this plan washed over him. That was what noble blood did for you, howsoever it was diluted. On impulse he said, "If they catch me, will you be my friend?"

"I would be. But how can I? You're not even real."

Looking out to check the corridor was clear, Oswy managed a chuckle. "Don't be stupid! Of course I'm real."

He turned back to say goodbye, but the room was empty; no clothes, no mattress and no boy. There was dust an inch deep on the floor except where Oswy had walked and sat. There were spider's webs around the doorway and in his hair. He thrust one grubby fist into his mouth and backed slowly into the corridor wall. It was cleaner there, the scrubbed stones a pale cream in the cool sunlight, but the hinges of that door were thick with rust.

"Sulien killed him," said Oswy softly to himself. "He must have come back and killed him."

He saw it all; the terrible murder, the boy's ghost condemned to eternity in the place of his death, the servants too frightened ever to come near the room again.

"Oh God!" said Oswy at last, "I've got to get out of here!" He turned and ran for the stairs.

They were the gentry stairs, whitewashed and painted with zig-zags and bright lines. Oswy's feet slapped sharply on them, the sound echoing up and down the spiral, but he was beyond stealth.

Where the steps were darkest there were lamps of glass. A smell of warm honey floated from the wax candles inside.

New friezes were painted on the walls, their gemlike colors glowing: A battle before the walls of Yocheved; the stars in their constellations; hunting at Shining Fell. It was not at all what Oswy had expected, and gradually the sheer beauty of it began to calm him down.

The stairs came to an end. There was a large ornate door to his right, but it was closed. The corridor stretched on before him.

Don't run, he said to himself firmly, *Sibyrt didn't run in the monster's den. Besides, they always stop you if you run.* Nevertheless it was a great effort to walk quietly down the corridor and look inconspicuous as he turned the corner.

There were the great doors of the keep, standing open, with the meadowsweet scent of grass streaming through them on a cool wind. And a guard's cell before them, the shadow of a guard huge on its wall.

Oswy dithered in the corner for a moment and then, taking himself in hand, he said a quick prayer and headed for the doors. He was just an inquisitive boy, the son of one of the servants, come in to gawp at the keep while the master was away. He strolled on.

The guard looked up from his knife curiously and watched him. Oswy walked on.

"Hey, Boy!" called the guard.

Oswy carried on walking. The man got up slowly, and Oswy increased his pace.

"Answer me," the guard insisted.

Oswy was almost past him by now, walking fast, his heart pounding.

"Here. Stop!" Yelling, the guard reached for his spear. Oswy began to run.

Nothing stopped him as he pelted out of the keep doors, the guard's footsteps loud behind him. Straight out and down the path he ran. It was past noon, bright and clear, the few people working in the enclosure could see him perfectly. Some paused in their tasks to watch.

The guard came running. "Stop him!" he shouted, "It's the new boy. Don't let him get away."

Oswy dived for the cover of an outbuilding. A workshop of some kind; tools were scattered about the floor, beams propped on trestles. The roof was falling in, rotten thatch trailing, and the upper level was rickety, swaying under Oswy's weight as he scrambled up the ladder. There was a worm-eaten barrel in one corner, filled with shards of glass. He wedged himself in the gap between that and the eaves.

Someone came in. He heard their feet shuffling in the sawdust, their breath soft beneath him. A second shadow darkened the door. Caught!

"He came in here," said the man below.

Chapter 1

"Nay," said the figure in the doorway, a woman by the voice. "He did not." There was a strange insistence in her tone. Oswy felt the man hesitate.

"Poor little lad," the woman went on, "would it be such a bad thing if he got away?"

There was a silence, and then the man said, "Bad for us maybe."

"Please..." prayed Oswy. There was the sound of movement at the foot of the ladder.

"Well," the man sighed at last, "I've looked and I can't see him."

"Oh Brand," the woman replied fondly. They went away.

He heard Brand shout, "Not in this one! Try the next," and the sound of heavy feet retreating, but he dared not move, not yet.

Hours, he waited, at first on tenterhooks between relief and fear, then, as the short autumn day dwindled and no one else came, in increasing misery. It was cold. The smell of mildew reached deep into his throat, and he was cramped and hungry. Worse than that, he had time to think.

He wanted to go home. He wanted to be in his place by the fire, watching mother stirring the great stew-pot, listening to Cine and Freda quarreling, Wulf intervening with his patronizing elder brother voice, father watching, silent and exhausted on his bench.

Oswy's mother always knew when he was afraid. She would come and sit beside him, busy with the baby, and tell him stories of the old heroes, in the days before the Holmr. He wanted very badly to be back there, for everything to be set right. He didn't even know if they were still alive. Perhaps the witch had gone back and killed them all, as the boy had said he would, but he would never know. They would look for him first at home. He could not go back, not even to check.

He would go to the city, and find a trade. The city was only three days walk away, and he wouldn't have any trouble there because he was ugly.

Really ugly? He felt himself prepared to cry even at this. Perhaps that was why they had sold him and not Wulf; they couldn't bear to look at him. Would anyone in the city want to shelter him? His own family didn't. And what if they brought him back, or the witch found him? Oh. He would be angry. It didn't bear thinking about. Maybe he would just starve to death on the way, and then everyone would be happy.

The sound of people coming in to the enclosure for the evening roused him. There was the lowing of cattle, the staccato beat of their hooves, and chat among the cowmen. By the sound of it there was a fair herd being brought in to the byre.

Oswy knew cattle; how to calm them and make them accept him. It would be warm to sleep among them, and he could get milk. He edged away from the wall, stiff and sore from sitting, and went down the ladder gently.

He waited while the herd settled down, watching through a hole in the mortar of the wall while the cowmen and herd-boys left for their homes outside the bailey. Gradually as the sky darkened the compound emptied, until only the animals in their pens remained.

He heard the slam of the gates, two guards talking, their voices carrying far on the evening air. There seemed to be only two guards for the whole span of palisade, and so naturally, with the master gone, they were together by the fire in the guard-house.

Under cover of a clamor from the kennels he slipped out of the door and walked as calmly as possible between the gardens to the byre. His heart was racing as he reached it, but there was no alarm. He found a mound of cleanish straw, burrowed into it and went to sleep, waking up in the middle of the night to take a drink.

When he was warm and fed, and with the familiar smell of cattle around him, he felt better: He would go to the city and do well, and when he was rich someday his family would come to him for help without knowing who he was, just like Saint Asaph in the story, and everything would be put right.

He awoke again in the bitter cold of the early morning, with the dreary light of dawn just showing over the battlements. The cattle were stirring, nosing him curiously and eating his bedding. He rubbed dirt into his face and hands and made sure his bare feet were thoroughly muddy, so that no gleam of white skin would betray him. Then, coming out around the back of the byre, he edged along the walls until he could hide again behind a pile of rubble just by the left hand gate-tower, and wait for the gates to be opened.

Soon after dawn a guard came, blowing on his hands in the chill morning, let down the bridge with a great rattle of chains, and opened the gates. People began coming in almost immediately, but going out involved passing the lighted gate-house and he could not bring himself to do it.

Chapter 1

The sky began to lighten. Two horses were led out to exercise by a vacant faced old man wearing a cast off tunic at least three times too large for him. Maids came in, barefaced, with empty pails, giggling. The cattlemen strolled in in a knot together talking stock, two herd-boys, exchanging insults, running before them. Oswy watched them carefully, with the glimmering of an idea.

He waited, losing more of the darkness, until the cattle began to come out. Then as they jostled past him he darted out of hiding and in among them. Shouting "Coo-oop" and hitting the bony rumps like a zealous herder he passed the shadow of the gate, turning his face away from the gaze of the guard.

At a brief glance the world seemed very wide to him as he passed into it. Then the cows barged into him and one of the herd-boys said "Hey! You're not..." and he was running again.

Down the steep hill he charged while the cattlemen conferred with leisurely dignity behind him, and across the boulder-strewn strip beyond. By the time they had decided to send a lad back to tell the guard he had passed into the forest and was hidden in the dense undergrowth.

He had made it. He was free.

Chapter Two

By afternoon Oswy was lost. He could not have said how it had happened, he had just been too eager to get away. Now he was surrounded by oak and ash in autumn gold, russet bracken underfoot, leaves falling through the cathedral hush. There were knotted branches and writhing roots in every direction; fallen trees holding up circles of earth, pits beneath them, toadstools in damp array on their sides. He found a great rose-bush - spotted leaves lying limply on a tangle of withies and thorns - and pulled off handfuls of hips. Their intense taste did nothing to relieve his thirst.

Every so often he would climb a tree and stand swaying on the top branches, trying to see some landmark by which to guess where he was. There was nothing but trees sloping up to the sky, or in places moor beyond the forest, brown and bare. He could not even see the witch's keep, though he knew it had stood on the high ground. He had thought he would recognize the shapes of the hills, but they looked different from here. First one then another would present a shape he thought familiar, only to change after a little walk. He had no idea where the road might be.

By the early evening he was getting desperate. He had found some late ripening brambles and devoured every berry, and there were thistles and pig-nuts to eat, but he was so thirsty he could barely think for it.

The night was coming and he had no flint, nor steel, no knife, no blanket. There might be frost in the night, or wolves. There were sure to be monsters this close to Shining Fell; spirits who drown children; trees who stalk; the winter Hags of the elder; and elves hunting for pleasure. He did not want to be alone in the forest in the dark.

A crow, frightened by his passage, flew up from the brush almost into his face. He cried out shrilly, clapping his hands over his face and sliding to his knees. Bats, startled, shrieked through the trees and about his head.

"Oh God!" he whispered, cowering, "Oh God, Benel, help me!"

Voices spoke around him in the trees. They were not human voices. He scrambled up and ran like a hart flushed from cover. Branches snapped at him, thistles and brambles scratching his feet and tearing his tattered hose. He

Chapter 2

kept running until he fell, his legs unable to bear him any more, his breath like fire in his throat, the world gray and silver before his eyes. He lay there a long time, listening, but there was no sound except the sigh of the wind in the trees. Whatever it had been he had escaped it.

When his sight came back to him and he could stand again he looked about for a tree to climb. One last attempt to find out where he was. Perhaps that mad dash had brought him close to the road.

Grimly holding on to his hope he shinned up a tall ash and looked out on the darkening valley. There, marvelously, only a couple of hundred yards away a pillar of white smoke showed. Then as he watched a second went up, sparks bright as flowers spiraling in it.

"Thank you! Oh thank you!" he said, gazing at the smoke with joy, and savored the moment a little before scrambling down and losing the sight.

He was careful this time, walking slowly, checking his direction often, and with the care he had time to remember that this might be outlaws, and that it needed careful handling whoever it was. As he neared the fires and could smell them through the trees he began to go stealthily. Finally he went down on his belly and wriggled through the bracken at the edge of the clearing stealthy as a serpent.

It was a fair camp, three spear-tents pegged between trees, a path cut to the further clearing, people passing to and fro, and a cauldron steaming over the fire. Now and then a face would be picked out by the flames, disembodied like a brief vision of the Abyss. Some were men whom Oswy recognized, vaguely, as villagers from Wyrmbank seen at the market in Scricleah. They were no outlaws, just plain men like himself. What were they doing here? Foraging? Cutting wood? It didn't look like it.

Still, they were ordinary people who might have sympathy for a boy lost in the woods, and by the look of the cauldron they had food to spare.

He left the shelter of the bracken and began to walk across to the fire. A youth with a bow, watching the perimeter, called out an alarm and two men walked out to meet him. Both carried spears.

"I'm so glad to see you!" said Oswy, earnestly, "Where am I?"

"Who are you, lad?" asked the elder of the two, a tall, graying man in a plain tunic of brown wool. There was a curious mix of suspicion and sympathy on his face.

"Cedda," said Oswy, "From Caster. My master sent me with a message to Hrolf Baker of Osford, and I got lost on my way back."

Witch's Boy

"How did you come to leave the road?" said the man, and Oswy, pleased with the attention, decided to elaborate.

"I thought I saw something." As he had seen his mother do, when she was storytelling, he threw a little doubt and disbelief into his face and posture, pausing for effect.

"What?" the gray-beard's voice was now no longer indifferent; he was hooked. Oswy smiled inwardly, and went on, hesitant as if he hardly dared speak.

"I saw a white lady," he said, "She was weeping and I went to comfort her. I don't know how to say it. As I got nearer she got further away. I followed her, all night, but in the morning I looked up and she weren't there no more. Then I saw I was lost. She was a very pretty lady."

The man was looking at him pityingly. "City lad are you?"

Oswy nodded.

"Thought so. A country boy would have more sense than to go traipsing after elves. Well, you'd better come and get warm. You can stay here tonight and we'll set you back on the road tomorrow. How's that?"

"Thank you," said Oswy happily, "It's all I hoped."

A little while later, warmed and fed, he was repeating his story, with embellishments, to three of the younger men, while the elders stood in small knots talking quietly over their beer. It was fully dark now, and the light of the fire was bright. Through the trees the blaze of the second fire and the flicker of standing torches could be seen. The sound of a lute floated on the evening breeze, and laughter, the loud assured laughter of men.

"Who's over there?" Oswy asked, nodding at the path. A young man named Ketil looked up,

"Sir Fulk of Kinridge," he said, "And Lord Robert of Rainford with their hunting party. We're beating for them."

A minstrel's trained voice, pure and sexless as an angel's, carried a strain of melody into the night. The fire crackled and flared. A tall red-bearded man came down the path and stopped at the sight of Oswy.

"Oswy son of Ottar of Mereton," he said, "What are you doing here?"

"Cyneheard!" Oswy exclaimed, and horror swooped on him. It was no use denying he knew the man; Cyneheard was a close neighbor and could not be fooled.

Chapter 2

He half rose, instinct again urging him to flee, but now every eye in the camp was on him, and Ketil had gripped the skirt of his tunic, holding him by it. He sank back into his place, defeated. All his plans, all his cleverness in affecting an escape, his day spent frightened and lost, all for nothing.

He looked up at Cyneheard with pleading eyes; "Oh please," his voice trembled a little on the brink of tears, "please don't send me back there. Please don't. You don't know what he's like. He'll kill me."

"Cyneheard?" said the greybeard who had first spoken to Oswy, "It's plain you know the boy, yet he gave a very different name. Why does he lie?"

"I know him well, Godwine." Cyneheard nodded to himself, "He's the son of a neighbor of mine, and he was sold yestereven to Lord Sulien of Harrowden. I spoke to Ottar, the boy's father, only this morning."

"Magister Sulien?" Ketil's eyes were wide.

"Yes," said Cyneheard, "Sulien the witch."

There were little movements throughout the group; men drawing back from Oswy as if from a leper. One or two made a sign of warding. Ketil let go of his tunic as though it stung.

Oswy knew the reaction; no one liked to be too close to misfortune. Not for the first time he felt how much it hurt. "Please," he begged.

"If Lord Sulien finds out we've sheltered him," whispered Ketil in a voice full of fear, "And he will find out..."

"Someone will have to take him back," Godwine nodded, "and quickly."

"Not I," muttered Ketil.

"Nor I," the hasty denial came from all sides.

Godwine looked around, "Do none of you dare take a little boy back to his master? There might even be a reward for him."

The murmur of denial increased. Godwine sighed. "Well," he said, "nor do I."

Oswy looked up hopefully.

"Sir Fulk would dare," Ketil suggested after a moment's thought. "Couldn't we turn the boy over to him?"

"Is he a good humored man?" asked Cyneheard doubtfully.

"He doesn't expect too much from us." Ketil shrugged, "And he can be generous. If he has had good cheer this evening it would be best to ask now."

The men of Kinridge nodded in agreement with this.

"Very well," said Godwine. "You can speak for us, Ketil, Fulk is your lord. I'll stand by you. Now find some rope and we'll tie the boy up."

Oswy fought fruitlessly against this treatment, earning himself a box about the ears and ensuring, if anything, that the ropes were tighter than they might have been. He was dragged along the path pleading and sobbing. The Lords paused over their wine to watch him.

They were sitting at the upper end of a great table, pavilioned in crimson canvas and lit by many lamps. The scent of the freshly split logs could still be smelled beneath the wood smoke and the wine. There were dogs at the feet of the lords, and hawks perching in the shadows behind them.

Oswy stopped his struggling to gaze at them; Fulk, a gray-haired man in a tunic of blue silk, with a kindly face and a broken nose; Robert beside him, a spare man with the sallow Holmr coloring, and a frown almost as dark as his hair. William, Robert's son, was looking on with amusement, and Fulk's two lads had only glanced up briefly before returning to their game. The household retainers, the minstrels, cwens, and hangers on were all too obviously waiting for their masters' reactions before committing themselves to anything.

"My Lord Fulk," began Ketil in a shaky voice.

Fulk regarded him for a moment, frowning with thought, and then ventured, "Ketil of Hulme farm?"

Ketil nodded, and Fulk put down his cup, saying "What is the trouble?"

"A runaway slave my Lord. We brought him for your doom."

"The boy? Let me see him."

Oswy was shoved forward into the light. The Lords made a brief assessment of him and seemed instantly to lose interest.

"He must go back to his master, obviously," Fulk said. "Whose slave is he?"

"Lord Sulien of Harrowden's."

There was a perceptible stir around the table. The minstrels looked up with eager eyes.

The cwens fluttered like bright birds, their heavy imitations of fine ladies adding a further touch of unease to Oswy's despair. He was not used to this Holmr custom; men allowed to become substitute women, while the real women were locked away for the sake of decency. Oddly, the idea scared him. As his mother had once said; "A people capable of that are capable of anything."

"Leave the boy here then," Fulk said, seemingly unimpressed. "One of my servants will return him tomorrow."

Ketil and Godwine bowed themselves away, smiling with relief. A knight of Fulk's party came forward and took hold of Oswy. At a nod from his lord he tethered him securely to a stake set well within the light of the fire.

It was a miserable ending, Oswy felt, to all his toil - tied up like a strayed sheep, alone and afraid in the middle of someone else's feast. Hoping for some act of kindness, some little gesture of pity, he began to cry, listening for a softening in the voices which spoke over his head. It didn't come.

"The boy should be whipped," Robert looked down with a face of prim disapproval. "I'll have one of my men see to it."

"I wouldn't advise it," Fulk replied.

"He has to be taught he can't run away just as he wishes."

"He will have lessons enough when he gets back to his master."

"'Lord Sulien!'" Robert scoffed, "There's not a drop of noble blood in the man."

"Ah," Fulk replied in a tone of reminiscence. "That's not entirely true."

"No?" William leaned forward, a larger man, with a more open expression than his father; curiosity written plain in every feature.

"No," said Fulk. "He is the son of Guimar Lord of Scricleah, and for several years was his heir."

"Guimar's wife only had one son, and that was Odo," said Robert skeptically.

"Oh yes," Fulk agreed. "Sulien's mother was Sceafn; she was taken as a trophy after the battle for Caster. Guimar kept her for some years, and raised the boy as his own." He chuckled, reminiscing, "Aldith was her name. A very pretty thing she was too, going about barefaced, the way the Sceafn women used to - even the ladies - and proud, though she was a slave. Her son is just as proud, despite his birth."

"Bastards!" William exclaimed, with a man-of-the-world air, "They're nothing but trouble."

"And the ones raised with expectations," his father agreed, "they're the worst."

"Don't say that too loudly in front of the King," said Fulk mildly. "You know what his younger brother is, after all," and he shouted for more wine.

It was late in the evening now, the first fury of merrymaking over; time to tell tales and savor the warmth of the fire, and for Oswy, sitting on the damp earth, his arms beginning to hurt from the ropes, it was perhaps the worst time of his short life. Time to wonder what would happen to him when he got back.

Nightmare images, each more horrible than the last, chased through his mind. He listened to the lords' voices with a kind of desperation, trying to drown out the thoughts, trying to glean some comfort, but the crying had taken on a life of its own, and he could not stop.

"I'll say this for Sulien," said Robert - the lords seemed settled now to the discussion of this painful subject.

If only they would talk about something else, Oswy thought, but they went on, and he went on listening, afraid to miss any small clue which might be of help when he was taken back.

"Because he's a witch," Robert was saying, "the peasants are terrified of him. I don't think they'd bring a slave of mine back with such alacrity."

"They're superstitious fools," said William. "'Trafficking with dark powers' indeed! If he really has such power behind him, why isn't he King of Sceafige by now?"

Robert turned in his seat nervously, as if the conversation irked him. "Stop bawling, slave!" he shouted suddenly, aiming a gobbet of half-chewed fat at Oswy's head, "Or I'll give you something to complain about. I hate whining children."

"Sulien doesn't frighten me." William was still talking, laying a heavy hand on the hilt of his eating knife. He was a tall, well built young man, and his easy confidence and swagger reminded Oswy of the village bully, before he had taken on a man-at-arms from Scricleah and been trounced.

There was a surprising amount of satisfaction in the thought of this complaisant invader taking on Oswy's master; being broken and shamed. Let him find out for himself why Oswy was so scared.

Fulk was looking at William with a slight smile, "Have you ever met him?"

Chapter 2

"No," said William. "And I have no desire to. What is he after all but a common slaveson who came to his manor by theft?"

"I used to be of the same opinion." A hound nosed at Fulk's foot and he paused to give it a bone from the table. One of the minstrels picked up his rebec and began to play quietly, a simple little tune without words. A jongleur got up from his place in the shadows, but was waved down again.

"I knew him when he was a child," Fulk went on, eventually, "and apprentice to Lord Tancred of Harrowden."

"Apprentice?" William scoffed. "Lords don't have apprentices!"

"Oh," said Fulk, "there's no doubt Tancred was a witch. Now there was an evil man; always on the lookout for someone to hurt. He could kill cattle just by looking at them and children by speaking their names, and he often did. A group of knights, about ten years back, went up to burn him out. They never got close to the place and by the next morning every one of them, and their families, were dead. Their lines are utterly obliterated and their manors have reverted to the King. Few people dare speak of it even now."

Fulk paused, motioning to his cup-bearer. The youth took up the wine pitcher and went round the table once more, refilling the cups of Lords and knights.

This is just a pleasant story for them, Oswy thought, bitterly, *with a bit of horror just for salt. But for me...*

Plainly his master's evil went back a generation; he had been trained in it, steeped in murder since childhood. Of course he wouldn't stop to have pity on a nobody like Oswy. The tears came faster. *I'm worth nothing.* Oswy concluded miserably. *They'll just give me back because I'm worth nothing to any of them.*

"When Tancred walked into a room," Fulk took up his full cup and continued, "it was as though Death himself had come in. Every eye fixed itself on him in terror, and silence fell. More often than not Sulien was with him, but he was nothing; a dog at his master's heel. I never knew him to speak, or even to raise his head and look at a man, but he was there. When Tancred desired a man's body-fat to make candles Sulien would be there holding the bowl. As he grew up he became very strong, and Tancred would have him hold the victims down for slaughter. He would do it surly as a whipped dog, but he would never refuse. He was far from innocent."

A nightjar called from somewhere close by, its eerie cry loud in the darkness. Oswy's heart spasmed, silencing him. Several men started nervously. Fulk smiled and went on,

"So, when we heard Tancred had fled, the four of us got together: I, Giles, your grandfather, God rest him, John of Wyrmbank and Odo of Scricleah (Sulien's half-brother, if you remember). We took our most renowned knights and went to raze his stronghold and burn Sulien out.

"We went in the broad morning because our men could not be commanded to approach the place by night. We found the drawbridge down, the gates open, the walls scorched and burnt, or torn apart; stone had been rent from stone as though a giant had smitten them. Not a living soul was on the walls or in the enclosure. We rode in, and there was absolute silence all about us; a silence of the dead.

"At the foot of the keep stair all five of my knights refused to go on. These were men brave as lions, tested in battle again and again. I would have trusted my life to any one of them. Yet here, before any threat had been made, knowing they faced only one man, they balked. Odo made much of it, until his men did the same. It was at that point we realized sorcery was being used against us. There was nothing we could do but go on ourselves, leaving them behind. After all, there were four of us, and we were not afraid.

"The stairs were strewn with loose stones, the treads at all angles and unsafe, the walls again were burnt and in places oozing with some slime which seemed to crawl upwards from the floor. Above the first level the spiral was broken and choked, impassable, and we had to make our way through the Great Hall and up the servant's stairs. Devastation was everywhere, and nowhere any sign of life.

"'He's fled too,' said Odo, his voice loud in the deserted corridors. (Odo was sixteen at the time, new come out of fosterage, strong as a bear and full of himself.)

"'No,' said Giles, 'Or our men would be here'."

"We filed into the solar, not knowing what we would meet, and he was there, waiting for us. He stepped out of the shadows by the side of the cold hearth and the sunlight picked out his face and hands. There was blood all over him, and burns, but he was smiling a little satisfied smile. We stopped, frozen like birds in front of a stoat."

Fulk shook his head, "Four knights in full battle armor, swords and maces in our hands, and an unarmed man cowed us with a glance.

Chapter 2

"'So,' said Sulien, looking at us all with contempt, 'You heard the master had fled, and you thought; Let's go and burn out the little weak apprentice.' He laughed. 'You failed to consider,' he said, 'what it was the master had fled from.'

"John and I exchanged worried glances; it did put a rather different perspective on our expedition. Sulien watched us with amusement.

"'Why don't you sit down,' he said, 'And we'll discuss my terms.'

"'Terms?' asked Giles.

"'Terms for your life,' said Sulien pleasantly, 'And for your freedom.'

"He was in a strange humor; exultant, like a soldier after battle when he turns to the villages, intent on looting and rape. I was afraid of him.

"'Who do you think you are?' Odo snarled - perhaps he remembered his childhood, being always the second-rate shadow in Sulien's wake – 'You should be pleading for your own life.'

'Plead?' laughed the witch, 'With you?' He shook his head at Odo's stupidity and stepped forward into the range of the blade.
'I'd sooner die,' he said. 'Strike me down then, if you can.'

"We watched as Odo struggled to move. He made what seemed to be a huge effort, straining until the sweat ran from him, but to no avail. Then Sulien took up a saw-edged knife from the table and pressed the sharp teeth to Odo's face. Not one of us could move.

"'I could kill you now,' said Sulien to his brother in a voice which was soft with pleasure, 'and, believe me, Odo, I would enjoy it.'
"He moved the knife slightly, smiling, and blood began to run down the blade and over his hand.
"'Shall we discuss terms?' he said.

"We discussed terms," Fulk concluded ruefully. "Or, rather, he set them down and we agreed to them. We counted ourselves lucky to get out of there alive, and by agreement we never spoke of it again. no one likes to be shamed. I'm sorry I had to tell this, Robert, I only did it because William here seems to have the desire to take him on. Don't do it, lad. Not unless you want young Henry to be your father's heir."

Fulk drained his cup abruptly and retired to his tent. The courtiers seemed not to know how to react to this tale of defeat and slipped away silently, one by one. Oswy wished he had not listened. He thought of the reception he would get when they took him back tomorrow and, loudly, he began to cry again.

Robert looked up, his face black with anger. "I've had enough of that boy's whining!" he shouted, "Hugh! Get over here and give him a good beating!"

A hard-faced man strode up to Oswy and, taking him by the hair, dragged him to his feet and held him upright. A second servant cut four birch twigs and with them, efficiently, he beat Oswy until the boy fainted.

When he roused, from pain and cold, it must have been little later - the fire had not sunk far - but still the camp had gone to bed. He sat alone in the silence for a very long time, and dared not even weep.

Just after dawn the man Hugh came back and wordlessly tied Oswy, hand and foot, over one of the pack horses. Then, silent and grim, he led it, none too carefully, out of the camp, into the pathless forest. Branches slapped and tore at Oswy's face and bloody back, but he lay quietly, certain now that nothing he could do would bring any gesture of kindness from anyone.

They passed out on to the road, and rain, in a fine mist unnoticed under the trees, began to soak their clothes and to spread, gentle and cold, into Oswy's cuts. Hugh muttered to himself, drawing up his hood. The horse blew at the cold droplets on its whiskers and put its head down. They trudged on, brown leaves falling on either side of them and the road turning to mud beneath them. Eventually, despite everything, Oswy fell asleep with his cheek against the horse's warm flank.

Sulien's voice woke him saying, with barely suppressed fury, "Who did this?"

"My master ordered it," Hugh replied, hurriedly.

Oswy opened one eye and saw Hugh backing away, face ashen with fear, Sulien stalking him, white knuckled, Leofwine watching with concern.

"Tell your master," Sulien's voice was harsh with the effort of restraint, "if he raises a hand against any of my servants again he shall rue it."

Hugh, quailing under the witch's stare, managed to stammer, "He thought it would please you."

"It has not."

Leofwine came to Oswy's side and, cutting the ropes, gently lifted him off the horse and set him on the ground. He took a physician's brisk look at

Chapter 2

Oswy's wounds, then got up and led the horse over to Hugh. Both Hugh and Sulien looked at him as if they had forgotten other people existed in the world.

"What!" snapped Sulien.

"The boy is fine." Leofwine's voice was gentle, reassuring, "It's not so bad as it looked."

"Lucky for Robert," said Sulien, grudgingly, and turned his back on Robert's knight. Hugh needed no urging but left without waiting to be dismissed.

The witch strode over to Oswy and looked down at him. His face was sullen with the afterglow of fury, his hands still clenched into fists. Oswy avoided his eyes, and eventually, after a hot, tense silence, Sulien sighed. Motioning to Leofwine, he said tersely

"See to him."

"Yes, lord," said Leofwine, with a half smile.

"And when you have finished," the witch-lord went on, "Lock him in."

Leofwine pulled Oswy to his feet and, keeping a secure grip on his arm, began to haul him into the tower. He gave a little rueful laugh, "He'll not get away again, my lord. I'll make sure of it."

This time there was no upstairs room for Oswy. Leofwine dragged him down into the dungeon and shut him in the single tiny cell. When he had turned the key and walked away there was absolute darkness in the room.

Oswy could hear the rats moving, scuffling and fighting in the straw, but he could not see how close they were. Rats had gnawed his brother Cine as he lay in the cradle. He remembered a night when two had come so close to his face that he could feel their breathing. Suddenly he forgot that he was too hurt to be frightened. He found the door by touch and beat on it.

"Leofwine!" he screamed, "Leofwine! Let me out!"

But it was a long time before Leofwine came back.

Chapter Three

Oswy stood pressed against the door, swaying a little with tiredness and hunger. He had shouted himself hoarse, uselessly, and was beginning to feel again how cold and wet he was. His back throbbed mercilessly and stabbing pains shot through his arms and legs each time he moved. He knew he should gather the straw together and lie down in it to keep warm, but the rats would be waiting for that. They would gnaw his face while he slept...

There was a clatter outside, and the sound of voices. Oswy backed away from the door as it opened and stood blinking. Leofwine was there, carrying a torch and an unlit oil lamp. With him was an old woman, stern as a grandmother, decently dressed and wimpled, but with her face defiantly visible to the world. A Sceafn Lady, obviously, accustomed to independence and command.

Leaning on her stick she regarded Oswy seriously. Her pewter-gray eyes were the same as Leofwine's, and there was a distinct look of kinship about those two as they stood in the doorway together.

"Hm," she said after a while. "Well, boy, I am Dame Edith, but you will call me My Lady. Is that clear?"

"Yes, my Lady." Oswy was awed.

She smiled and hobbled past him into the cell. "Light me the lamp then," she said, "and I'll see what I can do."

Leofwine lit the oil lamp and stood it in a niche by the door. The flame flickered for a moment and then bloomed strong and steady, casting a golden light over the rough walls and the old damp straw. It was good clean oil, there was no smoke.

"Be off with you now," the woman said. "And tell Brand to stop dawdling and get down here."

Leofwine took Oswy by the elbow and began to drag him up to the great kitchens of the keep. Out of the darkened cell, where the fear of rats had kept him standing, the pain and cold began to overwhelm him. His trembling legs weakened with each step, every pace jarring his wounded back. The lash cuts burnt now like hot irons, but his feet felt cold to the point of numbness. It

Chapter 3

seemed very dark in the stairwell, the air too bitter to breathe, so much effort just to raise a foot and climb one step.

Vaguely he noticed they had stopped and Leofwine was kneeling by him, looking into his face with concern. Then he was lifted and carried. He closed his eyes and it was as though he was five again, being taken in, too tired to move, by his father. A long day picking stones from the winter-hard earth was over with, and he was being carried home to a fire, food and sleep. But Leofwine didn't smell like a farmer, he smelled of parchment, and herbs, and the faint acridity of a mail-shirt. Nothing in this place smelled like home.

Oswy felt himself shifted awkwardly onto one arm as Leofwine opened a door. The air coming out was warm and full of steam, comforting to step into. There was the sound and brightness of a fire. He opened his eyes and saw a cauldron of soup bubbling over the blaze, and, standing by the hearth, a bath full of steaming water. Brusquely, like a knight physicking his squire, Leofwine peeled off Oswy's stiffening muddy clothes and dumped him in the tub.

"You're a fool," he said with annoyed concern. "Running off to the forest. You could have been killed."

"He was going to kill me anyway," Oswy murmured, soothed by the warmth and too tired to be afraid.

Leofwine gave a short laugh, "Oh yes? So why aren't you dead?"

Reaching out easily he pushed Oswy's head under the water. When Oswy came up again, spluttering and red faced with surprise, he said, "Do you think he couldn't have killed you if he wanted, at any time since he first saw you? For that matter, do you think he couldn't have brought you back - from wherever you had fled to - with a word?

"Why do you think there was so little hue and cry after you? We knew that as soon as he returned he would have you back. Escaping his power is not as easy as walking out of his doors. As it was he was spared the trouble. Which might prove well for you."

He shook his head in continuing disbelief; "Running off to the forest! Can you get any more foolish than that?"

Oswy could not answer, so he covered his confusion by yelling as his cuts were scrubbed with soapwort and hot water. He was beginning to feel much better - Leofwine's brisk ruthlessness reminded him of his mother.

"Leofwine?" he said, as he was lifted out and set before the fire.

"Hm?" Leofwine handed him a bowl of soup and looked about for a spoon with a puzzlement which showed him unused to kitchens.

"What is he going to do with me?"

The sound of footsteps went down past the door, heavy and slow as if burdened, and a voice cursed at the turning. It was the first sound of life Oswy had heard in the tower, but for Leofwine and the old woman.

"I don't know." Leofwine shrugged away Oswy's disbelieving look. "Truly. We were out riding. You were gathering straw and looked up to see a wild goshawk stoop.

"When my lord saw your face he started as though he had seen a ghost. He seemed both amazed and amused. Then he said 'Go on before me, I must buy that boy,' and I went. I know nothing more."

"Didn't you ask?" said Oswy, unsatisfied.

"No. I'll find out in time. But I'll tell you this: I've been told to treat you well."

He had a reassuring look, this witch's servant; his harsh, strong face made pleasant by the kindliness of his cloud-gray eyes. His long hair, the color of good soil, curled slightly in the damp air, and he wore it loose. Sometimes it fell across his cheek, a soft frame for those hawk features. Oswy felt a great desire to trust him. "Will you protect me from him?" he said, putting down his bowl to gaze earnestly at the tall man.

"Do you really think I could?" Leofwine replied, with a hint of depreciating laughter.

"You protected Hugh," Oswy said quietly, "earlier today."

Leofwine looked at him with surprise and pleasure, "You noticed? So. You're not so stupid as you seem."

"But will you?"

"Yes." There was a slight roughness to Leofwine's deep voice which was like the pull of calloused hands on silk, a catch that made it seem modest, unsure. "If I can. But remember, I am Lord Sulien's knight, I do what he says."

Oswy half rose from his stool, wincing at the sudden movement. He gaped at the man, aghast that he had been betrayed into such familiarity, and he thrust his fist into his mouth. It tasted strange.

"You're a knight?"

Leofwine laughed, ruefully; "I had hoped it was plain."

Chapter 3

"But you can't be," Oswy mumbled in self-defense. "Leofwine's a Sceafn name. The Sceafn knights died, in the invasion."

"Most died," Leofwine agreed, bitterly. "But some, by luck, or treachery, or sheer unimportance were spared. Their daughters married Holmr lords, and their sons became squires to the invaders, and hence knights." He bowed his head briefly, and when he looked up it was with masklike calm, masklike resignation.

"We are conquered," he said flatly. "We must learn to live with it."

Oswy's tact rose to the occasion. "But you're doing all this work..." he said apologetically, trying to turn the man's thoughts, and his own away from the familiar oppression.

"As for that," the knight smiled again, "I believe the last lord killed every soul in this manor, one way or another, so we must shift for ourselves."

He brought over the bundle of cloth he had been smoothing; a tunic of fine-woven wool. The dense indigo dye had faded over the tunic shoulders to a pale gray-blue, and in places the wool had worn thin as gauze. There was a dark band around cuffs, collar and hem where strips of embroidery had been removed. Oswy shrank away from it in dread.

"I'm not wearing that. It's his. It's got his shadow on it."

Leofwine looked at him sternly, "You'll wear what you're given." Dragging Oswy to his feet, he forced the clothes over the boy's head. "There," he said, "That's not so bad is it?"

"It's got his shadow on it," Oswy repeated, sullenly. "I don't want it."

"I don't know what you mean." Leofwine rolled up the sleeves until Oswy's hands showed, looking down on him with annoyance. "But what if it has? Are you too grand to wear cast-off clothes?" His voice shaded from irritation into anger. "Or is it just my Lord you're objecting to?"

Oswy quailed and abandoned the point. "Do I get a belt?"

"No," said Leofwine shortly. "There is more than one way of escape from a manor."

They returned to the dungeon, the knight picking a torch from a sconce along the way. The short autumn day was over and the passageways dark. Cold air blew down the stairway from the levels above, stirring Oswy's damp hair. "I don't want to go back down here," he said. "Why can't I go upstairs where I was before?"

Leofwine stopped, looked down severely. "You brought this on yourself, Oswy. You were trusted to stay, to behave sensibly, and you betrayed that. Now we know we can't trust you we must lock you up - for your own protection, as well as to retain three calves worth of property. The only room with a lock is in the dungeon. So that's where you're going. You might be thankful we're not throwing you in the pit."

"I won't try and run away again," lied Oswy, quickly. "Not in the dark. I promise."

Leofwine swung open the door of the cell. It had been cleaned and the old straw taken away. The packed earth floor was visible, with no hiding place for the rats, and gaps in the wall through which they might crawl had been blocked up. There was a pallet and a couple of blankets in one corner, a tinderbox and two tallow candles, one lit, in the niche in the wall.

"As you can see," said Leofwine, "you have nothing to complain about. Why not stop and think on that for a while."

With a gentle pressure on Oswy's salved and padded back he pushed him into the room, and then shut and locked the door. Oswy stood and listened to him walk away. Only when it was absolutely silent outside did he go and sit down on the bed.

Was that it, he wondered, a mild rebuke from a man who had worried about his safety? Was that all the punishment he was to get? It didn't make sense.

No. They were obviously waiting, waiting until he felt secure, so it would be even worse when it came. Who knew, in witchcraft? Perhaps today was just the wrong phase of the moon to murder a boy.

He lay down reluctantly and pulled the covers over himself, feeling heavy and stupid with fatigue. Snatches of this evening's conversation and Fulk's story floated in a garbled jumble through his head. The candle still burned tawny as a setting sun; there was a nimbus around it like the halo of a saint.

'The tiniest light can overcome great darkness, and one spark from the steel can become a great blaze.' Words from a sermon, little regarded at the time, now suddenly came to Oswy new-born and strangely comforting. He pulled one of his long sleeves over his face and wept into it, hiding from the pain and confusion of the world. The wool was soft and warm. Almost without noticing it Oswy fell asleep.

Chapter 3

He dreamed, but it was not his dream. The nightmare stole up on him as he slept, he felt it coming and tossed on the mattress, but he could not shake it off.

This time he was the boy whose ghost he had spoken to, and he was upstairs again hanging by his chained wrists from a hook in the wall. Oswy tried to shut out the sensation, remember who he was, but he could not. The dream was too vivid and the boy's thoughts too strong: His back was bleeding, pain, hardly bearable, forcing little whimpers of protest out of him. He was still determined. He would not scream; he would not scream. Let the bastard do what he will, he would not scream.

The flail curled around his shoulders and neck, one thong whipping across his face, cutting into cheek and lips, narrowly missing his eye. He cried out, he couldn't help it, and his master gave a little sigh of pleasure. Fury bore him painless through the next few strokes. He wrenched again at the chain, strove again against his master's power - the effort left him shaking, and it did no good. It never did any good.

Blood had begun to run from his back, trickling, tickling down to his bare feet. In his moments of sanity he felt it, but those moments were getting briefer, leaving him isolated in the dark world of his pain. He was close to fainting, and he longed for it, but without hope. It was too much to ask for.

The sound of the flail hitting the ground made his heart stop for dread. He could hardly breathe for it, as though every evil ever dreamed would come upon him at the next breath.

"Please," he prayed silently, "please not again. Please."

Then he was lifted and flung onto the floor, hitting the cold stone hard. He tried to get up, to get away, but the man pinned him down with practiced ease and bent down over him to lick at the blood on his face. He knew what was coming next - he writhed in the man's cruel grasp. Then, as he had never done in waking life, he screamed for it to stop. It did not.

Oswy woke, his own throat hoarse from yelling. It was pitch dark in the little cell. He grabbed his blankets and pulled them tight around him. His body was stiff and numb with fear while his heart hammered.

"Bastard!" the boy's angry litany echoed in his head, "Pox-ridden, nithing bastard! Fraecuth, cifesboren, slaveson bastard!"

The anger sustained Oswy for a while, but it was not his own anger and when it ebbed he found himself shaking. He crawled down into his bed and lay there, too appalled even to cry. The night dragged on, deep silence all around

Witch's Boy

him, and gradually the dream faded. He was still too afraid to move, but he began to think; hurried, feverish thoughts, incoherent and unstoppable.

That boy again! Why can't he leave me alone? I don't want to know what happened to him. Is he trying to warn me? How did he get in my dreams? I've got to get away from here! Who was that man? It wasn't Him. Who was it?

He could see the man's flushed face all too clearly, a wide, arrogant face with pale blue eyes. The man's dark brown hair had been cut close in the style of the Holmr barons, and his short beard had a reddish tint. Was he some servant of the witch, whom Oswy hadn't yet seen? Or perhaps a member of a coven with him? Was that to be his fate? Was he being kept alive in order to be delivered up to that man?

Suddenly he sat bolt upright, heart in his mouth. There was someone else in the room, a faint presence. He sensed its gloating pleasure at his fear. Slowly he edged towards the door and with trembling hands struck fire and lit the second candle. He stared around the room, eyes aching from the light. There was no one there.

The rest of the night he spent huddled in one corner, hugging the blankets to his chest and staring at the candle flame. The last shock, once it was over, left him too tired and weak to think, but he was determined not to sleep again. He wanted no more such dreams.

It was a wait as long as years. It seemed incredible, like a thing out of another world, when the key scraped in the lock and Dame Edith opened the door and stopped under the lintel to gaze at him.

"You've not been fretting all night, boy?" she said, with mingled pity and exasperation, "You look like death."

"I'm alright," Oswy's voice was thick with sleeplessness. He edged a little further back into his corner, unwilling to be touched. The woman looked him over with a measuring glance and shrugged.

"Well," she said briskly, "rise and eat."

She held out a bowl - its steam carrying the smells of rye porridge and pulped apple - but Oswy could not take his eyes from the black gape of door. "Is he there?"

Edith's mouth thinned with disapproval, she folded her arms. "No." Then, perhaps softened by his look of abject misery, she conceded, grudgingly, "Lord Sulien never comes down here, lad. Not once in the two years we've been with him. There's no part of the keep where you'd be less likely to meet

Chapter 3

him, if that comforts you. Now get up, there's a long journey ahead of you; so eat and make ready."

Oswy slid out of his blankets at last and took the bowl. "A journey? Where to?"

"Lord Sulien is going to Caster," the woman handed him the information with the air of someone handing out a sweetmeat to a spoiled grandchild. "And you are going with him."

Oswy looked up, sudden hope rising like the sun in him against the despair of the night.

"Truly? I'm going to Caster?" It was better luck than he had ever imagined, and he almost smiled at the joke. He had run away to try to come to the city and now, having been caught, they would take him there themselves.

"Truly." She nodded, "Now make haste. You're delaying them."

A little later, roughly washed and with the tangles hacked out of his shaggy hair, he was led out into the open air. It was a cold day, but the speeding clouds were breaking and sunshine moved over the castle like a living thing. At the foot of the steps a small travelling party had been assembled: A wagon; Brand and Gytha, busy with loading; Leofwine in mail-shirt, ax at his side, holding the reins of a roan and a sable horse.

Sulien stood there too - deadly as a blued blade - his plain tunic almost monkish in its austerity, but the hair which lay over his shoulder bright as gold in the morning sunlight.

Dame Edith coughed politely and Sulien glanced up. A moment later, as Oswy descended the steps, his gaze returned to the boy, and his dark eyes narrowed with displeasure. He waved the old woman away, and she returned to the keep hurriedly, holding her mantle tight against the cold autumn air. Then he said, with quiet anger, "Leofwine?"

Leofwine looked up apprehensively.

"How is it the boy is wearing that? Didn't I tell you to destroy it?"

Leofwine shrugged, puzzled, "It seemed a waste. And I thought, if it wasn't going out of the household..." he faltered, seeing the look on his lord's face. "I don't understand," he said.

"Because you don't understand my commands you don't obey them?"

Leofwine opened his mouth to reply and then, clearly thinking better of it, bowed his head and said frankly, "My Lord, I presumed too much. I'm sorry. Thankfully no harm has come of it."

"No harm?" Sulien turned to look at Oswy again. His gaze was like a thundercloud, heavy with threat. "Tell me, boy, have you come to no harm wearing this?"

Oswy stared. His mouth opened in horror. He could feel the blood drain from his face and his legs begin to shake. The witch knew! He knew about the dream!

It seemed intolerable to Oswy that not only had such a thing happened in this place, and he been forced to share in it, but that Sulien had known about it all along. He felt utterly debased and ashamed. Sulien had probably been watching, enjoying himself. His had probably been the presence which gloated in the darkness over Oswy's fear. Suddenly Oswy could no longer bear even to stand. He covered his face with his hands and crouched on the lowest step, crying.

He heard the ring of chain mail and knew Leofwine was coming to comfort him, but he felt that if he was touched he would not stop screaming for days.

"Leave him be," said Sulien dispassionately.

"But my Lord..." said Leofwine, and Brand's wife from the wagon said, "Oh the poor love!"

"Leave him be."

"But what's wrong?" Leofwine asked. Oswy sobbed louder; the witch would tell them, and then they would all know.

"Nightmares," said Sulien tersely.

"And this is my fault?"

"Yes."

After a while Oswy calmed down enough to look up, straight into the witch-lord's watching gaze. There was no pity in it and no pleasure, only a kind of grim curiosity, as though he had forgotten what human emotions looked like. Oswy was a little reassured.

"You'll ride in the wagon, with Gytha," said Sulien with a sullen calm which ignored the incident out of existence. Cowed, for the moment, Oswy crawled in and sat in a corner, hugging his knees. Leofwine gave him a worried look before climbing onto his horse, but he said nothing more as he lead the small party out of the bailey and into the early morning world.

Outside the bailey gate shaggy cattle and slot-eyed sheep were grazing on the heather above the tree-line. The potholed track led precariously down

Chapter 3

into the valley where an early morning mist still lay like a soft blanket clutched by a reluctant riser. Bright but cool, the sun glanced off the mist and the few tall trees which reached out of it. Above, on the high peaks, the first snow of the season glimmered yellow-gold in pure and careless beauty.

Oswy comforted himself with the sight. He could imagine himself as a mountain-elf walking alone in the high places, looking down cold-bloodedly at the world of men. What did it all matter anyway? He turned his face into the cold breeze and let it wash over him until his skin was icy. Gradually he began to feel easy enough to look around. Gytha was the first to catch his eye, he had the feeling that she had been watching him quietly all along.

She was a thin, slight woman, whose waefel - the shapeless, black overdress she would have to wear in a Holmr town to show herself respectable, - hung about her in empty fold on fold. Her face was hidden from Holmr sight by the grima - a masked hood of black wool with a slit at the front through which Oswy could just see her blue eyes. They were lively, and their corners crinkled in what he thought was a smile.

"I know it's hard," she said sympathetically. "Snatched away from your family - there's no wonder you'd have bad dreams."

"I'm fine," said Oswy, unwilling to pursue the subject, but he unclasped his hands from around his knees and gave her a wan smile.

The wagon jolted over the ruts in the road, sending up gushes of mud and water. Gytha, still watching Oswy carefully, took out a large bag and pulled several handfuls of raw wool from it. "Can you card?"

"Of course." Oswy was happy to have something to do. He took up a hank of wool and the combs and began to tease out the strands. The coarse greasy fibers felt good under his fingers, reminding him of evenings spent gossiping by the fire while Freda span and his mother beat the thread upward, with a satisfying swish-thwack, on the loom.

Gytha watched him for a while to make sure he was doing it properly, and then took out a piece of mending and began to stitch. After a little while Oswy shuffled up closer to her and she twitched her blanket over both their legs. Brand, reins in his hands, cursed at the tree-branches across the path and they drove on down into the cold embrace of the mist.

Drops of water began to bead on Oswy's black hair and to silver the dark tunic he wore. The forms of Leofwine and Sulien, riding silently ahead of them, were blurred and then disappeared in the fog. Gytha leaned forward. "He's not hurt you has he?"

Oswy thought about it and then, surprising himself, admitted "I suppose not."

"I'm no fool," said Gytha. "I can see there's something wrong."

Oswy drew back from her in shame. "It's nothing."

The mist thinned, showing all around them the black skeletons of trees, cold water dripping from their branches. A stag raised his antlered head and leaped away into cover. Pale light began to spill into the avenue of the road, making the cold dew glitter.

A little later, despite his best efforts, and the jarring passage of the cart, Oswy fell asleep and did not wake even when Gytha lifted up his head to put the wool-sack as a pillow under it, tucking the blanket a little tighter around him.

It was noon, by the sun, when a start and the sound of loud cursing awoke him. The smell of smoke and marsh-water was around him, a familiar smell. He looked up eagerly to find that they were in Mereton and the cart had slipped on the perpetually wet ground. Brand, grim-faced, was hanging on to the reins while the horse, white-eyed, skittered nervously in the shafts.

There was Oswy's house, still standing, the cottage-garden which grew half-heartedly in the sodden soil looking disheveled already by the coming winter. A gray reek was going up from the smoke-hole.

Silently, like wary strangers, some of the children of the village were watching as Brand struggled with the wagon. Oswy knew every one, and he could tell, from their several expressions of embarrassment and glee, that they recognized him. He needed, so badly, for one of them, only one, to smile, to show him they were there for him. He waited, hope transparent on his face. Then Alf Thatcher gave him a good long stare just to be sure he was watching and turned and said something to the others. They all laughed.

Oswy felt himself blush, he couldn't stop it. The throb of his back, the shocks and fears of the past few days focused themselves instantly into a wave of murderous anger and shame. Suddenly he was seeing Alf at work with his father, his foot slipping on the unbound thatch, falling, screaming, to the ground, both legs twisted under him. He was seeing his old enemy crippled for life, dragging himself around on a pallet, begging at the houses of his betters.

It was such a good picture! Let him laugh at that! All Oswy had to do was to say yes, and it would happen - he could tell them all later what he'd done. See if they'd laugh at him then!

Chapter 3

Absorbed in his vision he did not see the blow until it came - the slap hard over the bruise on his face.

"Stop that!" Sulien's hand was poised for a second blow. Leofwine stared at his lord in puzzled disapproval. Brand and Gytha pointedly looked elsewhere.

"Leave me alone!" Humiliation forced Oswy's words out; the recklessness of shame. "Leave me alone!" He knotted his fist clumsily - he had always been shunned, so he had never learned to fight - struck back, a wide inexpert blow.

Sulien caught the hand easily and held it until Oswy stopped struggling. Quick anger on the witch's face gave way to a look of awakened interest which frightened Oswy into stillness more effectively than violence.

An expectant hush settled over the onlookers. Oswy too held his breath and gazed up at his master in helpless supplication.

"Ill-wishing is dangerous," said Sulien after a while in a cold voice. "It quickly becomes a habit. Stop it now." He looked down at Oswy curiously and his face softened a little. "I can see I found you only just in time."

The wind blew cold spray into Oswy's face, whipping his ink-black hair into his eyes. Behind him one of the children laughed again, a spiteful sound. Sulien turned his horse and looked at the boy. The laughter withered under his gaze like straw in the fire. "I'll know you again," said Sulien.

As they drove out of the village Oswy craned his neck to look out into the marshes. With a great leap of the heart he recognized his mother and father in the distance, fishing the dirty water with a small net. The baby was riding on his mother's back, and Freda was following with a couple of sacks. They were still alive!

The relief left him light-headed, like strong ale. He could almost have laughed at the expression on his old friend's faces; terrified chicks in front of the fox. He didn't need their friendship - the cowards!

"He struck you for no reason." Gytha, low voiced but angry, brought his mind back from happiness and vengeance alike, "What did you do?"

Oswy considered. "I suppose... he may have known what I was thinking," he said. "I was wishing that boy would fall off a roof and break his legs. He seemed to think I could make it happen, just by wishing."

"If you wished that," said Gytha slowly, "I dare say you deserved a slap." Then she fell silent.

"My parents are alive," said Oswy a little later, as though saying it out loud would make everything better.

"Good." Gytha took up her mending again and sat bending over the needle. Without making any move she seemed suddenly to have withdrawn from his company. "Could you?" she said eventually.

"Could I what?"

"Could you have made your wish happen?" she asked, and pulled the waefel tighter around her legs.

Through long practice Oswy recognized, with a sinking heart, that his bad luck had followed him into the witch's household. She had been his friend for only half a day - and it had proved enough.

"Of course I couldn't," he said, but he was not entirely sure, it had seemed so real, so easy to reach out and make it real. His doubt showed.

Gytha stitched for a while, silently. Then she said "What does he want with you?"

"I don't know."

The sky had clouded over again and as they descended further into the wood a slight drizzle blew in their faces. The creak and rattle of the wagon, the sound of hooves and the chink of chain mail sounded loud in the valley's stillness. Oswy clung onto the side of the cart like a sea-sick traveler taking his last look at his home country.

He was trying not to think and for the first time in his life he was finding it difficult, so obvious some things had become.

He could never go back home, that was plain enough. He could make objects move by his will, he had dreams and visions, and now it seemed he could curse. The boy in the tower had been right. There was no place for him in the outside world.

Miserably he pushed the thoughts away, trying to convince himself it was just the cold, and the emptiness, making him think like this.

Even the air smelled strange as they turned to follow the stream, there was no hint of smoke or human habitation in it, only trees and moss, water and stones. They began looking about nervously, listening for wolf-voices on the air. Gytha and Oswy drew together again, taking comfort in each other's fear. Leofwine and Sulien up ahead spoke a little, softly, as they rode.

About an hour before dusk they drew the cart off the road into a small clearing surrounded by leafless beeches and clambered down. Sulien watched

Chapter 3

for a moment then passed the reins of his horse to his knight and strode off into the forest.

They made camp. Leofwine drew up the layout with a campaigner's eye. Brand and Gytha set up the tents and dug the trenches, while Oswy fetched and carried, bringing water from the stream and dead wood from under the eaves of the trees. He did not dare to go far into the woods to forage, they were dim and full of animal noises.

The sky darkened. Brand kindled the fire with the dry firing they had brought in the cart. The new wood, piled around the edges, hissed and sputtered as it dried out. Leofwine returned from checking on the horses and sat in front of the fire, moodily scrubbing at rust-spots on his helmet.

The drizzle abated slightly, though water still dripped from the tree-branches, making a cold counterpoint to the sound of the stream. Above Gytha's head as she stirred the cauldron the steam went up to join the breaking clouds. At the edge of the world the moon came out, and faint gray light spilled into the clearing.

Gytha took off the grima nervously to eat with her husband, put it on again quickly after. They had bread and cheese, a pottage of wheat and onions cooked with nettles they had found, still green, at the edge of the stream. Oswy, looking hungrily on, gazed at Leofwine imploringly but was told to wait.

He went and sat glumly beside Gytha, receiving the odd handout from her and trying not to think about what was happening to him.

Eventually Sulien returned, walking out of the trees as silently as he had gone. He threw down at Gytha's feet a brace of wood-pigeon and hunkered down wordlessly in front of the fire. There was a look of animal ferocity on his face which had nothing to do with the world of men.

His servants moved about him gently, careful not to attract his notice or come within his reach.

After a long silent struggle he sighed, his shoulders slumping, and held out his hands to the fire. The threat of immediate violence flowed away from him like blood from a wound. Everyone breathed easier, returning to their tasks with confidence.

The birds were freshly killed and bore the claw-marks of a large hawk or falcon. Gytha prepared them without comment and set them to roast over the fire. Oswy looked at them hungrily and wondered if there would be any scraps left for him, but he was horrified to be told to wash his hands and eat with the gentry. He would rather have gone hungry.

He did not enjoy the food. He was too aware of Sulien's presence, and the oncoming night. It was an uncomfortable meal. He hoped, once it was over, that he might be dismissed, but he was not. Pitchers, one of wine, the other of water, were put on the table, then Brand and Gytha went to their small tent, leaving Oswy with only Leofwine to defend him.

The waxing moon began to show above the trees. Leofwine poured himself wine and began to carve out a gaming board on the rough table with his knife, his hair glossy as a chestnut in the light of the fire. Sulien tore his gaze away from the flames and looked intently at Oswy. "What's your name, boy?"

"Oswy, my Lord." Oswy looked down at the table.

"So," said Sulien, "what were the two lessons?"

Oswy studied his hands, wringing them in his lap. He had forgotten about this. A curve of the witch's shadow, purple as a thundercloud, touched his fingers. He huddled away from it and thought as quickly as he could. Each second under his master's gaze was like another turn of the rack.

"You could have killed me then, if you'd wanted to," he said slowly, thinking back to his conversation with Leofwine in front of the kitchen fire. It seemed a very long time ago.

"And so?"

"And so," the answer surprised Oswy even as he gave it, "You don't want to." For a moment he felt reassured, but only for a moment. There were other things to be feared than death; there was no getting around that dream.

"Secondly?" Sulien poured himself a drink - he drank water, Oswy noticed, like a monk.

Oswy bit on his fist, reluctant to utter the answer. He knew it, of course, but once it had been spoken, he would have to accept it.

"Take your hand out of your mouth, Oswy," Leofwine said gently. "It's not seemly," and Oswy remembered that, if he said it, other people would know too.

"I..." He looked down intently at the wood-grain of the planked table, remembering good days; bringing the harvest in with music and dancing; ropes hung over the marshes when he was little - plummeting into muddy water and screaming with laughter.

Chapter 3

Eventually the sheer pressure of Sulien's silence wrung it out of him. With a sick feeling of loss he said "I'm a witch too, aren't I?"

Chapter Four

"Yes," the firelight reflected gold and amber in Sulien's brown eyes. "Yes. You are a witch."

Leofwine drew in breath, a quiet sound of surprise hardly to be heard above the rustling of leaves. Oswy raised his eyes a little and fixed them on the mage's white, well-kept hands as Sulien turned the crystal ring around and around on his finger.

"More truthfully," said Sulien softly, "you were born with power." His mouth compressed a little, as at a bitter taste, and he said, "Just as I was. But you must be trained."

Oswy felt a splash on the back of his hand and noted with withdrawn surprise that he was crying again. He did not know why, he felt perfectly calm. "I don't want to be a witch," he said. "I want to be a storyteller - a traveling storyteller."

"You have no choice."

Another tear fell from Oswy's eye, red as blood in the firelight.

Leofwine shook back the wide sleeves of his green mantle and said "I don't understand. I thought one had to seek this power, and study, and learn."

"There are ways to obtain it if you don't have it," Sulien agreed, and closed his eyes briefly. He took up his knife from the table and clenched his fist around the blade. Blood oozed from between his fingers. He went on, his voice level and cold, "The easiest way is to make oneself a whore for it, to sell yourself."

"To the Dark Ones?" Oswy whispered, and swallowed hard after he had said it.

"Yes," said Sulien, "And I've seen that done." For a moment he was silent, his face drawn and sickened, as though he relived the horror and vileness of it.

Then Leofwine reached out and touched his sleeve, saying, gently as he could, "Your master?"

Chapter 4

"No!" anger replaced contempt, Sulien tightened his grip on the knife. A little pool of blood began to spread out beneath his hand. The moonlight gleamed on gore and steel.

"Whatever else he was," the witch's voice, though with a faint accent of pain, sounded still unnervingly gentle and pleasant, "he was no fool. And you have to be a fool to make that contract. Who expects the King of the Abyss to keep his promises? No. He took the second way. He was a thief. He stole his power where he could, from objects, from books... and from me."

Although he hardly knew why, something in Oswy recoiled at that. Some part of his soul, unremarked in his life so far, but vitally important, understood enough to flinch. He looked up from his study of the bench to Leofwine's honest, puzzled face, and knew that the horror he felt was something he shared with Sulien and with no one else. He resented that.

Sulien opened his hand and looked at it curiously - the gash across his palm and all four fingers. Absently, without taking his eyes from Oswy, he picked up the salt-box with his left hand and poured fine white salt into the wound. "There are many such thieves," he said, "who would lose no time in using you in the same way."

Oswy shivered, feeling a dread almost as profound as he had felt in the night and hating the witch for making him feel it. He bowed his head again, scowling behind his long rough hair.

A moth flew into the oil lamp's bright light, casting huge wheeling shadows on the surrounding trees before its dusty wings went up in flame. Leofwine looked from Sulien to Oswy and back again, and stroked the fur edging of his sleeve as if he simply had to give comfort to something. "What could anyone do, with both you and I protecting him?"

Sulien glanced at him sharply, "Did you burn his old clothes?"

"No, my lord," Leofwine poured wine rather than meet the man's eyes. "I kept them by to be mended and given as alms." Meekly, perhaps remembering his blunder that morning, he finished, "What have I done?"

"You have put him in some danger." The witch-lord made a visible effort towards patience and began to explain; "An old, well worn garment, indeed any personal thing, will eventually come to carry the shadow of its owner."

Oswy looked up quickly and caught Leofwine's startled glance. He would have felt joyful because someone else in the world saw as he did; if only it were not this man.

"When that happens," Sulien went on, observing the glance but ignoring it, "the item becomes an occult connection; a link to the person whose shadow it bears."

"Do you mean," said Leofwine slowly, "someone would be able to work magic on Oswy through his old clothes?" He sounded both incredulous and horrified.

"And more," his lord agreed. "They could use him to observe, seeing what he sees; they could work their own magic through him, fueling their spells with his life's energy, making him feel and do as they desire; they could protect themselves from injury by transferring their wounds to him."

He paused for emphasis, still watching Oswy with a predator's patience, "If both parties are witches," he said, "then the connection works both ways, but, as in all things, the stronger has control. There are other uses too. Why do you think I burnt everything of my master's?"

"I had no idea," said Leofwine, and then, affectionately, "I thought you were just being wasteful."

Sulien laughed, an unpracticed sound. He took up the cup of water and looked at it without enthusiasm, putting it down again and sighing,

"It will probably go to some peasant." His mouth crooked in a cynical smile, "And when he starts having Oswy's dreams and thinks he's possessed, I'll get the blame for it, as I do for every piece of bad luck which happens within twenty leagues of my manor." He closed his hand on the crimson mess of blood and salt and traced a small sign over the back of it, sudden strain showing in the tension of his shoulders. When he opened the hand again it was healed - smooth and unmarked as ever.

Leofwine returned to his carving. Oswy twisted his bare feet together to keep them from the cold and fidgeted, trying to hold off sleep. The moon floated on the sky like may-blossom on a still pond. Oswy yawned.

Suddenly Sulien leaped to his feet, throwing back his head like a hound catching a scent. "Man-hunt! Coming this way."

Leofwine cursed, throwing off the fur-lined cloak which covered his mail and reaching under the table for his sword. "How many?"

"Twelve, maybe more, in full cry."

There was a faint sinister excitement about their lord, as though he felt the thrill of the hunt from afar and ached to join in. His eyes glowed with

Chapter 4

pleasure, and the cool voice rang; "Oswy! Get in the servant's tent and stay there. Leofwine, guard them."

The knight scowled, "I guard you," he said. "These packs have no respect for rank, no respect for anything but force."

"I know," Sulien smiled like a man contemplating an available woman. "Do as I say."

Oswy ran to the tent, flinging himself to the ground just inside and hushing Brand's sleepy protests urgently. He remembered a hunt through Mereton when he was nine; a village woman ridden down as they passed, her hand broken under a hoof; two of his friends struck aside with iron clubs - one died later; the fugitive caught at the edge of the village and smashed to pulp by mounted soldiers. He remembered being astonished at the noise; the cries - not like anything human at all. Then they had turned on anyone in sight. He had hidden for days after.

The night had quietened, the breeze dying down. Somewhere in the woods a fox barked and then, plaintive in the darkness, came the belling of a hound.

Brand and Gytha huddled together in frightened silence.

Oswy opened the tent flap a finger's width and peered out. He heard fast, ragged footsteps and behind them the sound of hooves. A shadow at the edge of the clearing lurched forward into the light of the fading fire and came to a sudden stop, taking in the campsite with rapid panicky glances. His eyes and mouth were so stretched with terror and his distorted face so slimy with blood and mud and spittle that it was difficult to tell what kind of a man he was. He trembled all over like a sick horse.

A high, excited voice rang out, "Over here!"

The hunted man ran forward and threw himself at Sulien's feet, grabbing at his ankles with shaking hands, pushing his filthy face into the fine supple leather of the witch's boots. "My lord!" he cried, "Protect me!"

Sulien looked down at him with distaste. "What have you done?"

"Nothing!" the man gasped, "My lord, *please*!"

The note of frantic conviction carried to Oswy even over the sound of approaching horses.

Sulien, looking as if he wanted nothing more than to kick the groveling wretch in the teeth, took a handful of hair and forced him to look up. Tear-filled amber eyes flickered for a moment like fire in the torch light as the witch looked down into them intently. Then he nodded. "I'll shelter you. Get in the cart and stay down."

Only seconds later the first of the pursuers rode into the clearing, following a brindled gaze-hound on a long leash. A young noble; his embroidered scarlet tunic grimed and smeared with mud, mud on his chainmail, mud and anger on his handsome face under the green lash cuts of tree branches. He took in the camp at a glance and, seeing only two men to oppose him, one of them unarmed, he sneered.

"Find him, lad," he urged.

The dog loped up to Sulien, nose-down, tongue lolling. Within a pace of him it stopped, yelping as though it had been bitten. Turning tail it ran belly-down back to its master, whining.

The sounds of snapping branches and the jangle of harness and mail came from three sides of the clearing. Glimmers of metal showed in the darkness.

The young noble gave the witch a measuring look, kicking his horse forward to within a foot of him. His gaze took in the long yellow hair and he sneered, "A little, rustic, Sceafn lord," he laughed to himself, and then, contemptuously, "So, serf, where is he?"

"In the cart." Sulien's voice was mild but his posture arrogant, affronted, "Under my protection."

The noble laughed. His mount, white-eyed, skittered nervously away from the blond man. He cursed and kicked it back again. "Don't give yourself airs, slave. Hand him over, before we take him."

The edge on the witch's voice was brittle as garnet now, "I am Sulien FitzGuimar, Lord of Harrowden. Begone, while you still can."

The horse backed away again, sweating. "You're Sulien? The witch?" The young man quailed for a moment, doubt and calculation visible in his eyes. But then a voice out of the darkness called "Hugo? What are you waiting for? Get him, you coward!" and anger seemed to fasten on him like a rabid dog. He flung the dog's leash aside, and wheeling his mount, yelled into the forest, "You slaveson bastard! Get out here yourself if you're so brave!"

Turning again, he swept out a great iron mace, the flanges on its heavy head sharpened into blades. He dug his spurs into his horse's flanks, riding down on Sulien like a steel-capped wave.

Chapter 4

The witch smiled. Hugo brought the mace down in a great arc, leaning his weight into the stroke. With more than human quickness, sudden as a stooping hawk Sulien caught the wrist and pulled down hard, following through the motion of the blow.

Hugo doubled over. The high front of his saddle slammed into his stomach, stopping him from falling, but driving the breath out of him in a huge cough. He straightened, gasping; risked a hasty glance to take stock of his companions, and while he was looking, Sulien stepped into reach again, still with that raptor's speed, and grabbed his weapon-hand. Holding the wrist steady, Sulien twisted it. There was a snap, barely to be heard over the sounds of chaos and fear, and Hugo screamed, dropping the mace.

Clamor pierced the night's hush: Men yelling in panic, the clatter of dropped shields, falling riders, flying hooves. From where Oswy watched on the outskirts the fire-stained darkness of the camp had become suddenly a chamber of the Abyss.

Hugo's companions, cursing with fury, were driving their terrified horses at the moonlit clearing as though it were a wall to be leaped. The chargers reared and snorted, white-rimmed eyes aglitter. Maddened, they tossed the men to the ground and tore away, the long gashes of spur-wounds like dribbling mouths on their sides. Thrown men lay senseless on the road.

Sulien released Hugo's wrist and the young noble, his lips ashen with pain, tried awkwardly to draw his sword with his left hand. As he was still fumbling Sulien picked up the mace and smashed his knee with it.

One of the other hunters swore and dismounted, tying his plunging horse to a low branch. He took one step into the firelight and stopped short, shaking, his face made vacant by fear. His friend ran to his side and then looked up. A shudder went through him like a crossbow quarrel.

"God!" he gasped, clutching at the other man's arm, "God! Let's get out of here before it sees us."

A man tossed by his horse in front of the tent came to and lifted up his head. "Benel protect us!" He began to crawl backwards, with painful elaborate care, towards the tent-flap. Leofwine grabbed him by collar and belt and hauled him away.

In the gray light, briefly, Oswy caught a glimpse of what it was the men were seeing. Although he knew it was not real, only an image of a real thing, he had to fight hard not to vomit. He wanted to crawl down under the blankets and pretend it was a nightmare, but Brand and Gytha were both asking what was happening, and he knew he must not leave the doorway and let them see. The bravery of the men who could stay standing long enough to flee from it astonished him. He wondered if Leofwine could see it and, if he could, how he could bear to stand his ground.

Hugo, seeing his followers unmanned, crawling crying out of the camp, turned his horse to flee. Sulien caught him by the edge of his cloak and pulled him sideways out of the saddle. The horse ran on into the night.

Hugo landed heavily on his broken knee and howled like a woman giving birth. As he struggled to rise the witch-lord, smiling with enjoyment, stamped on his elbow - grinding the heel down hard - and then kicked the sword-hilt from his opened hand.

Leofwine tied a final knot on the bonds of a captured man-at-arms. Wiping his hands on the grass he crouched and watched for a while. Then he came uncertainly into the light and stood just out of range frowning at his lord's brutal thoroughness.

Sulien got down closer to his victim, kneeling on the broken elbow, taking a hit across the face from Hugo's mailed fist with a little cry which sounded more like pleasure than pain. He straddled the body, pinning down the other arm with his knee and, with slow deliberate movements, drew off the helmet and coif and tossed them aside. Almost gently he slid his hands around Hugo's neck and began to squeeze the life out of him.

"Offer him quarter," Leofwine ordered, stepping closer, sounding disapproving and angry. Sulien said nothing, his gaze on the young man's face intent as a lover while he throttled the breath out of him. Leofwine grabbed his right arm and pulled the hand away. "Stop it."

"I fought him fairly."

"I know. And you've defeated him. Now let him go."

Sulien wrenched his arm out of the knight's grip, dealing him a back-handed blow across the face which cut open lower-lip and chin. "Don't tell me what to do!"

He closed his hands again around his victim's neck, but it was plain that the joy of it had gone out of him. Hugo had stopped struggling under the grasp and lay limp as a corpse.

"Guimar would be so ashamed of you." Leofwine turned away.

Like a man being turned to stone by a basilisk's stare the witch shivered at the words. Then, slowly, as though he had to learn the use of them,

Chapter 4

he unclenched his fingers, looking up at Leofwine's retreating back with hurt innocence. Hugo's first strangled breath was the loudest thing in the whole cool night.

Suddenly, furiously, Sulien flung himself from the body and stalked to the edge of the darkness. He stood there, arms folded, head down, silent.

Ghostlike, eerily noiseless, a white owl winged over his head, feathers like ice on the moon. Firelight picked out its molten gold eyes for a second before it passed on, hunting its furtive prey. The breeze of its speed blew back the hair from the lord's forehead, but he made no move. He seemed not even to see it, isolated as he was in some dark vision of his own.

"You can ransom him." Leofwine built up the fire, speaking kindly now, reasonably. He set one of the stools close to the blaze, and poured water into the cleaned cauldron. Taking off helmet and coif he turned his face into the breeze, combing his fingers through sweat-matted hair.

"Look at the clothes," he went on, "He must be worth a dozen serfs at least. And those I caught trying to flee, they'll be worth something too, though not as much."

He took a few paces towards his lord, head on one side, cautious and gentle. "What was that thing they saw?"

"A lesser Pit-fiend." Sulien flinched at the knight's touch on his arm.

"I'm glad I couldn't see it clearer." Leofwine towed him back into the light. The blond man followed, head bowed, sat down where he was told to, said nothing, biddable as a slave.

With a moan of pain Hugo stirred, and Leofwine left his lord huddled by the fire to go to his knees beside the broken young man. He looked at the ruined limbs and touched the joints carefully. Then he sighed.

"The wrist is a clean break," he said, "I could set it, but the rest is more than I can do anything about," and then, bitterly, "What kind of a life is he to have? I should have let him die." Blood, black and silver in the shadows, dripped from his cut chin and he wiped it away absently.

"Get Oswy out here." Sulien roused, standing, "He might as well learn something tonight."

Oswy scuttled further back inside the tent, grabbing some blankets and pretending to be asleep. It made no difference, he was hauled out anyway and thrust forward to where Sulien waited, silver as a lost angel in the cold light.

"See to my new villein," he commanded his knight. "Oswy and I will heal this one."

Oswy took a few steps closer, frost-brittle grass crackling under his bare feet. He was poised to flee, but the witch's listless tone reassured him, a little.

"Healing was one of the earliest magics I learned," said Sulien in the same remote accents, like a man speaking out of a fever. He handed Oswy a hand-sized block of wood and a small knife. "Carve him."

"What?" said Oswy, not sure if he understood.

"Make a carving of him," Sulien repeated. "Make it sturdy and be clear in your mind that it's him."

He hunkered down by the body, looking at it with a sort of puzzled curiosity, as though wondering what it had to do with him, and continued his lecture as he stripped the armor off and cut the sign of the sword on each of the broken joints.

"We'll stain the carving with his blood," he said, "To establish the link, and then transfer the wounds from him to it. As far as I know I am the only mage to use the mommet in this manner, they're more popularly used the other way. For torture." He smiled a twisted smile, mocking and bitter. "I'll keep it by me. In case he gives me trouble later."

"Why did you want to kill him?" said Oswy suddenly, almost comfortable with his master in this defeated mood.

Sulien turned his face away. "I am a monster." And then, in an awkward attempt at reassurance, "Don't worry, you'll soon learn when to hide."

When the healing was done it was late, and very dark. The moon had gone down into the sighing black trees and was lost. The fire was gray ash, baleful embers like elf-jewels in its center.

Hugo was sleeping under his bright red cloak, his hands and feet tied securely with his own sword and purse belts. The fugitive, Gunnar, was washed and tended to, sleeping in a nest of sacks at the bottom of the cart with his hand clamped tight around the pendant at his neck.

Leofwine had sat down for a moment in front of the fire and fallen asleep there, slumped uncomfortably with his head on his knees and his open hands resting on the trampled grass.

Chapter 4

"It seems we are the only ones awake," said Sulien softly. "Come here."

Oswy stood uncertainly, reluctant to obey, or to provoke anger by disobeying. Sulien took no notice, holding out his hands to the last embers of the fire, seeing them stained red by the light as if by blood.

"I worked all that magic," he said curiously, "Weren't you tempted even once to join in?"

"I..." said Oswy, in a yearning tone, his chest tight with guilt and excitement, "I don't know how."

"Let me show you." Sulien said a few nonsense words and there was light in his cupped hands as though a star of the heavens had flown down, like a tame linnet, to rest there. It nestled on one palm, a little round light the size of a ripe apple, pure as frost in the sunlight, but intense as the white heat at the core of the smithy fire. Oswy's lips parted and his eyes shone with wonder and delight. He still thought he should be afraid, but he could not be; such a beautiful thing!

The light shining between them showed him his master's face clearly; the angled brows and strong cheekbones, the wide mobile mouth softened now into a slight smile, the white scar on his lip which twisted when he spoke. "Well?" he said, "Shall I teach you this?"

"Doesn't it burn?" said Oswy, coming closer unconsciously, enchanted.

"Hold out your hands," said Sulien, and when Oswy had done so he tipped the little light onto Oswy's outstretched palm. It felt of very little; a feathery lightness, a faint warmth, and it dimmed at his touch almost immediately and was gone.

"Oh..." he said sadly, "Did I kill it?"

Sulien smiled, "No. Say this," and he said again the line of strange words with which he had called up the light. Oswy repeated them, so nervous he barely had the breath to whisper, and understood each one as he said it.

The feeling was pure joy. Like every lawful joy he had ever felt; the pleasures of food and fire, song and praise and story, the pride and laughter of watching Cine take his first step, the mystery and transport of a great tale by a winter fire. "Oh!" he gasped, "It's wonderful!"

"Yes." Sulien was smiling with delight, his face for once open and eager. "It's something worth living for."

For a moment Oswy returned the smile, like a son relishing his first triumph and his father's praise, the light shining in his cupped hands like a pearl. Then he remembered who he was smiling at and dropped his eyes hastily, studying the witch-light to cover his sudden dismay.

He was secretly a little disappointed with it. It had none of the superlunary brilliance or purity of his master's. It was like an elf-light, like mother-of-pearl; transparent and full of illusory shifting colors. "I didn't do it properly, did I?" he said, shaky now, as if he had run a long way or suffered a shock.

"Yes, you did," said Sulien, with surprising gentleness. "It's just that it's yours and not mine. You can tell a lot about a man from his witch-light, and yours is beautiful."

He put out his hand in a gesture that, in anyone else, would have seemed an attempt at reassurance. Oswy scrambled to his feet suddenly and moved back, afraid, and ashamed that for one moment he had had the witch's approval and been glad of it.

"For God's sake!" Sulien rose, with a look of baffled irritation. "What is it now?" He waited for an answer for what seemed like hours, and then sighed and turned away.

"Go to bed," he said, the note of annoyance still sharp in his voice, as though he knew he had been insulted. Picking up a couple of dry branches he stirred the fire back to life. "And don't try to escape tonight." he said, "I'll be watching."

Chapter Five

Oswy awoke to a dazzle, a shatter of light through the tent flap with a color cooler than the early morning sun. He crawled out quickly to see what it was.

Sulien and Gunnar were there, the witch holding something away from Gunnar's neck; a thing which glistened like sunshine on the sea. Coming closer Oswy saw it was the pendant on Gunnar's necklace.

"This is Elfish," said Sulien with surprise, and, to Oswy's astonishment he pulled the radiance down, bowing Gunnar forward, so Oswy could take a closer look. It came from a ring, the band old silver, scratched into softness, the stone changing from glance to glance, bright as the moon, clear as water. "How did you get it?"

Gunnar gazed up at his new master with an awe and fear Oswy found painful to see. He was a very young man, sixteen years at the most, and small, as peasants tend to be. His hair was a bright russet red and with his sulfur eyes he might have seemed fox-like, but for his innocence. "It's our luck, my lord. Me and my family. We've kept it."

"Since before the Holmr?"

"Long before. Just after the first church-men came to Sceafige, my mother said. During the god-wars. We were given it then. A long time ago. It's our luck. Please don't take it away."

Sulien looked again at the ring, dropping it slowly, as though reluctant. "Keep it. And if the time comes when I need to use it, I'll ask you." He turned to Hugo, who was picking burrs from the mane of his newly recaught horse. "This was why you were chasing him?"

Hugo shrugged. "That's what started it. One of the King's advisers wanted it and this peasant refused to give it up."

Hugo had awoken before dawn, abusive and afraid, and cursed until Brand and Gytha had scrambled up to tend to him, (leaving Oswy with the unknown luxury of being able to go back to sleep). Now Hugo was unbound, washed and fed, and had presumably given his oath not to escape, he was beginning to show a certain good humor.

"This adviser," a note like fear turned Sulien's pleasant voice sharp, "What was his name?"

"Adam de Limoges." The young knight shrugged again, "No birth and no family. One of the King's new upstart friends."

"This country is lousy with mages and herb wives and wiccan," Sulien said, suspiciously, "but I thought I knew them all. I don't know that name."

"Oh I don't think he was a witch." Hugo's green eyes widened in surprise, "He was staying at Earl Ranulf's house, and Ranulf is as pious as my father. I don't think he'd have a witch under his roof. Besides, it doesn't follow. The ring may be fae, or it may not, but it's still a pretty thing. A new man might seek it just to prove his power."

"True." Sulien nodded, swinging up into the saddle. He rubbed his cheek where a pattern of round purple bruises, livid against the cream skin, showed the mark of Hugo's mailed fist. "You don't seem to be such a fool this morning."

"The peasant led us quite a dance," Hugo laughed. "I was angry."

"Did you really lead them a dance?" Oswy asked Gunnar admiringly as the two of them piled tents and bedding into the cart, and climbed in after it. The cart ground to a slow start. Gunnar gave him a puzzled look, and then a sudden mischievous smile.

"I did," he said proudly, his golden eyes bright. "Through every bog and thicket in the county." The brilliance died swiftly and he shivered. "They had horses. I had to." He wrapped his hand around the precious ring and fell silent, rocking back and forth in distress. Oswy and Gytha exchanged worried glances over his head.

The cavalcade, a respectable size now Hugo and his three men at arms were added, set off and soon turned onto the larger road leading to Caster. Other travelers, peasants and merchants, gave way before them, stepping into the ditches on each side and standing, heads bowed, while they passed. The Castreld plain, with its brown fields and tidy villages, rolled gently out ahead of them under the milky white sky.

Oswy sniffed at the air with relief, the smells of smoke and dung were like a benediction after the wild cleanliness of the hills.

"So the King is in Caster?" the witch's tenor voice was unexpectedly audible on the peaceful air.

Chapter 5

"Not him," Hugo replied, scratching at his neat beard. "Just this advisor of his - Adam de Limoges. The rumor is; the King is thinking of giving him a woman who has lands in this area. Earl Hubert FitzGiles' daughter; Adele... Adela," he shrugged, "Something like that. Anyway, de Limoges came up to view the property - a nice little manor in the Fell Forest - but he leaves today. He may even have gone already and good riddance to him."

They rode on in silence for a while, a fugitive breeze ruffling Hugo's short-cut brown hair and rippling in the wolf pelts which lined Sulien's wine-colored cloak.

"I didn't expect to be still alive this morning," said the young Holmr eventually, smiling. "You had every excuse and, I think, the desire, to kill me."

"You owe your life to Leofwine," said Sulien, looking back at his knight with an expression which was difficult to interpret. "He pleaded for it, eloquently."

"Sceafns!" Hugo laughed, "They're so soft-hearted!"

In the cart Gunnar sat up suddenly, giving another of his mercurial smiles. "He's wonderful, isn't he?"

Oswy looked at him with sudden blackness. "Who?"

"Your lord," said Gunnar in the hushed tones of hero-worship.

Oswy lowered his voice so the gentry might not hear and said, angrily, "He's a cold-blooded murdering bastard and worse. I hate him."

"Oswy!" exclaimed Gytha, shocked. Oswy gave her a resentful look and fell silent, fighting, with limited success, against tears. He wanted to talk to her, to tell her about the ghost, and the dream, and the treacherous voice inside him which had awoken last night when he cast his first spell.

It said, *anything, anything. I'll bear anything if only I can have more of this.* Sulien had known, of course, how he would feel. He had known very well what he was doing, the bastard!

Oswy wanted to talk to her but he knew, even if she understood, she could do nothing, say nothing which would make it any better. So he kept silent, trying to comfort himself by imagining his forthcoming escape. It was poor comfort; the thought of losing the chance to learn more about his magic made even that prospect seem bitter as a drink of wormwood. The day dragged on, long and dreary.

By evening they had reached the city and found the gates closed for the oncoming night. They made camp under the shelter of the walls and ate, watching torches and moonlight striking glimmers from the helmets and spears of the patrolling city guards. The heads of criminals stared down at them from the battlements with crow-picked eyes. Their stench and the reek of the city gutters came fitfully down the night breeze.

Oswy, waiting clumsily at table, could not keep his eyes from the place; it was huge! He had never imagined so many people could live together in one place. The walls were like cliffs. He was sure he could get lost there easily, and Sulien would never find him. There might even be an alchemist (his mind stumbled over the word) in a city like that, who would be willing to take on a witch's boy and teach him. His heart lifted at the thought.

In the morning they entered the city with some ceremony. Leofwine and Sulien had put on their best clothes; the light glowed on strong colors and glittered from the gold and silver thread of embroidery. The two knights had put aside their armor, and combed their hair until it shone. Sulien's was braided in a golden rope down his back, so he looked like a Mearh raider, or one of the old Sceafn warlords.

"That hair!" Hugo had said last night, bright eyed and flushed with drink, "In a Holmr it could mean only one thing." Leofwine, half drunk himself, had risen to his feet in fury.

"I know what it means to the Holmr," Sulien had said with the quiet of precarious self-control, "But I am half Sceafn. Do you know what it means to us?"

Hugo had shrugged, "Do I care?"

"You should. You brought the subject up." Sulien held the young man's gaze, intent, using his knowledge as a weapon; "After the Broken Summoning, when the Dark Ones drove us out of our old homeland, we came here to Sceafige. The savages who lived here then were head-hunters - they would lop the head off, take out the skull, shrink the remains, and then tie it to their belts by the hair. Sceafn warriors took to wearing their hair long as an insolence, and a challenge; 'What a prize I'd make,' they said by it, 'but you're not strong enough to take it.'" Sulien had shifted forward, intimidating, making his point. "That is what you should see, when you see me."

Within the walls they picked a slow way through bustling market-day crowds, up to the central mound of the city where the castle towered like a brooding giant. They stopped, to Oswy's surprise, at the abbey guest-house.

Having dispatched the three peasants to the market to buy winter provisions, and given Leofwine charge of the hostages, the witch-lord leaned

Chapter 5

casually down and lifted Oswy off his feet, setting the boy before him on the horse.

"And you will come with me," he said, and rode out again into the teeming street. Oswy knotted his hands in the coarse hair of the horse's black mane and cringed away from his master's presence and the oppression of the city walls. Around him scores of strangers milled.

A gang of shrieking barefoot children ran past following a hoop of willow. The wind, changing, brought first the stench of a tannery and then the salt smell of the great estuary whose waters lapped at the dock timbers nearby.

A group of foreign merchants, their faces bronzed and their clothes exotic, hurried past talking of spices and trade-routes. Oswy was surprised he could understand them. A wildman, from Wyrmlige, sitting unheeding in the mud of the street with a horn of ale in his hand, broke into a song of his homeland. Urchins and dogs clustered just out of arms reach to listen.

They turned into a street full of booths. The houses on either side had trestle tables ranked in front of them and goods of every kind were stacked high there. The householder's wives - shapeless bundles of cloth with shrewd eyes - sat in their front rooms, behind wrought iron grilles, and haggled through the window with buyers.

Further along the crowded street a scream of pain and outrage went up then a grizzled man came out into the open wiping bloody hands on his stained apron. A youth staggered into the street, gripping his jaw - gore on his fingers and down his shirt.

Sulien passed the reins of his horse to an onlooker and, keeping a firm hold on Oswy's wrist, towed him through that door. Oswy's struggles drew laughter from all the passers-by.

Inside, he could feel the humming begin in his head; a sharp knife on the table quivered. "Stop it," said Sulien quietly, "They'd burn us both."

He picked Oswy up and forced him into the gore-stained chair. It had straps and buckles on the arms.
The grizzled man returned, grinning, carrying a pair of shears, and set to, cutting Oswy's hair. Oswy nearly fainted with relief.

"You must be very careful about this in future." Sulien fingered a shorn lock of rough black hair. He had waited until the barber-surgeon went out of doors before gathering up all the cuttings. Now he wrapped them in linen and stowed them in his belt-pouch.

"Either don't cut it at all, or burn the cuttings immediately," he went on. "That goes for your nails and your beard too, when you get one. They're powerful links. If an enemy mage got hold of them they could have you in their power in seconds."

By midday, after hours of being dragged around by the elbow to stalls and shops, Oswy was transformed. A visit to the tailor had provided him with madder-red hose, green braies and a fine white linen shirt. Over everything went a tawny yellow tunic with red banded sleeves, full-skirted in the Holmr style. They were very near his own size, ordered and never paid for by some noble for his son.

He admired them prodigiously, stroking the sleeves as though he was petting a small animal, and smiling with delight to see the street-children bow to him as though he was high-born. He was not so sure about the shoes; he felt incredibly important in them, but they hurt.

His master looked at him carefully. "Good. If you stand still and say nothing you might pass as my page. We're going to see the Bishop."

"Can you really set foot in the church?" Oswy asked, emboldened by a morning spent so domestically. He had heard Holy ground would reject the touch of a witch, searing their flesh like the red hot iron of the ordeal. It took the mage a little longer than he had expected to answer;

"I don't know," Sulien said at last. "But I mean to try."

He had sounded resolute when he said it, but he still paused before the open doors of the abbey church like a warrior taking stock of his enemy and finding him stronger than he hoped. A wisp of incense, heady as the roses of summer, floated out into the cold autumn air. Faintly in the dark depths of the building a voice chanted in solemn melody.

Oswy, who had not even thought of fearing for himself, imagined at first that his master was frightened of the threatened pain. He said, spitefully, "What's wrong? Are you afraid?"

Without taking his eyes from the gaping doors Sulien swallowed and answered quietly, "If it burns me, it means I'm damned."

Suddenly, angrily, so Oswy had hardly time to understand the fear and quail at the black despairing depths of it, the witch strode up the wide steps and set foot on the church's bright floor. He stood, looking up at the painted scenes; Benel at the head of his legions; the restoration of the Ruined Lands at the end of time; the damned tearing their own eyes out so they need not see

Chapter 5

what they had done, and only his labored breathing showed the extent of his relief.

When he had mastered it, he reached out and brushed his fingertips over the azure wings of a painted angel. Fleetingly an expression of dazed gratitude overcame his permanent scowl - as though he had been embraced when he had expected to be kicked. Oswy found it almost touching, and he was horrified at himself because of it.

In the hush of the holy place the chant came to an end. There was the sound of many feet pacing, the susurration of breath and of robes brushing the floor. The monks were returning to their inner world, taking with them a profound calm which made Oswy shiver. The flames of the constellation of candles bowed to them as they passed. Light and shadow chased over the tiled floor and among the curving archways like children playing tag.

A tall old man, in a purple robe so dark-dyed it was almost black, broke away from the procession and stopped just in front of Sulien. Yellow light gleamed on his ring and staff.

"You are very like your description," he said, offhand. The mildness of his tone did not conceal the fact that he was a fierce man. It showed in his eyes.

"Lord Bishop." Sulien nodded slightly, an acknowledgment and nothing more.

"When I set this place for our meeting," said the bishop, aggressively honest, "I hardly expected you to come."

Abruptly, Oswy realized the bishop was speaking Holmsh, and now he thought of it, Fulk had told his tale in that language, nor had Hugo ever spoken anything else. The words of the chant came back to him; how had he understood them? They had been in ancient Duguth, the scholar's tongue.

His heart beat heavily. Was this innocent - a new effect of magic - or had his lord cast some spell on him while he lay sleeping and unaware that first night at the keep? The thought made him sick.

He wanted to turn and race out of the doors, but though Sulien had dropped his wrist as soon as the bishop came in sight, he was still too close. Oswy told himself to wait. They would be deep in conversation soon, and he might slip away then without his master noticing.

"I had heard you were a witch," the bishop went on, filling Sulien's silence with words of his own. "This was a test."

"I know," said Sulien. "I passed it."

The bishop gave a humorless laugh. Oswy, taking a cautious step backwards, noticed how, out of long habit, the bishop's right hand hovered in the air where the handle of a mace would have hung. There was the scar of a sword-cut under his eye; he had not lived an entirely contemplative life. "I have heard stories of deeds of yours I would blush to recount in front of this boy." he said, stern as a Royal Judge about to pronounce doom,

No, thought Oswy, trying to look innocent as he backed into the shadows, *don't remind him I'm here!* Then; *what stories?*

"Are they true?" the bishop insisted,

"Yes," Sulien replied, "most of them."

Oswy took another step back, into the dense shade of one of the pillars. The bishop laughed again, appreciating the honesty, and said, "So why are you here?"

"Things have changed," said Sulien, "I want a priest."

"For confession?" the bishop's expression softened a little.

"For my manor. I'm building a church."

The old man looked shocked, for a moment. Then he folded his hands inside the rich cloth of his sleeves and said, "I'll need some persuading before I deliver a man into your power. Come, we'll talk about it." He turned and walked towards the monk's door, where dim yellow light showed the stone of the cloister.

"Don't remember." Oswy chanted silently, his heart beating fast. He put his hand over his mouth to silence his breathing. "Don't remember I'm here."

Sulien took a couple of steps after the bishop, then paused, frowning. "Don't remember," Oswy prayed. Instinctively, as he had done in Mereton, a picture formed in his head; Sulien turning away, following the old man through the door, oblivious to Oswy's absence. This time he said yes to it, with all his being, with such strength he swayed on his feet.

"Come," said the bishop again, with a touch of impatience. Sulien smiled his bitter smile and followed without looking back. Suddenly, simply as that, Oswy was alone. For a moment he could not believe it and stood, stupidly gawping, a darker shadow in the pillar's shade. Then he turned and, running down the church steps, he lost himself in the market day crowd.

Chapter 5

"I'm sorry, lad," the cooper rubbed his freckled face with a large calloused hand.

"Please."

"No," said the tradesman, firmly, "I've no need for an apprentice, and no need to anger a powerful man. I've a wife and children of my own to consider. Go back to your master and leave us in peace." He shut the door in Oswy's face.

Oswy stood and looked at it for a while, wondering if he should knock again and beg for food. Then, unable to face the humiliation, he turned out of the cooper's yard, kicking at the iron hoops as he went. It had been the politest of his many rejections - which made it no easier to bear.

He trudged further down the street, his feet slipping in the mess of entrails and blood which marked the butcher's yard. Even in the autumn cold flies arose around him in a carrion cloud. He swatted at them in disgust and went on.

A fair-haired skinny youth in ragged motley came past, towing a brown bear on a chain. The bear was muzzled tightly; the straps embedded in an ulcerated band about its head. Flies settled there in a crawling mass.

"Spare a coin, young lord?" the man begged, and hit the bear a couple of times to make it dance.

"I've got nothing. I'm no lord."

"Huh," the beggar sized up Oswy's face and clothes with an expert eye, "Some Holmr's pet then, and good for an eypence."

"I've got no money," Oswy insisted, and then, impulsively, "I'm running away."

"You're a fool." The young man doubled over, coughing as though he would spit up his guts. "What I'd give for a job like that!" He wiped a thin stain of blood from his mouth. His cuff was black with it. For a moment he stood, eyes closed, gulping air, then he gave a sudden brave smile, "Well, you come with me. I can teach you to juggle, and sing, and when I'm dead, which won't be long, you can have the bear."

"Thank you!" Oswy fell into step beside him, "What's your name?"

"Eaddi. What's yours?"

"Oswy," he answered.

The closed and curtained litter of a Holmr Lady, with a massive retinue of guards, came swinging up from the docks. They stepped aside to let it pass and gazed after it as every man in the street was doing. Outside the ale house a little lower down the hill one young man made a comment to his neighbor, and was hit across the face for it.

"Uh-oh," said Eaddi, seeing it, "let's get past here before the knives."

They edged forward, hearing the sound of mugs being flung, and the vintner shouting, "Now lads, calm down, I don't want any trouble."

The two outside, merchants' sons by the look of them, had come to blows. Their supporters, about four each, clustered in the doorway, yelling and throwing pots into the street.

"My crockery!" the vintner roared, "You'll pay for that. Get out of my house all of you!"

Eaddi and Oswy began to pass cautiously on the other side of the street. The vintner took one of the yelling crowd by his collar and threw him out, crashing onto the cobbles just by Oswy's feet. Rising, unstable with drink, he staggered into Eaddi. The beggar recoiled, jerking on the chain he held and the wounded bear roared, striking out with one giant paw. The drunk young man was hit in the side, hurling him into the running sewer at the center of the road, tearing a hole in his cotte and drawing blood.

There was a silence. The fight stopped and both factions stood, looking from their fallen friend to the beggar as though stunned. Then someone yelled "Get him!" and Eaddi, dropping the bear's leash, shouted "Run!"

They ran, pelting through the narrow filthy streets and down into the worst part of the town. The men they passed drew back into their houses and shut the doors. Their drunk pursuers were laughing behind them, healthy, well-fed young men enjoying their sport. Eaddi, his face gray and his breath laboring, slid to a halt in a small deserted square and coughed himself to his knees. "Keep going, damn it!" he choked.

Oswy hesitated, but not long. He could hear the running footsteps and shouts just behind him. "Sorry!" He fled, leaving his new companion to fend for himself, hoping they would be content with the beggar and forget about him.

He pelted through the square and up the muddy street beyond. The sound of desperate pleading, silenced by blows, followed him. His eyes filled with tears of shame and guilt, but he sped on, half blind. Then, from alleys on

Chapter 5

either side of his road, two of his pursuers stepped. Trying to stop and turn, the new shoes slid on the muddy track. He went down on his tail right in front of them and scrabbled in the mud like a baby trying to crawl. They laughed, and grabbing handfuls of his tunic and his hair, dragged him back to the waiting gang.

"Let me go! Let me go!" he shouted, "I haven't done anything!"

Hands pawed at him and voices above his head, in slurred excitement spoke at once.

"Why'd you run?"

"Look at those clothes!"

"Thieving urchin!"

Between their legs he could see Eaddi lying very still, his open mouth gaping stupidly in a mask of gore. His eyes, gray as a piece of fallen sky, reflected the speeding clouds.

"What shall we do with him?" someone said.

"He's a thief isn't he?" said the lad whose side was bleeding still from the bear claw, "Let's cut off his hand."

The youths burst into nervous laughter.

"Good idea," said the tallest, a man of about eighteen, with the long hair and short tunic of a cwen, a cwen's magpie jewelry aglitter on every limb, "But not here. We'll take him across the river."

"You don't mean it do you?" exclaimed another, sounding hesitant and a little afraid. The others hooted him down.

Oswy stamped down on his captor's foot and twisted in the slackened grip. A hand caught him by the hair and yanked. "Let me go!" Oswy yelled.

"Little bastard!" bellowed his captor, hopping, "You've broken my bloody foot!" and he drew the long knife which hung at his back. "Let's get him now!" he said.

It was only when Oswy saw the man's face clearly that he finally began to believe they were drunk enough to carry out their threat. Fear came over him like the sea and with it, welcome, almost familiar, the whine and hum of power. The knife twisted in the man's hand and he dropped it as though it scalded him.

"Leave me alone!" Oswy exulted, "I'm no thief, I'm a witch and I'll curse you!"

They froze, and Oswy laughed out loud. "*You're* frightened of *me* now aren't you!" It did not occur to him that he could not see the cwen until seconds before the blow came from behind and knocked him out.

The first thing he felt when he awoke, apart from the pain in his head, was the movement of the air - a blessed absence of walls about him. There was the sound of water. Then he realized he was standing, his hands tied together by the thumbs, a rope about his chest holding him upright. There was warmth about his legs and the comforting smell of wood smoke.

Fear hit him at the same time as the sickness. His eyes snapped open and he looked wildly around. He was tied to a stake and the fire was already lit beneath him. There was already so much smoke it was hard to breathe. He screamed from sheer terror and gagged, coughing, at the fumes.

Halfhearted guilty laughter answered him. Between the river and the pyre six of the gang stood watching him. From their presence he knew he was somewhere well away from any chance of help. They would not risk a thing like this where any passer-by might see.

It was growing hot very quickly. Yellow flame slithered towards him like a nest of adders. His taut face prickled and the skin of his hands, closer to the wood, tightened painfully. He should do something; work some magic, but what? He was so dizzy from the blow and the smoke and the heat.

Visions came and went in the fume: Flowers, and unicorns, like watching shapes in clouds; the boy from the tower, his blond hair ghostly pale, saying "Now you're dead too we can be friends." The smoke was white as the elf-jewel in Gunnar's freckled hand. White as the wings of angels.

Searing pain ended the dreams. A tongue of flame had licked his fingers. He screamed and breathed in furnace heat - his throat and lungs stiffening, burning. Panicked clarity showed him an eternity of this: he was witch-born, unshriven, the Dark Ones would come for his spirit now and forever there would be nothing but pain and heat and charring, and the stench of his own flesh going up in fire.

The shock of the cold nearly stopped his heart, as though he had plunged into chill water. He gasped and the air was clean, flowing past him like a little brook.

Panting in the blissful cool, he opened his eyes and saw the flames leaping and twisting in the air, fire pawing his body like a beggar's hands.

Through the furnace roar he could hear shrieking, see his tormentors on their knees, screeching like hares in a trap, doubled over, beating at their

Chapter 5

faces with flailing hands. There was a figure on the riverbank who was not screaming, but he could not see who it was. The fire burned fiercer. He began to shiver in the cold.

One by one the howling voices were silenced, the men lay still on the grass. The wood under Oswy was consumed and his bonds burned away. He fell down in the ash of the fire, too shaken to stand, and wept with fear and shock.

When he looked up again he saw Sulien take his hand out of the river and squeeze the cold water out of the little linen package of hair. Oswy crouched where he was, saying nothing, and his master picked his way through the bodies to stand over him. Sulien looked weary, like a man fretting over a task he does not understand,

"Why?" he said.

Oswy rubbed the back of his hand over his face, leaving a track of tears and soot. The clouds were breaking and the deep golden light of the sunset showing through, making his smoke-filled red eyes smart and water. He was too tired for all of this. Why not force the witch to kill him now and get it over with?

"You ran away, again," Sulien insisted, "Why?" He reached down to help Oswy to his feet and Oswy backed away from him.

"For God's sake!" the witch hissed, "I don't know how to be any kinder!" and then, unclenching his fists with obvious effort; "What have I done to make you so afraid?"

"You think I don't know what you did," said Oswy desperately, his voice trembling, and, seeing Sulien's frown of puzzlement, shook his head. "Not what you did to me. What you did to him."

"Who?" Sulien sat down in the ashes beside the boy. Sunset glory glittered on the bullion thread at his collar, and on his corn-gold hair.

"That boy," said Oswy, becoming angry in his turn, "The blond one. I saw his ghost, the first night I was in the keep, and I spoke to him." Despair and anger were making it hard to speak, he finished at a run; "You gave him to that man, the one in my dream - don't pretend you don't know about it. And then you killed him, like you wanted to kill Hugo. I bet you enjoyed it! Well you're not doing it to me!"

Sulien was gaping at him with a look of astonished enlightenment which could only be genuine. Oswy, who had expected anger, perhaps even horror, felt almost disappointed.

"Of course!" Sulien exclaimed, and laughed, "You didn't recognize me! And why should you? I've changed."

"What do you mean?" Oswy said, wretchedly. The surfeit of terror he had felt while burning left no room, at present, for anything else. He felt as spent as the ash settling softly all around him.

Sulien shook his head, a brief echo of surprise, and sat looking out at the river and frowning, as though dredging up old memories. Then he said, gently, "It was a long time ago, fourteen years ago, when I first saw you. I know you weren't born then." He shrugged, "Who can explain visions?"

His right hand, seemingly of its own accord, combed the cinder and closed around the few live embers. Remotely, out of the reluctant well of the past, he said "I was eleven. It was my first night in the keep, finding out what it meant to be Tancred's apprentice..."

He paused, struggling out of whatever private hell he had visited, and went on, half amused, "I thought you were escaping from him. I never dreamed you were fleeing from me!" He crushed the embers and wiped the soot-stained hand on his best tunic. "You asked me to be your friend," he said, with a little smile, "And I said I couldn't, because you weren't real."

"No!" Oswy shouted, scrambling to his feet, where he stood, swaying. "It's not right! It's a trick!"

"No trick," said his master, "It was me you saw, and my dream that you shared - I should flay Leofwine for giving you my tunic. Do you imagine I wanted you to know?" Then, seeing the boy still unconvinced, he traced the white line above his lip, clearly a bite-mark, long healed, and said "Look, I still have the scar."

Oswy sat down heavily in the dust, and put his head in his hands. The whole structure of his new world crumbled around him. He did not know what to think. The sun went down, slowly. One of the merchant lads, whom he had thought dead, moaned and, curling up on himself, began to weep.

"You didn't kill them," he said, surprised.

"No. I let them feel the burning. But I don't kill with magic. I wouldn't know when to stop."

"What about him?" said Oswy, his fear quickly finding another focus, "Tancred? Did you kill him? You said you would."

"No," Sulien shifted, frowning, "I... couldn't."

Chapter 5

"He was too strong for you?" The fear made Oswy's voice come out sharp, insolent.

But Sulien did not seem to notice, his expression was still puzzled. "I was the strongest. I had a spell poised which would have torn him apart. I simply... couldn't. He looked so betrayed. So pathetic." He shifted again, as if in discomfort, as if the taste of his mercy made him feel sick.

"You let him go?!"

"But I nearly destroyed him. He won't dare take me on again. You're safe from him. I'm sure of it."

The sky was darkening more quickly now, the first pale stars gleaming, like the points of leveled lances, between shreds of bright clouds. A breath of frosty wind stirred the ashes of the fire.

Oswy looked down at the singed hems of his new clothes. It dawned on him that Sulien had saved his life.

"Master?" he said finally,

"Hm?" said Sulien, rising.

"If you don't mean to kill me, or to use me, what did you buy me for?"

"I should have thought that was obvious." The witch reached down and pulled Oswy up by the collar. "You are my apprentice, of course."

Chapter Six

Adela, daughter of Earl Hubert FitzGiles, shut the door of her room with excessive gentleness and leaned against it as if her slight weight could keep the monster out. There was a smell in the air - ambergris, dried blood and sulfur. The smell, Adela supposed, of Adam de Limoges. For a moment she could feel nothing but disbelief and violation.

"How?" she breathed at last, "How did he get in here?"

The thought made the hairs on her neck stir with disgust. He had somehow got past Sister Fidela, Sister Ursula, who stood on guard outside the compound. He had opened the locked iron gate, and walked through the anterooms where the children slept, turning their curious faces away. He had come here, secretly, into her haven, proving he could enter whenever he desired. What if she had been here? What if he came again?

"How? How could this happen?"

"Don't know, m'lady," said the maid, Gunnild, her voice subdued, but her eyes full of fury and fear. "I happened on him. He give me a grin, bold as brass, like he'd fixed this up with you. But I knew that weren't so. You wouldn't risk the shame, and the pyre. Not for him."

She held out a silver brooch. Leaning close, Adela saw the design: a snake writhing together in a knot with the end of its tail in its teeth. Her own eyes looked out at her, dark blue, imprisoned on the gleaming back as though it had already begun to devour her. She recoiled.

"He said to give you this," Gunnild continued, "As a tryst token, and he wasn't going to wait no more. But, lady, he had a girdle of yours in his hand. That one."

It lay awry on the sheepskins of the floor, an old girdle, much worn, mended in a dozen places with stitch-work ranging from childish to expert.

"He dropped it, guilty, when I saw he had it." Gunnild's voice rang with challenge, "I reckon he put some spell on it - and the brooch too; he took that off his own cloak."

Chapter 6

"Throw them away," said Adela, outraged, "Throw them both away. No! Bury them! I'm not having anything he's touched near me."

She saw the thought drift across Gunnild's square face - anger descending into calculation - and shook her head. "Don't keep it, Gunnild. It's not worth the risk. You don't know what spell he's laid on it. Could you bear the chance of finding yourself enslaved by love to Adam de Limoges?"

"No. No, you're right, lady" the woman admitted, with a show of teeth which might have been smile or snarl, "And it should be flung out just to spite him. I'll get Steven to throw it into the mill-race. Will that do?"

"A child? Do you think...?"

"He's canny, Steven, and he's almost old enough to go out to the men. He'll do all as I ask."

"Very well." An anger of her own rose through Adela like an itch. She looked around at her ruined sanctuary - the rumpled sheets where he had rested, rugs kicked aside on the floor - and she straightened her back. "Now I want you to go through this room and clean it well. And, after I've brought scented flowers to mask the stench, I'm going to the Queen. She will have to speak for me now. If anyone can change the King's mind she can. For God's sake! The king owes his life to my father. You'd have thought he'd treat me better than this."

"Rather you than me, my lady," said Gunnild frankly. "Don't like the Queen - I can't get over the way she's colored like a fiend. And when she smiles! You know, in Mearh, we reckon the Swertings eat people. Just for the fun of it, like."

"I'll take Godgifu with me." Adela recovered her humor a little, "She'd choke anyone."

Queen Olufemi - the foreign queen, black and yellow as a tiger in her cloth of gold gown - was pacing the confines of her gilded rooms. She had done away with her petticoats and underskirts, raised her hem to the ankle, so she could stride. The stiff material creased into sharp ridges around the shapes of her legs. "Why haven't I seen you here before?"

Her eyes - elfishly slanted under swags of fine, copper-tipped braids - were alight with curiosity and something hot, something which might, Adela thought, be banked anger. The flash of her teeth was indeed startling.

"I have been in mourning," Adela said carefully, "for my father."

"That would have ended three months ago."

"Yes. But I had nothing to ask and... I feared to come to your notice."

"Because I am a fiend and a cannibal?" The question whip-cracked in Adela's face. She stepped back, remembering Gunnild's comment, her own laughter, guiltily.

"No, lady!" she exclaimed, "Because I had thoughts of going into a nunnery! Because I feared to be married off!"

Queen Olufemi paused in her pacing and looked at Adela, startled. "But you *are* to be married off."

She had good spies, Adela thought, or a great deal of wit, to pick the truth out of the clinging spiders-web of court gossip. "Yes. And I've come to ask you to beg the King to release me."

Adela looked around, saw the wives of great nobles sitting poised at their embroidery. There was a slide of eyes away from her, but otherwise the finely clothed statues did not stir. Their disapproval did not need to be signed - it came out in the careful blandness of every face.

She rubbed moist palms down the sides of her blue gown then gambled desperately, playing the truth. "It's not just because I wanted the Church, I simply don't want him. Adam de Limoges! He is vile! He..."

"No!" the Queen raised a hand, varicolored and, Adela saw with amazement, calloused like a man's. "No, don't tell me."

Her smile was lightning - sudden and fierce, "You know, I hope, that last week, for the first time, we were permitted to attend the council, and to speak?"

"I know."

"Good. Last week was petty: an argument over jewels; the disciplining of a spoiled child. This week they will hear your case. Then they will know that women also have serious concerns."

Adela pushed back annoying tendrils of her beech brown hair - veiled, because there were only women here to see, by a flimsy circle of yellow gauze which floated airily about her hot face. Her inner petticoats had begun to cling - a flush of sweat dampening all her linen. The urge to kick them away was a nagging torment under the dread.

"My case?" she said, "At the council? Before the whole court?"

Hisses of in-taken breath melded with the fire's sibilance. Behind the queen tiny shocked movements ruffled the drape of perfect gowns, set gusts of perfume adrift on the warm air. But it was left to Adela to voice the fear: "A

Chapter 6

woman, saying in public whom she'll marry? I'll be lucky if they laugh! More likely they'll punish me - to put me in my place. It will ruin all my hope! Please don't make me do it!"

But, from the look on the Queen's face, she could already tell she spoke in vain.

Adela focused on the ironwork, the ornamental curlicues like writhing mercury suspended in the air. On the other side of it the Great Hall was a weight of color and light, filled with a low murmur; courtiers leaning together to discuss the judgments, petitioners self-consciously coming and going, presenting their cases in muted tones, the occasional snap of the king's voice - impatient.

The grille itself should have been a comfort to her; it had been blessed by the Bishops with every conceivable prayer. It kept out the bodiless Dark Ones who cause miscarriage, madness, and the birth of foul things. The ingenga, who enter through the eyes and devour their victims slowly, walking about in the shell, might conceivably pass through it, as contagion, on a direct gaze from one already tainted, but she was not going to encounter a direct gaze - no one would be so rude. And the iron itself kept her safe from any physical attack.

Behind that screen she was as securely protected as a woman of the Bad Times, when the Lords of the Abyss walked abroad, corrupting and destroying whatever they touched. So why did she still feel afraid?

Behind her - she looked back a moment, trying to gather support - sat ranks of black, shapeless things, with living eyes which rested on her. It was disconcerting to see them all; her friends and her enemies; the companions of her life, thus shrouded from the world, reduced to darkness and anonymity. For as long as Adela could remember she had heard her nurse, Godgifu, curse the grima, and, at the sight, she briefly understood why.

Turning her head, as though it had to be winched, she forced her gaze through the protective cage, blinked away the sting of light and color.

King Drago's men were bright as dragon's trove. His own cloak, the purple of a shaded amethyst, carried gold and emerald embroidery which stretched it over his shoulders, dragging toward the floor. His dark beard too hung heavy, forked and threaded with a spilled gore of rubies.

So many bearded faces! It had been seven years since she became a woman, confined to the cage, with only supervised visits from her father, or the occasional unsatisfactory suitor. Now every time she looked out - at a Friday

Feast, or at council, like today - the sight of men had become more strange. It was as if, each time she went back into the cage, they grew a little more inhuman.

Her gaze slipped away from the true men - slithered over the fluttering brilliance of the cwens, registering the gilded eyelashes, brimming with light, the shaved, smooth cheeks, disturbingly feminine on these alternate women - and came to rest relieved on the branded face, the shaved, exposed head of Sister Ursula, on guard before the door. Nuns were, of course, deemed to be sexless as God, but Ursula had still been born a woman. If she could function as an adult in this outer world, why should Adela not?

"Where is the girl who refuses to marry as I decree?" The king had risen, come close, peering in through the lattice of metal, the half-light.

Trying to see me! Despite her resolve Adela shrank back, her feet fouling in lace, heat pressing against her face beneath the woolen grima. *I'm hidden for my own safety, doesn't he know that! He shouldn't be looking at me! Unless...is he a shell? Is there a demon in there, trying to get to me?*

The movement betrayed her. The brown eyes found hers and narrowed. Breath stopped in her. But no inganga passed on the gaze; she was still herself, with the blush draining away, leaving her clammy and cold.

"Well? What do you have to say?" The voice was too deep, the face masked in its hair almost as thoroughly as hers was masked. For one insane moment she thought she saw pity in the earth-colored glance, but it could not be.

"I..." If she broke now she would agree to anything. So she took a shaking breath, closed her eyes and leaped.

"I won't marry him. I'm a Benelite, and he's a witch. It was the witches who let the Dark Ones out of captivity. They nearly destroyed everything. The Church says they should be burned for that, not rewarded, not kept at court and given honor and lands.

"Besides, he is a vile, cruel man, and I have a responsibility for my people, to keep them out of the hands of men like that. I won't!"

"Won't?!" If there had been sympathy it was gone now. He was turning - embroidered emeralds dragging through the strewed herbs, scent of trampled wormwood rising like spice - "Who says 'won't' to their King? If I command, you do."

Chapter 6

She heard a faint sigh to her right, where Godgifu sat, and thought the pile of cloth that concealed her had settled into lines of defeat.

"As for your responsibility to your land," the king said, "you're no more than the keyhole of the box. Your responsibility is to open to whomever I choose to bear the key. Sit down and don't give yourself ideas. Next case."

That was it? Outrage burst her shyness, drove her forward to clutch the bars, "Wait!"

"Wait, sire." Sister Ursula stepped out, staff in hand; a lean, hard, ugly woman with the brand of the church like a sore on her cheek. "She has all but pledged herself to the Church."

"The Church!" He swung around, his great bulk moving swiftly, bearlike, "The Church has had enough of my property. Time the Church learned to shut up!"

"Wait!" Adela shouted, "Wait, please. I didn't mean..."

"No! Ah! I am surrounded by hags and harridans! Sit down and shut up! Or shall I have you gagged?"

She reeled back. Breathed; breathed as an act of will, breathed past the tears, glad to be hidden in her smothering wraps. *They are cruel! They are so cruel!*

But the thought sobered her - she realized the king was alone among them. He had no cage to hide in, no protection from the intrigue and treachery but his own wits. He had to show himself always strong.

If she forced the issue, here in front of all these men, of course he would have to do what he threatened. He could not afford to give in to a woman.

The vision of him, struggling in the circle of predatory eyes, trapped as she was trapped, flooded her with astonishment, rocked her world.

She pressed wool onto her face - the tears soaked away - then bowed shakily and collapsed into her seat.

"Well!" said Godgifu, her nurse, "When I was Reeve of Grandscir I often spoke before King Edwy - and heard other women do it too. But I never heard woman or man address a king like that and get away with it. Whatever possessed you? I thought you were going to beg!"

She shook her head - a vigorous motion under the cloth. "You should have begged. Made it an opportunity for him to show his generosity. Not that he would have said yes in any case - such a precedent to set! But you might have got a fairer hearing."

Adela's outrage rose again. "What do you mean 'not that he would have said yes'?" she whispered bitterly. "What was the good of making me expose myself like that if you knew he was going to say no? And not just you - the Queen! Was she making sport with me, sending me out here to be mauled - like badger baiting, with me as the prey?"

The nurse paused, smoothed the coarse black wool over her knees with age-spotted hands. "I am always forgetting," she said slowly, "How cloistered you Holmr women are. God knows how I forget, in this cage, but I do. The mind isn't what it was, before the Invasion, in Edwy's day, when I was young. But don't you see that today we have broken new ground? Today a woman stood up in front of the whole court and spoke in her own voice about an important matter; something which affects men's property, and lives.

"It would have been too much of a change to grant your request, but he heard it, and the next woman who brings an important case to court - if she's more humble than you were - she may actually succeed. Or if not her, then the next."

"That will be fine for them," Adela said pointedly, feeling hurt and slightly betrayed at her nurse's wider interests, "But what about me?"

She took out her embroidery, the rough work because her hands were not yet steady, and stabbed it with the brass needle as zealously as a saint mortifying his rebellious flesh.

"Now you can fall back on the underhand ways of the Holmr, and do it privately, through the Queen."

"If you think she'll listen."

"Of course she will, child. She owes you something now." said Godgifu and looked out again with shrewd interest at the newly accessible dealings of the court:

"Right," the king was saying, "I don't want to hear anything more from women. DeBourne, I'll hear you now. And then I'm going hunting."

Guillem DeBourne. Adela knew his name from her father - they had been friends. He was also the king's friend, she understood. As he edged somewhat reluctantly onto the flagged floor she put down her sewing to attend.

Chapter 6

"It should rather be related in private, my liege." One hand fiddled anxiously with his ornate silver belt-end, and his feet shuffled - trying to make an escape.

The king snorted, "Private!" he laughed, "In this court private just means they find out tomorrow instead of today. Come now, spit it out."

"Well..." DeBourne obviously knew better than to argue. His voice took on a storyteller's poise, and he relaxed into watchful competence, "Just yesterday," he said, "I was visited by a youngster - the servant of a certain Sceafn hermit, Wulfwine; a very holy man, so it's said. "

"We all know about the holiness of the Sceafn. It didn't save their lives or land in the war. Get on with it."

"Well, my liege, the lad said his hermit had received a warning for you, in the form of a dream."

"This should be entertaining," scoffed the king, "go on."

"He dreamed he saw you go into the great hall - he described it, though he could never have seen it - and there on the floor there lay a pool of darkness so deep that though hundreds of candles were burning in the room, no glimmer of light showed on its surface."

The king stirred, and his eyes grew hard, but he let his friend continue, speaking into a well of dreadful quiet.

"The darkness tempted you, he said, and you knelt down and put your hand in it. When you pulled your hand away it gave you visions of glory. But, he said, when you reached out to it a second time it took you, and pulled you in, and though God's angels came for your soul it could not be found, either in heaven or in earth."

A chill silence descended on the court at his words, the silence which might have followed a sword being drawn in a holy place.

"I would not have expected this of you, DeBourne."

"My lord," DeBourne looked up frankly, understanding; "If I had thought - as you suspect - the man meant the Queen by this, then I would have killed him where he stood. But I do not think so. It chimes with something I feel. There's a darkness in our midst - something more than the usual backstabbing, something... spiritual."

He turned his head, slightly - a well brought up man, he could not bring himself to look directly at the women - but Adela knew his glance lay fleetingly at her feet. "Maybe the girl is right, and we shouldn't be harboring witches."

"Do you forget how we won this country? My father's witch, John, was worth more in that battle than a hundred knights. He was a weapon in my father's hand without which he may not have conquered. Why should Adam not be to me what John was to my father? Do you expect me to cast such a weapon away?"

"If it turns in your hand, yes. The dream! It warns of something which promises glory but then sucks us down to damnation. Draws you down Lord. The warning was for you."

Horror settled on Adela, and again, a sense of empathy; her own trouble was only part of a larger plot, a web in which even men could be caught.

Perhaps they're not so unlike us after all.

But the king had begun to laugh. "A holy man, this hermit, eh?" he said, smiling, "Perhaps I'll make him an Abbot. Give him something better to do with his time than dream. Maybe you'll go and join him there? Since you've clearly turned to religion yourself."

He threw the rod of judgment down on the table like a gnawed bone, swept up the sword which stood propped against his stool. A clamor of half-heard requests broke out, but he wheeled and strode away. Bauduin, his younger brother, nodded with sympathy to the unheard plaintiffs as he quietly tucked the discarded rod into his sleeve. Then he went out, with the rest of the King's party.

"That's a good sign." Godgifu rose, stiffly, rubbed her back, as the ladies began to clump together, chewing over the vision like stoats worrying at a dead bird.

"A good sign!" Adela gasped, "Our king is the prey of some dark design, and you call it good?"

"Oh come, child," the old woman moved slowly through the iron-bound door, held it open, gazing out at the light and air, until Lady Cruce - wife of the new ruler of Grandscir - took it out of her hands and shut it.

"Don't be credulous," Godgifu said, ignoring the slight humiliation, the implied rebuff. "There is darkness at the center of every estate, and, unresisted, it draws us in to our destruction. Wulfwine could have sent the same message anywhere and it would be true."

Chapter 6

She wrestled with the folds of waefel and grima, emerging at last slightly breathless. The Sceafn style wimple which she wore still, despite the mockery, had been pulled awry, showing a coiled pile of ice-white hair. She covered it quickly, talking on. "What I meant was this; the king has had the chance to show his power against women and the Church, and his fearlessness in the face of fate. He has come out of the council looking strong, and now he has an afternoon's hunting to sweeten him. Speak to the Queen soon, and perhaps she can catch him in happy humor."

"I'll go now." Adela said, but instead she stood listening to the scrape of wood on tile behind the door, the voices of slaves, sullen, as they began to set up the trestle tables for this evening's banquet.

Eventually she asked, softly, "Do you think I'm a fool to contest this match?" and plucked off the grima, ducking her head to avoid looking at her nurse's face.

"No," Godgifu replied, with what was, for her, extreme gentleness, "I have watched Adam every Friday Feast - carefully as I could, with my bad eyes, behind this wretched cage - and he makes my thumbs prick. Now there's a "pool of darkness", if you like. Look closely and you can see the devils thronging in the air around him like flies over bad meat. I pity anyone who once comes under his power, and I pity the king, who knows no better than to show him favor."

"I didn't know you felt like that!" said Adela in a whisper of gratitude, "I thought no one would understand."

"Oh," said the nurse, snapping back to her usual ruthless self, "Adam de Limoges I loathe, but it doesn't mean I agree with you not wanting to marry at all. You are a great lady, you could do some good."

"You heard the King!" Adela exclaimed, "I'm just a keyhole, but in the Church...."

"In the Church you could have freedom, and learning, and respect." said the nurse, with a grave face, "I understand. But do you realize there are women outside the Church who want those things too? That's what the Queen is doing, what she has just used you for, if you hadn't guessed it yet; trying to get those things for ordinary women. You could be helping her, not taking the easy escape."

Adela was brought up hard by the words, troubled enough to think deeply about them.

"Things could be changed?"

"Of course. The trick is to do it without making everything worse."

Adela stepped out into the enclosed park known as the Women's Wilderness. Her quiver was tight around her - the waefel's folds bunched uncomfortably under its strap. Inexplicable, and horrible to have to wear this here, where only women came. Here she had been used to run in her shift on the soft turf, hunting the half wild deer barefoot through the managed woods. Was the command to wear the coverings here some ploy, to make her realize how truly hateful they were?

Queen Olufemi sat on a camp-stool beneath the first of the great oaks, and seemed a twin of the descending sun - its rays caught, magnified, brightened by her golden gown. When she moved it blazed, and shadows scattered away from it under the trees.

Behind her, washed out by her radiance, were the shapeless black pillars of two handmaids, and Mother Beatrix, lance straight, iron gray in the oak's shade.

This was serious then, Adela thought, uneasily. "My Lady." she bowed, "Mother Beatrix."

"Adela." The Queen rose, heedless of custom, came forward, her eyes downcast, apologetic. "I used you, to your humiliation, to prove a point. I'm sorry."

There was a rustle of grass behind her, the scratching of loose twigs being drawn across the ground. Beatrix' face tightened, prudishly, and the Queen lifted a glad smile over Adela's shoulder.

"I have given some thought to how I could help you," said Olufemi seriously. "I would not hear your plea before. But now we will both listen, and we will both take you seriously."

She gestured. Adela turned in response. The sun filled her eyes, and a huge shape loomed over her, black against the sky. It laughed, and the deep roaring made her shrink away, prickly with cold and shock.

"You didn't tell her!" Drago was laughing at his Queen - a laughter which sounded to Adela like slaps.

"I told her to wear the coverings." Olufemi seemed light-hearted under the onslaught, and unrepentant. "But I thought if I told her she would not come. She is..." her flexible voice with its soft, full accent, shaded into contempt, "She is well brought up."

Chapter 6

"So she is." He was studying her again, trying to see her face. She leaned away, but dared not move - her legs trembled, she might fall.

"Well," said the King at last, in a soft voice, an almost human voice, "No sense in wasting an evening. You can talk and walk, I assume. Bring your bow and we'll see what we can find in this park."

He went into the wood, bracken crushing into powder under his feet, squirrels whipping like red lightnings into the boughs. Their warnings - eck eck eck - were passed from tree to tree, indignantly.

Olufemi gestured Adela forward, and followed close, like a bright southern angel at her right shoulder. The other women came behind.

Breath returned to Adela as she walked and an unexpected measure of ease came with it - it was like being a child again, this walking with men. She had done the same on her father's estates in the North, when she was tiny, before her brother was born, before her mother died.

Without noticing it, she had come up beside the King, was walking there like a daughter, watching his shooting, trying to match it.

I'd forgotten, but this isn't so dreadful. What was I afraid of?

With a lift of the heart like the bird's sudden flight, she let fly, bringing down a plump wood-pigeon.

"Good shot." Drago broke his silence with genuine praise, "I should have you training my bowmen."

"Thank you, my liege," said Adela nervously.

"Sensible of you to shut up when you did, this morning." Drago stopped at the sight and scent of an unexpected rose. It was twined in a tangle of white and gold flowers around a rowan, petals peeping out among the tree's red harvest.

"I suddenly understood," Adela agreed, reassured now he was not looking at her. "I knew you couldn't change your mind in front of all those people."

"What a bunch of canting prudes and spongers they are!" the king laughed, "I can't do anything in front of them without one side or the other thinking I'm the King of the Abyss himself."

He stepped, with surprising lithe grace for such a big man, over a brook which sped its leaf-flecked way down to meet the River Windel. Under the ribbon of clear sky it shone like a school of silver fish, and the sound was cool in the late afternoon sunshine. Adela leaped it, her soft shoes coming down lightly on the springy turf. Then she laughed, silently under the grima, seeing the maids mincing over the stepping stones.

Laughter faded quickly, under the nagging fear - Adam had been in her room. What if he came again? "Please don't make me marry him."

"This looks like a good spot for otter," said the king, "They make good gloves, if we can catch them."

"Please," she insisted. "I'd rather die than marry him."

There was a fallen tree a little away from the brook's edge. Its topmost branches trailed in the stream.

Drago sighed, in good-tempered resignation, and sat down on the mossy trunk. "Come on then, let's get it over with."

"Oh." Adela sank to her knees in front of him. Suddenly it seemed impossible to explain; a little girl's foolish whim. "I don't know why, my lord, but I'm terrified of him. There's something about him, something unclean. Even through the cage, across the whole length of the Hall I can feel it." Then, half crying, in a sudden rush of words she had not meant to say; "He tried to put a spell on me! He has no... no decency! Oh, what does he want with me? I've never given him any indication of favor. Surely he must be able to see I loathe him! Why should he want to marry a woman who hates him?"

"Petal!" exclaimed the king, shifting on his perch like an awkward boy. One booted foot now dangled in the water. "Plenty of reasons why he should want you, willing or no. Just like a woman to think it must have something to do with love!" He began to prize up flakes of peeling bark and throw them into the stream.

"Listen," he said, as he watched the ripples being smoothed over by the hurrying water. "I shouldn't tell you why he asked for you, but I will, for your father's sake. I don't forget him you know." he stopped, rubbing the heel of his hand through his cropped hair and looking uncomfortable, as though he had never worked out how to give praise.

Adela sat on the springy turf, conscious of the Queen settling just behind her, and of Beatrix, still standing, inappropriately military against the evening's sweetness.

From the opposite bank the pungent smell of wild garlic gusted on the dancing breeze. She watched the splashes from Drago's idle missiles and wondered. They had told her - when they brought her father's body home from Holm - he had died well, making himself a shield for the king.

Chapter 6

She had never questioned that. It was right to die for one's lord. Still she could not imagine what it was really like either to give or receive such a gift. She thought, after all, the king was right to pass over it in silence.

After a while he began again; "Adam has a son. And the lad's a grown man now." He sighed, whether at his own childlessness, or for some other reason, "When Adam left for the center of the World two years ago he left his boy in charge. To be honest, I think they had some kind of argument. I don't think he expected to come back.

"Anyway, the lad's had two years of being his own master and lord of a manor. It wouldn't be exactly fair to come back and take it away from him. At least, so Adam thinks, and it's a gentle thought." He smiled bemused approval, and she remembered he had fought all his life to keep his inheritance.

"You see now," Drago said, "Why Adam asked me for lands bordering his son's holding? So he could be close to him without interfering. Your piece of forest in the Fells borders it."

Adela shook her head in a rush of sudden relief mingled with puzzlement. She could not believe this talk of a son, it sounded good, but it was not in the man's character. Adam had a smile like a pike's smile as it waited for its prey to come within range of its teeth. His eyes too, pale sky-blue, were as dead of human feeling as a fish's eyes. Only when a man was badly hurt at the tourney, did they show any emotion at all, and then, especially if he screamed, they filled up with lust.

The king kicked out at a round stone under the stream's dappled surface. It went flying, trailing water, and flushed a startled squirrel out of the undergrowth. "Damn! There's one we missed." He looked down at her and said, gently, "A man who can be so considerate of his son can't be all bad can he?" Then he laughed. "Dark Ones know how he managed to get a son! His taste is for little boys, not women."

"Then, Lord, I'm freed," she said, and rose, lifted by relief and happiness. "Because, when my mother died and I inherited our family lands, I gifted that manor to Giles, with my father's permission. I hold nothing in Castreld now, my estates are all in the counties of Scarfeld, Stanscir and Caldland."

"No!" said the king in astonishment, coming down in the stream with a splash which made Adela giggle, "He told me all about the manor in Castreld. How special it was to you."

Painful, even now, to speak of such things, to speak of the place where she had been young, but she swallowed it and explained. "It is special. I was brought up there. But then my mother died, and my father couldn't bear to live there without her. None of our family have set foot on that ground for ten years. But we knew Giles could go back without pain - he was too young to remember her. So I gave it to him. I can have the deeds brought to you."

"Well," said Drago, briskly, though his square hands were fidgeting with embarrassment. "That's different. I can hardly give him the boy to marry, whatever he might prefer. It seems the wedding's off after all."

He bowed, mockingly; "Keep an eye on him at this Friday Feast, and maybe you'll get a little revenge. We'll see how well he takes it, eh?"

Chapter Seven

The banqueting hall was packed and roaring, smelling of smoke, roast meats, sweat and perfume. The din of conversation quieted a little as the second remove was brought in; woodcock and pheasant, roasted, with stews of mallard and goose; pike presented in green sauce and turbot in a sauce of red rose-petals. The carcass of the boar and the dishes of venison were taken away and in their place was set a whole swan, its flesh gilded with gold leaf, and a subtlety of pastry in the shape of an embattled castle.

Adela wiped her hands with a napkin, dipped for her in a bowl of cool water by a solemn little page. The water felt very good. It was infernally hot in the hall on this balmy evening. Torches and candles blazed in a reek of smoke, and the fire in the great hearth roared like an exultant giant.

The golden light cast a shimmer over the gem-bright colors of the men's clothing, the silks and rich embroidery. It flattered plain faces and gentled harsh ones. Even the nuns were smiling as they stood by the cage's open gate, watching the children go in and out, laden with food.

There was a kind of spell to the radiance, which made the world seem a kindly place, and Adela relished it, welcoming wholeheartedly the feeling of happiness it brought. It was the first time she had felt anything approaching content since becoming a ward of the king's court.

As the minstrels began to play again the older and more trustworthy pages came forward to carve the roasts and place the meats between diners.

Giles, his corn-blond hair gleaming in the candlelight, wore a half frown of concentration as he served the barons. He looked younger than his twelve years, with his new blue tunic and his serious expression, but he had been singled out to serve at the king's table, and he was determined to do it well.

Adela smiled under her mask, knowing he would keep her awake long into the night with his chatter about this great honor. Let him! She would lose him soon enough. In a year he would be old enough to go out to the men, and she would be finally alone in the cage.

But tonight she was safe, and a year was a long time. She pushed the sadness away, listened with delight to the music, let herself dwell with fond pride on her brother. So mature he was! So composed!

It seemed no time at all since the days when he would rush to her, permanently grubby, to have his scraped knees bathed or splinters pulled. Now look at him; a thoughtful, deft, graceful boy who increasingly reminded her of both of her parents. Their father's hair had been the same shade of gold, (a rare and much prized color she wished she had inherited herself), but the mischievous green eyes, veiled now with responsibility, were their mother's eyes. It was a source of unexpected pleasure that every time she caught the sidelong glint of Giles' emerald eye she was reminded of her mother, dead so long ago.

As if he sensed her regard he paused, looked curiously at the women's enclosure. She had sat close to the wrought-iron deliberately to be in his view. She waved, and he grinned back, pleased with himself.

Turning away in high content her glance fell on the face of Adam de Limoges. His posture was relaxed, complacent, but his gaze was on the king, and the malice in it shocked her. He had been told then, she thought, and now, under the ash-brown of his fading hair his face spoke of treason.

He should not have been able to hear her indrawn breath, but still he looked up and met her gaze and smiled.

She leaped to her feet. Why did it feel as though he could see her? As though his look could pierce straight through the grima and slide over her naked face? Her instincts screamed: *Move back! Flee back into the half-light. Get away from the grill!* But she could not. She thought he had made some slight gesture - the rings on his right hand had flashed in the light. Now she stood paralyzed, like a wren pinned down by a serpent's gaze.

"I'll have you," he mouthed, and smirked to see her fear.

"Adam!" The king's voice rang out, loud, mocking and merry. A spasm of intense fury passed across Adam's wide face and was gone in an instant. He turned to face Drago with a smile.

The hall hushed, the diners looking up from their trenchers, awaiting the king's pleasure with amused curiosity. Adela, released from the spell, sank onto her bench and gazed up at the king with invisible gratitude. The court might believe he was doing this solely for his own amusement, but she doubted it. The timing had been too good.

Chapter 7

"Are you well, my lady?" the page whispered, as her dining companions made noises of sympathy.

"Yes," said Adela, and strengthened her trembling voice with sheer will. "Thank you. Do you think you could bring me some more water? The heat...."

On the other side of the barrier, the King said "I've had enough music." and grinned to hear the untidy winding up of the minstrel's song. He leaned back casually in the gilded chair and fixed a mocking gaze, on Adam's toothy smile. "I've a mind for something more exotic. You have a name as a witch. Show us some magic."

Blue flame leaped up in Adam's eyes; fury, plain for all to see.

A murmur of fear and disapproval went round the hall. One or two of the braver diners risked the king's wrath by openly making the sign of God. The Archbishop rose, bowed, and left the room.

"That's set you by the ears! You two-faced, spineless cowards!" Piety threw the King into a ferment, as usual. "You're quite happy to gossip about it. You're quite happy to eat and drink with him as long as you don't have to see what he is? I put him to the test and suddenly you're all innocent?"

He swept the avenues of well-dressed diners with a glance of contempt; "Well, if you don't like it you'd better leave now," and he gestured expansively at Adam, who stood, his face a brutal mask of anger, below him. "Get on with it then."

"I am not some sideshow conjurer!" Adam exclaimed, his beautiful deep voice growling with rage, his big hands clenched and white.

"I'm putting you to the proof, Adam," the king mocked, and his Barons looked down on the witch with icy distaste, "I've had a certain amount of inconvenience over you, and I want you to prove your worth. Are you any kind of a conjurer at all?"

"Shall I conjure you a fiend?" Adam replied. It came short of a threat by the merest breath. For a moment the air in the hall hung heavy as the two men locked glances, like battling rams. Then Adam came to his senses with a visible effort and gave a suave bow. "I am at your command," he said.

The king motioned good humouredly to his cup-bearer, and the lad came forward and filled up the golden goblet with wine.

"Not a fiend, I think," he said, and cast a brief glance in Adela's direction; "I'd like to see something more welcome than that. I want to see this son of yours."

"Very well, my liege." Adam backed away from his bench - still a menacing power in him, despite his age, still bodily strength and something more. His face was serene again, only his ice-blue eyes still brimmed with rage like a hotter echo of the massive fire. He stopped there, in front of the blaze, and the fierce light stained his beard red, so he seemed to turn a severed head to glower at the court.

Adela's page was coming from the kitchens, intent on his bowl of water. Adam caught him by the hair, dragged him into the firelight. The bowl went spinning, bursting into pieces against the cage. Metal flashed. There was a gust of coppery reek, and blood, bright life's-blood, pumped out of a wound in the child's hand and spattered on the floor. Adam held the screaming boy by the wrist until there was a puddle of it.

"Let him go!" shouted the king, aghast, and, pushing the boy away, Adam nodded complacently.

"Of course, my liege. I just need the blood of a child for the spell."

"No more of that." Drago's eyes were sharp as broken glass. Under cover of the boy's stifled sobbing he muttered to Bishop Ranulf, who was rigid with disapproval and horror, "I begin to appreciate the church's point of view."

The witch put his hand in the pool of blood and, with the elegance of practice, drew a wide circle on the floor. Then he scribbled runes and signs all about the outside of it with a finger dipped in gore. The blood began to dry, glistening stickily.

Flames hung inside the circle, writhing, as though the wild light of the fire had been trapped there and now struggled to be free. There was a noise, very soft, like the sound of despair, and gasps of awe and fear from the watching crowd.

Adam grabbed the box of salt from the nearest table and flung it into the center of the flame. It went up in blinding flashes of light, white and blue and palest yellow. Then, his deep voice like a bull's bellow, he shouted out a long sentence of meaningless words, shapeless and sinister. His stained hands were closed into fists as though he could beat the light into doing his bidding.

Inside their red necklace the flames paled, faded until they were like ribbons of flayed skin. The labored breathing of the hurt boy was the loudest thing in the hall as the ghoulish things began to coalesce into the shape of a man's face. It turned in its frame of flame-yellow hair and looked out at the frightened banqueters, a face beautiful as a drawn blade, hard and sharp and brittle as flint.

Briefly something about it touched Adela, as though she had seen that face before - in dreams, maybe, or in some other world. She strove for the memory, but then, with a moan of exhaustion, the wounded page slipped to the floor in a faint, and the image went out like a snuffed candle.

"So that's your son?" the king broke the long silence which followed, "He doesn't look like you."

"But he takes after me in other ways," Adam said. Something in his voice made Adela shudder, something very different from fatherly pride.

The court physician, stirring out of his shock, gently lifted the fallen page and carried him away.

"Was the business with the boy really necessary?" said Drago coldly. It astonished Adela that he had the courage to speak, and to sound so unimpressed. The faces surrounding him were gray and frozen with dread. The men, forced to acknowledge the supernatural world, must be considering their own frailty.

The witch shrugged; "We have to make a few sacrifices for our art."

He had frightened the court into silence, and that lit in Adela a spark of defiance. Deliberately feigning unconcern she picked up her knife and began cutting up her food into pieces tiny enough to be discretely introduced beneath the grima. As she worked she talked, holding one half of an uneasy conversation - about the virtues of the new palace - with her stunned neighbor until, reassured by her mundane tone, the woman began to stammer some responses.

Gradually the braver men, remembering their reputations, began to joke about the vision, their laughter loud and forced. Adam sat down again on his bench, his neighbors edging nervously away, and eyed the pages with a face of frustration, like a man turned away from his lover's bed.

Adela watched him, as she might watch a wasp crawling over the walls of her room. When he rose as if to go she sighed in relief, and looked down at the small breath ruffling the surface of her wine. Then, with a sociable smile, she turned to reply to some pleasantry of her companion's.

Adam's big, bloodstained hand came down over hers.

She cried out - she couldn't help it. The shock! He had thrust his arm through the cage. He was actually touching her!

How could he dare! How could he dare do something so abhorrent? And in public! Someone would come, soon and take him away - and stop him. They would have to stop him now.

But the men were watching another entertainment - one of the cwens ribbon-dancing in a clash of anklets and thrown coins - and the women had shrunk away, too astonished to act.

He was leaning on her hand now, heavily, grinding the bones against the hard oak table. The touch made bile rise in her throat. She tried to pull free, but could not.

Her struggle seemed to amuse him, so she turned her face away from him and sat silent with forced indifference.

"You have made a contest of it now, my lady," he said. His voice was quite gentle, while the pressure of his hand increased until she could hardly refrain from crying out. "We can get married this Autumn, he went on, in the same polite, smug tone, "On your manor in Castreld."

"That land is Giles's!" Adela exclaimed indignantly and Adam laughed,

"Oh yes," he said, relishing the words, "Your brother... such a sweet boy. He and I must get better acquainted."

Horror made her turn her head. "Keep away from him!"

He smiled with pleasure at her reaction. Then he released her hand, licked the dried blood from the ends of his fingers, and went off, whistling.

The fox cubs were rolling over and over in a tight ball of joyously snapping teeth and pawing feet. They seemed to be grinning at one another as they wriggled, and their excited barking covered most of the sound of the two boys edging up through the undergrowth to peer at them.

"They're fighting," Richard whispered.

"No," said Giles, quietly, "They're just playing." He put his head down on his hands and watched them for a while. The light began to strengthen, the sky showing pink and gold through the spread leaves. Slowly the gray world of dawn began to fill up with color.

Chapter 7

"They're definitely getting bigger," said Richard. A shaft of yellow light moved over his hair, russet as winter bracken, and lit on the blue glass bead which fastened his shoe, so it glowed sapphire.

"I think my sister's going mad," said Giles reluctantly.

"Did you know," Richard whispered, taking a deep breath so he could get it all out in one, "When a fox is hungry it makes itself look like it's dead. Then when birds come along to pick out its eyes it snaps them up before they realize."

"Is that true?" Giles was surprised out of his reverie. His friend nodded.

"Father Guilo told me. It's written in one of his books. What's the matter with your sister?"

Giles sighed and sat up. The fox cubs whisked away to earth. "She's worried about Adam."

"The witch?" said Richard, with quick interest, "Did you see what he did? It was amazing!"

"He wants to marry her." Giles puzzled it out as he went, "And she doesn't want to."

"So?" said Richard, brushing the leaf-mold from his green tunic as he rose.

"She seems to think he might hurt me." Giles rubbed at the gold stubble at the back of his neck where the hair had recently been cut. He was beginning to feel a little guilty for evading her precautions and slipping out into the forest before dawn. He had gone with Richard to watch the foxes every Sunday since they were born, it was a ritual. It was nearly a duty: Richard, who was probably his best friend, would have been hurt if he had refused to go. Still, he knew Adela would worry and now he regretted it.

"That's stupid." Richard, who was approaching thirteen years of age felt himself to be very much a man of the world. "It stands to reason," he said. "If he wants her to marry him then he'll be extra nice to you."

"That's what I thought," said Giles, climbing to his feet with a frown, "If he wanted to kill me he'd do it after they were married - so there'd be nothing she could do. But she made me promise her not to go out alone."

"You're not alone." Richard shrugged, and began to work his way further into the forest. "Come on, if we hurry we can get to the gyrfalcon's nest before that old wineskin of a steward misses us."

"She's set all the servants to watch me." Giles pushed through the undergrowth in the wake of his friend. "I had the devil of a time getting away from Aelfric this morning."

Richard was silent, and Giles, more nervous than he cared to admit, said, "I should go back now, before I get him into trouble."

There was no reply. Above Giles' head the tree-limbs swayed, leaves rustling. An animal sense for danger told him something had changed. In the growing yellow light the wood seemed suddenly an alien place, unfriendly. The squeal of branches startled him like enemy trumpets. "Richard?" he said, and was ashamed to hear his voice waver.

There was a scream, loud, shocking and angry. He felt his heart stop, and then race.

"*Giles*!" it was Richard's voice. He was not pretending, that scream must have rent his throat.

Giles paused, panting. He wanted to run away. He wanted it very badly, but he was no peasant who could do as they liked, he was a nobleman's son, with obligations. So he picked up a fallen branch, and, cursing himself for his cowardice, he pushed aside the undergrowth and ran into the clearing to do battle.

He saw very little; a brief, blurred impression of open sky; Richard pinned improbably to the falcon's tree, blood running down his arms; the witch, Adam, turning at the sound of his footsteps. He hurled himself at the man, slashing the branch through the air. It shattered over the witch's back, sending jagged splinters flying, but it was Richard who jerked from the blow and cried out. Adam laughed, and made one slight gesture with his right hand. Giles was stopped. It was sudden and implacable as being turned to stone.

It felt to him exactly as it does in a nightmare; when the evil thing is coming up on you and, sobbing, you command yourself to move, trying and trying with all your might, and you cannot even raise a foot.

"Leave him alone!" he shouted, trying to cling on to his anger, so he did not have to admit he was scared. "What are you doing to him?"

Adam came softly over to him and sat down, taking a long, pleased look at both boys. Richard, still making little sounds of agony, was hanging by his hands from the trunk of the ash-tree at the center of the clearing. His hands were overlapped, one on top of the other, and driven through both wrists was a wide-shafted crossbow bolt. Blood was dripping onto the gray bark like a strange rain, and Adam had bathed his hands in it until they were entirely red.

Chapter 7

"I'm drawing power out of him," said Adam, in a gentle whisper, as he took hold of Giles' wrist and forced him down onto the turf beside him. "And I'm using it to fuel the spell that's keeping you so tractable."

He looked at Giles with a smile of anticipation which made the boy want to scream.

"My son tells me," he said, in the same gloating voice, a voice of sensual pleasure, "That it feels to the victim as though you are reaching deep inside them and defiling their very soul. He says the shame of it never goes away."

He reached out and stroked Giles' hair, from the nape of the neck to the crown. Giles tried to flinch, but could not.

"And now for you," Adam said softly.

Chapter Eight

"They wouldn't even let me see him!" Adela wailed. She was stamping in an anguished circle around her room, blind with weeping and rage. She had beaten the walls and her own face in her distress, and her throat was raw with shouting in fury and despair. "Giles is dead, and they wouldn't even let me see him!"

Godgifu, crying quietly herself, did nothing to stop the outburst, but said, gently "There were foxes there, they would have chewed the lad when he was dead. You wouldn't have wanted to see him like that."

Adela rounded on her violently, "Not foxes! Him!" she shouted, "You know it was him! Whatever was done - whatever was so horrible they won't let me see - He did it. You know that!"

She began to pace again, something inside lying to her, telling her she could walk away from this - if she could only walk far enough, fast enough, it would not catch her. A brittle energy drove her, but the walls met her at every turn, and there was no way out.

"Oh God!" she burst out suddenly, "Oh God I wish I was a man, then I'd kill him!" She slammed her small fist into her best glass beaker.

Shards scattered, raking through her skin like cat's claws; the pain finally brought her to herself. She sank down to her knees and wept in earnest for a long, bitter time, while her nurse crouched beside her and rocked her as though she were still in the cradle.

"Damn him!" Adela whispered, wearily. "May the Dark Ones eat him."

"I think they've already begun," said Godgifu seriously. Then she brought Adela quenched red wine in a wooden cup and said, "But now we must make sure he gets sent to the Abyss, soon as may be."

"It was my fault," Adela whispered, covering her face, "my fault. I should have told the Queen he'd threatened Giles, I should have made them protect him. It was my fault."

Chapter 8

"My lady," said Godgifu sternly, "There's no time for this." Dashing the tears from her own face with a ruthless hand she poured out water into a pewter basin and began to wash Adela's cuts, talking patiently as she did it.

"For now," she said, "because he knows no better, the king will think it was another revenge attack - Sceafn peasants taking their grievances out on the weakest of their oppressors. He will see no reason now not to marry you to that man as he promised, after all, Giles' lands will revert to you."

"I don't care," said Adela with quiet misery, "I don't care, he can do what he likes with me."

"Don't be so selfish," said Godgifu ferociously, but, gentler than her words, she began to comb her lady's disheveled hair, reassuring as memories of childhood. "How many innocents will be blamed and punished for this if you don't tell the king who really did it? Do you think he'll go easy on Sceafn serfs who dared kill Holmr nobles? He can't. Unless you tell him who's really responsible the villages around here will be razed and the people hacked apart. Is that what you want?"

Tears brimmed again in Adela's dark blue eyes, like softer echoes of the flying glass. Her nurse pressed on, relentless, "And what about the other children in this court? Don't you think they need protecting?"

"If I marry him," Adela sobbed, "He won't have to kill any more."

Godgifu snorted in disgust. "A man like that doesn't kill a child because he has to," she said, "He does it because he enjoys it, and he is happy to be offered the excuse."

"I can't believe that," said Adela, in a numbed voice, "no one could be so evil."

"No?" said Godgifu, harshly, "You should have seen what the old king's soldiers did to the folk on my estates, in the Invasion, and they were just ordinary men who had let themselves get a little excited. Imagine what Adam could do to your people if you let him."

The tears were spilling onto the floor now, spreading under Adela's splayed hand, darkening the skirts of her drab gray dress. She sniffed them back and sat for a moment biting her lip to stop them coming again. Then she murmured, meekly, "Thank you," and squeezed the old woman's hand. Getting to her feet, she smoothed down the damp cloth and said, "If you'll help me get ready I'll go to the queen now."

"What do you think I'm doing, child?" said Godgifu fondly.

Queen Olufemi was in her solar, sitting reading in a pool of late afternoon sunshine, with a cup of warm, pale wine resting at her elbow. When she had heard Adela's story she rose.

"Go and get your coverings, we will see the king at once."

The King greeted her with an awkward gentleness which made her want to weep. Then he stood, lost as a cowherd in the face of court etiquette, turning over in his big hands a whetstone warrior from a game of tafl.

Adela knew she should feel exposed, out here in the men's world. She should feel daring, embarrassed, even ashamed, but there was nothing of it left in her. Instead she too stood, numbly, until Guy, the King's squire, gestured her to a seat and settled her there with tapestry cushions, wine in a chased silver cup, and sweet pastries.

Does he expect me to eat with the mask on? To drink? A tremor of anxiety surfaced; *or to take it off?*

She watched carefully as he effaced himself, retiring into the niche of the deep window and leaning there, his arms crossed, looking out on the lush land with peaceful hazel eyes. He had put out no reed for her to drink through, no knife to cut up the pastry into manageable pieces, and he showed no signs of ever doing so. *No,* she decided finally *He simply hasn't thought about it at all. I don't suppose he's ever waited on a woman before.*

He did it very graciously, she thought, treating her almost like another man, with no sense that this was an appalling break with centuries of tradition. He had, she supposed, been ordered to treat her so, but he did it with an unstudied air. She doubted whether, in ordinary circumstances, she could have been as comfortable.

The squire's carefree expression plucked at her as she turned back; he seemed so pleased with the world and with himself, and why should he not be? He was handsome, sleek with muscle, confident of both his martial prowess and his perfect manners. He would probably be knighted this winter.

A pain moved under the surface of her calm - the thought that in five or six years Giles might have looked just the same.

The pain pushed its way into her throat. When she was invited to speak she found she could not. Instead Olufemi, who had stationed herself like a bodyguard behind her husband's chair, repeated Adela's accusations in a level voice.

Chapter 8

There was a long silence. The scent of spiced wine and honey-cakes mixed with the fragrance of candles and the tang of new linen. From outside came the shouts and clatter of a mock duel. The world was going on without Giles, as though he had made no difference at all. Anger began to stir in Adela, forcing the pain aside.

"It makes sense," said the king at last. "I couldn't believe, when I heard it, that this was the deed of some Sceafn." He half rose, then hurled himself back into his chair - the legs shrieked against the floorboards. The Queen stepped back, unperturbed.

"It's not like them," Drago growled. "To be honest I don't get particularly upset if a gang of them ambushes a Holmr knight in the forest. It shows they've still got spirit, and any decent knight should be more than a match for a bunch of serfs." He rubbed an open hand over his face, grimacing.

"But to kill two little boys?" he said, his light tone no longer concealing the shock, "And to..."

He bit off the end of his thought as though he was biting on a leather strap while they pulled an arrowhead out of him. Adela forced the pang of horror aside; she did not want to know, she really didn't want to know whatever it was he was trying not to tell her. "It's not like them," he repeated, weakly.

"It wasn't them." Adela confirmed. She took up the silver cup, and gripped it so hard it was bent out of shape. "It was Adam."

The king leaned back in his chair, balancing it on the back legs, and fixed her with a sharp look. "What was it he said, exactly?"

"That we would be married on my lands in Castreld. When I said those lands were Giles's he said... he would get to know Giles better."

Drago got up, very quietly, held still for one long moment, while his face went blank with thought, then he swore like a Wilmlander mercenary and kicked the table over. Stone tafl-pieces scored long gashes on the new floor. The King's cup went skittering in a flood of pale wine, rolled, flashing in the strong sunlight. One of the guards looked in and was hauled back quickly by the other.

"Adam is dead!" the king shouted, "He's dead! I'm going to kill him!" He strode to the doorway and seized the inquisitive guard by his chain mail sleeve. "Get Adam de Limoges and bring him here! If he escapes I'll have your head for it!"

The guard hurried away, smirked at behind his back by his companion.

Drago paced, while his squire silently put the room to rights.

"He was going to be the sword in my right hand," Drago said, resentfully, "He was going to be to me what the colleges were to Varian. Sceafige was only the beginning. With his power behind me I was going to conquer the world - make a new Empire."

His pacing brought him to the Queen. The line of gold thread around her grima glittered as she looked up at him. Within the enveloping wool the light picked out her fierce brown eyes for a moment, before the movement took them back into shadow. Outside the women's enclosure she too wore the coverings, but her indignation seemed to seep through every heavy fold.

"I was going to make a new Empire," Drago said, "for our son to rule."

"But the price is too high," said Olufemi calmly.

"Yes," after a pause, a breath, his face closed again on private thought, he nodded. "Yes, if this is his price then it is too high."

"There should be a public trial," Adela suggested, hearing her voice weak but determined, "so everyone will know he's been brought to justice for what he did. So there will be no reprisals against the Sceafn peasants."

"No," said Drago, thoughtfully, "no trial. What evidence have we got? Your word against his and you're a woman, irrational and overcome with grief. no one is going to believe you. I'm only surprised I do."

"But you wouldn't just have him killed..." Adela breathed, and stumbled for words to express her discomfort, "Like a murderer yourself."

"Oh, no," said the king, with some bitterness, "I can always find an excuse." Then he grinned at her, until she wanted to slap him. "As for Adam," he said, "I can have him burned as a witch. I don't think anyone can deny that would be just."

She remembered, suddenly, clearly, the heat and crush of the banquet; the frightened silence; the ghostly face in a circle of blood.

Green sap sizzled on the room's small fire, filling the chamber with the fragrance of apple-wood.

"You did it on purpose," she said, wonderingly, feeling unwonted respect for his cleverness, and distaste. "You made him show everyone what he was, just in case you might have occasion to get rid of him."

"And no one noticed," Drago agreed, happily. "No one expects strategy from a great oaf like me."

Chapter 8

Adela looked down at the wine-cup she held. In its shaded depths the liquid was the color of Mearh amber.

"And the Sceafns?" she said softly.

"Ah," said the king, with a touch of guilt. He picked up the carved warrior again and tapped it on the table. It had lost two of the fingers which gripped its graven spear, the new stone showed silver-gray beneath. "I'll see to it they get a couple of hours warning," he said, "before my men arrive."

"My liege," said Adela, her voice unsteady between indignation and regret, "that's not the memorial my brother would have wished."

She put the cup back on the table, willing the hand to be steady. Grief turned all emotions to weariness, but beneath it she was conscious of a twinge of satisfaction: She had just rebuked the King! If she could do such a thing, then surely she could learn to go without the coverings and the walls - to walk the world barefaced, as nuns had to do.

"What do you want from me?" Drago mocked, not unkindly, "You think I should tell all my outraged courtiers I've had a fit of mercy for the sake of my soul? They wouldn't believe it."

"You must do what's right," said Adela wearily, "And your soul could probably do with something."

The squire, Guy, forgotten in his alcove, gave a muffled snort of amusement and bent his head - black curls falling over his smile like a veil.

The king put his game-piece down with great delicacy, and burst into laughter. "Gods! You are like your father! He was a fool too, but a holy fool. Alright, petal, I'll see to it, somehow, that no one gets hurt."

There were sounds outside the curtained doorway. Raised above the tramp of feet, the metal whisper of chain, were the guards' voices, slurred and puzzled. Pouring through and over them like dark honey the brown-gold voice of Adam dripped reassurance. He sounded not at all like a condemned man, not at all like a man with anything on his conscience, merely gracious and slightly amused.

"By the Moat of Blood!" The king's face was red as the jewels laced in his beard. He sprang up. "I didn't ask the damn fools to bring him here like a guest. What the hell do they think they're doing?"

"Um," muttered Guy uncertainly, "Should the Ladies be here for this? He may offer some offense."

"Don't be so bloody proper all the time!" Drago snapped, "Adela's the last one left of her family, of course she should be here, and as for the Queen, if you can order her to do anything you're a better man than I. Now bring him in, and stand ready to knife him at the first sign of magic."

The squire's eyes rounded with apprehension, he had clearly forgotten what kind of a prisoner he had to deal with. It was with a very sober tread that he went forward to draw back the curtain and usher the witch into the room.

Adam came in smiling, and favored each of them with a long look of approval, like a cat choosing between mice. Drago scowled in return and, taking one long step forward, belted him across the face, sending him hurling into the wrought iron candle-holder which stood by the wall.

He landed on his knees in a tangle of tapestry and a spattering of hot white wax. For a moment there passed across his face a look of intense terror. He cowered, clasping his arms about his face, while the iron stand went toppling, the candle-flames tracing transparent gold arcs across the smoky air.

If the king had been as ruthless as he liked to pretend he might have ended it there - kicked the groveling man in the head until the skull crumpled under the fading hair, or simply taken his notched sword and hacked until the witch was dead.

Adela watched him struggle with the temptation, a hard-headed little voice in her shouting *yes! Do it now! Kill him while you can!* Ashamed of herself, she said nothing.

Soon, as if afraid Adam's cowardice might be catching, Drago backed away from the man and stood watching with a frown of contempt.

Adam uncurled, peeking up through his linked arms like a bullied child. In his astonishment he looked almost innocent. Then he smiled and easy confidence came down over his face like a mask. "Mercy?!" he mocked, "How admirable. But then I always knew you were a fool."

He got to his feet, age beginning to show in the stiffness of his movements, and stood in the center of the room, gazing at the king with derision. "You are probably starting to regret it even now."

Then he made a graceful gesture with his right hand. The carved jewel in the great red-gold ring flashed green with inner fire, and with no more effort, he froze all four of them where they stood.

"Dear, dear," he said, "I thought it might come to this." Then he walked forward and spat in the king's face. "That's for hurting me. Don't do it again."

Chapter 8

"You're dead!" shouted Drago, "You're a dead man! Guards, get in here!"

"I don't think so. Your guards are fast asleep, and you're in no state to harm me."

Adam strolled to Guy and prized the drawn scram from the squire's clenched fist. "This was meant for me, wasn't it?" he said, flourishing the heavy blade under the youth's angry eyes. "I hope you appreciate that your tardiness has sadly endangered your king. You traitor!"

A slight flick of the wrist and the scram laid open Guy's cheek to the bone. He made no sound, silent as a well-trained squire should be in the presence of his betters. Then Adam wiped his fingers through the blood, the hand lingering just long enough to be a threat. The were-fire died in the green ring, but Adela felt the spell tighten around her, wrapping her around like filthy bandages.

"There," said Adam with satisfaction, "It doesn't do to waste an item when you can use people."

"What the hell do you think you're doing?" the king growled, sounding as belligerent and unafraid as always. Adela admired him for it and breathed as deeply as the spell would allow, working hard to show the same lack of concern.

"A small demonstration," said Adam, "to sweeten the proposal I intend to offer."

He drifted over to Adela, slid his hand under the grima. It touched her neck like some questing maggot - her heart lurched, she tried to flinch, but could not. Then he yanked off the mask, pulling a handful of brown hair after it. The air hit her face - she felt her skin blaze with blood and heat - and his gaze crawled over her, inch by inch.

"Perhaps I should take her here," he said, "In front of you." He slid his hand down her neck and under her collar while she bit on her tongue to stop herself making a noise. "Then you'd have to marry her to me."

Her silence annoyed him, perhaps. With a sudden flash of petulant anger he hit her hard across the face. Her lip burst and blood poured from her nose and mouth together, staining the oak floor. She yelped.

It pleased him - he continued more urbanely. "But I do so hate to restrain myself. And for now I need her alive."

"What's the proposal?" said the king, with a sigh of impatience at which Adam scowled.

"I don't ask much." The old mage sat, pointedly, in the king's chair. "I want to live a quiet retired life in a little part of the country I can call my own. I want my son back and I want to indulge myself in my old age with a few simple pleasures. It's not too much to ask, is it?"

"You want me to give you this woman," the king said in clarification, "knowing that as soon as you have her lands you intend to kill her?"

"Yes," said Adam, shrugging. "What is the difficulty? She's only one woman. And I could make you king of the whole world."

"What?" said Drago, sharply. Adam smiled.

"A servant of mine is arriving back in Sceafige soon," he said, "with a certain relic he acquired in Yocheved." He paused for effect, smirking. "It is the scepter of Emperor Varian of the Duguth, with which he commanded the Dark Ones to do his will. When I have it I will be able to do whatever I wish."

He drained Adela's wine, crushed the cup, tossed it aside.

"I could hand you an Empire greater than that of Varian himself. It's what you want, isn't it - you've told me often enough - an Empire for your sons. I can give it to you, for the temporary use of this one woman and the grant of her lands."

"Emperors..." said the king, meditatively.

"Just reach out and take it."

No! thought Adela, shocked. *No my lord you can't... you just can't!* For a moment, only the spell stopped her falling to her knees and begging.

"My sons could be Emperors..."

"Slaves!" The Queen's voice rang out unexpectedly, contemptuous; "They would be this man's slaves. Maybe his victims too. Have you forgotten what you said? The price is too high."

Adam did not even turn to look at her.

"The Noir whore thinks she understands politics," he said gently, "But she should go back to her loom. This is men's work. Now, Drago, what do you say? Will you do what I ask? Or will I have to kill you?"

"How dare you?" the king replied, so softly Adela was not certain she had heard him aright. "How dare you!" he shouted again, and her heart leaped for joy.

Chapter 8

"How dare you threaten me in my own bloody room!" he yelled. "How dare you hold me against my will? How dare you hurt my squire and threaten my ward and then try and bribe me? I'm the bloody King here! So kill me now if you're going to, otherwise when this spell wears off I'm going to have you flayed!"

The sun, setting, glared in at the narrow windows with a brazen orange fire which picked out harshly the lines of age on the witch's astonished face. As it does with many monsters of the night the light seemed to have turned him to stone. His gray brows came together only very gradually as he came to terms with the king's refusal, frowning over it as a backward child frowns over some hard teaching in the schoolroom.

"You'd rather die?" he asked. "Are you mad?" and then disgust replaced his curiosity. "Oh, I understand. You're being noble. You're out to impress the underlings. Well, let's see how impressed they are when you're dead."

Getting up he spilled the wine cups and flagon on the floor, tore down the nearest tapestry and hurled it into the fire. All this as casually as a man taking up his cloak upon leaving.

"I won't kill you straight away," he said, edging towards the door, "I'm going to see what your brother Bauduin thinks of my offer. A slave's son needs to take all the friends he can get. As for you, you can wait for death, a little while - a few days, a week - It'll give you time to look forward to it properly."

He laughed, "Sweet dreams," he said and strolled out, whistling.

By the time the spell had faded enough for them to move Adam had vanished out of sight. Though every guard and every servant was turned out to search for him they had no sight of him before the dark night came down.

The following morning a Queen's maid, with an escort of two sturdy nuns, arrived at Adela's door to bid her to attend on the King. She had spent a long, wearisome night of warring fear and duty, brooding on what it was right to do, and had concluded, in the intense hush before dawn, that she must offer to undertake this marriage after all. She had no right to place the king in danger simply to save her own life or honor.

She had meant to see the message got out to the king this morning. Yet, perversely, she was annoyed to be summoned, and suspected that Drago had also had second thoughts. It did not please her to think he intended to take away the virtue of her self-sacrifice by ordering it.

She pushed away her untouched breakfast, collected her coverings - with little thought now of the impropriety, so quickly she had grown used to this - and, with a guardian on each side, she followed the girl to the king's private chambers.

Guy let them in, looking as weak and wan as a man who has been cured of a long fever only by means of a severe bloodletting. The gash in his cheek had closed, but looked swollen and hot against his pallor.

She felt distantly angry about it, as she would have felt had someone deliberately ripped her best dress - the sense of a fine thing wantonly spoiled.

"Are you not well?" she said gently.

He shook his head, slowly, "That spell..." he said, his voice slurred and tired. He shuddered. "I feel as though I had lost half my life's blood, not just taken a scratch." He breathed, swallowed, "Go in. He wants to speak to you."

Inside was a scene of disarray, parchment pages drifted over the bed and floor like heavy fallen leaves. The king, his black beard straggling uncombed over the deep blue of his robe, was toying listlessly with a tray of food while he peered at the monkish handwriting of one scroll. Three clerks, perched uncomfortably on folding stools, were poring over tally rolls; arguing over property values and tithes. From the burnt down candles they had been at it for some time. Certainly Drago already looked fretful and annoyed.

"Take your arguments elsewhere for an hour," he said to his exchequer when Adela entered with her escort, "And when you get back I'll expect them to be solved. I expect everything to be finished by the evening, if not then we work through the night. Understand?"

"My liege!" the eldest exclaimed, in a soft, reasonable voice, "Some of these matters need not be dealt with until the new year. "

"Tonight," said the king finally. "It all gets finished tonight or not at all. Now get out."

The clerks gave Adela a variety of scandalized glances as they flapped past her, black as crows. Their conversation, as their sandals slapped down the corridor, was in Duguthan, the sacred tongue, but it did not sound at all edifying.

"My liege," Adela began immediately, still standing, her small fists clenched in an effort to steady her voice. She was uneasy - speaking before she was commanded to do so - but she wanted to offer this freely and she was afraid he was going to command it.

Chapter 8

"My liege, let me marry him. I don't want to put you in danger. Maybe I can't fall in battle for you, but I can, and should at least do this."

"What!" the king exclaimed, leaping up as if hurled by a mangonel, "Do you want to marry him?"

"No, of course not!" Adela's reply was rather more vehement than was polite.

"Well then," said the king.

"But I should," Adela insisted, pleased and surprised to see he was not as mean-spirited as she had thought.

"What kind of a coward would that make me? If I let you die for me?" He began to pace, irritably. There was a new note in his voice. Something had changed about him. A malaise was following him like the gray whisper of plague. With sudden horror she saw it: He was afraid.

She made a small noise of pity in her throat, quickly muffled in case he should hear and take offense. He stopped pacing, eventually, and looked her in the eye,

"Petal," he said, resolutely, "I owe you."

"Oh!" Adela hurt for him. She drew breath for a long impassioned repetition of her offer, but he forestalled her, kindling into his old self and storming; "And if that man thinks he can threaten me, he can choke on it!"

"But..."

"Sit down!" snapped the king, pointing to one of the camp stools at the foot of the bed. "And shut up. The question is closed."

By now she too knew better than to argue with him. She sat and kept quiet, and it seemed to her more difficult than anything she had ever done, except perhaps for casting the first handful of earth on Giles's small coffin.

"You heard DeBourne's dream," he went on quietly, when she had settled and the room was still. "I didn't think anything of it at the time, but now... it looks like I've no hope of eternity. The Lord of the Abyss will have me."

He shook his head, forestalling Adela's cry of pity and disbelief, shrugged, "But, if I am to die," he said, "I'd as lief do it somewhere where I'm glad to be alive. I will leave tomorrow for my hunting lodge at Kingshurst. Such a move should also," he looked at her soberly, "draw Adam's attention from you, buy you some time. It's a poor repayment for your father's debt, I know. I'm sorry."

In a small unworthy corner of her mind she agreed with him, but she said "You've done already more than you ought."

Feeling herself close to tears she turned away, picking at the stitching of the stool's leather seat until the urge to weep had passed.

"As soon as you can when I've gone," he said, "leave the court. Bauduin changes his allegiances so often his word is worth nothing. He won't be any protection for you."

"Oh, my liege," she said - one long sigh of regret that she had done this to him.

"Go," he said, "start to make ready. The sight of you distresses me."

She did as he said, throwing herself into the work as some relief from her feelings of guilt, and all the time, with mounting anger, she knew her misery and his fear were exactly what Adam had designed when he gave them this hopeless reprieve.

In the morning the children told her Drago had not slept at all. Servants had heard him pacing from one end of his chamber to the other, endlessly, until the sound lulled them into nodding themselves.

But Gunnild's messenger, Steven, said that, soon after dawn, he had seen the king harry his disgruntled foresters out of their beds, turn the court into an uproar of packing, and ride out for his hunting lodge in the eastern forest.

"In the best of spirits, lady, and in rude health," said the boy, appreciatively, and grinned.

Chapter Nine

"The king is dead!" The sound of running feet, a voice crying it in the passage, then doors opening, men calling out in dismay.

Adela's hand shook, the shears nicking her jaw. A lock of hair fell into the fire and was burnt in an instant, the stench making her choke.

"May God and Benel have mercy on him." Godgifu filled Adela's silence with sober practicality, "And for everyone's sake may we have a new king soon. Here, let me do it."

She took the shears and cut off her lady's hair, the spilled, waist-long tresses falling over her hands like heavy silk.

"There," she said, eventually, "it should do, at a distance. Now put these on and we'll try the whole effect."

Steven had brought clothes from Adela's Sceafn groom, Aelfric. They were the horse-boy's second-best garments - brown woolen hose and a weld-yellow tunic in the Sceafn style; long, split front and back for riding. It had been patched with faded green. Though Aelfric was a small man the clothes hung amply on Adela and she belted them loosely with Giles's most worn belt.

Aelfric had also sent her his knife, unasked, giving up the symbol of his freedom to her need. It was probably the most valuable item he possessed. The generosity made her weep - everything made her weep at the moment - but it lightened her heart as she hung the long scabbard from her waist.

A large brown hood altered the shape of her shoulders, and bulky leg-bindings straightened out the curve of her calves. Godgifu nodded with cautious approval. "If Adam does have a watch set on you, you should slip by it like that. With God's grace he won't know you're gone until the new king sends for you. Even if Bauduin moves like lightning to seize the crown, that shouldn't be for at least a week. You can be half way to Castreld by then."

She sat down on the bed, an end of one white braid peeking out beneath her wimple. There was a terrible silence.

"Gunnild's writ of manumission is on the table," Adela said, to be saying something. "Make sure she gets it. If things go wrong, at least she'll be free to return to Mearh."

Standing, she took up her bow and her stuffed saddlebags and cast one last look around the room - her bed with the green hangings; the nurse's pallet, neatly made; the truckle-bed rolled under her own, which had once been Giles's; the empty cedar wood chest which had held his clothes, gone now to the poor; her father's sword and shield leaning against the wall. Ever since she had arrived here it seemed she had done nothing but mourn.

"What a terrible place this is," she said. "I'm glad to be leaving."

The old woman, her pale eyes full of tears, got stiffly to her knees and plucked at Adela's hem. "Please, my lady. Please let me go with you. You're like my own daughter. You're all I have left. Please let me come and protect you, or at least be with you at the end."

"Oh!" Adela gasped, hurt even in her numbness by her old friend's sudden vulnerability. She fell to her own knees and hugged the woman tightly - the silk wimple and the old skin equally creased against her cheek. "Godgifu! Why do you think I want you to stay? You've been my mother all these years. I need to know you are safe. You must stay. I couldn't bear to put you in danger too."

"But you surely won't go alone?"

"Who can I take? He knows all of my servants. He would follow any of them."

"Wait just a day, so something can be arranged," Godgifu pleaded, but Adela rose and slung the saddlebags on her shoulder.

"No," she said, "I want to go now. Don't fret for me. I will stay alive; I know my duty."

She went out, through the tapestry-hung passages, the niche candles flickering in her wake. The air was warm and stuffy, smelling of stale perfume and dust - the smell of her enclosed life.

At the children's gate she paused, reached for the latch. Her fingers brushed the cold metal and her hand stopped as though frozen: How could she think of doing this? She who had been trained to be useless! She would fail! She would become prey.

The outside world was full of horrors - fiends, and fiends who wore the skin of men; devils and fae and monsters. She knew that - it was why Holmr

Chapter 9

women suffered such extravagant protection. And now she was going to pit herself against them, alone.

Air moved against her bare face. Godgifu came up behind her, reached over to lift the latch.

"There are no fiends out there any more," she said. She had, Adela thought, a mother's way of reading thoughts. "They're all imprisoned behind the Moat of Blood, and even if they weren't, you know there is a Moat around your own heart, keeping you safe. No one has needed the cage, or the coverings, since Benel died." She tutted in feigned annoyance, "You should know that. For heaven's sake! Why don't you Holmr believe your own faith?"

The gate swung open. Sister Ursula looked in and away again in swift complicity.

"Go now." said Godgifu, "And God be with you, Adela."

"And with you, mother," said Adela and slipped through, doing the unthinkable in one quick step.

She strode down the cool stone corridor and out into the blazing sunshine and disarray of the courtyard. Noblemen stood bareheaded in the dust, frozen with shock. Servants milled, exchanging the news in hushed tones. There was a ripple in the crowd and, heedless of solemnity, shouting out breathless answers to the flung questions, a dust-covered messenger came pushing toward the steps.

"Make ready! Bauduin's but an hour behind me, coming for the crown! No, no. They've taken his body to Aldminster - on a cart."

Adela moved through the stricken crowd quietly, seeing what servants' see, invisible as they are to their masters: A monk smirking behind his hand before he composed his face to sorrow; young men frowning over their own future; knights who had fought beside the king paling in genuine grief.

"The blood sprayed their faces until they were as dark as the queen," the messenger replied with relish to one whispered inquiry. He was close to her now, glowing with a sense of his own importance.

Adela herself felt nothing - a core of panic, squeezed, by its own tightness, into nothing.

By the outer gate Aelfric had picketed a horse for her, a dull-coated, bony farmer's cob, such as would not cause an instant cry of 'Thief' being seen under a lad so scruffy as Adela. She patted its white whiskered nose absently before remembering that no servant was rushing to her aid. Then she slung the saddlebags inexpertly over its back, scrambled up and rode out - not the first messenger to do so.

The road - dusty earth and stones hemmed with brambles and broom - was wide enough so an Earl and his retinue might travel along it without forcing the common folk to step into the gutters. It was newly made. Stumps of felled trees stood up like sentinels from quick growing nettles along the way.

Adela rode along it at a steady pace, walking and trotting and walking again, and for a while the seed of panic slept quiet as she marveled at the sheer eeriness of being alone.

It felt so strange! Strange, but good; peaceful, undemanding. Freedom made her drunk with possibilities - she might go anywhere; go to Greatburgh and take a ship; go to the fabled center of the World, to Echianopolis, or Yocheved itself. She could see wonders, and experience firsthand the things she had only read about in marvelous books.

While she thought, the plow-mare plodded on. Travelers exchanged nods with her. She hogged the shade and drew her face back into her hood. Freedom's intoxication ebbed. Realizing she would not convince for long in the tight confines of a ship she put the dream aside, and was surprised at the ache of regret when she did so.

An hour or so later she turned onto the Empire Road which led up first to Sancte Wilhelmton and afterwards to the North. There was a small lake by the side of it, and the ruins of strange walls - the stones seamless, perfectly white, twisted at the top into shapes of liquid decay; like ice dissolving into water.

She dismounted and filled her water-skin at the lake. Then, letting the horse drink, she sat down a moment in the ruin. The ground was as level as a pavement. Idly, she brushed at the dust, wondering if it covered a paved floor and if, perhaps, this had been a church under Sceafn rule.

Instead flecks of color began to show under her fingertips; she felt, under the grit, an astonishing smoothness, as though marble had been poured and set like glass. It was pleasantly warm to the touch, even in the deepest shadow, and the colors were bright, dyed into the slickness of the stone.

Standing up she saw the picture; an unveiled woman, confident and beautiful, with rouge-red lips and coiled sable hair coming down on her shoulders. Her saffron gown billowed in the same powerful curves as her hair. Symbols, some barely discernible - lemon or gold against the yellow material -

Chapter 9

floated at her command. In her left hand she had a staff, orb-tipped, and on her forehead was tattooed a crescent moon.

The edges of the pavement, drifted over by centuries of dirt, faded back into the soil.

Adela sat on her heels and looked at it. The woman's face seemed to change as the leaves moved overhead; her smile flickered in the dancing summer light.

A witch of the Duguth Empire, Adela thought uneasily, dredging up remote history, and present religion. Was this the face of one of those who had taken part in the Broken Summoning - who had enabled the Dark Ones to open the Abyss and come out? She was so young! Could she have seen all that terror; the Ruination of Firentharf and the Amyrred Lands; the Empire's renunciation of magic and espousal of the struggling church; the Bonfire of Witches?

No! She looked too happy. She must have died long before then; when the witches were the Emperor's left hand, and the armies his right.

"Here, lad, get away from there!"

The voice startled her to her feet, it was deep and reproachful, speaking untamed vulgar Sceavish. She grabbed the reins and vaulted onto the horse's back, kicking it around to face him, wary and prepared to flee.

It was a pilgrim, leaning on his staff, his bronzed face shadowed under a wide hat. When he saw her fear he put down the staff at his feet and held out both hands.

"I mean no harm, lad," he said, a little more gently. "It's an elvish place, that. You shouldn't go near it."

"I didn't know," said Adela, gruffly. The pilgrim smiled,

"They're heathens, them elves," he said, "Or fiends maybe. Even a young un like you should know better than to sit in one o' their places."

"Sorry." Adela kept her head bent as if in shame. Her heart was hammering; he could realize any moment what she was. She felt acutely conscious of her faint Holmsh accent and aware, more than ever, of the legacy of hatred the old king had left behind. She nudged the horse forward cautiously.

"Eh, lad," said the pilgrim, oblivious to all of this, turning to walk beside her, "what was it you saw?"

"A lady," said Adela in a surly tone of voice and urged the mare to a trot.

"Ah," the pilgrim nodded with grave wisdom as she drew away; "That'd be like them."

She hardly dared breathe again until he had dwindled to the size of a hand behind her.

The road, now straight and efficient as an arrow's flight, began to oppress her. It was too smooth, too unweathered, too permanent. There was a smugness about it. 'I outlasted my creators and I will outlast you,' it seemed to say. 'Little creature of flesh. Hide if you can.'

But she could not hide - walking this road she was visible to every traveler before and behind, as far as the eye could see.

The seed of fear began to sprout. She was a Holmr woman, at large and undefended in a country whose whole population had at one time been outraged by Holmr might; she was fair game, and she knew it.

By the time she reached Sancte Wilhelmton it was twilight and she was desperate for the reassurance of walls about her. The cob, which had seemed so placid for the first few hours, had caught her fear, and the last part of the ride had been a constant battle for control. She was exhausted, and ravenously hungry, and having felt neither sensation before they struck her like calamities.

It was a shattering joy to see the town; even the ancient road seemed to leap with a certain flourish to the shining walls, glad of reunion with some kindred work of stone. She made the tired horse trot the final mile, eager to get out of the threatening darkness, to find an inn, and food and rest.

The gates were closed. Guards, patrolling, told her to be off - they would not be opened again until dawn. She had just sense enough to get off the road and into the shelter of the trees before sliding from the horse's back and collapsing in tears. Now she had to make camp; and she was so tired, and so alone.

When the fit passed, and it passed quickly, she took her saddlebags and bedroll off the horse's back, and tied the beast where it could graze on the road's grassy border. Deeper in the shelter of the woods there was a hollow lined with plantain and yarrow. She dumped her things there, gathered wood, and made a ring of stones for her fire.

It took at least an hour, crouched over the steel, to strike a spark which would catch on the cattail tinder. The night came down around her as she worked, and with it all her primal terrors; wolves, demons riding on the

Chapter 9

soughing wind, human men coming on her at unawares, while she was alone. When the spark finally caught she almost put it out again with tears.

She fed the fire for a while, knowing she should take off the horse's tack, and then set the dried meat and oatmeal from her saddlebags to soak for the morning. Fatigue pressed her down, and she did nothing, while around her the night darkened, and her fire blazed in the hollow like a fallen star.

Then - and it felt like all she could possibly endure - she unbuckled her heavy belt, strung her bow and set it within easy reach, and, lying down in the blankets, was almost instantly asleep.

Voices woke her, men's voices. Her heart raced and she willed it to calm, listening with her whole being. There was the faint shivering ring of chain mail, and the glint of it in the moonlight on the road. Her own fire had died into ash; she was hidden from them.

Gingerly, very slowly, she rose, putting an arrow to the string. Her heart sank; she had heard two, but she could see only one.

"He turned off here," the shadow at her arrow-tip said, in Mearh-tinted Holmsh, his accent as uncouth as Gunnild's. A man-at-arms, thought Adela, reassured, with no real cause to be brave, and, doubtless, second-rate mail on his back. She had a bodkin point to her arrow. It would get through.

"Shut up then," said the second, in an urgent hiss. "Do you want to wake the whole town?"

Adela pulled back the bow, aimed for the shadow's unprotected throat, the weight of the draw pulling painfully on her stiff shoulders. She hesitated.

"Look, there's his horse," said the shadow in a quieter tone. "He's camped near here for sure."

"Come then," whispered the other, "let's go tell his lordship."

The shadow hesitated, silver glistening like spilled water down his arm. "Why don't we just go and get him?" he said.

You move one step closer and you're dead thought Adela. It was astoundingly good, having him at her mercy. She felt almost as though she was riding on the arrow-tip - she was made of sharp steel, focused and cold.

Then the other man hissed, "He's an archer, the lord said. He'd have at least one of us before we got to him. Now come away before he hears us."

They moved away. She heard them walk a short distance and, after a pause, hoof-beats muffled on the grassy bank. The sea-sighing of the leaves drowned out the sound quickly, but, just before the quiet drumming faded she thought she heard it stop.

She snatched up her knife-belt, buckled it on, looked at her bedroll - no time to pack it up and take it - then she grabbed the saddlebags and ran out to where the cob was drowsing. The rope took precious seconds to unknot. She fumbled with it and cursed herself as she worked.

Even now she was still unafraid, concentrating on the next thing to be done. She spared no energy on wondering who these men were, or what they wanted with her. They were her enemies; she must get away.

Scrambling onto the mare she kicked hard, sending it into a reluctant canter. The great hooves sent dirt flying, the din of them on the ancient road like a battering-ram coming down on an oak door.

The town, a looming mass of dark gray speckled with torches, rose up before her. Under its stony skirt, a deep fosse ran, filled with the night's darkness. A path circled it. She hauled on the cob's hard mouth, turning her onto the narrow track.

Behind her broke out a sudden clamor of angry shouting, the half-mad neighing of horses trained for battle, and the sound of flying hooves. They were faster than she was, she could hear it.

She thundered on. The wind whipped dust into her streaming eyes. Mounds of refuse, thrown down from the walls, fouled the horse's straining legs. She was going to be caught. Already they were gaining on her.

There was a pile of hazel withies drying by the path. Adela grabbed one and clumsily twisted it into the mare's mane. It slapped the beast's side like a riding whip. Then Adela threw her saddlebags into the ditch. In the darkness she could not see whether the fosse went down to stones, grass or water. She had to trust. Panic-stricken, a little voice in her was screaming; *You'll get hurt! Don't do it!* But she let it wail on, as though it was no part of her.

She flung her bow into the fosse. Then she took a shuddering breath, and in a moment of numb courage she hurled herself off the galloping horse into the steep darkness of the ditch.

She landed on her shoulder, bit back the howl of pain, and rolled. Her cheek hit a stone. She put out her good hand to grasp for support - the dry grass cut and burned it. Her fingers grazed the wood and leather of bow and quiver. She closed her hand on them and slithered on, down to the marshy depths of the long slope. Still she made no sound. Something within her, some icy part of her soul which she had never guessed at, was in control. She had no

Chapter 9

more fear, and felt no more pain than an arrowhead does cutting through steel and bone.

At the bottom of the fosse a necklace of fetid pools ringed the city. Tall marsh grasses grew there, fresh among the city's debris. She wriggled into their cover and lay invisibly among the fish-bones and the pale flowers of the flag iris.

The horse, lashed by the withy, galloped on. She heard the pursuing horsemen round the first gate-tower and sighed - she had been just in time. Any later and they might have seen her, even in the night, as a dark shape diving from the mare's back. Now they would follow the sound of the horse and she could lie hidden here until morning. Then she would find her saddlebags, go into town and buy replacements for what she had lost.

The horsemen approached. She held her breath, pointlessly. They passed and she breathed again.

Her shoulder began to ache. She tried to move the hand and could not. Best not to think about that. Instead, now she was safe, she began to wonder who these men were. Could Adam have found out already she was gone? How?

The answer rose up like despair. He must have learned it from her nurse. Godgifu would not have given such information willingly. He must have wrung it out of her with torture. Oh God! She had left the old woman to bear his rage while she made off to safety herself! She should have known! Of course Godgifu would have been the first person he turned on! She should have known!

She desperately wanted to cry and to shout, and yet she did not seem to be able to. Her hard-hearted voice was saying; *Very well, she's dead. But at least you're safe. Lie quiet and be safe.*

Then she heard the horse coming back.

One horse, not her own, was walking back from the pursuit. She pressed herself further into the soft ground and lay listening. A man dismounted. She could see him silhouetted against the gray sky, standing on the ditch's rim. His shape was entirely edged with silver, as though a monk had drawn him to illustrate an armored knight in the edges of a psalter.

He was looking down. She thought perhaps he had guessed her trick, but he had no way of knowing where, in this city-wide ditch, she was. Let him search along the whole of it. If he came down here she would shoot him. Only, she prayed, let him not come down here.

He stepped forward, cautiously. She took her numb hand and closed its fingers around the bow. They stayed closed. Then she pulled. The pain bloomed behind her eyes like a vast black rose. Her aim wavered and returned. Moonlight struck the tip of the arrow like a silver flame. The man froze. He had seen it.

She knew she had to strike now, before he rushed her. Her fingers eased their pressure on the string.

"Lady Adela?" The whisper slid reassuringly into the night. The voice was familiar. "It's me," he said, "Guy."

She almost shot him in the sheer weakness of relief.

Chapter Ten

The fire wove a red-gold tapestry in the center of the men's camp. It had its own fierce life, shouting for joy when another branch crumbled into ash beneath it. Adela watched it silently, feeling she understood the world of the flames much more than she did her own.

She was safe. She kept repeating it to herself, as though it should mean something. It meant nothing. She had no idea what to do next.

"It's not broken," said Guy, in a reassuring tone. He laid a hand on her misshapen shoulder, and another on her arm. "I'm going to have to touch you to put it right, and it will hurt. Please try not to scream, my men are listening."

Then he twisted, hissing with the effort. The dislocated shoulder ground back into place. The world swam blackly out of focus, and then slowly returned. Adela, still numb from fright and flight, was absolutely silent.

"There," said the young man, with satisfaction. He moved her arm a little, watching her reaction, and smiled in encouragement. "It's as good as new."

Then he pushed into her hand a cup of hot red wine, steadying it against her trembling, and made her drink. His fingers over hers were warm and strong, calloused by spear shaft and sword hilt. Something numb eased within her at the wine and his touch, but the easing had a pain of its own.

"I am so sorry," said Guy, looking into her face with concern. "My men have as little tact as charging boars, and I made things no easier." He sat, wearily, and cradled his own silver cup in both hands. "But then," he said, "to be fair to them, I didn't warn them you were so brave or so cunning. I had no idea you'd give us such a chase."

He brushed the black curls from his forehead and sighed. Firelight bathed his face in gold. His glossy hair was tied back with an off-cut of braid, so the length was not visible. Adela thought he looked better for it; less like an older man's plaything, less like a cwen. Without the soft frame his face seemed gaunter, hardened, the gash standing out, angrily.

His agate-colored eyes were red-rimmed. Adela recognized that at some point since yesterday he must have found the time to weep. She envied him. Quite suddenly, thinking of his sadness, she felt her own again, blacker and heavier than ever before. She tried to cling to the numbness. It fled like mist.

"We must have scared you half to death," Guy said, kindly.

She scrambled to her feet. How dare he, she thought, how dare he, in his pain, still have time to stir up hers? The ache in her heart writhed, turning into anger, and then fear. And then all the unresolved emotion of the night came out of its hiding place with a howl.

Trying desperately to keep control she paced to where her exhausted horse had been picketed. Her movements seemed stiff and unreal even to herself. The horse rolled a white eye at her, as though it sensed her turmoil. Guy rose, concerned. She hated him for his gentleness.

"Your horse too is more of a warrior than she looks," he said with a smile, reaching out an uncertain hand to touch her arm. She flinched away. "What do you call her?"

She knew he was humoring her, as an adult humors a frightened child. She would not be talked to like that! And yet, oh she wanted to cry! "I call her Petal," she said, bitterly, and recoiled from the spiteful gesture even as she made it. She could feel herself trembling so hard she could no longer stand up. She clung to the horse, and it shied away from her. Her hands shook, her teeth chattered, and then, with a great *Oh!* of anguish, she threw her arms around Guy's neck and wept, shatteringly, in the circle of his arms.

He drew her back into the warmth of the fire, holding her lightly, comfortingly. She clung to him, burying her sobs in his wide shoulder, while he, tentatively, stroked her shorn hair. The rhythm of it soothed her. After a long time, she lapsed into silence, breathing hard, suddenly aware of him, his warmth under the light summer tunic, the movement of his chest with each breath, the hardness and strength of his arms. He smelled good - a smell of hazelnuts and horses and steel.

Without thinking, she looked up - how beautiful he was in the firelight – and, taking a handful of his soft hair, she drew his face clumsily down to hers to be kissed.

The shock and shame of it struck her at the same time as the pleasure. She wrenched herself away, swaying on unsteady legs, and would have run, but for his grip on her wrist. For a moment she thought the worst - and God knows she had encouraged him - but he looked almost as aghast as she.

Chapter 10

"Oh God!" she collapsed into a graceless heap. "What must you think of me? I'm so sorry! I'm so sorry! Oh God!"

"No!" he had caught some of the horror - he was backing away wide-eyed, "No! I'm sorry. My fault! I forgot you were a woman! I forgot I shouldn't touch you. That you're too pure. My fault! I'm sorry."

A silence, and then, together, they began to laugh.

When it passed he raised her up again, setting her on his own stool and sitting beside her on the ground. "Strange," he said, his green flecked gaze turned on the fire, "to think we should be so alike - the way you reacted. After my first battle I was just the same. My lord said I was cool, and brave as a lion, during the fight..." he shook his head, in depreciation, "But afterwards," he said, "I went all to pieces, just like you."

The smile broadened, "King Drago says," and then faded like ashes as he corrected himself, "he said it was a good sign. Some people get the reaction in the midst of the fray, and they don't come out alive."

"And did you fling yourself at the first man who offered you comfort?" said Adela tartly, guilt beginning to nag again after the laughter. She had not thought herself so wanton.

"To tell the truth? Yes I did," said Guy, kindly. "It's part of the same thing, I think. The body just demands reassurance. 'Am I really alive?' it says, 'Prove it!' It means nothing."

She smiled at him, feeling a great rush of affection for him, almost as though she had a new brother. Then she caught sight of herself in the polished side of the silver goblet he held, and was horrified. She looked like a street urchin; a grubby child with a bruised face, tears making scant tracks in the dirt. No wonder Guy had mistaken her! She laughed again, grateful to him for making her think of such a foolish thing as her appearance. Just briefly she had forgotten everything but the two of them. She appreciated it.

She slept that night in the servants' tent under the eye of an old Shipeld washerwoman, whose accent she could not understand. In the morning she washed carefully, and combed the dust and fish-bones out of her hair, before shamelessly joining her young host at the head of the small column.

They passed through the town while it was still sleeping, the stench of it rising up around them like the dew, and were on their way briskly, making for Passanham, or maybe even Tofecaster before night fell.

The day promised to be cool and still. A stream, winding its luxurious coils now on this side of the road, now on the other, chuckled softly to itself.

The stone street cut through its curls like a butcher's cleaver, the low arches of its many bridges giving back an echo of their hoof-beats as they passed.

They rode for a long time silently, respecting each other's sadness, while the guards' voices chatted behind them, staccato as woodpeckers. From the sound of it they were discussing some scandal, but they spoke the Mearh language, keeping their secrets from their Holmr lord.

"Did the king ask you to look after me?" Adela asked, eventually.

Guy took off his heavy helmet, and pushed back the coif of mail, wincing as the rings pulled at his hair. "No," he said, honestly. "The truth is, for my own part I will be safer now away from the court. It's well known what Bauduin thinks of his brother's favorites." He laughed, indulgently, "It must have been impossible to grow up, a slaves-child, with two legitimate brothers, and not to hate them."

Then he burst out, in sudden bitterness and anger, "But I'm not going to pretend I'm ashamed, and stay, slinking about court, fawning on him for favors. There'll be many who do, but I'm no such turncoat, and I want him to know it." He hit out at a tree-branch above his head, showering them both with yellowing leaves - an early hint of autumn - and then he smiled at her alarm.

"So," he went on, more gently, "I was leaving anyway. When your groom told me you had set off for Castreld, and in such a manner, I thought I could serve both our purposes in catching up with you - giving you such protection as I can."

The trees thinned as they came out into tilled fields and it was suddenly warm under the watery glance of the veiled sun. A short distance from the road a small manor house stood. It still bore scorch marks from one of the king's campaigns. Villeins, toiling in the demesne land, looked up and gaped at them as they passed. A Holmr knight, with his retinue, talking on equal terms with a scruffy boy on a bony cob. Adela smiled at them and they looked away with scowls of distaste.

"But you think I'm right to leave the court?" she asked, feeling glad to talk, and in almost a holiday mood riding so carelessly and in such good company.

"Certainly," he said, and returned her smile. "Bauduin is a schemer - I have played tafl with both of them. Drago thought, what, four places ahead? Bauduin had the whole game mapped out from the start. He will give Adam whatever he asks (all the more gladly if it means he leaves the court and goes off to some God-forsaken region in the Northern wastes) and he will wait until

Chapter 10

he can strike him down in safety. But if you've fortified your manor in the meantime, and are sitting there surrounded by your household knights, well then, he may think again."

"I'm really thinking of defying the king over this!" Adela marveled, "I'm thinking of going to war!" She shook her head in horrified amazement, "How can I do it?"

Guy gave her a smile of such warmth that she blushed, looking away from him. "The man has already killed one king," he said, and a note of implacable hardness came into his tone. "To my mind you have every right not to marry a traitor. Bauduin should appreciate it, if he has any sense. As, to be fair to him, he does."

They watched the hay being stored, nut-brown boys scrambling over the ricks with handfuls of hazel pins while their fathers thatched the stacks like houses.

"Are you coming all the way home with me?" Adela asked, hopefully.

"Of course."

"What will your men think?" she asked, lightly, and he laughed.

"Oh," he grinned with a sidelong glint of his tarnished-bronze eye which made him look twice her age, "I know exactly: They think I'm keeping you for your pretty face. Miles has had to pay John two crowns on a bet that I preferred boys to men, despite the long hair. It's a good enough cover. I see no reason to disabuse them. Do you?"

Adela felt the blood rush to her face, hot and shameful. Guy rode beside her smirking over it. It took all the self control she had not to be toweringly angry with him. After all, she told herself, he was infinitely more experienced than she. It was only human of him to be a little amused.

"It is for the best," he said, kindly, relenting after a couple of miles of her charged silence. "It'll stop the servants trying to interfere with you, and it'll explain why you're not helping with any of their work. Didn't they gossip about you at court?"

"Yes," she said, dubiously, "But never about... never about... things like that."

"You are incredible!" he laughed, "You're fleeing for your life, and you're still concerned about your reputation?"

"A woman's reputation is her honor," said Adela, firmly.

"No," Guy shook his head. "Honor is honor, reputation is just what other people think. If it makes you easier, I think you have a great deal of honor, and I don't think reputation matters at all."

"It matters to me," said Adela, and fell silent.

For a few days she felt it acutely; ashamed to meet the eyes of any of the servants, blushing painfully when the men-at-arms spoke over her head in obviously ribald Mearsh. But gradually, without noticing it, it faded from her mind. She began almost to enjoy herself, as though this were a pilgrimage, a short time taken out of her grim life to go riding through the summer to worship at some flower-laden shrine and rest, afterwards, in the company of a good friend.

On the fifth day of the journey they reached Castreld and began to climb into the sweet-smelling heather of the Fells. That night, under the opaque darkness of the ever-present clouds, they first heard the howling.

It was colder than a wolf's voice, tormented, hateful. It belled across the huge emptiness of the hills like the crying of a lost soul. At first it was faint, a gray thread of sound in the distance, like the memory of a nightmare, like waking up in a cold sweat in a dark place and thinking 'Was that a noise?'

Faint at first, but all through the night it grew louder, and more vile. The servants huddled together, weeping and praying. The men-at-arms, gray faced, made jokes to convince themselves they were not afraid.

"Adela?" Guy asked, gently, his face calm as he fed the fire, putting on a pretense for his men.

"Yes," she said, wringing her shivering hands. She had guessed his question; "I think it's *him*."

Dawn came, gray and cold. They began to travel as soon as they could see the road, going up now slowly into the hills. The slopes before them rose up into mist. Behind them the foothills descended, rounded and gray as clouds.

"How much further?" Guy asked, sharply.

"Two days, I think," said Adela, shakily, feeling already the jaws of the trap closing about her.

"Too far," he confirmed her fears. "Whatever it is, I think it will attack tonight."

Just after midday they passed through a small village, perched on the steep slope like a gannet's nest. Guy left the servants there. They went on with only the two guards.

Chapter 10

"Please!" Adela begged, trembling between fear and desperation, "Let me go alone! It will follow me, not you," and then, in a shameless outcry; "Oh God! I don't want you to die!"

"Do be quiet, woman," he said irritably, "I'm not leaving you."

They climbed out of the fog, up onto the barren cold peaks of the hills. The wind tugged at them, moaning among the scree of shattered rocks. Rings of gray dolmens stood up from the brown heather like the picked rib-bones of huge beasts, and the ruins of stone huts littered the bleak heights.

The road ran down into the dark swell of the Fell forest, the tips of the trees just showing under the veil of mist. The sound of sighing leaves came fitfully up to them on the ever-changing wind. Twilight came down.

"We'll camp here," said Guy, picking his way over the strewn boulders at the highest point of the hills. The ground went down all around them, and they could see the further peaks, stretched out under their coverlet of moss and gorse like the shapes of sleeping giants.

"It's just about defensible," he continued, leading his horse into a tumbled circle of rock. "And we'll see it coming, whatever it is."

The two men-at-arms exchanged glances as they lit the fire and picketed the horses. "My lord?" said one, "John and I would like to know what's happening."

"Keep a lookout," Guy commanded, and then, at a nod from Adela, began; "This 'boy' is Adela, a noble lady and ward of the court. She is fleeing for her life, from the attentions of a witch," and then, with a flash of bitter grief, "The same man, incidentally, who killed your king. I have given her my protection. Now I think she, and therefore I, am about to be attacked by some hell-wight under the witch's command."

He looked at their astonished, frightened faces, and swallowed.

"I don't command you to stay," he said, with resigned compassion, "If you want to go you may do so without dishonor, but go now, while you can."

The older of the two, Miles, recovered from his fright with a smile.

"Lad," he said, "I'd rather face all the fiends of Hell than tell your father I ran out on you just when you needed me. I'm sure John feels the same; don't you, boy?"

The younger man nodded, slowly, and then turned away, his face drawn with fear.

Night deepened. The moon came out, washing the curves of the land with a dreary light. The voice came again, bitter as gall and ashes, and was answered by a second. Guy and Adela exchanged glances of terror.

"There!" cried John, pointing.

They moved over the hills like the shadow of sharks on the ocean's bed. Deeper than the shadows of the stones was the shade they cast, darker than the black sky. They were swathed in gloom, lit from beneath by dingy flame. The shape of them could hardly be guessed - the eye flinched away in horror – hound-like, perhaps, with their bloody muzzles pressed to the trail. And they moved fast, scudding across the silver tors like driven clouds. There were three of them.

"Sweet Benel save us!" Guy whispered, as petrified for an instant as the standing stones. Behind him John slipped to his knees, too terrified to stand. Adela, sick with fear, stood shivering like a doe at bay before attacking wolves. She had thought she believed in the Dark Ones before this, but seeing them. How had she dared live?

Pain brought her out of her horror. Looking down she found she was gripping the tumbled stone wall so hard that her hands were bleeding. She unclenched them in a daze and strung her bow.

A stench of carrion hit them. Guy stirred, drawing his sword. Adela pulled the bow and fired, twice. The arrows passed through the hell-murk and through the beasts like water. Flesh flowed together after them. They left no mark and made no wound.

The first hound opened its mouth and howled. Deep in its gullet tainted fire flickered, reeking of carrion. John scrambled out of the ring and ran, flinging aside helmet and shield to go lighter. There was a sound like bestial laughter, and one of the hounds followed him.

Adela backed away, until she was pressed up against the low wall of the ruined tower.

A hound put its forepaws up on the rim, saliva dripping from its hollow teeth. With all his strength Miles buried his sword in its chest up to the hilt. It leaned down casually and closed its gaping jaw around his arm. He screamed, and screamed again as Guy pulled him away, battering at the beast with his shield rim. The arm, under the silver moonlight, was burning with a red flame, juice dripping from it like a roast over a fire.

"Get away, Adela!" Guy shouted, "Run!" and he hacked at the creature's slimy muzzle. The sword cleft through it like mist. It closed up

Chapter 10

behind, unhurt. He threw away the useless weapon, bent to pick a stone from the ground.

The hound leaped the wall, landing with a crack on Miles' peeling sword-arm. Its tail, a scorpion tail, lashed out at Adela. She threw herself over the stone wall, slithering into the night.

Miles crouched under his shield, trying to stay out of reach of the thing's snapping maw. The linden board shattered beneath its claws. It tore the wood apart. He tried to fend it off with the shield-boss. It laughed its fiend's laugh again before putting out its needle teeth and ripping open his guts.

The second beast looked straight at Adela, malice and cunning in its dead eyes. She crawled away. It howled at its companion - the other went on eating the fallen man. Then it began to pace towards her.

"Run!" Guy yelled again, and threw himself on it, ramming the sharp flint into its throat. It tossed him away, long teeth shredding his steel helmet, grazing his forehead beneath. The gash smoldered. Blood ran into his eyes. He got up again and grappled it with his hands.

Adela ran.

She heard the scuffle, and then a howl as it sprang on him, knocking him to the ground under its infernal weight. She looked back. He had it by the throat, trying to force the head away from him. Then it put its taloned paw down on his chest and kicked. She heard the crack from half-way down the slope.

He lay so still that, for a moment, a drop of blood glistened on one eyelash like a perfect copy of the silver moon. Then the hound put its head down and began to feed.

Adela fled, hurtling down the slope blindly, hearing behind her the shrill neighing of terrified horses and the insane cackle of the hound's laughter. She poured all her strength into the flight. Night air whipped at her face. She did not feel the jagged stones under her soft shoes, or taste the tears streaming down her face. Panic took her. She had to get away!

She was down on the level ground, pelting towards the forest. A hound yowled behind her. It was answered, twice. Then she heard them begin to run - their weight shook the ground. They were coming.

Under the trees she darted like a greyhound in full flight. The cover felt good - but it was illusory. She knew these things could follow her anywhere. Despairingly, she put her head down, her breath already a torture in her throat, her legs shaking, and ran and ran, skidding around tree-trunks, tearing through broom and bramble, until finally she could run no more. In a glade, bordered by holly and birch, carpeted in bracken, she fell and could not get up again.

She saw them drifting through the trees like smoke; struggled up to her knees, trying to pray. She was too scared to find the words. They were silent now, a darkness among the dark branches, flickering with grimy flame. Their heads were slimy with her friend's blood.

When they were only a few paces away terror opened her mouth. She was going to scream, but words came out instead;

"Who is mighty, but God?

And where is there safety, except in my God?"

The hounds spat sparks, howling.

"He has hung strength from my belt," she went on, struggling to keep her voice level, to stop the fear in her throat from gagging her. "And armored me in light..."

Were they mocking her - stopping so close? The hatred, the inferno of envy and pain in their burning eyes was almost like a physical blow. Oh and they stank! She lost her place in the psalm. Her mind, bewildered by fear, threw up lines and verses at random.

"For He will surround you with angels," she began again, and suddenly her courage flared. There were angels looking after her - the poem promised it. Under the protection of those awesome beings; dragon-slayers, winged and luminous, how could she be afraid of anything?

"For He will surround you with angels," she repeated, singing it out in a clear voice,

"And their swords will ring you in fire.

Light is falling from their wings,

Like the wings of seagulls in the noonday sun."

She had stopped them. They backed away from her, calling in despair, trying to drown the sound of her glad voice, pawing at their muzzles in pain.

But they did not go far.

The night darkened. The hounds waited, their angry eyes fixed on her. She became aware of how terribly thirsty she was, how hoarse from running. Her muscles stiffened and cramped after the headlong flight and she had begun to feel the pain of her feet and ankles, grazed and bruised on the rocks. The

Chapter 10

hounds waited. She sang on, knowing when she stopped they would tear her apart.

A breeze sprang up, she shivered in her sweat-soaked clothes. The moon began to go down. Her voice croaked out one of Emperor Varian's songs of exultation, faded to a whisper in her dry mouth. A hound edged forward. Adela's spirit faltered; she could not keep this up.

Just behind her she thought she caught the gleam of a wood-fire; a warm fire, amber and gold and red in the black night, very different from the murky glint which lit the beasts. She shrugged it off - it was her exhaustion, playing tricks on her. It had seemed to her as though the blaze was floating in the air like dandelion seed.

Her voice faltered again. The lead hound got to its feet, laughing its demon's laugh. The fire was clearer now, falling, like hair, around a golden face. The face was watching her, with ravenous curiosity.

Adela could feel herself slipping into dreams. Only the ferocious ache of her parched and strained throat was stopping her from fainting. She thought of the men who had died to give her a chance at living, and grated out, through sheer willpower, another verse.

There were golden hands with the face - shining faintly with their own light. They were stringing a bow.

Adela's voice slipped into silence. She closed her eyes, resigning herself to death. The Hell-hounds gave tongue, whooping out victory and contempt in a clamor which split the night.

There was a long sound like tearing silk then the dull thud of impact. The howling broke off suddenly. Adela, hands clenched, awaited the rending pain of their teeth. When it did not come she opened her eyes again, reluctantly.

The beasts were lying on their sides, while their own dull burning crawled over them like worms. In the necks of each a long, gray-fletched arrow quivered, the shaft of it black with poison. The hounds crumbled to ash as she watched, sinking in on themselves, leaving nothing but sulfur and soot.

The archer unstrung his bow, wading through the bracken like a nymph in the waves of the sea. He was clothed like a nobleman, and as beautiful as an angel, light and lithe and dangerous as a walking flame. She did not know whether she should run from him or fall down and worship.

"Make it again," he said, in a voice as golden and as unemotional as sunshine. "Make the light."

"I don't understand." she said, wondering how she had passed into a dream without falling asleep. Was she dead?

"Are you an angel?" she gasped. He had wild green eyes, and hair like fire. He shone in the darkness with his own light. But, somehow, she could not imagine him in any church.

"I am no one's messenger," he replied, as unaffected by her question, and the shudders of her reaction, as tree-roots are by pavement.

"Come with me," he said, and walked away. She stumbled after him, frightened to be alone again in the night.

"Who are you?" she stammered, and then, "What are you?"

He paused, and looked at her with that curiosity which was the only thing she understood about him.

"You may call me Torch," he said. "Has it been such a long time? Can you have already forgotten the elves? Now come. I will take you to my king."

She remembered the pilgrim's horror of elves. She remembered his warning, but she was lost and frightened. She followed the elvish man down into the secret heart of the forest.

Chapter Eleven

"Come here, lad. We have a buyer for you."

A stab of despair, of desolation, turned Oswy's soul cold. He knew his legs had weakened at the words, the muscles spasming, but, oddly, he could not feel it happen.

Why can't I feel my legs?

His father's face was gray with exhaustion, drawn, haunted. Looking up at it brought the darkness back - it felt as though a pit opened, and he fell into darkness; weeping and weeping, knowing no one cared.

"I don't want to go with him!" He flung the words into oblivion; no one would answer. No one cared. "I don't want to!"

And suddenly his father was kneeling down on the autumn stubble beside him, his face kindly, eager. "You don't have to be his. I can save you."

No. The thought came out of nowhere, *No...this isn't right. This isn't what happens.*

"I'll protect you," his father said, the tones of his voice subtly changed; suave, reassuring, "I know what to do, but you must trust me."

He smiled. He had never smiled like that in all of Oswy's life.

Horror came to join Oswy's despair, came to push down on his chest. Not my father! The realization was a primal thing - a grip on the throat which stopped his breath; it's not my father! He could see now how someone was working the face from within. Something was moving under his father's skin like a maggot.

"Give me your hand," it said, "trust me."

"No!"

Oswy turned to run - and the meadow crumbled, frayed away into nothingness. The world ended in front of him. He turned back - and faced a second abyss. A narrow path rose out of it on a knife-edge of earth. The thing who wore his father stood there, blocking the only way out.

"Don't go," it said, "I want to help you."

"Who are you? What are you doing?"

The face still carried its carefully crafted smile. "I want to protect you," it said. The voice dropped to a whisper, a murmur of dread, of secrets too horrible to reveal. "I know what he intends for you."

"Nothing!" Now the earth at Oswy's heels had begun to unravel. Darkness ate its way towards him, pushing him towards the stranger - who waited with a smile.

"You know nothing!" Oswy shouted again. Unimagined shapes of terror were coming with the nothingness, driving him forward. There was barely a step between them now. The stranger's smile was full of teeth.

"Go away! Go away!"

But the man walked forward.

Oswy felt a hand snag his sleeve - a touch like slime - and, with a sickening wrench of panic, he flung himself over the edge of the cliff.

Immediately it was sky. He flew away, soaring on black wings, the stranger left astounded on the narrow track.

Then the path and the man folded themselves, first into a jewel, and then into light; a brassy reflection of candle-flame stabbing out from the dirt floor of Oswy's room.

He woke up, and lay in the pitch darkness of his dungeon cell, with fear pressing an icy pillow over his face. He listened for his life. Rats were scraping at the mortar of the walls, but there was no other sound.

Just a dream then, he thought at last, feeling his heart slow, the sense of pressure on his chest ease until he could breathe again. Just a dream. Only...

It nagged at him; the feeling that, under the skin, he had seen that man before. There had been something half familiar about him, a half remembered smell, maybe. Or the sense of slime.

And what did the last image mean - the yellow blaze lancing up from the floor? It had been so real he could no longer remember if he had been awake or asleep when he saw it.

Moving slowly, curiosity goading him out of the safety of his bed, he unwound himself from his blankets and went on hands and knees over the floor, brushing the surface with an open palm.

Chapter 11

He was afraid of what his hand might touch; the matted fur of a rat, the yielding softness of a spider which moved suddenly against his fingers, a man's stealthy foot; but he had to know what the topaz glint had been - truth, or dream.

He searched the floor from wall to damp wall, jarring his hands as he came upon them suddenly. It was bare.

Shivering and gasping - the spring night was bitterly cold - he crawled away from the mystery, back to bed, and lay there, waiting to warm, waiting for sleep to come again.

Snatches of memory, scenes from the past few months fluttered and wheeled, like butterflies, into his tired mind. He pursued them, intrigued by their brightness.

He remembered, long ago it now seemed, leaving Caster. He had thought they would be coming straight back to Harrowden; to the cold and empty hall of Sulien's manor. Instead they rode in to John of Wyrmbank's prosperous fief and were greeted with ceremony, but not much warmth, by John himself.

"We will be staying for the Midwinter feast, and maybe beyond," Sulien had said, as though he had been coming into his own house. John bowed, a glint of resentment in his speedwell-blue eyes.

"Father!" a boy came running, graceful as a skimming swallow. The pale light of winter flowed over him, making his short hair shine like polished brass, darkening his steel-gray eyes to the color of slate.

He flung himself on Leofwine, giving the knight such a bear-hug that the breath was forced out of him with a grunt. Then he stood, poised, smiling, every inch the little lordling from his neat Holmr haircut to his blue-dyed calf-skin boots. There was a roguish glint in the gray glance which was turned on Oswy.

Oswy remembered, with embarrassment, how that day he had been tied into his saddle to stop him falling off.

"Oswy, this is Edward, my son," Leofwine had said with pride, while Sulien turned his back on the boy and stalked off, his mouth twisted as though he had tasted something bitter.

"Edward," Leofwine commanded, fondly, "I want you to take Oswy in hand. Teach him some manners."

It had not been the best start for a friendship.

Oswy grinned into his rough woven blankets thinking of Edward. Only yesterday, before Oswy left, they had finally got their own back against the bullying Holmr boys. They climbed the tower, going on tiptoe past the witch's room, scrambled out onto the roof, seeing their enemies far below them, remote and scurrying as woodlice.

Then they turned the bucket upside-down. The water came out of it thick as the neck of a horse. It poured, like dragon's venom, the whole height of the keep, landed on Gilbert and Rufus. They disappeared in sparkling flume, reappeared dripping and cursing.

Oswy and Edward had leaned back against the shingles of the roof and whooped with laughter.

Oswy tossed, winding himself further into the swaddling wool. He was warmer now, but not at ease; it was his first night back in this room, and already he had suffered a second nightmare. Did he dare sleep again?

The dream's taste still lingered in his mind, and his muscles ached from the long ride home. He yawned and in the twilight state between waking and dreaming memories floated like balls of witch-light.

Bright sun on a snowy field. Leofwine and Hugo practicing their sword-play with red faces and red chapped hands, while Oswy guarded both their cloaks by wearing them.

His hands aching, cramped with the cold, as he copied letters onto beeswax tablets, the wax brittle in the bitter weather.

"No, no, no." That was Father Paul - their new priest - correcting him again, patient and gentle as a plow-ox in the field. "Oh, but you're too cold to write, come away into the warming room, you can read me this book."

The moment when the written words began to make sense! Eagerly following them, his finger pressed hard to the parchment.

"No, no, no." Father Paul again, "Don't touch the page, you'll wear it away." Shyly, he had given Oswy the present of a pointer - ash wood, pale as the winter. He had carved it himself with the figure of Saint Corineus - who had journeyed in every country of the world. The saint was grinning with the excitement of travel.

"Every book is a journey," Father Paul had said.

Oswy wormed a hand out of his blankets, found and fingered the polished wood, smiling again. He had enjoyed those lessons; sitting on the hard stool in Father Paul's narrow cell, the light brilliant as a coating of ice on

Chapter 11

the white walls. Piecing together the words, while from their shelf above his head the three great, wooden-bound books gazed down at him solemnly, promising more stories than even his mother knew.

He sighed, and snuggled into the pillow, but, instead of sleep, desire for magic came unexpectedly over him like ravenous hunger.

It had to be fed. He called the witch-light from memory - and saw suddenly the damp walls of his room gleaming peridot green, lemon, silver, the scuffed dirt floor swept over by wings of glory - but it wasn't enough.

Frustration snuffed it out. Why had he been taught nothing else over the winter? Letters, horse-riding, etiquette - they were all very well but they were not what he wanted. And Sulien must know it. Why - having given him this itch for magic - why wouldn't they let him scratch?

He sat up again, his eyes gritty with tiredness, but his mind entangled in suspicion. Had Sulien changed his mind perhaps, and decided simply to use Oswy's power for his own ends, as his master had used him? Was that what the dream meant; what the stranger had tried to warn him about?

Or was it just that, in the company of so many decent people, Sulien was ashamed?

The witch had certainly kept to himself all winter, brooding in his tower room, coming out, in human form, only for music, and, unexpectedly, on Midwinter's day.

He had sat at the feast like a specter of Death, with the merriment falling silent around him. Oswy remembered the stony politeness of his face, while he wound the crystal ring around and around on his finger like a man winding up a crossbow to the notch.

The memories went wandering, growing in significance, in clarity. He was barely aware of lying down again. The colors deepened. Everything was warmer - and the sounds more rounded, mellower. There was a fire in an old fashioned fire-pit, and the smell of mead, and the sound of lord's voices, talking Sceavish.

I didn't know John was Sceafn, Oswy thought, with pleasure. And it seemed to him obvious now how the Invasion was just a dream he'd had, in another world, and how really he was free, not a slave at all.

Light awoke him, and the noise of Brand whistling tunelessly through his teeth. His cell door had been left unlocked during the night, and Brand had pulled it open with his foot, one hand cradling a loaf and a small pot of honey, the other holding high a sputtering, pitch-coated torch. Heavy black smoke descended over him like storm-clouds moving down over the hills.

"Never thought I'd be reduced to waiting on a marsh-fisher's bairn like you," he muttered awkwardly, as he passed Oswy the food. "You've landed on your feet alright in this household."

"Hm," Oswy replied, as he rubbed at his tired eyes. He scowled at the loaf, feeling grim and dreary.

"I'll have it if you don't want it, lad," Brand said, seeing his hesitation over the food.

Oswy smiled at the thought, remembering days when a loaf this size would have had to feed his whole family. Impulsively he broke it in two, offered Brand the larger half. The servant took it slowly, frowning, and watched while Oswy smeared his half with honey and ate.

"Was that knightly virtue or plain human kindness?" he murmured, warily, and then relenting; "I'm sorry, lad. I just don't know what to make of you any more." He hesitated again, wringing his hands. It reminded Oswy, bleakly, of the Holmr judges, who wash after passing execution, to take off the taint of blood.

"I thought you were a Sceafn churl, like me," Brand went on, "And my lass, well, she's that fond of you. But look at you! You look more like the Lord's son than his slave, and sometimes you act it too. How am I supposed to treat you now?"

Oswy put his bread down on the dirt floor and looked away. He did not know what to say to this. A familiar ache began in his chest - the pain of losing a friend. He knew it so well; he had been judged and found "different". "Do what you like," he said sullenly.

There was a hot, heavy silence and then Brand sighed, wiping his soot-greasy hand down the side of his tunic.

"Ah, lad," he said, "I know it's not your doing. We all must do what He commands. Don't take it to heart so." He reached out as if to ruffle Oswy's hair and then thought better of it.

"Come then, if you will," he concluded, still with a touch of deference which indicated a boundary crossed, a relationship changed forever, "And come quick. Father Paul is leaving. You'll want to say goodbye, I dare say."

"Leaving now!" Oswy exclaimed and jammed on his shoes, forgetting instantly anything but the urgency of the moment.

Chapter 11

"Aye, now." Brand backed into the stairwell, flakes of burning pitch floating about his head in the moving air. Oswy tumbled out after him, hurled himself up the sharp-edged steps.

"Hey lad," Brand called after him, his voice hushed, secretive even in the private darkness of the dungeon. "Go quietly," he warned, "Your master..." and he paused, "Well, he's not happy."

Oswy came out cautiously into the early morning. Spring sunshine, pale and warm as new milk, splashed over him as he emerged from the keep gates. He breathed deep, scenting snow-bells blooming, heather and grasses drenched under dew. The wind came fresh over the tree-bare hills, carrying a sense of wildness and freedom.

Through the outer gates - flung wide and packed now with jostling cattle, the shouted commands of the herder boys shrill as seagulls - Oswy could see the Fells, emerald and beryl green and ocher, gray outcroppings of stone shining like silver. Then, driven swiftly on the moisture laden air, a cloud came scudding, passing over the high places like a frown.

Close to the keep door stood Father Paul, his hair ragged as thistledown, hoar-gray as the snow which still clung in pockets of shade under the stones. With jerky, repetitive movements, he was stroking one ear of a dove-gray mule; the beast's soft nose was in his other hand, nuzzling for oats. Behind him, trying to look inconspicuous, two guards were leaning on their spears, both of them assiduously studying the growing grass. It might have made a peaceful, domestic scene, but for Sulien.

The witch wore anger like a suit of mail. His fists were clenched and his eyes were like dark embers. He was speaking softly, in his most gentle tones. It was plain the priest, studying the patterns of sunshine on the hills, dared not look him in the face.

"You risk the boy's damnation," said Father Paul, sounding browbeaten but determined.

Oswy understanding instantly that they were arguing about him, froze into the shadow of the doors and watched, wide eyed.

"There are men out there who make my master look like an April lamb." Sulien replied, his voice low and intense. "As soon as they know he exists every one of them is going to come for him. His blood alone is worth its weight in silver!"

He stalked forward, knotted his hands in the mule's halter. The beast trembled at the touch, tossed its head away, ripping the rope through his fists.

Father Paul moved to keep the animal as a shield between himself and the younger man. Leofwine, in his accustomed place at Sulien's right hand, stepped forward too, calmly, easing the threat of violence by his mere presence.

"Still no reason to turn him into a witch," Father Paul went on, doggedly.

"No?" Sulien mocked, "His power won't just leave him, you know, no matter how hard he prays for it to. And if I die, leaving him untrained, defenseless. Who will protect him then? You?" He laughed, the sound of it bitter as a cry of pain. "I could kill you with a single glance."

"The church..." Father Paul began, uncertainly.

"The church would burn him alive!" Sulien shouted. Leofwine put out a broad, brown hand to restrain him, a crescent scar on the back of it pale as the dew. Angrily, the witch slapped it away.

"God would protect him," Father Paul concluded, resolutely.

Sulien's dark eyes kindled into red fire. His face paled with fury. Then, quicker than a striking snake, he took the old priest by the hair and smacked his face hard into the mule's bony shoulder. Dragging him over the animal's plunging back, he flung him to the ground.

Paul curled up, sobbing with pain, breath whistling through his broken nose, bright blood oozing between the fingers he pressed to his face.

"Even as He protected me?" Sulien hissed, and kicked viciously at the priest's stomach and ribs until Leofwine ran forward, locked massive arms around his waist and dragged him away.

"For shame!" the knight exclaimed, while Sulien struggled, cursing, against his grasp, "Look at him, my lord. He's an old man!"

And Sulien, his voice full of desolation, as though he had been betrayed, cried; "I told him everything! Everything! Is he stupid! Didn't he listen?! Or is he just laughing at me!"

Shakily, still holding one hand to his wounded face, Father Paul got to his feet, came sidling towards them.

"My son," he said, affectionately, while the blood ran down his fingers onto the grass, "Hush! I am not laughing at you. I am asking you to think."

He came closer, reaching out with his free hand to touch and comfort the witch.

Chapter 11

Sulien recoiled from him, pressing back into Leofwine's restraining embrace, his eyes widening with apprehension and fear. Leofwine caught the priest's gaze, shook his head slightly.

"Don't," he murmured, and Father Paul stopped, stood uncertainly for a moment, and then lowered himself carefully to the ground. A daisy, still dew-grayed in the bailey's sweet turf, poked up between the splayed fingers of his supporting hand.

"Think, Sulien," he repeated patiently, sniffing the blood back between his words. His voice trembled with shock, but his tone was gentle.

"The boy is a peasant. He was born to be under protection, not to have to protect himself. You will be asking of him something which, by nature, he isn't fitted to do."

Sulien gazed at him for a moment, the panic and rage fading from his face, guilt and confusion replacing it. His struggles subsided, until he was standing quiescent in Leofwine's grasp. Then he sighed, bending his head. His heavy golden hair slid from its tie, fell forward, covering his face as he withdrew into himself.

"You don't understand," he said, hopelessly.

One of the two guards, running fast, returned with a helmet full of water from the well, bathed the priest's face with the soaked hem of his woolen cloak. Father Paul spared him a smile before turning back to where Sulien stood, head bowed, arms folded, sullen as a chided schoolboy.

"Make me understand," he commanded, and, rising, took a painful step forward, putting on authority like a robe.

"No," Leofwine murmured, firm but quiet, his dark head bent protectively over his lord. With an indrawn breath, a tiny frown of resignation, he released the grip he had on the witch's slumped shoulders, led the priest gently aside.

"Don't press him," he whispered, "Not in this mood. Not if you want to live," and loudly, turning the priest's face into the pellucid light so the bruise stood out, purple as a bishop's stole; "Now, let me look at that."

In the fleeting silence a lark, flinging herself joyfully into the pale sky, sang notes like sweet rain. Then the servants - the cattlemen, the shrouded washer-women, the goose-girl with her snake-necked flock - who had been frozen into frightened stone by the argument, began to edge away about their business. A rumor of voices, spiked with horror and glee, drowned out the bird's music.

Oswy shivering in the cold shadows, understood something of Sulien's feeling of betrayal. Was it Father Paul who had kept him from his studies all this time; who had frustrated him; who had not given him what he wanted?

He had assumed the man who had taught him to read would feel only sympathy for his desire to learn. Instead it seemed clear it was his fault Oswy's wishes had been thwarted.

He felt, suddenly, overwhelmingly angry with the stupidity and hypocrisy of the church, furiously contemptuous of this ugly, dried up little man who was trying to deny him knowledge which was rightfully his.

The feeling rose up like a black wave, like a wave of blood, salty and stinking. It rolled over him, left him gasping at its intensity, and then was gone, as though it had never been.

He shifted from one foot to the other, frowning, threaded both arms back through his sleeves and hugged them about himself.

What had happened? Had he really felt that? It had seemed more as though, briefly, a Dark One had made its home in him. He made the circle over his heart - the Moat of Blood - frightened. Then, as he shuddered, Sulien raised his head, his eyes bleak as the Ruined Lands, and stared straight at him.

"Oswy," the witch said, in cold acknowledgment, and Oswy wondered how much he had sensed of the black moment, and how much of it, if any, had been his doing. Straightening his back, hotly aware of all the eyes regarding him, he came forward to make his farewell to the priest.

"Child," Father Paul greeted him fondly, stood leaning, with apparent nonchalance against his mule's strong neck, only his hands were trembling as he soothed it.

Oswy looked to his master for permission to speak, received a curt nod.

"Goodbye Father," he said, very decorous, running through in his mind how Edward would do this - because Edward would do it properly; "I hope I can come and see the new church when it's built."

"I expect to see you, and your master, there every Feastday," Father Paul returned, smiling, "It belongs to him after all."

"That must hurt," Oswy said, and gazed ingenuously at the priest's broken nose, "I expect I could heal it for you, if my master showed me how."

And he noticed, with some satisfaction, the quirk of a smile on Sulien's lips. It felt odd to have the witch as an ally.

Chapter 11

"No," Father Paul replied, uneasily, "I want nothing to do with this magic of yours. Nor do I want you to have anything further to do with it."

"It will come out," Sulien said suddenly, the words halting, as if he spoke against his will.

"And if he isn't trained it will come out wild." He sighed, twisting the band on his finger, his light voice toneless and gray; "The worst magic always comes instinctively. "

"It's true," Oswy leaped in, vehement with enthusiasm, "I nearly cursed someone, and I didn't even know I could do it."

The priest drooped against his mount, uncertain under this paired attack.

"It takes years of training," Sulien pressed on, "just to learn how to prevent yourself from doing magic. Be thankful I have that training. By now, if I had not, we would be digging bleeding pieces of you out of the walls."

At Father Paul's shaky signal one of the guards came forward to help him up into the saddle. The gates had cleared, the shaggy cattle were dispersed, grazing over the hills.

A shepherd child, blowing on a set of wooden pipes, hugged the gate-tower, looking into the enclosure with feral curiosity, then ran still playing, back to her small flock. Sulien's eyes followed her, his face softening briefly into a weary beauty. He dragged himself back to business with obvious reluctance.

"I have two errands for you," he said, sounding numb and dispirited, as though he were very, very tired.

"The first is to ask Sir Hugo's father whether he intends ever replying to my demands, or shall I assume he doesn't want his son back?"

The priest nodded, rather absently, a worried frown still creasing his forehead. The bruise was beginning to spread out over his face like spilled wine on old linen.

"The second," said Sulien, "is to get a message to Gunnar's family. Tell them he is now my freedman, and if they wish to put themselves under my protection I will free them also."

"They are someone else's villeins?" Father Paul sounded disapproving, "I can't countenance that. It would be theft."

"They belong to Robert of Rainford," said Sulien, a vague twist of amusement under the deadness in his voice; "His father and I had an agreement. He has had long enough to mourn. Time now to remind him the agreement hasn't lapsed."

"As you wish," Father Paul brushed aside the business with a wave of his hand and looked down seriously into the witch's closed face. "I have to write to the Bishop," he said, "I have to report to him on your spiritual condition, recommend whether or not you should be re-admitted as a member of the Church."

"And?"

"If you intend to corrupt this boy by teaching him witchcraft, in all fairness, I cannot recommend it."

"You'd rather the Dark Ones ate me?" Fire stirred again among the ashes of Sulien's mood. Father Paul, seeing it, clucked amiably to his mule, began to ride toward the cloud-swept hills, saying, over his shoulder, "No, no, no. Never forget God's mercy. But I can't emphasize it enough; do not teach the boy magic."

Oswy watched him dwindle, rapidly, as the mule picked a delicate way down the steep slope of moorland to where the road lay, just visible through the mist of color - the bronze and apple green - of the budding poplar and chestnut trees. He turned to his master, desperation making him brave.

"You're not going to do as he says are you?"

Sulien sighed. For a moment he looked older than the priest, weary to the bone.

"No," he said, "I don't think I can."

Then, putting on pride and arrogance like a cloak, he turned his face away from the road, looked up to the high peaks; the granite tors stained with sulfurous lichen, the pure sky. He held out a demanding hand in summoning to Oswy.

"Come then," he said. "Let us make a start."

Chapter Twelve

Oswy stood, reluctantly, on the great gray boulder which balanced on the very top of Hammer-and-Anvil fell.

Ahead of him the sun, glowing like a disk of dragon-gold, drove up into the sky. Very far away she seemed, whipping up her horses until the clouds sprang from their mouths red-tinged. Birds circled beneath her, and Oswy, breathless at the height, looked down on them as though he were a god.

Below him the Fells marched far away, gold washed green, and then blue and purple against the pale sky. Behind him the smooth moor swept down to wooded valleys.

A cold wind tossed the budding tree-tops, came whistling through the broom and gorse to tug at his clothes, and nudge him, ever so gently, towards the edge.

Just one step away was a long fall, straight down, onto rock-strewn peaks. He could almost feel the tumbling through the air, the urge to go closer and closer to the drop, the urge to step off and feel for one moment the rush and thrill of the dive. He stood very still.

Sulien sure footed and silent as a cat, came up beside him, looking out on the wild lands with satisfaction.

"A good day," he said quietly, glancing down on Oswy with a smile. "Let's get away from all of them. Let's fly."

"Fly?" Oswy gasped, feeling his mouth open wide in a foolish smile, his mind filling up with his mother's tales: Owl-wives, hiding the knowledge of secret hunts from their stifling families; the old gods, falcon-cloaked speeding, winged and fierce, over the Earth. Incredulity and delight warred for possession, left him speechless.

"If you want to," said Sulien, suddenly uncertain.

"Oh yes!" exclaimed Oswy, "I want to! How?"

The witch got down on his knees, leaned out over the cliff like a boy birds-nesting for gull's eggs. The wind, flinging itself up from the edge, hit him in the face, lifted his yellow hair into a blaze like a comet's trail. He laughed, a real, easy laugh, before sitting back on his heels again and thinking about the question.

"I'll cast the spell," he said, "you watch, feel the shape of it, and remember it for when you will be able to use it yourself."

"Will I need to remember gestures, and words?" Oswy asked, all eager, steeling himself to memorize every one.

Sulien shrugged, "If it helps you," he said, "but I don't find them important." Then, relenting, he smiled again, a reflective, almost shy smile.

"This is an art we practice, Oswy," he said, "Perhaps, in the days of the Duguth colleges, words and formulas and spells were important - I can see it would be simpler if you were trying to train mages to work together. But these days, when we prey on each other like beasts, everyone does his own will.

"Some spells are useful to remember. Some," he shrugged, "you see the knack and never need the words again. I can guide you, but you will have to find out what works for you."

Then, rising, he placed his hands on Oswy's shoulders, took a good long look at him, his face curious and his eyes very intent. "I would guess a raven, or maybe a crow. Watch me now."

He closed his eyes, and taking his hands from Oswy's shoulders began to make slow, controlled gestures, elegant against the sunrise.

The shadow in which he moved, purple as the robe of an emperor, spread out from him like ink in water until Oswy, and the tor on which he stood, and the very sky above him, was stained with his influence, enclosed by and subject to his power.

The touch of it was strangely intimate - like touching the naked soul - and Oswy gasped as the edge of it hit him, terrified by its sheer, nonchalant strength.

Then Sulien began to change the pattern of the world, gathering its fibers into his hands as though he were weaving. Oswy saw the shape of it, understood where the threads were to go. He could hardly stop himself from shouting aloud. It was so obvious!

Pressure began to build up, squeezing him tightly. He felt the sky above him as a great weight, the earth rise to press him against it. He could hardly breathe - his very bones cried out - while the world rejected him, pushing him into a shape too small to fit.

Chapter 12

Dimly he saw his master holding back the final hammer-blow, like a man putting his shoulders to a bursting door. Then, leaning forward, Sulien traced a small sign on Oswy's forehead, saying one word, very softly; hardly to be heard over the hiss of the wind. The hammer-blow struck.

There was for a brief moment a great light, fierce and bright as burning salt, and a clap of sound like thunder. Oswy felt a dizzying rush of movement, a swirl of air, and a lightness so terrible he thought he must be sick.

Then he noticed the strangeness of his vision; the way he had to turn his head to see anything clearly, the way it all seemed flat, like a painting plastered on a white wall. He craned his neck around to see himself - a sleek bundle of sable feathers, gleaming like blued steel - and he laughed and laughed with delight.

The sound came out harsh, the raucous caw of a great carrion bird, shocking him at first into silence, and then into more laughter.

He felt the wind then, pulling at him, lifting his feathers with a cold breath, roaring and whispering like a million voices speaking at once. He grasped the sweet turf with both feet, frightened to let go, afraid of being swept away, buffeted, helpless, by this ettin of air.

Sulien leaned down and picked him up, cradling him carefully in both hands. It was more frightening than the blast - his ribs felt parchment-thin against those fingers. Then the witch tossed him, just like a child's ball, over the edge of the cliff.

The up-draft hit him. He put out his arms to save himself and the fan of his wings caught the wind. He was tossed up, tossed by the wind like a baby tossed into the air by a doting father. He felt no more fear of falling than a baby does as it yells with delight at the high point of the arc.

Up and up he circled in the draft, rising like a mote in a shaft of sunlight, until the world below him was smoothed out into one green plain, and the sky seemed like a sea - filled up with craggy islands and swimming monsters of cloud.

The rising air slowed, leaving him to drift, effortless among the currents and eddies of the air, cocking his head to try and take in, all at once, the gold-bordered wilderness of the heavens, the tapestry-like remoteness of the world of men, and the moonstone-sheen of the wind in which he swam.

He had passed beyond laughter now, into a joy which was all the more shattering because it was quiet. He felt again, as he had when he had called up the witch-light, that he had touched a truth - touched reality, and found it good.

He opened his mouth in praise, to shout out his thanks - to God, to Sulien, to something - and the terrible cruel cry which emerged set him laughing again.

Then, like ashes, clinging and dirty, in a voice too cynical to be truly his own, the thought came to him;

"Do you really think this is what magic is about? You're only playing at it," and briefly, even buoyed up by the warming morning air, he wanted to weep.

A cloud just beneath him burst apart in a fountain of rainbows. He was spattered with spray - bright as pure gold - which beaded his black plumage. The gyrfalcon turned fast in the air, looked at Oswy out of a burning yellow eye. Its white feathers and blue-gray markings caught the sunshine and blazed briefly silver, before it plunged back through the vapor like a loosed arrow.

He recognized it by the violet shadow of its magic, and drifted on the wind incredulous and delighted, watching as his master danced on the air; larking about like a boy let off from work on a spring holy-day.

The joy came back as he watched, and he would have joined in, but the raven-shape was not made for such feats. He had to follow the falcon more sedately, down out of the high reaches of the sky, until they were skimming close over the moors, feeling the warmth and coldness of air over grass and bare stone, running water and still.

Over the fells the air was tinted with the faint smell of magic. A power was there, holding the rocks and gorse and scrub in thrall. Oswy felt it was a masculine power; like the boldness of a man secure in his own strength.

Then, just briefly, they flew over the edge of the forest, and the feeling changed. There was another power at work here, closed in, kindly, but shy as a young fawn hiding in the grass.

Oswy back-tracked, stitching the border with his flight, making sure the sense remained. It did, and he wondered what it could mean.

Eventually by the banks of a small stream, its borders thickly grown with reeds, they landed, and, in a flicker of darkness and silence, became human once more.

Oswy sat down quickly, his shoulders already beginning to ache, but his heart so full of wonder he felt he could neither stand nor speak.

Sulien sat and watched him for a while, his face more peaceful than Oswy had ever seen it.

Chapter 12

"My master taught me that," he said, his voice gentle, regretful, soft as the voice of the brook where it rolled clear as glass beside him. "It was... generous... of him. Having no magery in his blood, it was not something he could do himself, not even with borrowed power. The body has to be capable as well as the mind."

He shifted on the soft turf, smiling, speaking now so quietly Oswy was not sure if he was meant to hear. "My master taught me many things in the early years - things I didn't have to know to be of use to him. He gave me what I now live for - my craft." He finished in a whisper which Oswy knew was not meant for him, "I would have loved him for it, but that he was so cruel."

Then the witch lay back against the short-cropped grass, his jasper-red tunic like a splash of newly spilled blood on the verdant ground. He folded his arms behind his head and for a long time he was silent, gazing up at the flying clouds.

Oswy let him be for as long as he could bear it. He recognized that Sulien was at ease, and he doubted if such a thing could happen often. Nevertheless, after what seemed like a long wait, he said "Master?"

"Hm?" said Sulien, still looking up at the pale sky.

"Did you feel the way the..." he struggled for the words, "Well, the feeling of the land changed?"

"Of course."

"What does it mean?"

"You feel the influence of the elf-lords," said Sulien, and smiled with obvious enjoyment at Oswy's widened eyes, "Crow the secretive," he continued, "and Icewolf, Lord of the Tors. They will want to see you, quite soon."

"They kidnap human children!" Oswy exclaimed, half horrified but still filled up with ravenous curiosity. He had heard all the stories, but he had never yet seen an elf. "And they send a tithe of them to the King of the Abyss!" he finished, triumphant, indignant and eager to hear more.

"Perhaps," Sulien admitted, calmly, "perhaps they feel they have no other choice. They seem to be as confused as I am about these matters."

"When can we go and see them?" said Oswy eagerly. He felt dizzyingly happy; his new life was turning into something glorious and exciting. He was glad now he wasn't doomed to be a farmer, glad he had been sold. Even, with a certain reservation, he felt glad that Sulien was his master.

"Not yet," said Sulien quietly, "I would want to see you a good deal better prepared first. Icewolf collects interesting humans. He may want to keep you."

Oswy shivered. "Would he send me to the Abyss?" he said, in horror.

"I don't know," Sulien replied, and his dark brows pinched together in a frown of uncertainty. "It may be," he said, and the shadow of his magic deepened around him, darkening with his mood; "It may be I am about to take you there myself. The priest is right. The practice of magic is so rarely innocent, so often leads to damnation, that I wonder how I dare think of teaching you."

"But..." Oswy's mood too plummeted back to earth, and, rising up to meet it, the yearning for magic came over him like an ache. It wasn't fair, this, he thought; to be given a gift and then have it taken away again.

"But the flying..." he said.

"Was one of the few purely innocent things I could think of," Sulien finished for him. "Healing magic too I could teach you with a clear conscience, but as for the rest..."

"But you said you would," Oswy insisted, knowing he overstepped the boundaries of what was expected from a slave, and not caring. "I want to learn everything," he said, "I want to."

"Yes," said Sulien, and turned to watch Oswy's face, as intense and as threatening as ever, "And this morning I wanted to kick the priest until there wasn't a bone left unbroken in his body." He snorted, "since when has desire been any recommendation?"

"But you said..." Oswy whined, turning his face away from the dark gaze, feeling its continued pressure with resentment. All his easiness in this company, even the dawning fondness he had felt for this man, fell away, and remembering the witch's sudden rages he grew silent, hugging his knees for the illusory feeling of defense.

"Yes," Sulien sighed, "I said...." And he leaned forward, intent, the pressure of his regard like a wrestler's hug - tight enough to choke. "But remember, this is not a game. It's not for children. It's deadly serious."

He paused, searching for the right thing to say, then went on, with increasing force, the words pouring out of him like confession: "Bad magic is so easy to start, it looks so innocent, but it's like... it's like a drink of salt water to a thirsty man. It does him no good. While he's drinking it there is perhaps a

Chapter 12

tiny relief, but the thirst grows worse and worse with each mouthful until it's a constant torture, and suddenly he can't even dream of stopping. "

He turned away, rubbing his open hand over his face as though he felt ill. His rings, brown agate and crystal, set in gold, glowed in the light like the powers of earth, water and fire, but his voice did not echo the image of strength. It was unsure, reflective, personal.

"It will drain everything of value from your life," he said, "And replace it with a parched, frantic scramble for some thrill which turns your stomach even as you lust for it. And all the time you will be growing more and more inhuman, until you could look at one of the fiends from the pit and see your own reflection."

And now, in distress, "God knows I know what I'm talking about. You must have heard of some of the things I have done."

Oswy, horrified and fascinated at the same time, hints and rumors taking shape about him like a dark smoke, remembered suddenly Fulk's comment 'surly as a whipped dog'. He remembered too a nightmare - a boy, his own powers bound, screaming defiance - and, surprising himself, he asked

"Willingly?"

"No," said Sulien, surprised too, but honest,

"I did none of it willingly, and yet it still snared me, and now, when I can do whatever I want, I thirst for it."

He looked down at his open hands, frowning, and his face took on the intent look of a man trying not to be sick.

"You don't understand what that thirst is like, Oswy. There are still days when I long for my master to return and force me back into evil; so I can have what I secretly want but still be able to say "It's not my fault. He made me."

"And how can I even blame him? I know the force of the desires which pull at him - who better? I feel, every day, how nearly impossible they are to resist, once they begin. Most of the fault must lie simply in taking the first step."

His gaze lifted, grazed Oswy's face, and fell away. "But the first step is so easy, always... almost innocent. I might be taking it for you, just by teaching you. That's what Father Paul thinks. How do I know he's wrong?"

Sound carried to them in the sudden silence; the bark of a fox from the forest below, the sibilant hiss of the wind as it flattened the grass, the squabbling of rooks and crows as they fought over a dead hare, its soil-brown fur appearing and disappearing among the clot of black.

Oswy's eyes rested on them while he tried to work out what it was he felt. Impatience to learn, certainly, but also a new fear - fear of making the first step, by accident, onto the downward path his master described, fear of not having the strength to come up again.

Then another voice spoke in his head, gray as ash, the voice which had briefly taken all the pleasure out of the morning; "He wants to keep the knowledge to himself! He's trying to frighten you off so you won't ever threaten him," and the revelation cast him into even deeper doubt.

Silently, they got up and walked, until the tip of the keep tower, its new coat of white-lime dazzling in the sun, showed itself over the crest of the last hill.

Then, calm and distant again, as though he had shared nothing with Oswy, and expected to receive nothing in return, Sulien said

"This afternoon I have two parchments for you to read and remember - the one on astrological sympathies and medical uses of various plants and stones, the other on methods of defense against rival mages. Tomorrow I'll ask you questions about both."

Oswy nodded, looking yearningly at the bright sky. Then he sighed and prepared to follow his master into the cold stone tower.

"Once you're content you've mastered the lists," Sulien continued, his tone slightly tentative, like a man finding his way around a strange town, "you can do what you like with the rest of the day."

Oswy leaped at the chance. "Please, my lord," he said, "might I fly to see Edward? I just have to show him what I can do!"

"No," said Sulien, his face surly at the mention of his friend's son. He sat down on the pile of rocks and rubble which still littered the space under the guard tower. Under the gleam of his hair, golden as an Eldryhten coin, his eyes were shadowed, but angry. His servants, going in and out, hugged the far wall in their efforts to keep away from him.

"I kept your form in my mind, because I worked the spell," he said with careful clarity. "For you to work it on yourself you would need to know the structure, the limits of your own body, to control them, to be able to bring yourself back."

Chapter 12

Frowning, he picked up a piece of broken flint, rubbed his thumb back and forth on the sharp edge.

"There are a few ways of giving you such control," he said, and, with a short laugh, "they call them 'Ceremonies of initiation'. A grand title to try and conceal how unpleasant they are. Nevertheless I won't really be able to teach you any serious magic until you have gone through one."

He shifted the flint in his hand, so the edge bit deeper. "The easier methods are vile," he said darkly, "but the two clean ones are so painful you might die from them. I have to decide which one to use."

Oswy gulped, biting his fist in sudden fear. Catching the witch's disapproving look he lowered the hand awkwardly, feeling unprotected without it. His breath was coming fast and hard with the thudding of his heart.

"Die?" he whispered.

"Did you think this came cheaply?" said Sulien.

Rising, he strode away. Oswy stood a long time, his eyes locked on the treeless horizon, his mind and spirits in such turmoil that he saw and knew nothing. Then, blindly, he made his way into the keep and down the steep stairs, to collapse in his cell as though his bones had dissolved.

There were two parchments stacked on his pallet, almost the same color as his rough cream blanket. They were folded neatly into quarters, crammed with careful black writing. He knew they were precious, but, after one brief look, he flung them into the far corner of the room.

"What's the point of learning it if I'm just going to die?" he shouted at the inoffensive booklets.

At the sound of the word 'Die' his voice faltered, and he had to bite his lip to stop the tears. He hugged his arms about himself and put his head down on his knees waiting for the terror to pass.

Outside the open door of his cell the amber glow of a torch flickered in its veil of smoke. Faint sunlight filtered down the spiral stairs to join it and the two lights warred with each other, fluttering and swirling like bats in the draft. He thought at first it was their voices he heard, faintly, speaking words of comfort, reassurance, unconvincing words of love.

The fear ebbed a little as he listened harder. It was not two voices but one; one voice with all the smutty grayness of the hot torch ash, with the fainting warmth of the far away spring sun. It was a beautiful voice, sticky sweet as honey squeezed out of the comb, and, after a little thought, he recognized it from this morning's flight.

"Who are you?" he whispered, still uncertain as to whether it was all in his fear bewildered mind. The answer came back, like a thread of smoke.

"I am your friend."

"But who?" Oswy insisted, stopping his ears, trying to work out if he heard the voice or if it merely spoke in his head. The voice whispered on.

"I can't tell you," it said, "not while you're under His influence. Don't you know that names are power?"

"No," said Oswy, "I didn't." As he spoke he was chasing an elusive memory. Hadn't he heard this voice in a dream? Its slightly artificial gentleness reminded him of something.

"I knew he would teach you nothing," it said dismissively.

"What do you want with me?" Oswy demanded. He was not sure he liked this disembodied creature, and yet it was nice to talk to someone who seemed to care about him.

"I'm watching out for you," it said. "You know he's going to kill you soon."

"No!" Oswy leaped to his feet indignantly. Hadn't his master proved and proved again that he did not mean to do him harm?

The voice's laughter was like a cloud of steam, gentle, but clinging. "No?" it said, "Didn't he just say you might die?"

"But it's necessary!" Oswy hissed, with anger born from fear. He wasn't quite sure why he was defending his master, when Sulien clearly didn't care what he felt, and this voice did.

"Is it so?" mocked the voice. Its murmur now was as loud as his own speech in his ears. "I notice he didn't offer you a choice of one of the safer options, even though he admitted they exist. You heard him, telling that hag-ugly priest how much your blood was worth. Well it's worth much more if he can get you to go to your death willingly. Why else do you think he's being so friendly? It's hardly in his nature you know."

"How do you know what's in his nature?" said Oswy, striking out suspiciously in a sudden fog of confusion. He didn't trust this voice; but why hadn't Sulien given him a choice?

Chapter 12

He felt the voice recoil from his attack, scuttling back into his mind like a scorpion scuttling under a stone. Then, gathering itself together again, it said, plausibly; "These are Sulien's dungeons. This was my cell once."

It paused, as a man pauses to draw breath, to steel himself for speech. "He tortured me for some months," it said, "before he killed me."

"A ghost!" Oswy spun on his heel, peering wild eyed at all the dim shapes and shades which fluttered in his room.

"Yes," said the voice, gently, and yet, under the gentleness he was quite sure it was gloating at his fear. "I don't mean you any harm," it said, reassuringly, "I just know he wants to kill you. And I intend to thwart him."

Oswy pushed the heavy, iron-studded door of his cell as far open as it would go. He leaned out. Ragged shadows swooped at him, circling up and down the stairwell, rushing past him into the darkness where the pit was, and the bricked up holes in the floor where men had been walled in and forgotten.

The blended lights could not reach so far. The corridor stretched out into blackness. Oswy imagined, suddenly, all the unshriven dead men waking, clawing at the stones with the fragile bones of their hands and screaming. The sound would be very faint from here, very like the moan of the wind and the scritching of the rats in the walls...

"Don't go," said the voice, anticipating him. It was so gentle, so protective, he would have flown into its embrace, if only it had arms to hold him. "Before I died," it said, "I managed to make an amulet."

From its tone Oswy could tell it was extremely pleased with itself, "And I hid it from him," it finished, "Knowing it would protect whoever came after me. Now I give it to you. Come back into the room."

He seized the torch from its iron bracket, the light of it felt like walls of magic, like a globe of defensive force tamed to his hand. Then he went back, just as it asked, the lure of protection battling with his fear.

The corners of his cell were dark even in the dancing amber light. Propping the flaming brand in the center of the room - precariously balanced against his hard stool - he wondered how many other men had died in this cell, and he wanted very much to flee, but the bribe of magic drew him, stronger than a candle-flame draws a moth.

"Why didn't it protect you?" he said, like a buyer haggling over a pot, scowling at it as though he expects it to burst apart in his hands, when all the time his fingertips are caressing it and his eyes are saying "I must have it!"

"The power in it," the voice said, persuasively. "Came from my death," and it laughed. "Has he not even told you about death-magic?"

"No," said Oswy, frowning. The words kindled some deep revulsion inside him, but sensing the voice's amusement at his naivety, he said nothing more.

"He does keep you ignorant!" it chuckled. "Open your mind now, and I will take you to it."

It was an over-sweet vapor, the touch of the ghost, like a breath from a grove of rotting roses. Oswy felt it beat upon him, trying to ooze into his closed mouth, into his nostrils and the hollows of his ears. He closed his eyes quickly and it seemed to pluck at his eyelids, trying to squeeze in under the lashes. He could feel its glee and excitement. He held his breath, driving it off with sheer willpower, and his body moved of itself, kneeling, scrabbling at the dirt floor.

"Get off me! Get off me!" he yelled, in sudden panic. Fear fueled his power. His head felt it would split with the shrieking of it. There was a clap of noise like thunder, and the walls shook. The mud and straw, blocking up the rat holes, crumbled and the dirt whirled about Oswy in a cloud. The stench of the ghost was torn away like a lady's veil in a storm. He could breathe again.

When he had stopped sobbing with relief he found himself on his knees. He had dug down into the packed earth of the floor and his filthy hands were locked around something which glinted saffron-yellow in the dim light. Shakily he wiped it down, held it out into the flickering torch light, and drew a long sigh of pleasure at the sight of such a valuable thing.

It was a brooch of gold, made in the likeness of a serpent, whose body writhed in a complex knot, and whose silver teeth closed on its own tail. The eye of yellow topaz glittered like polished brass. He felt an immediate desire to possess it and keep it safe.

"Don't do that again," he said, looking up from the jewel for an instant, protesting the attack despite this prize. "Do you hear me? I don't want you ever to do it again..." Then, when it remained silent, "are you still there?"

"Yes I'm here," it said, the coating of gentleness worn very thin, resentment and anger barely reined in beneath the surface. "Keep it on you all the time," it said, its accents surly, but its words still generous, "On you, or near you, and he won't be able to kill you however he tries. And obviously," it concluded reasonably, "Don't let him know about it, or he'll take it away."

Chapter 12

Oswy looked down at it again, thinking. His eyes looked darkly back, captured on the gleaming metal. Perhaps the ghost was lying, and Sulien didn't intend him any harm. Oswy had misjudged his master before.

But, even if Sulien didn't intend him to die, he had said himself it could happen. The initiation would be dangerous; Oswy might not survive. There couldn't be any harm in having an amulet to ward against the chance, could there? No, there couldn't be any harm in it.

He unwound the length of braid which he wore as a belt and pinned the brooch beneath his tunic at the waist. When he had put back the tie and knotted it even the pin was covered. The metal of the jewel felt cold and hard, digging through the fine linen of his shirt. He expected it to warm quickly, held against the heat of his body, but it did not. It lay cold as a dead man's hand against his skin. He found himself leaning away from it, and yet he had no desire to take it off. It was too beautiful, and it made him feel safe.

"I am so cold," moaned the ghost, its voice faded to a whisper softer than the fluttering of the parchment pages in the gusting breeze. "Oh! I am so cold!"

"What is it?" Oswy demanded, edging once more towards the door. He wondered if it would follow him out of the room, or if it was trapped there. He hoped it was trapped. He wanted no more of ghosts and darkness and the memories of fear. Noticing the jet-black bead of a rat's eye staring at him out of the wall, its whiskers twitching at the smell of him, he flinched. How would he ever sleep in this room again?

"It has taken so much of my strength, talking to you," the ghost whispered, "and I'm so cold. Raise power for me boy, before you abandon me. Feed me."

"How?" Oswy gasped, his eyes widening with apprehension.

"It's not much," the voice whispered, pervasive as the sighing air, "not much. And it will teach you blood magic. Give me your hand."

There was the sensation of coldness, an icy fist slipping inside his arm, putting on his hand like a glove. He pulled back in horror, and it slid away as if it could not get a firm grip.

"Let me," it begged, "you must let me. After all I have done for you..." and softly, temptingly, "He'll never teach you this. He doesn't know. I thought you wanted to learn everything."

Oswy gulped, frightened and excited at the same time. Suddenly, puzzlingly, he wanted this above all things, to learn a secret Sulien himself didn't know. To spite the arrogant bastard! Steeling himself for the touch he reached out his right hand, choked back the cry of disgust as the ghost slipped within him, fought it, feeling its frustration and rage, until it had possession of his hand and nothing more.

The hand stretched out, faster than Oswy had ever moved, with an adult's sureness and purpose. He felt it close around the neck of the rat - damp matted fur against his fingers, the lash of a naked tail - and lift it, struggling, into the light. Its hand-shaped paws scrabbled against his skin, tearing dirty furrows into his palm and wrist. It squirmed, chittering fiercely, and sank its long yellow teeth into his thumb. He yelled, and, at the back of his mind, heard the ghost give a little sigh of pleasure at his pain.

"Tut tut," the ghost mocked, "you don't have a knife. Never mind. Fire will do." And it moved Oswy's hand, the struggling animal still clamped in its grip, towards the flames of the torch.

"What are you doing?!" Oswy yelled, horror coming over him like a wave of blood, "What are you doing! I don't want..."

His fingers locked around the rat's forepaw. Even as he shouted his denial he was holding the tiny, delicate foot into the scorching flames.

The rat screamed, shrill and bird-like. He felt the shock of agony go through it; all its muscles stiffening under the pain. The flesh of the paw melted, blood bubbling up and blackening in the fire.

"Stop it! Stop it!" he pleaded, turning his head away so he need not see, while tears of pity and remorse spattered on the churned ground. The little heart was beating in frenzy against his palm. He tried to pull his hand back but instead its grip tightened. It was clenching into a fist.

"No!" he wailed, while bones broke under his fingers. His thumb found the spine and pressed. The smell of burnt meat was everywhere. The bone snapped like a winter twig. The heart fluttered and stopped. The tiny body went limp in his hand.

And then it hit him: Power! It rose through his arm, his shoulders, flowing into his body like warm oil. He felt huge, strong, reckless. He wanted to smash this place, find his enemies, pulp them like fruit and drink their blood.

As suddenly as it had come it was over. He fell on his knees, shaking, his eyes tightly shut, and tried to deny he wanted it again.

It didn't happen, he said to himself. It was a dream. Just like before. But, when he looked, there was the body, and his hand, bloodstained, reeking of death.

Chapter 12

Scrambling up, blind with weeping, he ran for the door, hurling himself out into the darkness as if he were hunted. Only the ghost's voice followed him, growing fainter with each step. He was leaving it behind. He could pretend he had not heard it saying, "If that's what a rat's death feels like, imagine what it's like to kill a man!"

Chapter Thirteen

Oswy stumbled, still weeping, out of the keep's postern door. The guard on duty looked after him curiously but said nothing. He could feel the eyes on his back, and shame drove him on faster. He was sure the man-at-arms had seen his gore-blackened fingers, smelled the carrion smell of him. He would go to the well, draw up bucket after bucket of cold water and wash until he was clean of it.

Right over the kitchen garden he ran, the turned soil soft under his feet, the aromatic scent of trampled herb seedlings rising up around him in the thin afternoon warmth. A woman in an undyed dirty dress straightened up and cursed him for treading down 'her' plants. He bolted past her, hardly seeing her bare, work-worn face through the glitter of his lashes.

Scrambling over the raised edge of the herb-beds he almost fell onto the mossy flagged pavement which ringed the well. He rushed forward, and then balked. Someone was already there.

The young man's bronze-brown hair had been untidily hacked with an eating knife to keep it short. By the uneven look of the back he had done it himself. He was wearing a tunic of Leofwine's. A good one - the dark green color still emerald-intense, vine scroll embroidery delicate around collar and cuffs - but it was much too wide across his shoulders and the sleeves hung down over his hands. It was Hugo, solitary and morose, sitting on the low lip of the well, frowning and tossing pebbles into the darkness as though only his pride prevented him from following them.

Dithering in the shadows Oswy watched him for a while. He thought perhaps Hugo was brooding over his captivity, maybe even missing his family and friends. If that was so he could understand very well how the young man felt.

Part of him yearned to go and offer sympathy, but another said practically; 'Do you think he would want pity from a Sceavish slave?' A third yammered in panic, 'get him out of the way! I want to get to the well!' And another, terrifying him, whispered 'wouldn't it be good to tip him over the edge, listen to him scream as he hit the water.'

Chapter 13

He moaned, clutching his head with his hands. What was happening to him? Was he going insane? He remembered Sulien's warning - was it only this morning? - with a stab of despair. Had killing one rat been enough to enslave him to black magic for ever? Oh why couldn't he have been more careful?! He rubbed the tears from his eyes and then gagged, realizing he had smeared the blood and grease all over his face. He had to get to the water and wash this all away.

Hugo looked up at the noise. His green eyes, emptied of their usual flippancy, narrowed with concern.

"God's sword!" he said, "What's the matter? You're bleeding!"

Oswy shook his head, his eyes filling up again at this unexpected kindness. His voice choked in his throat. He gestured wildly at the well - the mossy, green rope coiled in the empty bucket - and, with quick deftness, the Holmr knight drew water, and set it down in front of him as carefully as a servant.

When Oswy had washed for the third time, soaking his sleeves up to the elbow, drenching his face and collar and hair, Hugo caught him by the chin and made him look up.

"So," he said, thoughtfully, after one long glance, "it wasn't your blood after all. Tell me what has happened."

"I..." stammered Oswy, reacting instinctively to the tone of command, "I killed..." and he choked again on the long explanation which Hugo would probably neither comprehend nor believe.

"Ah," sighed the young knight and rocked back on his heels. His face became stern, but his eyes were still not without sympathy or concern. "I understand," he said, "and now you think you will never be clean again. The feeling will pass. I assure you."

Oswy looked up at him in astonished gratitude. Was this really the man who would have torn Gunnar apart over a ring? And then Hugo said, "So, who was it you killed, and why?"

"No one!" Oswy exclaimed, shocked to the core by the thought. His voice was more indignant, angrier, than it would have been had he not just been imagining tipping Hugo to a watery grave in the fern-grown depths of the castle well. "It was a rat!" he shouted.

Hugo stared at him, astonished, and then burst into a peal of relieved laughter. The sound echoed in the well shaft until it was a mocking roar which startled the white doves off the tower's slate roof. Oswy felt himself redden under it as though it were a wind of searing fire.

"It's not funny!" he protested, and Hugo, wiping tears of mirth from his moss-green eyes exclaimed,

"All this anguish over vermin? God's Sword! I knew you Sceafn were soft-hearted, but this!"

"You don't understand," Oswy sighed, hearing in his own voice an echo of the frustrated loneliness he had heard this morning from his master. He knew, very well, no one would understand except Sulien, and to Sulien he could not speak. The doubt the ghost had planted in him set a numb hand of dread on his lips, cold as the amulet pressing against his ribs. You don't understand," he said again, despairingly.

"No," Hugo replied, gently, bowing his head again over the water, "I don't. But I'm sorry I laughed at you boy." Oswy looked up, hearing in the hoarse voice a grief as profound as his own.

"I could wish," Hugo murmured, almost to himself, "that my father was as soft-hearted as you. Half a year I've been in bondage here and not a word from him."

He shoved back the cuffs of his long sleeves with a movement so practiced he seemed hardly to notice it. "If I had known before," he said sadly, "what value he placed on my life, maybe I would have spoken softer in front of your Lord."

"I'm sorry," Oswy said awkwardly, shaken a little out of his own concerns. He knew what it was like to find your family values you somewhat less than you hope. He wanted to say as much, to try and offer some comfort, but the gulfs of race and status and age kept him silent.

"It's nothing," said Hugo eventually, gathering his dignity with visible effort. Then he grinned. "Maybe you should go and tell your rat story to Leofwine," he said, "I dare say he's soft enough to understand you."

"Yes." Oswy sighed with relief, feeling propriety come back between them, welcome as cool water on a hot day. "Yes, Sir, I'd like to. Do you know where he is?"

"In the Hall, I think," said Hugo, turning away to drop a pebble into the echoing darkness and counting off the numbers in Holmsh while it dropped.

"Don't just barge in," he said sternly when the distant plunk had died away and the wavering reflections had stilled. "He's holding petty court."

Chapter 13

At first sight the Great Hall looked like a forest fire - a vaulted darkness filled with smoke and moving lights. White wood-smoke coiled in the wide bolts of primrose light which poured through the clerestory of arrow-slits high above Oswy's head. Torches and candles glittered like huge jewels of polished amber in their own greasy reek, and the red fire in its long pit spat drifting ashes into the air.

Below the dais, where Leofwine sat in Sulien's carven chair, a fog of rumor and lowered voices mingled with the fume. Supplicants, and their relatives, their witnesses, their oath-swearers and their animals, were dawdling on their way home, watching the last case of the day as they might have watched a troop of mummers on a summer evening - content to take whatever entertainment was offered. Not even the choking acridity of the smoke could completely mask the stench of them.

"A theft of this value is a hanging matter," Leofwine's soft dark voice slipped gently into Oswy's hearing as the boy moved up toward the dais. "I hardly call that petty, do you?"

"No, my lord." The accuser was a brown, weather-beaten man, gnarled and strong as old oak. He spoke meekly, but there was a hint of insolence in his tone.

Leofwine sighed, squinting through the band of sunlight which lay like an aura of gold over the bench. The blaze picked out the prancing unicorn of the tapestry behind him, the glint of a plaited silver chain around his neck, the sudden whiteness of the clerk's hand as it moved out of shadow to dip the gray quill.

"How many times must I tell you, Ulf?" said the knight, patiently, "This is not within my authority. You must come before my lord Sulien."

Even in the witch's own hall there was a murmur of dread at that name.

"I'd rather you tried it," Ulf stated, harking back in his boldness to the time before the Invasion, when any free man might speak his mind to his lord without fear. Oswy felt the tug of nostalgia sweep through the onlookers; the plain faces brightened with cautious hope. Leofwine reacted to it too, with a smile.

"I'm sure you would," he said, "because I can't tell if you're lying just by looking at you, but he can."

Ulf opened his mouth to reply, and Leofwine silenced him brusquely.

"I've heard enough. Either you return tomorrow to bring the charge in front of my lord or the decision will be made against you." He leaned forward to look the man in the eye, "In which case," he said, "I shall expect you to pay Alfward heavy compensation for the time you've made him spend in the pit."

Pointedly turning away, he asked the clerk who sat, head bent, below him, "Are there any more cases?"

The farmer slouched out, muttering. The clerk shook his head, his shorn flaxen hair and white face like the blur of smoke in the shadow. He blew on the last line of ink and then rolled the records up and carried them away, his black robe fading into the shade and smoke like a cloud. There was an eddy of movement in the crowd as men and women rose to go home. Leofwine and Oswy stood where they were, and soon they were alone, while the lowering sun filled the huge room with light the color of flames.

"Weren't you supposed to be reading?" Leofwine asked, with a smile, as he came down to stand by Oswy's side.

"I can't!" Oswy exclaimed, and the act of speaking brought it all back to him, so he had to squeeze his eyes tight shut against the tears.

"I can't go back down there!" he gasped, making great empty gestures to help the words out. "Don't make me sleep in there tonight! There's a ghost!"

"What!" Startled, Leofwine went down on one knee to look in his face. His smile faded rapidly at what he saw.

"Hush there," he said with quiet concern, reaching out to lay a comforting hand on Oswy's arm. "You're safe enough, and this panic isn't fitting for a boy your age. Now come out into the air and we'll talk."

They sat with their backs against the stone wall of the workroom where Oswy had hidden when he was running away. It had been repaired and was now solid, giving back the feeble heat of the day in a welcome glow. Oswy hugged his knees and watched the demesne workers trudging out of the gates to take the steep road down to Harrowden village before darkness came. Occasional laughter floated on the air. A guard came out of the keep and kindled the torches on the outer walls. Slowly, struggling to keep his composure, so Leofwine would not be completely ashamed of him, he began to talk.

He told the knight about the affectionate voice of the ghost, about his ravenous curiosity, and then about how he had allowed the creature to take his own right hand and torture another living being with it. Finally, drawn out by Leofwine's grave silence, he tried haltingly to explain about the rush of power when the rat died, and how good it had felt.

Chapter 13

In all the long, costly confession, it never occurred to him to mention the amulet. Nor did he notice how his elbow was pressed against it, making certain that not even the shape showed through the fine-woven wool of his yellow tunic.

"Oh," said Leofwine, when Oswy was finished, then he too was silent a long while, watching the pink crescent of moon floating in the still blue sky and frowning with thought.

"You know it's Sulien you should be speaking to," he said eventually. The rough silk of his voice was calm, without the condemnation Oswy had been expecting and dreading to hear.

"I can't," said Oswy miserably, "I just can't." How could he possibly explain to Leofwine, who seemed so decent, and yet so utterly loyal, that he was half afraid his master meant to murder him? "He frightens me," he admitted, weakly.

"Huh!" Leofwine exclaimed, as if in exasperation at this foolishness. He pushed back the hair from his face and the smell of wood smoke drifted from it, reminding Oswy, irreverently, how very hungry he was.

"Well," the knight continued thoughtfully, "You seem at least to have learned your lesson. I don't see you doing it again, do you?"

"No!" Oswy exclaimed, "Never!" And he was overwhelmed by the feeling of loss. Why was he casting aside such easy power? Wasn't there some way he could have it without the killing? And, a more sinister whisper, why was he getting so worried? It was only a rat after all.

But he had been warned. He recognized this as the beginnings of the thirst his master had spoken of, and he knew the only way of escape was to stop it now. With every ounce of his will, his face solemn as though he were making a binding oath he said; "I will never do it again. I promise."

Leofwine smiled slowly, a smile of true delight. Then he reached out and ruffled Oswy's hair until Oswy had to yelp and scramble away, choked with relieved laughter and indignation.

"You're a good lad," said Leofwine, while Oswy re-tied his leather headband and stuffed the errant hair back into it. "And I'll not mention this again. As for your room, since you've stopped running away it makes sense to move you back upstairs where you'll have better light for reading."

"Reading!" Oswy exclaimed, leaping to his feet in horror, "Oh my God! I was supposed to be reading. He's going to test me tomorrow, and I haven't even looked at it yet!" He ran off and back again in agitation.

"The parchments are in my room," he said in hurried supplication, "I don't want to go back down there. But he's going to kill me if I haven't learned anything."

Leofwine's smile had broadened into an indulgent grin, "Calm down," he laughed, "I'll get your books for you after dinner. One thing at a time; are you sure this ghost of yours can't come out of there?"

"Yes," said Oswy, and hoped fervently that he spoke the truth.

"Then I'll lock it up until Father Paul can come to deal with it." A frown of thoughtful sadness passed over the knight's face like a cloud. He was sighing as he pushed himself to his feet. "Perhaps you were right to bring this to me," he said. "If you had told Sulien he would have felt obliged to go down there, and after last time I wouldn't want to put him through that again."

"He saw it too?" Oswy asked, eagerly. It was becoming a comfort to him to know he was not alone in his visions. But Leofwine shook his head with a look of puzzled sympathy.

"We were cleansing the keep," he said, "but the memories were so strong down there he could see nothing else. Can you imagine it? Having nightmares open-eyed; not being able to wake up. He hasn't been there since, and from what he told me, I don't blame him. no one should have to face that twice."

Then, before Oswy could ask him exactly what he knew, he said, briskly "Come with me, I have something for you," and he strode off through the gathering twilight toward the windowless bulk of the kennels.

The hounds' voices rose up to greet them as they plunged into the warm darkness of the wooden building. The dogs strained at the end of their leashes, tongues lolling, tails flailing at the air as they tried to hurl themselves on Leofwine. The yammering made Oswy's ears ring, but the sheer joy of the animals made him smile.

The three blood-hounds which had given Leofwine such a rapturous welcome came sniffing around Oswy's ankles as he followed the tall man into the musty darkness. He waded through them with some trepidation.

"Don't worry," said Leofwine, from where he knelt at a pen at the sheltered end of the cot, "They're soft as butter. They've never hunted men. Come on."

He edged his wide shoulders out of the way so Oswy could see.

161

Chapter 13

In the pen there lay a gaze-hound bitch, a massive animal whose brown coat was brindled with gold. Her black arched ears were alert and her wolfish amber eyes full of self-satisfaction. She sniffed at Oswy's outstretched hand with all the dignity of a great lady examining a suitor.

A knot of pups was asleep in the straw against the warmth of her long belly, their paws twitching in infant dreams. Oswy smiled at them with delight. They were such ridiculous things; little mops of brindled fur, their skins baggy and over-sized, wrinkled and folded about them like an elder brother's hand-me-down tunic. Their brows were furrowed as if in deep thought.

"I've decided on a fitting punishment for you," said Leofwine in a whisper. He leaned forward to stroke one of the puppies from nose to tail, so gently it hardly stirred, "Something to make up for what you did."

Oswy sighed, imagining labor and drudgery, trying to look studious and rather innocent. The effort was wasted, Leofwine was not looking.

"Here," said the knight quietly, and, turning, he placed the smallest puppy in Oswy's right hand. The creature woke, briefly, gave a yawn which showed a rose-petal tongue and the needle-sharp points of white teeth, and then put its head down again on Oswy's fingers and went back to sleep. It was almost exactly the same size and weight as the rat he had killed.

He looked at it foolishly, wondering what this meant, not daring to move in case he should do something wrong. While he was still silent Leofwine said,

"This runt isn't thriving. It seems a waste to leave her to die, but we have no kennel hand, and I can't afford the time to nurse her." He drew breath, watching Oswy closely, "So I'm giving her to you. Whether she lives or dies is in your hands."

Oswy looked up into Leofwine's shadowed face, catching the candid glance of the steel-gray eyes. He looked down again at the puppy lolling on his hand - her little sides going in and out like bellows. The meaning of it came over him suddenly: He had been trusted. Unashamedly he began to cry again, guilt and gratitude and joy all mixed into one, while the burly, brown-haired man leaned back against the kennel wall and watched over him quietly.

"How did you know?" Oswy sobbed, in such a mix of grief and happiness that he hardly knew what he felt. "I thought I could never make it right! How did you know?"

"You took a life," said Leofwine, shrugging, "of course you would want to give one back. Now do stop crying, you're worrying the hounds."

Oswy pushed one of the other puppies aside and placed his down in the straw with her black nose pressed up to her mother's nipple. She stirred slightly and began, sleepily, to suckle. He immediately felt stupidly proud of her.

"Leave her there for the moment," said Leofwine quietly. "You go and get dinner. I'll see about your room and fetch your books."

He was only a moving shadow in the warm darkness now, a shadow with a deep, soft voice. Impulsively, full of gratitude and love, Oswy threw his arms about him and hugged him fiercely.

"Will you be my father now?" he said, "You're so much nicer than my real father."

"Hush!" said Leofwine, with a half laugh of embarrassment and pleasure. He put one arm about Oswy's shoulders and drew him out into the cold blue and silver twilight.

"I'll be your friend, certainly," he said, smiling. "But it's not my son you're destined to be."

~

"Please! Please! Don't hurt me! Don't touch me! Go away!"

Oswy was panicking, pulled along by the wrist, his heels dragging furrows in the waterlogged ground.

The time had come for his initiation. Yesterday they had searched the keep from top to bottom to be sure no enemy mage had left an occult link there. Dame Edith had returned from Harrowden village with Oswy's old ragged clothes over one arm, and they had burnt them to ashes in the great Hall's long fire-pit.

"Here," Sulien had said, casting onto the fire the linen package of Oswy's hair which he had carried with him since Caster. "This should help to prove my good faith. I no longer have any link to you. You are safe from my influence."

Chapter 13

He had seemed more than usually brusque, angry at the whole subject, "You will be very easy to enslave or control," he had said. "We must be very careful to make sure no other mage has the means to do it."

The same night, at midnight, on the moon-washed cold floor of the great hall the witch had drawn up runes of protection - a circle of arcane fire around the keep and all the demesne lands.

"No sorcerer will be able to walk through that," he said, a note of satisfaction in his voice as he contemplated the work. But Oswy had wondered even then if the walls were there to protect him or to keep him from running away.

This morning he had done quite well. He had washed and eaten, keeping his hands from trembling and his knees from giving way by filling his mind with his mother's stories. But then he had gone to confession and suddenly the thought of death was real again, and he could not get off his knees. When Sulien had come to take him for the trial, he had had to carry him, and only the thought of the amulet, held tight against him under his woolen tunic, had stopped Oswy from kicking out and trying to flee.

Now not even that could calm his panic. He bucked and wrenched at his master's grip like an unbroken colt.

"Let me go!" he shouted, "There's an easier way, you said so! I don't want to die!"

"Be quiet!" Sulien smacked him across the face with his free hand, and then, grudgingly, muttered "You know it has to be done."

"You're behaving like a peasant, Oswy," said Leofwine sternly and prized Oswy's clinging fingers from the iron ring of the postern door. "I am a chireugeon, my lord is a healer. You're not going to die."

But Oswy just dug his heels in and screamed for help.

The guard at the gatehouse began to sing to drown out the noise of them, his voice loud and untuneful as he whetted his ax. He kept his head down, his eyes fixed on the gleaming metal as Leofwine slammed the door shut behind them.

The frightened whinnying of horses broke out as, in the stable, the half-witted old groom reacted to Oswy's yelling with a high-pitched wail of terror.

Sulien's temper snapped.

"You don't want this?" he shouted, amber glints flaring up in his brown eyes like fire, "You don't want control? You don't want to be able to do real magic? Fine! Go back to your sty!"

He dropped Oswy's wrist and gave him a shove which sent him sprawling.

"You're free," he said. "Go back to your parents, if that's what you want. Go and wait for some other witch to come for you. I've had enough of you!" He turned his back on Oswy, and folding his arms watched the black clouds seethe over the peaks.

"He's just frightened," Leofwine said, reasonably. "And he is a peasant. You shouldn't expect too much from him."

His words stung Oswy more than the slap, but worse still was this sudden release. Trust Sulien, he thought, trust his master to make even the gift of freedom seem like a kick in the teeth. He scrambled to his knees, wiped the mud from his face and plucked at the hem of Sulien's blue tunic.

"I don't want to go," he pleaded, "I want to stay here and learn magic. I want it more than anything."

Sulien turned his head and looked down on him distastefully. "Then stop being such a coward," he said.

"You said there was an easier way," muttered Oswy, staring at a grass-blade bent over under the weight of a bead of water, expecting another slap for his insolence. "Why can't I have an easier way?"

There was a sigh and Sulien crouched down to look him in the face.

"The easier ways are disgusting. This way is only painful."

He frowned, putting his words together as carefully as an armorer twisting rods of metal to make the heart of a sword. "The memory of pain fades quickly," he said, "but the memory of shame can torture you forever...." There was a pause, barely two heartbeats long, while he held Oswy's gaze and then Oswy looked away, cowed by sudden understanding. In the steel-sharp, cold voice he used when he was one step away from violent rage, Sulien said "Now get up and do what I say," and Oswy rose and followed him like a perfect slave.

They walked slowly down into the shelter of the trees, pushed their way through coppiced hazels on the borders of the road and into the wild woods. The clouds thinned above them into a roof of pearl-gray light. The snapping of twigs under their feet was loud in the moist quietness of the

Chapter 13

morning. When they came out into a long clearing, the scar of some ages-old fire, thin warmth from the veiled sun stroked Oswy's dirty face.

Ahead of him the treeless plain went up into a fold of the hills. The breeze scattered flying stars of dew from the swaying tips of the plants which grew waist-deep there, thick as a planted field.

"Listen to me," said Sulien intently and shook Oswy by the shoulders to be sure he was paying attention. "You will want to flee from this pain. You must not. Do you hear me?"

Oswy nodded, swallowing, his eyes wide with fear.

"Be with it when it breaks you apart. Let it show you where the limits of your body are, and when you know them bring yourself back."

"What if I can't do it?"

"If you don't die," said Sulien with a touch of morbid humor which Oswy resented, "then I will consider trying the second method, which is more painful, and more dangerous."

Oswy turned to look again at the green valley. The sky above it was white as the membrane inside an egg and the wind was cool. His heart began to throb in the base of his throat, and breath felt heavy. With shaking hands he unwound the securing wool and tugged out the ring-pin which closed the neck of his tunic. He dropped it on the ground beside his belt and then pulled tunic and shirt together over his head. Laying them down neatly he made sure the amulet was concealed in the folds of the skirts before clambering out of hose and braies and standing bare and shivering in front of the long slope. Whatever happened, however painful it was, he swore to himself he would get back to his amulet and it would not let him die.

"You will do it," Sulien said softly behind him, and his heart raced with fear, thinking the witch had read his mind, before he realized the man was only trying to be reassuring.

"You are stronger than you think," his master said, "and you have an instinct for this. You will do it. Now walk."

Tentatively Oswy edged forward until he was right at the shore of the sea of nettles. The older shaggy plants were chest-high on him, new leaves showing bright green everywhere. The ground was covered with fresh growth. Nettles, their surfaces furry with stinging spines, swayed gently in the breeze.

He put one foot forward and it was as though he had stood on a mat made of red-hot pins. He yelped and threw himself back to safety, holding his stung foot clear of the ground. It had begun to throb and burn as though the blood running through it was heated in flames. The very thought of going further into the green cauldron made him wince.

"Walk, Oswy," said Sulien calmly, and calmly, with a hand in the small of his back, pushed him into the wavefront of the wind-tossed plants.

It passed very rapidly from discomfort to pain, and then to agony. As he stumbled through them, walking initially from force of will, and then because he could not think clearly enough to stop, the stinging spines brushed gently over his legs and flanks and chest, leaving tracks of pain over belly and groin worse than any whipping. He felt flayed, as though sand, borne in a hot wind, had rubbed all the skin off him, and every grain of it had carried poison. The venom worked into his blood, making his bones throb and stars of silver swim on the edges of his vision like stinging insects.

In the center of the mile-long valley he stopped, head thrown back, gulping air, his eyes tightly shut as he fought to stop the pain from overwhelming him. His neck and head had not been stung, and that helped, slightly. It was an anchor, a line flung out to reality, to a world which existed apart from him and his agony. He knew he was crying, but it seemed to him his blood was so hot the tears flashed into steam as soon as they fell. He tried to blot everything out but the touch of the cool breeze on his unhurt face. If he could only concentrate on that, until the pain passed then he might just be able to get through this without going mad.

There was a rustle behind him and his flayed body felt the presence of magic, just as a swimmer feels the flickering of a school of tiny fish against his skin, and the almost nauseous shock that there is something alive in here. Then Sulien kicked the feet out from under him and he fell backwards, screaming, with the sky swinging out of place below him and the green waters rising up to drown him. Nettles stung his throat and cheeks, reached through his thick hair to prick his scalp.

"Stop fighting it!" Sulien was yelling, "It's not going to work if you fight it!" and jamming a foot under Oswy's back he levered him over, pushing his head down with one hand, forcing his face into the verdant cushion of stinging nettles. They pierced his face and eyelids like thousands of hot knives. He opened his mouth to scream "I hate you! I hate you!" and the spines brushed against the thin skin of his lips and tongue.

But now it felt far away; he could track the pain almost dispassionately, as though it was connected to him by a thin red cord. He was a bundle of red cords, tangled and intricate, and he could see how they were

Chapter 13

woven and where they touched the threads of the outside world. Curiously, the pain held away from him, acknowledged but no longer felt, he began to map the lines of his body, working out where they went and what they did. He did not notice he was being dragged face-down through the nettles by his hair. Nor did he notice the point at which it ceased and he was lifted up and carried, his tunic tucked around him with rough care.

Vaguely though he could feel the weight of the amulet pressing on his belly and see it through his closed eyes like a dark thread in the world's pattern of white and red. Its coldness penetrated the wool in which he was wrapped, spreading like balm over his swollen skin.

It was a complicated process to move his arm, but he did it. Lifting the limb up and letting his hand fall over the shape of the brooch he hugged it to himself, and it seemed the dark thread brightened into saffron-gold, and he felt a sense of great gladness and triumph.

He woke up, becoming conscious of unbearable irritation and itching. The smell of dock was everywhere, sweet and green as a mown meadow. It was so hot, and the scent made him more aware of how parched he felt. Surely his blood had boiled off and his body was now desiccated and empty, light enough for the drafts to blow it out of the door and over the battlements like thistledown. His tongue was so swollen in his mouth he had to labor to breathe. Where was his protection? His hand groped among the sheets for the serpent-brooch, his assurance of survival. It was not there.

There was a sound - the door opening. A shadow detached itself from the wall, where it had been sitting, watching him, and strode out.

"My lord?" it said. It had Leofwine's voice.

"Will he be alright?" that was Sulien's half-Holmsh accent. He sounded anxious, if such a thing was possible.

"I think so." The dark voice seemed doubtful to Oswy. He pushed himself up on his elbows, the weight driving hot pins of pain into his arms. Where was his amulet?

"He has a fever, but at least he's moving now; he looks like an ill boy rather than a carving."

There were his clothes, dumped in a heap by the side of the bed. He had only to lean down and pick them up. The amulet was still concealed there, he could feel it. The golden thread was between them, fixed to his belly like the cord of a newborn baby. It tugged at him, insisting he pick the brooch up. He began, with infinite labor, to edge towards it.

"Go and sit with him," Leofwine was saying. "He'll be glad to see someone familiar when he wakes."

"I did this to him," the lord of this keep sounded angry and guilty together. Oswy had no idea why, or what it all had to do with him. He could begin to bend down now and stretch this empty arm of his toward the one real thing in the room. It was very hard to move a body as hollow as this.

"I am the last person he will want to see."

The voices were still speaking, lowered in consideration for a sleeping child. Oswy listened to them vacantly, and his body moved without him. The pain of the effort wheeled through the sounds like a shower of sparks. He watched it without interest.

"That's not so." The knight, Leofwine, spoke again, his tone mild and reasonable. "Do you remember," he was saying, fond as someone recalling good times, "when Guimar had you whipped for speaking Sceavish to me in front of his guests?"

There was a pause, then Leofwine went on, more insistently, "And you caught the wound-fever and nearly died from it?"

"I remember."

There was a certain warmth in the cream-colored voice which answered, as though the speaker counted even this as a pleasant memory. It seemed to Oswy, half-delirious as he was, that a faint light shone through the partly closed door, and a freshness, like the silence very early on a clear morning. He clung onto it eagerly, even as his body moved closer to the inferno of power he could feel like a greasy darkness around the golden brooch. His fingers touched and closed on his tunic, the calluses snagging on the close-woven cloth, and he wondered suddenly why he was doing this.

"It was still Guimar you cried out for during the fever."

That was Leofwine. He was only a few paces away. The thought came to Oswy like a vision of heaven; he had only to call out and Leofwine would come, and bring him water, and take this frightening thing away from him. But then he might die. He hesitated.

"Guimar was my father," Sulien again, "I loved him."

Chapter 13

Sulien would know what to do with this. But he would be very angry to find it there. Weak as he was Oswy did not think he could bear such anger.

"But this boy neither loves nor trusts me."

The witch's voice was full of the ruthless honesty which Oswy had learned to associate with hurt. It amazed and confused him in equal measure. Was it possible his master actually cared about him?

He tried to draw his hand back to listen more closely, but it edged forward against his will and all his strength could slow it only a little.

"How do you expect him to learn to do either," Leofwine said, his light tone smoothing the reproach, "if you won't make the first move yourself?"

Quite suddenly Oswy realized that if Sulien did not want him dead then the ghost had been lying to him for purposes of its own, and what paltry strength he had left fainted away in dread.

"Oh Leofwine," Sulien sighed, his quiet voice full of weariness, "I dare not," and the pause which Oswy knew so well, while he fought to explain.

"He is right not to trust me. All that power, lying there, ready to fall into my hand..."

The sound of steps, then silence. Oswy could almost see him turning away, gazing at the horizon of his inner world with his arms crossed, scowling at his own honesty. "No," he said, eventually, "I am too like my master. I dare not go near him until all this is over."

Oswy's fingers closed about the slick cold metal of the serpent brooch. The voices faded immediately. His hand was caught, as though in a powerful fist. Then, in a rush of dirty fire, the ghost was there, rising out of the amulet, up into his arm, sinking into his blood and veins, pouring into him like a stinking wave.

He fought it feebly, and it laughed. He opened his mouth to scream for help and it thrust a heavy fist of vapor over lips and nose and pushed until he kicked like a man on the gibbet. And all the while he sensed it gloating, taking its time, playing with him. It had no doubt and he had no doubt which of them was the stronger.

It had his body now. He could feel it lying within him like a second skin. When he tried to thrash, to yell with all his might, it was like pushing on a locked door: nothing happened. It was like waking up from a long sleep to find, just above you in the darkness, the rough wood of a coffin lid, knowing from the silence that six feet of packed earth is pressing down above you, and the coffin lid is nailed shut.

He tried again to scream. Nothing. Then the ghost touched his mind briefly and he flinched under it, as he might have done from the touch of a leper's suppurating flesh.

"I could take this too, you know," it said, glee pouring out of it like thick oil. "But I think I'll let you keep it. You can watch what we're going to do. That will be more enjoyable for both of us."

Then, burrowing deeper within him, like a maggot in his living body, it found and touched the source of his magic, a secret place within him he hardly knew himself. It had walls about it, and the ghost threw them down and went in, wrapping the tendrils of its power around him like filthy rags. His spirit reeled and wept, crying out at the violation, howling with disgust and desolation and despair, but his body lay peacefully, like a boy asleep. Leofwine, returning, walked softly to his stool, careful not to wake him.

"I don't think you're as strong as he was," said the creature in its beautiful voice, "but at least you're a good deal more biddable. When we have nursed your body back to health I think I can make some use of you."

It paused, and Oswy knew it was waiting for something; the terrible intimacy was charged with expectation.

"Don't you want to know who I am?" it said, hopefully.

"No!" he cried. As if they were in a room together he huddled away from it, trying to escape from its invasive presence.

"You little worm," it sneered, "You're pathetic," and its contempt filled his soul, scalding as bile.

"Tell me then," he sobbed, trying to placate it with instant obedience while he struggled to make one sound which Leofwine would recognize as a cry for help.

"I am the lord of this castle," it said, with deep malicious satisfaction. "I am Tancred, lord of Harrowden, and I am about to take back what is mine."

Chapter Fourteen

Dame Edith smiled down at Oswy, her fair skin like creased linen around the cobweb wrinkles of her mouth.

"I have a present for you," she said, and took out of her folded apron a belt with buckle and strap-end of gleaming brass, the red leather tooled with a design of flying birds. He put out his hands for it without looking up.

"The belt," she said, seemingly surprised by his lack of reaction, "is for this," and, lifting it in both hands, conscious of the symbolism, the seriousness of her gesture, she held out to him a long, scabbarded knife.

He sat over it for a long time, his face blank as though he had been presented with some device whose purpose he did not understand.

"It's the mark of a free man," she urged, the wrinkled skin tightening into a frown, while her hands unconsciously smoothed out her skirt. "And a generous gift. You should say something."

"Thank you," he said then, his voice sounding distant, as though he still spoke out of his fever. "Thank you so much."

Then he looked up and smiled, a sudden, wide, friendly smile, out of keeping on his shy face. "I'll think of you when I use it," he said, and there was a little laugh in his tone which made the words seem less than pleasant.

"It isn't from me," she said, answering his smile uncertainly with her own. "But my congratulations go with it. Lord Sulien told me you had been made free. He gives you this so everyone will know it."

The smile disappeared with a flinch of... something. The head bent again, stooping over the knife.

"Now," Edith said, briskly, as though she was trying to dissipate the last clinging shreds of his illness with her own energy, "I daresay you're well enough to break your fast with us in the Hall. Be as quick as you may. You've lain a-bed long enough as it is."

She walked away, the skirts of her red gown trailing wilted strewing-herbs out of the door as she went, leaving him gazing down at the weapon like a beggar counting the coins in his bowl.

It was a beautiful thing. The hilt of gray bone was polished until it shone like pearl and bound in patterned brass at either end. The matching brass fittings of the red-dyed scabbard glittered like gold as, with a smooth, practiced motion, he pulled the knife out to gaze at it.

The blade was as long as a man's hand from finger-tips to the bracelets around the wrist, sharp, and mirror-smooth. He weighed it in his hand, tested the edge and the point by driving it into his own thumb until it hit the bone - all this as expressionless as an animated statue. Then, angling it so the light fell on his face, he studied his reflection for a long time.

"Both the gambeson and the mail-shirt have leather lacings up the back," said Leofwine, turning them to show the buckles. "Which makes them easy to untie - when the knight is so badly injured that pulling them off might kill him." He handled both with long familiarity, as a farmer pats the work-smoothed handle of his scythe. The heavy canvas gambeson, with its stuffing of wool, filled Oswy's outstretched arms awkwardly, he lowered it to stand, held upright by its own rigidity, on the armory's echoing oak floor.

"When you polish the weapons and helm," Leofwine continued, his strong brown hands reaching out for it, running an absent thumb around the triple-sewn collar, "Be sure to rub oil or grease into the armor lacings to keep them supple." And he paused, as though sensing something wrong.

"I understand," Oswy said, and turned his face away, so the knight could not look in his eyes.

Leofwine frowned, pushing back his thick, chestnut hair with a broad gesture which managed to convey both exasperation and worry.

"Though you are to be Lord Sulien's squire," he went on, absently, while the frown still shadowed his gray eyes, "this part of your duties you will do for me."

He opened up the great chest in which the gambeson had been stored. The mown-hay smell of sweet-woodruff, and the spicy pungency of wormwood billowed from it, almost overcoming the gambeson's scent of oiled metal and untreated wool. Torchlight swooped over the faded yellow of the outer canvas layer of the padded armor, making it bright gold for a moment before he laid it back on its bed of moth-killing herbs.

"My lord was never trained as a knight," he explained, with a faint pride, as though he spoke of a favorite younger brother. "And so he rarely uses armor or bears a weapon. As you've seen, he scarcely needs to."

Chapter 14

And he turned again, swiftly, to see the flare of anger and jealousy pass like a reeling shadow across the boy's unguarded face.

"What is it, Oswy?" he said, and knelt down in the patch of pallid light which stroked the floor beneath the slit window. If he had expected Oswy to come and stand before him, letting the daylight fall on his face, then he was disappointed. Milky light striped his long hair, the heavy bones of cheek and jaw, glimmered pale on his silver chain and the small scenes of harvest and hunting embroidered on his collar, but Oswy stayed where he was, almost invisible, sullen in the shadows.

"Do you still not feel well?" Leofwine asked, "My mother told me you were not yourself this morning." And he watched with puzzled eyes the start of shock and guilt, the pause of hidden thought and then the way the young face put on confusion like a mask.

"Oswy?" Leofwine reached out, touched the boy's sleeve fleetingly, an habitual gesture of reassurance which did not lighten the wariness in his eyes. "Is this something we should take to Sulien?"

The hiss of the boy's in-taken breath was almost lost beneath the sudden sputtering of the torch as it burnt itself out and died. In the darkness which followed the fleeting look of calculation passed unmarked, and then Oswy gasped "I'm sorry" and sagged against the outstretched hand as though he was still unbearably weary.

"I'm just so tired," he said hopelessly, "And during the fever I saw so many things that weren't there. I don't know what's real anymore."

"I understand." The lines of suspicion around Leofwine's mouth eased a little, though his frown remained. The gray eyes were still alert as he watched Oswy's face, but he said only "Coming so close to death always changes you a little," and with sympathetic firmness "try not to push us away while you get used to it. Now, what can I do?"

"I'm so tired of being in the keep," Oswy said, his voice a despairing monotone. "Can't we go for a ride or something?"

"I do have an errand out to the village," Leofwine said, studying Oswy speculatively as he spoke. "Gunnar's family is newly arrived, and have yet to be told what land they will be holding."

His dark voice took on a tone of practical compassion; "Judging by their state when they presented themselves yesterday they'll be terrified to be visited by even a Sceafn knight. Your presence might well reassure them."

He picked the mail-shirt up from the floor, the cords of his wrists standing out with the strain, and let it fall in slithering folds into its heavy canvas bag. "Come with me then," he said. "And as you're so eager to get out, we'll go now."

As they entered the stables the old groom scrambled up from a nest of hay and stood warily, watching them. Dried grasses and flowers clung to him, tangled in the sparse white hair, and long strings of goose-grass trailed from the ragged hems of his loose tunic, so he appeared only half human. The other half might have sprung into life out of the straw, as maggots are spontaneously generated from rotten meat.

For a moment he stood tall, poised, like a knight in a peasant's dwelling, conscious of his own quality, and then, as if something broke inside him, he was crouching, backing away with his deformed hands over his face, and mumbling a string of hopeless apology in pure, perfect, upper-class Holmsh.

Leofwine moved swiftly away from the door, where he would be, to the old man, only a dark shadow against the morning's shifting light. Then he paused, holding out his empty hands to the cowering servant and speaking in soft reassurance.

"Will? It's only Leofwine, and the boy Oswy. You remember us."

The groom peered up at him between his twisted fingers. The undyed, slave's tunic he wore was many times too full for him, hanging on his skeletal thinness like a shroud. A seal-ring of heavy gold swung loose from the shriveled skin-and-bone of one finger, held on by the swollen knuckle. His golden-brown eyes flicked nervously to Oswy and then back,

"Leofwine?" he whispered, cautiously.

"That's right," Leofwine spoke with deliberate clarity, as though he were talking to a very small child, "Now, I want you to help Oswy saddle Amber. The pony, Will. Help Oswy saddle the pony."

"The pony?" Will took one hand away from his face and put the other to his mouth, biting the red stumps of his nails.

"Yes, Will," Leofwine smiled kindly, "saddle the pony." and he gave the half-wit a very gentle push toward the stall where the pony, Amber, stood looking down his fallow nose like a disapproving bishop.

Chapter 14

When the old man came close enough the pony lifted its head with a welcoming nicker and began to lip at the straw in his hair. His face lit with a child's smile and he reached out automatically to brush his gnarled white hand down the sleek neck. Then, with surprising competence, he fetched saddle and bridle, twitched straight the worn sheepskin blanket and began to buckle on the tack.

He spoke as he worked, exhorting the beast to good behavior, promising it love and reward, like a lord with his man, or a father with his child. His voice creaked and whispered—the print, unmistakable as a necklace of bruises, of a strangler's hands—but his tone was content. He might be terrified of strangers, but among these animals at least, he was king.

Oswy let him be until his mount was ready, though his smooth young face began to contort with rage at the half-wit's obvious pleasure.

Will was humming now, a tuneless, grating murmur in his throat. He straightened up to stroke the pony's soft nose and there was a certain unconscious grace about the movement which sat strangely with his newborn smile; like a jester wearing the jeweled sword of a prince.

Leofwine was invisible in the next stall, stooped down to tighten the girth-strap on his horse.

Oswy drew the long knife from its scabbard at his back, reached up to take a handful of the grimy tunic at the groom's skinny chest and drew the suddenly frightened face down to his.

"William FitzBaudoin D'Arcy," he said, in an icy whisper which made the old face crumple into infantile terror. The scarred hands came up like a shield over his eyes.

"Kneel, William," said Oswy coldly, "your master is back."

The tall old man slid bonelessly to hands and knees in the dirty straw and began crawl slowly backwards, whining in a desolate whisper. Oswy kicked the supporting arms out from under him, and the old man went down on his face and groveled.

"Silence!" Oswy hissed. The keening stopped with a little whimper.

"If your proud family could see you now!" the boy gloated, and paled with rage when only confusion answered him.

"You don't remember them do you?" he said with false sympathy, "You were never the same man after the water..." A shudder seized the groom's skinny frame, and Oswy smiled, saying gently, "Do you remember the water,

William? The noose and the water rising? Trying to tear the noose off with your poor hands?" He laughed, "I've never seen anyone go so long without breathing, and still be alive! But you were worth something in those days. "

With the very point of his new knife he traced a long red line from the corner of William's eye to the rapid beating pulse at his neck. He pushed a little, testing the ease with which the blade severed skin and flesh. Blood began to slither like a venomous serpent down the dirty skin. Trembling a little Oswy reached out and wiped his fingers through it, lifting them up to admire the ruby liquid.

Quite suddenly, as if the sight had triggered some unbearable memory, William began to scream, his eyes and mouth wide open with terror, the sound pouring out, high pitched, inhuman and unstoppable.

"What the...!" Leofwine's voice shouted in surprise as he struggled with his frightened horse. Oswy rubbed the knife and the bloody hand clean on his red hose and turned with a face of innocence. The groom crawled away into the darkness. The sound of his fear, bodiless as a banshee, wailed on for a moment and then was silent.

"Oswy!" Leofwine caught Oswy by the collar, pulled him to the doorway where the misty light was strongest. Chill vapor coiled in it, like a phantom drifting facelessly from the Well of Cold.

"What were you doing?" he demanded, raising a broad hand threateningly, looking for the first time like a man who has been trained to kill. "Answer me quickly. What were you doing?"

"Nothing!" Oswy gasped; the sound of panic genuine enough, "Nothing! I just wanted to show him my new knife - Have you seen it? It's so lovely! - And he started screaming, and I didn't know what to do."

Leofwine looked him over, the gray eyes stern and unsatisfied. "Even if it's true it was a stupid thing to do," he said, "stupid and cruel. And I'm not certain you're telling me the truth."

He lowered his hand and, sighing, took a step back. "Something is wrong with you," he said slowly, pushing the hair back from his face with a gesture of weariness. "I am minded to take you to my lord right now. He'll get the truth out of you."

Oswy stood for a moment, his face tight as though he fought back some overwhelming emotion. Charged silence settled like the threat of thunder over the dark spaces of the room. Mist breathed clammily through the open door.

Chapter 14

Then, suddenly, the boy sank to his haunches by the wall, putting his head in his hands, and began reluctantly to speak. "He's the whole problem. He nearly killed me. It really hurt! I don't want ever to see him again." The voice trembled on the edge of tears, "At least don't make me see him today," it said. "I just need today to get myself ready."

"So that's it!" Leofwine laughed, shaking his head with quick relief. "Sometimes," he marveled, a smile lightening his face, his whole posture eased, "Sometimes you two are so alike! Do you know he's been avoiding you for the same reason? And yet both of you were agreed it had to be done!"

He shook his head again and turned away to reach for the bridle of the black stallion which stood blowing nervously in the stall behind him. As soon as his back was turned Oswy's face took on such a fixity of rage and malice that it seemed for a moment to be the face of a fiend, not of a child. A decision must have been made because the rage was replaced with a satisfied smile. Even that was smoothed away by the time Leofwine turned back.

"It will be best for the two of you to get this over with soon," the knight said kindly, and in tolerant indulgence, "But we'll go to Gunnar's first. When you hear what they have been through you may change your mind about my lord's harshness."

All of Gunnar's family seemed to be perched on the sagging thatch of their new house - faint shapes in the thickening fog. The coppery hair of the young man himself was a sinister red against the white sky, like the first flames of a line of hay-ricks going up.

A carter was passing bundles of combed straw and supple hazel-withies to the newcomers, shouting up good humored questions. In the vegetable gardens of the cottages within earshot the goodwives were idling over their hoes, listening with interest, occasionally putting back their veils to shout their own queries.

Beside the ringing voices of the Harrowden men the new family's replies seemed subdued, and they were working fast, heads down, as though in fear of reprimand or beating. Perhaps they were merely eager to get the gaps in the thatch closed before the mist gave way to rain.

"And from the stone known as the Emperor's Tally Stick, following the stream until you come once more to the three quickbeams by the spring."

Leofwine traced the boundaries of the family's land in the loose earth of the hearth. He sat in state on the only stool with a cracked pot of untouched ale wobbling by his foot. His voice was calm, and by slow degrees Gunnar's father, a flax-pale ghost of a man, edged into the firelight until he was poring over the map with astonishment.

"This is so much."

The middle girl, a thirteen-year-old with a ripped grima which showed her watered-gold hair, coughed hackingly as she sat on the damp earth of the sleeping bench. Her younger brother hushed her urgently, but she coughed on, muffled, into her hand.

The hut was beginning to smell of soil and steam as the powerful fire dried out the earth floor and the loose packed benches. The new thatch whispered in the updraft of heat and its scent of summertime drifted wistfully among the smoke.

In one cleared corner of the fire-pit a gruesome bag of bones and hair was lying - the remains of the folk who had lived here last, dug out from among the ashes this morning. None of this family gave it a second glance: They had seen worse.

"We will provide you with seed, and remit taxes for the first year. After that you'll be assessed to see how much you can begin to pay."

"How can you afford it?" marveled the farmer and then cringed back, aghast at his own boldness. Leofwine laughed, softly, his exuberance tempered to soothe their fear.

"This manor is not listed in the king's books," he said, "and by my lord's craft it has passed being noticed by his tax gatherers. We will pay when we can afford to, and not before."

Peasant and knight shared a secret smile at the Holmr king's expense before the farmer beckoned his eldest son out into the firelight.

"Gunnar here wants to come and work for you permanently," he said, his eyes downcast, watching the back of his hand as it tugged on one side of his long fair beard. "Up at the keep."

Gunnar nodded in vehement agreement. Even over the winter the starved lines of him had begun to fill out, the freckled face rounding almost into comeliness under the astonishing ember of his hair. He was a far cry now from the wretch who had flung himself at Sulien's feet, begging to be saved from the man-hunt.

Chapter 14

"It's true," he insisted, glowing with a suppressed fever of joy strangely incongruous in the shabby household. "I can't do anything to repay... I mean I owe... so much..." His hand was knotted in the collar of his alms-chest tunic, gripping tight the luck-ring where it hung concealed.

Leofwine's harsh face softened with a wry smile as he watched the freedman struggle with the words. "I understand," he said, accepting the wordless tale of a life saved, loyalty pledged in gratitude, the liegeman's joy at finding a worthy lord. They were both Sceafn, with a common heritage of tales; of course he understood.

Gunnar fell silent, content that his eloquence had reached an informed hearer. He fixed Leofwine with anxious eyes, like a toddler angling for an apple.

"Such goodwill should not be denied," said Leofwine softly. A flinch of hopelessness went through the pallid cottar and his silent wife, but they said nothing.

"Come to us at the end of harvest then." The knight rose, dusting off his hands on the split skirts of his old-fashioned tunic. Alone among the folk in the small house he had to stoop to brush past the soot-stained beams, so he was not looking as the frost of despair eased.

"Time enough for us when your family's stores are full," he finished, as though answering the very thoughts of Gunnar's work-weary parents; "It would hardly benefit my lord to starve his newest sokemen out for want of labor.

He angled himself out of the low door. The wood of lintel and joists was silver with age. Mist dripped on it, so it seemed utterly in keeping that for so long it had been the door of a tomb. Someone had carved there scenes from legend: Erian, god of order, tearing apart the jaws of the wolf of night; the earth goddess, Hearru, driving an ox-cart through a wheat-field which bowed down in waves all about her. The maker's hand no-doubt rested now, fallen into nameless carrion in a sack within the house.

Leofwine turned back to admire the carvings, to take a courteous farewell.

The moist quiet was torn suddenly by the scream of a horse. He turned instantly, scram out of its scabbard without thinking.

The dun pony was rearing, striking out at the air with its hooves, its head back and all the yellow teeth bared. Oswy clung to it with a face of frightened desperation. Then it came down with enough force to scar the ground, lashed out with its heels and tore into the mist in a breakneck gallop which bore it out of sight almost at once.

There was blood on the ground where it had stood, but Leofwine stopped neither to look nor think. He was on his horse and following before the peasant family had thought even to cry out.

Mist parted before them, clinging to the ground. Hollows were hidden; hollows where a pony's foot might founder, the leg crack, the rider be thrown headfirst onto stony ground. Even the best of riders might have been afraid to gallop in such murk, and Oswy was far from being the best.

Leofwine rode fast, head down, following the tracks and the sound of the drumming hoof-falls. Now and then he spared a glance about him as though expecting to find the boy already tossed into a broken heap on the ground.

Fog opened reluctantly before him, closed eagerly behind, stroking past his face like cold wings. The sound of the pony faltered, slowing. There was an animal noise - pain and outrage - and the hooves were flying again, the speed panicky and frightened. Leofwine frowned as he rode.

The mist thickened. The trail led downwards. The sound of water hissing through reeds, the cold voice of a stream began to filter through the insistent heart-beat of the hooves. Leofwine, riding carefully now, wiped the dew-drenched hair out of his eyes as he peered at the ground. Sounds had dimmed. He was falling behind.

Fog thickened around him, lifting off the dark water like frosty breath. He could now barely see the damp earth from the neck of his horse. Soon, for his own safety, he would have to dismount and follow the trail on foot. Faintly a horse's whinny of protest, the sound of renewed speed came again.

"Little fool," Leofwine muttered under his breath, his voice tight with a mix of worry and anger; "I'll wager he's trying to run away again. Will he never learn?"

Silence now, except for the rush of the water, its whisper in the grasses by its banks. He lit down from his horse, padded lightly over the boggy ground. Cold water began to seep through the leather of his boots. His hair clung to his face in long wet curves.

In the moving chambers of fog once or twice a colorless voice spoke to him; beautiful, meaningless words. White figures in the mist showed him half-transparent smiles before melting away like smoke. Water-elves were raising themselves from the river, drifting away on the air like scarves of fog. They

Chapter 14

had shadowy steeds, with manes like shreds of cloud; their cloaks trailed like gray vapor; their hair like winter moonlight laid on the clammy air.

As long as the mist lay on the land they would be riding, taking with them disease and inspiration. Leofwine wiped his face on one sleeve and walked through, head down, following the pony's tracks with frowning intentness. Only the set of his shoulders showed he was well aware of being watched.

Sound, menacing in the quiet, came to his ear - a high-pitched creak, a violence of splashing and thunder. The stream ran on swiftly towards it. Dimly a dark shape loomed, crouching over the water like a troll-wife washing the blood out of her hair.

The water wheel turned and thundered, the shape came out of the fog gently, resolving into the gray timber and mossy thatch of the old mill. The pony was tied up in front of it, knife wounds dripping on its lathered flanks. Leofwine shook his head over it angrily before tethering his own horse and walking warily toward the door.

Mist stole in with him, curling over the shrunken boards of the floor. It was cold inside, and the scent of decay was heavy. Five years it had stood empty, the stone dismounted, the wheel turning a barren shaft in emptiness, wooden cogs wearing themselves smooth while rats swarmed over the miller's body and the abandoned wheat. Now even the rats were gone, only the wheel still turned, working shaft and cogs and stone endlessly, uselessly, against nothing.

"Oswy?" Leofwine's whisper died unanswered against the echoing darkness of the mill.

Dust and threads of sacking clung to his feet as he walked. Small bones cracked under his tread. His movements had begun to take on the stealth of a hunter; or a hunted thing. His voice was sharp with growing unease as he called out again. "Oswy? Come out now and stop this foolishness. What good is it doing you?"

He stood uncertainly in the center of the empty dark and a rain of dirt and webs scattered gently around him: Someone had moved in the room above.

"If you make me come up there," he insisted, anger in his tone now, "You'll regret it."

And distinctly, over the shudder of water, the grinding of wood, he heard the boy laugh.

The ladder swayed under his weight, the treads slippery with damp and wear. It was darker up here, the dingy light filtering reluctantly up through the trap door. The mill down-shaft turned and turned, groaning and squealing like a soul in torment. Wooden teeth bit together and apart in eternal unsatisfied hunger. Trailing a hand idly over the spinning column Oswy stood like a poised shadow in the center of the room. It was hard to tell in the darkness, but he seemed to be smiling.

Leofwine took two steps forward, still gentle, still self-controlled, waiting for an explanation. Then Oswy made a slight gesture with his right hand. With the thoroughness of a great-ax blow - the blow which can cut through a mounted knight and his horse in one - Leofwine was stopped.

"No! No! No!" In his mind Oswy was screaming, sobbing, hurling himself again and again at the sharp wire of Tancred's spell. He thought his soul was being cut to pieces. "Stop it! Please stop it! I don't want to..."

But even as he screamed he had taken hold of Leofwine's hand and was pulling him forward, positioning him, like a child with a doll, exactly as he wanted. Through the restraining spell Oswy could feel the knight's struggling, insignificant as the scrabbling of the rat before he had held it in the fire. All the man's great strength, all his warrior's training, came to nothing against that half-mastered magic. It was... *unfair*.

Leofwine's face was sleek with sweat as he strained against the invisible bonds. Hoarsely, the words full of distress and puzzlement he asked "Oswy, why are you doing this?"

"I'll tell you a little later," the old witch replied in Oswy's voice, his tone urbane, amused. Then he took Leofwine's left hand and fed the fingers into the cogs of the mill.

Bone shattered, blood spattered the cogs as one by one the knuckles burst beneath them. Leofwine screamed, a sound of astonishment as well as agony, all the muscles of his body rigid with shock. The mill-shaft slowed a little and then ground on.

When the hand was gone; a shapeless mass of gore and splinters of bone, Oswy pulled it away and let the knight fall to his knees and cradle it, struggling to draw breath against the pain.

"Oh God!" Oswy was praying now, in the little prison in his own mind. "Oh God I'm sorry! Oh God, Leofwine! I'm sorry!" But his voice was saying softly "I hate you," as he kicked his friend in the face.

Chapter 14

Even under the grayness, the contortion of pain Leofwine flinched a little in hurt at that.

Oswy wanted to shout at him "I don't! I don't hate you! I didn't mean to do it!" But the words which came out were "You were supposed to be on my side, but you never were. You're his friend, not mine. I hate you!"

And, with satisfaction rich enough to taste, Tancred laughed at them both.

Sudden hatred flooded Oswy's mind, hot as molten lead. He called out to his power, the white core at the center of his being which now lay swathed in the dirty grasp of Tancred's spell. Faintly, weak as a sparrow in a man's brawny fist it answered him, fluttering against the witch's grip. He howled in dismay; it was so little, and so useless.

He had drawn his new knife now and was amusing himself by cutting small wounds all down the length of Leofwine's throat. He took the undamaged hand and nicked the great vein in the wrist so that slowly, second by second, the man began to bleed to death. The blood's life-energy licked at his sticky fingers, teasingly.

"I think you will enjoy this," Tancred spoke gently to Oswy, the mental voice breathy with anticipation. "It will be a thousand times better than what you've done before. Trust me."

"I won't enjoy it! I'd sooner die!"

"Oh I don't think I could allow that. I have many more uses for you alive."

His mind sharpened by anger Oswy could sense Leofwine still struggling, setting all his will on one small movement of his maimed hand. It seemed pointless, hopeless, Oswy did not understand what it meant to accomplish, but it was clear to him the knight still had some plan. Hurriedly, while Tancred was distracted with his pleasure, before the loss of blood could weaken Leofwine too far, Oswy called his power again and joined it to that effort.

It hurt so much! It hurt like the moment after he had lost his temper and all the pots in the house had burst apart; the moment when his family had first looked at him and been afraid. He wanted to run away, as he always had done, but he could not: If he stopped now, Leofwine's death would be his fault, because he had not done everything he could.

Suddenly the bond broke. Tancred felt it fail. He slapped Oswy back; poured over him contempt like acid, hatred and rage and fury like blows.

Oswy tried to cringe away from him, but there was nowhere to go. The spell of possession which had stopped at the borders of his mind began to tighten again. He felt his very self being torn away in severed, bleeding gobbets.

Closer and closer came the old witch's mind, like a dog on a battlefield nosing a dying man to see if it is safe to start to eat. Oswy cowered, waiting for the teeth to close on him.

Leofwine lifted his mangled hand, slid it along his silver chain until it was resting on whatever pendant hung there. Something changed in the air of the room. Oswy could feel it even through his terror - a sense of expectation. Then, with a sigh of exhaustion, Leofwine crumpled heavily to the floor.

Pressure on Oswy ceased. Tancred stooped down over the knight's body.

"This had better just be some pointless holy sign!" he threatened and tore open the pinned collar of Leofwine's tunic. The pendant was small, and covered with blood, and no symbol. He wiped it gingerly, seeing on it the lowering purple stain of magic power, and it glimmered like water in the gray light.

Two circles of rock-crystal - the stone of seeing at a distance - had been married together, held with a band of silver. Between them, like a sheet of beaten gold, the frayed ends of it matted with blood, gleamed a lock of yellow hair.

"Damn you!" Tancred shouted, the sound of it wild and shrill in Oswy's small voice. He kicked at Leofwine's unconscious body so viciously that ribs broke under the blows. "Damn you! I'm not ready!"

Something wavered in the corner of the room. A ripple went through it as though the shrunken wood, the grimy light and dust-filled air, were all figures on a summer tapestry, and something was moving behind it, like an assassin behind a curtain.

"Who are you to be wearing this!" Tancred demanded, hauling up Leofwine's head by the hair. Only the ragged gasps of labored breathing answered him. Furiously he slammed the head back into the hard oak floor.

"Well?" he hissed at Oswy, dependence and need and jealousy pulling at him like a whirlpool in a dark tide, "Who is he? Sulien wouldn't hand out occult links to just anyone. Tell me!"

"I... don't know," Oswy stammered, astonished by the old man's sudden loss of control. "Honestly..."

Chapter 14

In the corner of the room points of light had begun to swim dizzyingly in the air. There was a scent of beeswax candles and the impression of a fire. Then, horribly, within a circle about two paces wide, the world began dissolving away.

Tancred's questioning stopped. He dithered - should he slash this man's bared throat, or prepare defensive spells?

The corner had become a gateway now, the edges of it patterned with chaos. The room beyond it was blindingly bright - a confusion of colors and candlelight.

He bent to cut the throat.

Force, impersonal and violent as a siege catapult, picked him up and hurled him into the wall. Timbers splintered and burst. The upper story of the mill swayed under the impact. Oswy's shoulder ground out of its socket, and the collarbone cracked. Sulien walked into the room.

A pause which seemed like forever as Sulien looked down at the knight's body, his angel-of-death face utterly still.

Tancred shrugged the pain of injury off onto Oswy, and with it a deluge of emotions and half-recalled images of the past - Pain and the ache to cause pain, nostalgia, hatred and love. His wish for revenge had begun to fade under the desire that everything return to how it once had been.

"Oswy?" Sulien asked, his tone as gentle as the brush of a cat's paw. The very stillness of him seemed a threat, like the set jaws of a man-trap waiting to snap.

"I didn't do it!" Oswy whispered hopelessly. The sound went no further than his own mind.

Oswy's power was torn out of him and as Tancred shaped it into a spell of ravening fire their minds came close in a strange intimacy. Oswy could feel, with astonishment, the depths of Tancred's doubt; his unaccustomed pain of actually caring; the agony of faint hope. Perhaps the boy would come back on his own, if he was only asked.

Strong with a lifetime's habit voices were wheedling at Tancred, insisting that to ask was to be weak, that asking meant certain rejection. Better to take and be sure. He did not fight them, he had learned very early he hadn't the strength.

'But,' he said to them, cunningly, 'persuasion is less risky than force. Twelve years must count for something, and the boy has always been sentimental.'

He levered Oswy's body to its feet, passing the pain of movement over casually, not even pausing to enjoy its affect on Oswy's mind.

'And,' he finished, with satisfaction, 'even if he comes back willingly, he will still need to be punished.'

"You have three seconds," said Sulien, intently, "before I kill you. Now talk."

Oswy's body took a step forward, smiling. It held out both hands. "Sulien, my love," it said, "I've come home."

The rage died to ashes in Sulien's brown eyes. He recoiled. A parade of emotions passed across his suddenly open face; dread and weakness and something very like relief.

Time stopped again. Beneath the stridor of turning wood a silence gathered in which, very faintly, Leofwine's gasping breath could be heard, growing shallower. Oswy felt his own screaming should be audible in that terrible hush - 'Don't listen to him! You hate him, remember?' - but it was not.

Sulien looked up, oddly vulnerable, a child confronting an abusive parent, hoping that, against all the odds, this time it will be different. Tentatively, while Oswy screamed at him to do something, to take control, he said

"Master?"

And Oswy despaired.

Chapter Fifteen

Sulien retreated one step, still looking boyish with fear and disbelief. His foot came down with a sticky splash in the spreading pool of Leofwine's blood. It had begun to fill the room with its coppery sweet reek and to patter like rain through the warped boards and onto the dusty floor below. The knight's white face stood out from that red pond like bleached driftwood. The bruised lips gaped like another wound. It was very hard to tell now if he was breathing or not.

Sulien shuddered from head to foot, like a man awakened in an instant by a breath of icy air.

"You bastard," he said softly, lifting up a face suddenly wiped clean by rage. "You bastard!"

He came at Oswy like a wolf, teeth bared, his eyes mad with unleashed fury - and was knocked sprawling by fire. Dull orange fire poured out of Oswy's outstretched hand, fastening itself around Sulien like a living thing. It moved like slime; a cable, a thunderbolt of slime, but it burnt whatever it touched.

Oswy was screaming again. The fire was being torn out of him, ripped out of his spirit. It could not have hurt more if it had been lengths of bleeding skin being torn away.

Sulien tried to get up. The fire fastened itself on him like a leech, knocked him back down, probing for some gap in his defenses. The acrid stench of burning began to overpower the reek of blood.

"Enough!" Sulien gasped, his fists clenched so tight that the nails bloodied his own palms. He spoke a word of command, his light voice hissing with effort. The flames died. He rose, panting, from his knees, his golden hair all dusted over with brown ash, and strode forward.

A second firebolt hurtled into him, covering him in claws of flame which ripped at him, scrabbling and scratching over the shield of his magic like a plague of tiny insects. Grimacing with strain and disgust he hurled them away from him. They spattered the far wall of the mill and smoldered there, writhing like a nest of lice.

Oswy felt sick now, hopeless. He wanted to die. He wanted just to lie down and die. He could feel Tancred drawing the power out of him, draining it to the very bitter depths. It had felt as though the first spell had been fuelled with all of his life and spirit and soul. How could there possibly be anything left?

He cried out in silence as the wells of his power were drained again. There was nothing left. There was nothing left! Tancred had taken everything and wasted it. He would never be a real witch now, he would never work magic of his own. Tancred had taken it all.

Sulien swayed with tiredness where he stood, putting out a hand to keep himself from falling. It slithered in the gore which striped the spinning pillar of the mill's down shaft. He pulled it away as though it had been burnt.

"Let Oswy go, you bastard," he said, as he took another step toward the boy. His face was smudged with brown ash, and drawn, but it was sane again. Sane and cold. "This is between us."

Oswy's body edged away from him as Tancred summoned once more the depleted depths of the boy's resources. There was not much there.

"Perhaps I might," he said mockingly, his old man's smile vile on the young face. "If you begged me to."

Sulien flinched with weary distaste, as at the call to play some too familiar obscene game. "I don't beg," he said harshly.

He lunged, tangling one hand in Oswy's banded sleeve, pulling the boy towards him. Behind him, where the nest of fire still wriggled, the mill wall caught suddenly, flames licking up toward the damp thatch. Glossy yellow light outlined his intent face, leaving it unwarmed.

He grabbed Oswy's jaw, twisted the head up, looked down. A gush of spectral fire hit him in the face, snapping his head back, enveloping him in a gray and weary blaze, pushing him step by step into the burning wall.

"Give up." Tancred mocked him, the sound of it strange in Oswy's shrill voice, "You know you can't retaliate without killing this child. And none of this is discomfiting me at all."

Sulien was trembling now, Oswy could feel it in the hand which still gripped firm around his jaw. The grasp tightened, purple bruises began to show under the fingers, tears stood out in Oswy's coal-black eyes.

'You're hurting me...' Oswy whined, silently, his bravery all used up along with his magic. Then, ashamed of himself, hoping against faint hope that

Sulien could hear, he shouted out; 'Please help me! Please don't give up. Kill me if you have to. I don't want to go on like this!'

Sulien took an absent step away from the conflagration, as though he hardly noticed its heat on his back. He slid his other hand over Oswy's face until his white, uncalloused fingers rested on the closed eyes.

Oswy's body spasmed as Tancred tried to wrench him from his master's grasp, tried to throw him into the scorching blaze. Spells of paralysis, weakness, entrapment and exhaustion pinwheeled about the younger witch in a dirty cloud, pressing at the ragged edges of his shield. The purple shadow in which he moved was now no thicker than a second skin. The spells mobbed it on all sides as Tancred threw into the battle the powers of every amulet and magic item he possessed.

Sulien's grip on Oswy intensified, as though it were all that was keeping him standing. Slowly he forced Oswy's eyelids open, tilted the boy's head up and looked down into the watering eyes.

His gaze was like a scramaseax; the needle point of it so fine you think it can do you no serious harm. Then gradually it widens, the pressure behind it splits open the links of your mail, forces its razor edge and its thumb-thick back into your suddenly unprotected flesh. With terrifying, nonchalant ease, the gaze pushed into Oswy's soul, the mind behind it following, deliberate and unstoppable. There was immediately another presence in Oswy's head.

It was sharp and hot, that mind, enveloped in darkness, like a sword which has been heated until it smokes, and the fuller of it was a ribbon of white uncorrupted flame. It cut through the bonds of Tancred's spell like a cauterizing knife, and Oswy shrank screaming before it, terrified by its merciless anger.

His body was convulsing now, being shaken from side to side like a fox in the jaws of dogs. Warred over by two terrible minds, each stronger than his own, he was not sure any longer who he was, or where he began and ended.

"Leave me alone, damn you! Both of you! Just leave me alone!" he shouted, and his voice sounded out, loud beside the shrieking of the mill. Joy, unexpected, fleeting but intense, came over him suddenly: He could speak again!

The last bond holding his body was severed with quick ruthlessness. He fell from Sulien's grip, prostrate into the pool of blood. Flames licked across the floor towards him but he could not move. The battle for possession had centered on his spirit, on the drained source of his magic powers, and it was so violent he could hardly see for it.

Tancred had used now all the amulets he possessed, he fought no longer with magic; he had begun to hurl at Sulien images of the past. The pictures were so clear they blotted out the real world: the burning room; the dying man; Oswy's own body lying perilously close to the fire. They were so horrible he wished he could flee out of his own mind to escape them.

Images of shame, blood, death again and again, each more grotesque than the last, beat at Oswy until he wanted to die simply to make them stop. In the chaos and darkness of his embattled mind he groped towards his master's spirit for comfort: To be with him, to be with anyone would be better than being alone with this.

He found Sulien more horrified than he was; held captive by guilt, struggling to hold on to anger against the terrible desire to weep: It was his fault! All of this was his fault! If he had only not been what he was then, perhaps, none of this would have happened.

Only pride and habit - not to give the other man the satisfaction of knowing he was hurt - was holding him steady against that onslaught, and they were very bitter companions indeed.

Oswy came closer, but now he was afraid to break the deadly balance of his master's mind, afraid to turn it to despair and lose them both.

Another scene began to build: It was a long time ago. He was a boy again, standing in a meadow full of the bleached stalks of dry plants, the empty seed-cases rattling in the chill breeze. A gray river wound through it, cold under the cloud-filled sky. Dimly, in the distance, he could see something move in the water.

"I don't want to see." Sulien pleaded - Oswy's terrifying master pleading like a child.

Dread tightened around Oswy's mind. He knew a nightmare was coming and he could not wake up. The scene changed; the thing in the water came closer. Moved by some will which was not his own he stepped up to it and gazed.

It was a woman. Her long golden hair eddied in the currents like weeds. In amongst it, wrapping themselves gently around the glinting strands, entrails, washed clean, floated like pale ribbons. She had been split in half up to the navel. Eels wriggled in the cavity, feeding. In the socket of one eye a

Chapter 15

water snail had left a nest of silver. The other, newborn blue, stared from a face which had once been very beautiful, emptily up at the gray sky.

She was naked. She had been dumped naked in the stream, like a whore, for everyone who passed to gawp at and snigger over. It was that, above all, that he could not bear.

"I *said* I didn't want to see!" Sulien hissed in weak anger at himself.

"Who was she?" asked Oswy timidly, realizing suddenly that he had to bring his master out of the trap of the past. He felt Sulien's jolt of surprise gladly: until that instant the young witch had clearly forgotten he was no longer alone.

"Don't look!" Sulien's grief flared instantly into devouring fury, "Don't you bloody dare look at her! That's my mother! I'll bloody kill you if you look at her!"

The knife-edge of rage split Oswy apart. He cowered back, making himself small, waiting for the death blow.

Sulien turned on Tancred, the old witch clinging on to Oswy's soul like a spoiled brat clutching on to someone else's toy.

"As for you," he shouted, "Get out of him now, or I'll break you. You know I can. You've used up all your petty magics, and I haven't even started."

Oswy felt Tancred's grip on him loosen, reluctantly. His soul came back to him in pieces. Pain began to fill him up, as though he was trying to walk on two broken legs.

"Of course, my love, you only had to ask," Tancred lied suavely, the taste of it unmistakable in the forced intimacy. "This was only a trial of strength."

He shaded abruptly into truth, "The real attempt comes later," he said, amusement creeping into the mental tone. "When I have acquired a certain item which neither of you have the strength to resist."

The voice faded as Sulien hit out at the last shreds of its power, but its amusement grew.

"When that comes," it said, "I will have both of you. The boy and I will meet in person. Won't that be nice."

And finally, almost too faint to hear: "In the meantime occupy yourself with this thought - while you wasted your time fighting me, your friend has almost certainly bled to death."

It was gone. With abrupt violence Sulien's heavy presence also withdrew. Oswy was left alone with himself. The emptiness ached. His body seemed unbearably tired and cumbersome. He wanted to sleep - forever - and the thought of Leofwine, his new father, dead at his hand, made tears leak from the corners of his tightly shuttered eyes. He lay there a long time, praying for the world to go away.

His master was speaking words of enchantment, the pale, polished voice shaking a little with weariness. The mutter of the spreading fire died down. The trickle and splash of new blood slowed and stopped. Hope stirred grudgingly in him.

He stretched out his senses and pain answered him everywhere. Fumblingly, not certain if he was doing it right, he opened his stinging eyes, levered himself up out of the clotting puddle of gore.

Outside the mist must have been thinning. A faint saffron light began to filter up through the open trap-door defining Sulien's drawn, hard face in strokes of gold. He had bandaged Leofwine's maimed hand firmly in strips of linen torn from his tunic. Now, grimly, he was tying a long, narrow rope around his own left wrist, pulling the knot tight with his teeth.

Oswy edged carefully to his feet, stood swaying a little while he remembered what balance was. Oh! his shoulder hurt!

"Can I help?" he asked tentatively, afraid to speak, but desperate to drag Leofwine back from death, with every means in his power.

Sulien looked at him. Then, calmly, deliberately, he punched Oswy so hard in the face that the boy was lifted off his feet and slammed brusingly into the wall.

"Don't you think you've done enough?"

Oswy lay passive, sobbing with pain and guilt, not troubling to defend himself from whatever might come next. But Sulien had already turned his back on him, and was kneeling down beside his dying friend, taking the unharmed corpse-pale hand onto his lap.

Oswy lost himself for a moment in misery: It was all his fault! If he had trusted his master for one instant this would never have happened. Now even the chance for that was over. They were enemies again.

There was a resigned sigh.

"Oswy?" the witch's voice said wearily, something of an apology in its tentativeness, "Come here. I need your help."

Chapter 15

Oswy crawled numbly out of his corner, took the strip of linen Sulien held out, all without looking up into his master's face.

Sulien drew his own knife, laid it in front of him as carefully as a priest positioning the sacral sword. It glinted like far-off lightning in the weak light.

"I will slit my wrist," he said calmly, "And his. When I have done it you must bandage them together as quick and as tight as you can. Do you understand?"

Oswy looked up, his mouth falling open in surprise. His master's beautiful face was masklike, telling him nothing.

"Will you die?" he said, aghast.

"He and I may both die," Sulien replied, and in the same level tone, as though he was explaining some minor detail in the bookroom, continued, "When you have done that, tie the end of this rope to one of the beams: The spell was not designed for a willing donor."

"I don't want you to die!" Oswy exclaimed, brushing the words aside in desperation. He felt suddenly bereaved and could not explain it, except that he had spoken the truth.

Surprise and self-hatred fled unwillingly across Sulien's closed face. He turned his head away. "I'm sorry," he said.

Dust filtered softly through the faint sunlight like dim hangings of fine gray gauze. The rope made elegant curves across the floor, sinuous as a black snake. Leofwine lay drowned very deeply in a cold sleep, lapped in a blanket of rubbed, worn sheepskin - the horse's saddlecloth. Oswy had brought it up into the dark room a very long time ago, it seemed. Now he crouched in the corner, grief coming over him as silently as the falling dust.

Sulien still knelt by Leofwine's body, his head bowed. At first he had looked to Oswy like the carving of some martial saint; his still face ivory-pale under the gilt-work of his hair. But now some human flaws had begun to show - cold sweat on his brow, his lips blue and bruised, shadows gathering in the sockets of his eyes.

A fit of shivering came over him. He fought for breath, short, shallow, painful gasps. A lock of his long hair, darkened by moisture, clung to the corner of his mouth. He lifted his bound hand as if to brush it away but could not. The hand dropped, exhausted. Then, silently, with an old man's painstaking weary care, he put his head down on Leofwine's wide shoulder and closed his eyes.

Oswy saw it clearly - a darkness gathering over both of them like a pair of dusky wings; an angel maybe mantled over them like a hawk over its prey. Blood began to leak from between their locked wrists, making a spreading stain on the worn wool.

"No!" he shouted, and crawled forward. The shade twitched away from him, unthreatening, patient.

"No!" he yelled again and pulled at his master's hand, "Wake up! Don't go to sleep! You'll die!"

Sulien turned his head, slightly, grimacing, as if trying to retreat from the small voice, the insistent tugging.

"You can't die!" Oswy yelled, not certain what he was saying in the urgency to get through, "You owe me! It's your fault he's coming for me. You owe me! Now wake up!"

He hauled on Sulien's arm until the witch was kneeling again.

"Can't..." Sulien whispered.

"You must!" Oswy shouted, shaking him. "If you sleep you'll die," he hissed, vehemently, "You mustn't die! I need you."

He swallowed, hating himself already for what he was about to say, hating its womanish acceptance of defeat, its callous practicality:

"This is Leofwine," he said, speaking rapidly, as if to get it out before the shame closed his throat, "I love him. I don't want him to die! But if there's nothing you can do, if he's going to die anyway, don't kill yourself trying to bring him back. Don't make me guilty of killing you too. Please!"

"No..." Sulien labored for breath, his body shaking with the strain of speech, "No, it's not... it's not got that far. I can still do it... if I stay awake..." He paused, head back, gulping air like a runner whose heart is bursting.

Oswy shuffled closer, trying to give him strength by his mere presence, and gradually he forced himself into calm.

"You don't understand," Sulien whispered, "I can't... I can't let him die. He's my shield - against the world... He's my conscience."

Outside the little room noon had broadened into a bright day. The light which struck up from the trap-door was golden now, picking out swags of spider's web gray with dust, glistering on Sulien's discarded knife and the

Chapter 15

crystal pendant lying in the hollow of Leofwine's throat. A pulse was beating there - the stone rocked a little, and a bright gleam told out time, triumphantly.

Sulien watched it, his eyes dim with the need for sleep, his face weary beyond feeling. Tentatively, like a man opening himself up for censure, or for friendship, he began to speak. His voice was like polished ivory which has been smashed into splintered pieces.

"He was Guimar's squire," he said, "When I was Guimar's son. He was... five years my senior, my hero, everything I wanted to be."

He turned his head slightly, looked at Oswy with the ghost of a smile. "You understand... what it's like... to be different," he said. "He was - the only Sceafn squire in a Holmr household, and I was... half Sceafn, witchborn, a slavechild. Sometimes it seemed we stood together against the whole world."

The smile died. His dark brows drew together in a twitch of pain. "Maybe you understand this too. He's all I have left - of those times, of my father. He remembers me... as I was... when I was clean. Before..." he stopped, bowing his head as if to hide from Oswy's gaze, "Before Tancred."

Oswy twisted his hands together in his lap, looking down at them, concentrating on the pain in his shoulder, trying not to cry. He understood all too well. Guilt rose over him like dark waters.

"I'm sorry," he said and his voice shook shamefully with tears, "I was afraid. I didn't mean for this to happen. I fought him - as hard as I could, but he hurt me. I'm so sorry."

Flicking the rope out of the way, Sulien put his bound arm around Oswy's shoulders and hugged him awkwardly. His body tensed with reluctance where Oswy touched him, making it a very cold and formal embrace.

The pressure drove red-hot darts of pain into Oswy's side but still he rested in it with a certain astonished comfort, a sense of no longer being alone.

"I understand," said Sulien quietly, "I understand perfectly, and God knows I've done worse things than this for him."

He sighed, some of the strain passing out of his face, and at the same time Leofwine made a small moan of protest, trying to open his eyes.

Joy rose up in Oswy like a sparkling spring. The very air of the room seemed lighter. Too full of glee to sit he wriggled out of his master's grasp, bounded to his feet.

"I must go and get help!" he exclaimed, everything seeming clearer and easier now, "I'll get Father Paul, and Gunnar!"

"Oswy! No!" Leofwine reacted in weak panic to his voice, covering his face with his maimed hand, turning away.

"It's alright!" Sulien reassured him, while Oswy stood as if petrified, joy turned to sorrow, a weight of grief and pain settling on him like a cloak of lead, "It's alright."

"My lord?" Leofwine opened eyes washed clean from every adult subtlety by the nearness of death, fixed them on Sulien's tired face. "He..." he whispered, accusingly, and paused, grimacing, to breathe.

"Not him," said Sulien firmly. "My master had possession of him, God knows how," and he gave Oswy a level dark stare promising judgment. "We will have to settle that later. For now it's over, trust me."

Sunlight picked out the white scar on his lip as he gave a wan smile, "Leofwine," he said, his bastard Holmsh accent making the meaning stand out as clear as water - dear friend - "You are the only person close to me who has ever survived a meeting with Tancred. You've changed my luck."

Leofwine returned the smile - a flicker on the deathly pallor of his face, "Little brother," he said.

"Truly now," Sulien replied fondly, showing the bound wrists, the shared blood. "You'll find yourself casting spells before the day is out."

A whisper of laughter answered him. Looking up, still with the weak smile warming his face, he nodded at Oswy as if to say "Go," and Oswy stirred out of his paralysis, climbed down through the trap door obediently, blocking off the light for an instant with his body.

He went out into the astonishing brilliance of daylight. A breeze plucked at him with cold freshness and he shivered, feeling wrung beyond bearing by possession and liberation, grief and joy. The thunder and rush of water seemed to shake him with their violence. His legs trembled beneath him. He wondered suddenly if he would make it back to the village, or faint somewhere in an empty place far from human aid.

Mounting the pony was a torture which left him reeling. He lay down for a moment sprawled out over the beast's neck like a casualty of war, telling himself he deserved this; it was his penance. Then, feebly, he put his heels to the pony's dripping flanks and set off at a slow shambling walk to find help.

Chapter Sixteen

Was it singing, or the sound of running water? Adela stopped, crouching down over her ruined second-hand shoes, her bruised and bleeding feet. Dawn was coming, slowly. Twilight picked out strange shapes in the trees - a bird sleeping headless on a bough, the curve of what looked like a shoulder frozen into the bark, a mouth laughing soundlessly. Faint silver-gray light made a cage of black bars out of the branches, a treasury of pearls out of the cold morning dew. The sound of the brook, or the voice, shimmered on the still air as equivocal as the dawn. Adela shivered.

Torch walked on a little way, though she knew from the angle of his head that he had heard her stop. He paused himself, eventually, stood glimmering between the dark trees like a glimpse of sunrise. There was a hint of transparency about him in the broadening light, like a candle-flame brought out into the day. His voice was as enigmatic as buried gold; "Come," he called.

"I'm thirsty," she said, and rose like a sleepwalker to brush aside the ferns and bracken, to push her way through the pathless forest towards the water.

"No!" There seemed to be some emotion in Torch's voice as he cried out behind her. She did not wonder what it was - she had done with emotion. This calmness was best; she could live in the present, deal with her simple needs, never have to deal with loss and grief again.

The sound grew clearer, cold, lilting, spilling in and out of the sliding water like chilled wine. The sheer beauty of it brought a stir of wonder to her numbed heart. Surely here she could do no damage, the singer of this song must be as fair and as untouchable as the falls she saw glistening through the trees, brushed gently by the silver-pale dawn.

It was a wild thing singing, she could hear its shyness under the ripples of laughter and power. With a hunter's instinctive caution she crouched down, creeping through the last wash of bracken silently, with expectant, tremulous care. She had no desire to frighten the glorious thing away.

At first she saw nothing, only the falls coming down in argent splendor over their bed of glossy stone. The rising sun splashed golden light over the tips of the trees, and russet and rose and yellow leaves made a sudden fire against the paling sky.

Then Adela saw her; her hair and long white flanks like curves of foam in the falls. Not a woman, for she was made up of shades and shapes of water and the light moved through her, flashing from her trailing hair. She had lifted her long slender hands almost into the air, welcoming the sunrise. The river slipped past them unruffled. Her radiant face, raised to the sky, was altogether innocent as the pure and perfect music poured out of her.

Adela was suddenly ashamed. She had trespassed on this being's solitary, intense privacy. To go on spying on the graceful girl seemed indecent. Her heart had been eased by the fleeting beauty; surely that was enough.

She took a step back. A dry twig cracked under her foot, a tiny sound, almost inaudible beneath the rush of the water. The creature in the falls looked down, her mouth opening in a startled 'Ah!' Then she saw Adela. Horror swept over her smooth face, contorted her long slender body with an agony of modesty. She covered her silver-gray eyes with her hands and keened, a desolate, cold whisper of shame.

"It's alright!" Adela could not bear the cringing, she stepped forward comfortingly, "Don't be ashamed, I'm a woman like yourself."
But the long legs were melting into the stream, the face, turned away from her, began to dissolve. The clear cold voice wailed on.

"Please! What are you doing?" Adela demanded, horrified herself now, "Sweet lady what are you doing?"

The girl's hair was now no more than a silver shade on the surface of the water, her body elongated, thinning. Her shadowy flesh melted into liquid. The 'Oh!' of her mouth stretched, was silenced, and then was washed away. The river ran on, emptied. Birds began to sing in the dawn, just as though nothing had happened.

"No!" Adela shouted, her calmness shattering, "No!" She found herself shaking, "No!" she wailed again. Memories, suppressed by grim need, leaped on her weakness, tormented her with images: Giles's little coffin, Drago, pale and diminished by fear, Guy lying pinned under the monster's claw.

"It's me!" she cried, choking under the impact, "It's me! I kill everyone I meet. I'm cursed! Oh God..." And the tears she had tried to ignore came flooding out, racking her with sorrow, falling off her concealing fingers into the stream.

Chapter 16

Torch came up, curiously, and stood watching while the light broadened around him. When she had sobbed herself silent he pulled one of her hands away, examined it, and her swollen eyes.

"You have created water," he said, with what seemed like a flicker of awe. One gilded finger touched her cheek briefly, and then he lifted the tear to his lips and tasted it inquiringly. "Does it mean something?" he asked.

"I killed her, didn't I?" Adela demanded shakily.

He shrugged unconcern, the movement graceful but artificial, as if he mimicked something he did not understand. "She was a mortal thing. Now or later, what does it matter?" Then, as though it explained everything, he finished; "She was an Asrai."

"I don't know what to do here," Adela said, weakly, "I want to go home."

He hunkered down in front of her, intensity breaking the surface of his calm. For the first time she saw him in the light - an insubstantial shape of ghostly beauty, crowned with fire. Adela was suddenly afraid for him, he seemed so fragile.

"No!" his voice was like bells chiming at a distance, "You can not go home. The Bright One brought you to me."

Swinging from his deerskin quiver, among a clutter of uncut gems and pendant glossy feathers, hung a bronze bowl with a carved silver fish flashing in the bottom of it. He unslung it, dipped it in the stream - the liquid broke about his glimmering hand as it would around flesh and bone. Lifting it, dripping, from the water he offered it to her.

"The Bright One?" she said, while a wholly irrational feeling of hope came over her at the words. The water tasted like a glimpse of heaven, but she put it down to urge him to speak.

"One of the Bright Host," he replied and combed the grass with his long fingers, "He told me to go to you and save you from the Horde."

She thought at first he had said all he was going to say. He tied up the bowl again, his movements stiff, as though he felt affronted.

"At first I thought; by what right does he command me?" He turned, with a smile which had about it the same quality of uncertainty as his shrug, "But I was curious. The Bright Ones rarely speak to us. Why should he thus single me out?"

He plaited a lock of his long hair, like weaving flame, the ears beneath it were as pointed as the ears of a fox. "When I saw you," he said, "I knew: He had brought you to me because of my quest."

"You didn't think," Adela asked, fighting against a wave of astonishing laughter, "that he'd actually brought you to me to save my life?" She was almost shocked at her ability to laugh, something about this whole subject filled her with inappropriate joy.

"It may be," Torch replied and stood up, waiting for her to struggle to her feet so they might go on. She sat where she was.

"The Bright Ones often accomplish three or four things at once," he offered, reluctantly.

"Describe him," Adela demanded, "I have to know before I decide whether to go with you or not."

"You have already decided," said Torch.

"I can change my mind."

The sun showed now, a brilliant saffron arc above the treetops. Warmth began to spill down onto the riverbank. Adela lifted her face to it gladly, felt it soothe away the strains and bruises of her flight. "Tell me," she said.

"I do not know what you would have seen," Torch began. He held out his hands to the sun as if to gather it to himself. They grew more solid as she watched. "They are like us - they can change their shape at will. This one appeared to be an elf, or, perhaps," grudgingly, "perhaps a very beautiful human."

The smile returned, more fitting this time, wild and eager. "But, Ai!" he said, "The wings!"

Her heart leaped: "Wings?"

"Mmm... Azure and indigo and sapphire, all shot through with silver like a net full of stars. Ai! I would have plucked every feather and made myself a cloak. The Icewolf would have eaten himself for envy!"

"An angel!" Adela whispered in wonder. "You saw an angel!" She hardly dared think about this in case, somehow, her very thoughts sullied it. Yet, despite her restraint, when she looked up the world around her had become suddenly more luminous, more wonderful; the colors brighter, the blue dusted shadows more mysterious.

Chapter 16

"I tried to believe it," she said, the depths of her own unbelief opening themselves for her to see, "I thought I had brought myself to believe that God had sent his angels to watch over me. But you saw it! He spoke to you?!"

"I have said so," Torch began to drift away from her, picking a weightless, effortless course through the long reeds, over the trembling waterlogged grasses at the marshy edge of the stream.

"Wait!" she cried, scrambling to her feet, looking, she guessed, like a herder boy in her tattered, second-best tunic; a herder boy brought awe-struck into the king's hall. "You truly think he meant me to come with you?"

A fleeting darkness coiled beneath the elf's bright emerald eyes. She had the impression that his face changed; something moving within it. There was a glimpse of spite and wrath like deformities under the skin.

"This is abominable!" he hissed. "The second time you have questioned my word."

Some instinct held her back from apologizing - the same instinct perhaps which holds a man calm before a vicious dog. "I don't doubt your word," she said, stiffly polite, "I just want to hear it again."

"And now she asks me to repeat myself!" the elf snapped, his body wavering like smoke with the intensity of his grievance. His eyes paled, even as she watched, into a sinister, serpentine yellow. The texture of his red hair changed, it clung about his face as stickily as if it had been bathed in old blood. A stench came off it.

She recoiled, half drawing her knife, seeing in him as he dimmed a likeness, a kinship to the infernal hounds which at once horrified and intrigued her.

"No!" he cried, but not to her. He was struggling now, unaware of her fear or her interest, like a man whose whole mind is obsessed with one temptation. The candle-flame of his body guttered, writhing into strange tormented shapes as wrath twisted it. Light and darkness warred in him like madness.

"No!" he said again, desperately, as though he was pleading with his gods; "I will not make this choice. Not yet." And with a shudder of effort he threw off the deformed shapes, burned once more into fiery and luminous beauty, but Adela thought he was now more transparent than ever.

"You made me angry," he said to her then, kneeling down in front of her. His weight left no print in the spongy moss. "I had forgotten you were so ignorant."

She hardly dared answer him, but sat for a long time wondering about what had happened. Had he been cursed? Or was this some feature of the nature of elves? She remembered, all at once and unwelcomely, Godgifu telling her that the elves pay a tithe of souls to the King of the Abyss. The memory brought heart-wringing overtones of comfort and friendship and home. She looked up from it with a shiver, and found him watching her.

"When I was new," he said, in the voice which was like tuned sunlight, its sound so beautiful it was a little while before she could attend to what it was saying; "My mother named me Torch. She made a foretelling over me, with all her power and her lore: She said 'He will bring a great light to our people.'" Softly he finished "Her name was Joyful in those days, but the foretelling took away her voice. We call her Silence now."

"I'm sorry," said Adela softly, and he looked at her in suspicion.

"Why?" he said, "What hand did you have in it?"

"None!" she said with a quick, decisive shake of the head, "Of course. It's something men say when we wish to show sympathy."

"Like thank you," he laughed. "One of your empty gestures which make us angry. Do not say it again."

"I'm..." said Adela, and caught herself. "I won't."

"I believe," he began sailing fallen leaves on the current as he spoke, putting pebbles in them, like a human child making boats, "that if the prophesy could be fulfilled then her voice would be restored. So for over a thousand summers I have searched for the light Silence spoke of. I have brought home so many dwarfish baubles, so many lights and lamps and jewels that my Lord's palace, under the Tor, shines at midnight like a star. And all of them are trash."

He shook his head - she recognized her own gesture carefully mimicked.

"The last time," he said, "She wrote me a note: 'You are looking in the wrong places.'

"'Tell me then what are the right places.' I said, but she could not."

He watched the autumn flotilla float erratically away, like a party of pleasure barges with drunken steersmen. Absently, while he went on with his story, he pried up a handful of slimy stones from the river bed and pitched them at the moving targets, sinking them one by one, unerringly.

Chapter 16

"I despaired," he said, the words sitting strangely with his carefree occupation. "I said to my mother, I am taking my life away from you. I give you back the name of Torch. I am going to search for a new name.

"And I came away."

He gave her suddenly the wild eager smile which she was sure was his own. "I had not been walking even a moon," he said, "before the Bright One brought me to you."

"I still don't understand," she said, quietly, a little afraid to find herself part of a quest which had continued over a thousand years. "What have I to do with any of this?"

He looked at her as if he was trying to gauge whether she was foolish, or dishonest. There was a hint of incredulity in his lilting voice. "But the light which surrounded you when you sang!" he exclaimed, "Nothing in all the nine worlds is other than a shade of darkness compared with it. Even the Bright One's face, which I could barely look at - it burned me - even that was like only the shattered reflection of it in a dark mirror."

"I saw nothing," she whispered, awed, "Nothing at all."

"You didn't see it keeping the Horde at bay?" he demanded, almost pleading with her. "You didn't see it summon me, and nearly break my heart with yearning for something I did not understand? I am still sick with it!"

"I was singing from the books of our faith," she whispered again, and an idea touched her gently, like the brush of a sapphire wing, "I was singing about God."

He sprang up as if lashed. "I don't want to hear," he said, "I have seen your churches and heard their bells. They give me pain. I need no speech about God from you. His blood cries out to me from the ground five thousand miles away, where you humans killed Him."

"The Moat!" she said, and saw again how little she had really believed in her faith, "The Moat of Blood is real too?" But he only shuddered and began to walk again.

She followed, with the new idea settling in her heart like an inspiration. Quite suddenly the day seemed full of excitement and hope, and she welcomed it eagerly as she walked.

All that morning they went downwards into the center of the wood - a dim place, full of hush and watching eyes. There was a haudh there, written over with spirals and circles, and a thin writing like the scoring of rat's teeth.

The inner room was lined with silver-gray stone, and when midday came a shaft of light speared it, making the carvings shine out as if written in gold.

"Let me sleep here?" Adela asked, faintly, as they came to it. Walking had become a torture to her - her bloodied feet hurt so, and her legs trembled. She had spent all her strength in the flight from the hounds, and now she walked on will alone. It wasn't enough - hunger and lack of sleep gnawed at her, and the world wavered at the edges of her vision, pulsing in and out.

"Sleep?" said Torch, in what sounded like disbelief, passing the shelter by and going on, without breaking pace, "Do you have no compassion at all?"

She did not want to anger him again - it felt too perilous, and besides, the chamber itself was pagan; the haunt of feral gods, and not the safest place to rest. So she forced herself on, and gradually the draining weariness eased into a dreamlike state, where some things were intensely colored and shaped, and others were shrouded in mist; a grayness which grew slowly as the afternoon wore on.

They began to climb again, out into lighter woodlands where mountain ash raised their crowns of brilliant berries against the hazy August sky. A hedge of blackthorn, twisted and stark, marked the end of the trees. In among the long thorns creatures were sitting at their ease - black, spiky things with pearly white eyes, clad in scraps of leaves. As Adela and Torch pushed through the blackthorns' raking branches the creatures watched them, silent and intent.

"What are they?" she asked him. He shrugged again, the movement more practiced this time.

"How should I know?" he said, "They are themselves."

Beyond the barrier, moorland swept up in billowing rises to a higher hill, and then to a sharp peak crowned with a tumble of gray boulders and another thicket of thorn. The last sunlight of the day lay like spilled mead over the heather and gorse. The bare hills shone like a child's face scrubbed for a festival. A wind came over the cropped turf, smelling of warm earth and wild herbs.

"Here we wait," said Torch, and sat down beneath the thorny hedge. He brought out cheese, bread and a parcel of berries from his scrip, and from a red-dyed pouch which hung from his quiver two green and golden apples with a smell like white wine.

Chapter 16

Adela collapsed onto the ground, feeling that she would never get up again. "Oh! I'm so hungry!" she said, the scent making her at once ravenous and nauseated.

Torch smiled, the courteous, learned smile which seemed out of place on his feral beauty. "Have one of these," he said, and held out an apple to her. The setting sun polished it, and the smell was now like honey and flowers.

She took it gently, careful not to bruise the smooth skin. It felt firm and full of sweetness. She nearly forgot herself and bit it right then, but habit intervened. Putting it down beside the other things she began the simple grace which Sister Ursula had taught her. The words were so familiar that on many days they had been just another pre-dinner ritual, like washing her hands, but now she said them with real thankfulness; this food might just stop the unraveling of her world, keep her upright a little longer - she felt as if she was going to faint.

When she opened her eyes again and looked for her apple it was gone. A small pile of withered leaves, yellow and green, marked the spot where it had stood. A drift of the same slipped from Torch's open hand as he watched her with something like shame in his eyes.

"I had to try," he said, his flexible voice carrying overtones of wry apology, "I have a fine collection of other lights. I had to try to keep you too."

She gazed back at him in puzzlement, knowing that something important had happened, but not knowing what.

He tossed back his head suddenly, and then rose to his feet in one lithe weightless leap which reminded her of flames.

"What is it?" she said, and he said "Hush!" at the same time.

Adela rose with an effort, straining her eyes to see what he saw, but the sun was lowered behind the far hills now, and in the blue twilight even the familiar things looked chancy and strange. Up in the sky - or was it the crest of the hills - a new star kindled, white-blue and fierce. Then it shattered, and pieces of it began to pour across the moors. Leisurely they looked at first, like candles floated on a stream, and yet she felt somehow the excitement of speed.

Beside her Torch had begun to sing under his breath, the sound of it sharp and bitter, like the warning cries of crows. The hedge rustled behind him and the thorns turned outwards branch by branch. With a creaking, eerie chatter the white-eyed creatures picked up tiny spears, headed with slivers of flint, and began to dance, brandishing them.

"What is it?" Adela asked again, and the elf cut off his song in irritation.

"Keep down and silent," he said harshly. "This is nothing to do with you."

There was a sound now, a flat, dull droning, like a fly trapped inside a horn lantern. It grew louder and louder, a dismal noise, wearisome and spiteful as an old quarrel. Louder again it grew, like the humming of flies over a corpse full of maggots. Adela found herself shrinking back into the thorns to get away from it, shaking her head like a horse tormented by insects in the summer heat. Still the noise grew.

Behind it, where the lights floated, there came a ringing of horns, silver and valiant. Torch drew his sword - it shimmered with cold white light, and runes stood out on it in burning gold. Then he laughed, an utterly inhuman sound, like a wolf's howling. Voices rang out in answer, a pack of them like a pack of hunting wolves.

The buzzing grew. Then Adela saw it; a heavy thing, scudding close to the ground, half scrabbling with its many clawed legs, half flying on membranous wings the color of gut. Wasp-like, huge, it turned its head and she could see the intelligence there, the malice of it. It saw her too. It opened a mouth full of mandibles and leered at her.

She scrambled up. It turned towards her, its black bristled legs gouging out long tears in the sweet grass, the soft abdomen swaying behind it, swollen with poison. Backing away was impossible; the serried hedge pressed against her. She stooped for a stone to hurl at it.

"Do not dare touch it!" Torch shouted at her angrily, "It is ours!"

It was now barely five paces away, filling the cool air with the scent of ordure. Torch stepped forward silently. It swung about, bringing the long dripping sting to bear on him.

The lights swept over them like a wave breaking. Adela saw elves on twilight horses, their swords scintillant brands of light. She saw wolves, coming down in a pack, silver-backed and shimmering.

With a lunge of hideous strength the thing arched, thrusting the poisoned sting at Torch's chest. He moved - a blur of speed. The sting plunged into the blackthorn hedge. Thorns scored long scratches down the bloated belly - it dripped red, glossy, human blood. The hedge-creatures creaked in triumph. Torch put back his head and laughed aloud.

Chapter 16

It wrenched itself from the black branches, the ragged wings beating out such a stench that Adela gagged. Three clawed legs swept toward Torch - the hairs on them glinted like metal. He dodged two, whirled and in a double-handed blow brought the sword down on the third with all his strength. The impact shuddered through him; he fought for balance. A tiny wound opened on the chitinous leather and bled a trickle of yellow liquid before closing.

The creature chuckled - a grating buzz of sound. Knotted flight muscles raised the wing, hitting Torch in the face, knocking him off his feet. He scrambled up, but now he was trapped between two of the staff-like legs. They squeezed him, and he cried out, struggling, the long bristles cutting into him like knives.

A pure, piercing voice yelled a war-cry. One of the elves - a young maiden, heartbreakingly delicate - leaped from her running horse onto the demonic head, covering its insectile eyes with her body, sawing at the thin neck with a glowing dagger.

It dropped Torch - he came crawling over to Adela, grinning like a madman, all his fine clothes tattered and rent as if by sharp wire.

"Get back there and help her!" she cried, disgusted with him.

"Needle?" he laughed, "She's as vicious as a stoat. She needs no help of mine."

"Do you have no honor at all?" she snapped, "Letting a woman do your fighting for you!"

"I have had my stroke," he shrugged. "She is taking hers. All's fair." And he sat up eagerly to watch.

Needle still clung to the creature's narrow face, hacking with a puzzled fury at the neck. Elves and wolves waited, watching her, spread out in a loose circle around the monster, shouting out encouragement, but giving her no help.

The creature stooped its head, brought up its two pincered forelegs like a fly washing and brushed her effortlessly, into its mouth. The chitinous jaws worked, for a while. The girl's harp-sweet voice screamed, briefly, then it flung her aside. She landed sprawling and lay very still.

A howl went up. A sleek white wolf leaped out of the circle of onlookers, buried its teeth in the swaying abdomen. It broke off, whining and spitting, streaked back into safety with its red jaws covered in foam. Blood oozed glistening down the huge curve of the dark one's belly.

So it went on; the combatants changing place with a bloodthirsty politeness which infuriated Adela. "Why can't you just all mob the thing and have it over with?" she demanded.

Torch looked at her with disgust. "That would be no fun at all."

She mirrored his revulsion. "Fun?" she said, "A young maiden, one of your own people is dead because of this. You call that fun?" and she crawled away from him before he could answer.

Below the writhing branches of the thorn hedge a stand of archangel had grown, its clusters of white flowers swaying amid the nettle-like leaves. Into that soft bed Needle had been tumbled, and she lay as though she was sleeping. Adela knelt there and looked at her; the great wound in her side where the monster's mouthparts had chewed. Her white face, nodded over by the white flowers, was pillowed on a gossamer cloud of hair, silver as the moon. She seemed drawn out of strokes of moonlight, impossibly fragile, and now broken. Adela wept for her, a spattering of tears for the waste of it and for the callous disregard of her own people. The pale face seemed to smile, just slightly, at her grief.

A howl of triumph went up. She turned and saw the elven lord bowing to his followers over the body of the demon, baring long wolf-teeth in a mocking grin. She knew he was their prince, knew it instinctively - the lethal grace of his movements stirred her warrior blood.

The tidy circle of fighters broke up into chaotic celebration - some danced, some leaped to their horses' backs and galloped in breakneck races over the hills, some drew their weapons and fought each other furiously while the wolves yipped and tore in reckless chases among their legs.

The lord crouched down and began to clean his white sword and bright dagger on the wind-bleached turf. In the blue twilight his hair shone like ice gilded by strong sunlight, but his eyes were a smoky amber-brown which flashed into delighted warmth when he saw her.

She found herself standing, smiling, all without knowing she had moved. Then Torch came out of the shelter of the hedge and threw himself down in the grass at his lord's feet.

A huge silver wolf, with a gray stripe like an arrowshaft down its spine, came racing out of the pack to fawn on the lord like a lapdog. When he had patted its shaggy head it lay down, a moony crescent of muscle and fur, and he sat leaning back into its warm flank just as a human king sits on a cushioned throne.

Chapter 16

They began to talk, Torch and he. Adela was certain they were speaking about her. She edged forward, half guiltily.

"You invited her to stay, of course." The lord's voice was soft, earthy; it drew her closer almost against her will.

"I gave her the apple," Torch said apologetically, "but she unmade it somehow. She didn't eat."

"No," he was aware now that she was watching him, though Adela didn't know how she knew this. He smiled, "She is too fine for such clumsy enchantments."

He looked up, turned the smile on her. There was a long moment, and Adela felt something happen - like the world being made. She seemed to be standing in a wash of strong light, a tunnel of golden light which pulled at her.

For the first time in days, she remembered that her face was naked. It burned.

Her heart was pounding. Her eyes were fixed on one small detail - the lord's slender hand as it idly stroked the wolf's neck. With a wrench of dismay she realized that she envied the beast. She stopped in her tracks and covered her opened mouth with her hands.

You're disgusting, she said fiercely to herself, *He's as alien to you as any animal. Have you no discernment or self control?* And she forced herself to look up and take note of his fanged mouth, the deformed ears, the womanish lounging indolence with which he sat.

Manlike, he had turned to other matters.

"That hordeling, the monster," Torch was asking him, "It was Tinder wasn't it? I thought he was close to his choice when I left."

"No," the prince was saying, so sad that Adela felt her own sorrows up to now had been nothing, "No, Tinder is dead. That thing could never have been a subject of mine," but he was nodding 'Yes.' to Torch's question even as he denied it.

Adela's rational mind was shouting at her frantically - This is too strong! It's too sudden! It must be a spell! He's cast some kind of spell on you. Get away from him now, while you still can!

But still she walked closer until she was standing at Torch's shoulder.

The wolf growled at her - its white muzzle wrinkling, its thin black lips stretching over gleaming teeth. The lord leaped to his feet.

"Torch!" he exclaimed, "This is the first lamp you have brought me which has ever truly lightened my heart." And while he smiled, Torch rose to introduce them.

Adela wavered on the edge of panic. 'I must get away!' she thought, 'I can't let this creature have such power over me! I must get away now!'

"My lord Icewolf," said Torch formally, "I have called her Starlight."

"Oh no," the lord laughed gently and stepped forward. This close to him Adela could feel the power coming off him like a perfume, allure as a heat.

She turned to run. He caught her hand - his hand and arm stained up to the elbow with the monster's blood - and stopped her as finally as death.

"Oh no," he said, softly, "Between us there can be no question of use-names." And in a whisper, "My true name is Gennan, and yours?"

"Adela, my lord," she said, and without even regret she became suddenly his, body and soul.

Chapter Seventeen

Gennan dropped her hand and sighed unhappily. The huge wolf butted its black nose into his leg and he rubbed it behind the ears with an absent fondness which seemed to relieve his melancholy not at all. Adela's heart ached for him.

"You seem sad, my lord," she said. "What is it?"

"Today I have lost one of my subjects," he answered her, "Horribly. Should I not be sad?"

Like a thing from another life she dimly remembered the girl's half-eaten body lying sprawled on white flowers. She felt ashamed at the way Gennan's touch had so easily driven it from her mind.

"She should have a great funeral," she said, generously. "A warrior's funeral - she was so brave!"

"She?" Gennan glanced at her with puzzlement. In the dusky evening light he shimmered slightly, inhuman as a statue of ice.

."Needle," she insisted, and shuddered with frustration and distress: Why couldn't he understand her? What was she saying wrong?

"Oh!" the sigh spoke a wealth of realization, "Needle!"

His tone had changed again, slipping over into something much lighter than grief - glee perhaps, or mischief. Looking up quickly she caught him exchanging a slow wicked smile with Torch over her head, like boys deciding on a prank. Fury almost choked her, and then shame because she felt so fiercely possessive.

"A funeral for Needle..." She could see him savoring the idea like a strange fruit, and wondered why it was so foreign to him.

"An interment," he pondered, smiling with pleasure - his fangs pressing white marks into his lower lip as he grinned - "A funeral! Yes! It will be a welcome novelty indeed. Starlight, my lady, you are a box of delights. Come walk with me."

Witch's Boy

He offered her his left hand, this one too gloved with drying blood. She took it gladly and was shocked anew by the strength of her reaction to his touch.

"What's the matter with me?" she thought, horrified, "I'm not like this. What's happening to me?" But when she tried to analyze it the thoughts slipped like water through her grasp. Everything was coming apart now - her mind curiously far away and her emotions bitter-bright. The grayness at the edges of her vision had crept forward, she felt she stood in a dark room, looking out of a high window at the world. Silver sparks shuttled across the light. She clenched her fists - she had to hold on, just until she could sit down, eat, sleep.

"Lightning," she came to her senses briefly to find Gennan smiling down on his white wolf. "Take my horse and go ahead. Tell them to make a chamber ready for the lady."

The wolf yawned, showing a great gape of jaw filled with white fangs. Then, without rising from the ground, it began to stretch, arching and contorting as if in pain. Its limbs lengthened, changing shape as easily as a reflection changes in the curve of a silver spoon.

It took barely ten heartbeats for the wolf to distort into an elf; a splendid youth with butter-yellow hair curling crisply over the silver-sewn collar of his white tunic. He grinned at Adela, his indigo eyes brimming with pleasure at her shock. Then he bowed mockingly and raced off.

It was too much. The strangeness knocked the last prop out from under her. She revolted from it. The ground swayed slowly, nauseously, from side to side beneath her.

Gennan was speaking to her, something a little like worry in his lupine eyes, but she could not understand the words. Torch, behind him, was studying her with a frown. It was as if they were standing beyond a window of glass; moving, silent pictures. The window became the mouth of a well - shrinking as she fell. She was going to drown in the dark water.

"I'm going mad!" she wailed in despair, "Dear God I'm going mad! Help me!"

And suddenly she was able to pray, brokenly at first, and then, as the shattering emotions fell away like banished demons, in blissful, confident calm.

Something wet and warm dragged itself across her face. She opened her eyes with a start to see a very intelligent amusement flicker through the

Chapter 17

sky-blue eyes of the wolf which had licked her. Another, its moon-silver fur soft and warm against her back, was lying pressed against her as she sprawled on the ground.

She realized she had fainted indeed, and she felt recovered enough to be somewhat embarrassed. The feeling increased when she looked up and saw ten, or more, courtiers gazing at her with rapt interest, whispering to one another as they saw her rouse.

As she tried to struggle to her feet Gennan reached down and lifted her - she had an impression of strength totally out of proportion to his slightness. He looked alarmed, as if her faint had startled him as badly as the werewolf had panicked her. When she saw it she knew one part of her prayer at least had not been granted. Love tightened around her like a chain.

"You went away!" he said, reproachfully, "You made me frightened. What happened?"

"I'm..." she said, and choked back the automatic 'sorry' before she said it, "I went a little mad, I think. Everything is so strange here."

In lieu of an apology she put her hand back into his, smiled, and let herself be led up onto the bare slopes of the hills.

"It intrigues, and disgusts us a little," he said suddenly, his soft voice shading into the breeze like a thread of russet smoke, "to find other beings with minds and souls, whose bodies are made up of meat. We are - with the Horde and the Bright Host - the masters of matter. We are above it. It obeys us, we do not obey it. Some of us find it an abomination that rational creatures should be tied down to obeying physical laws, but some, like myself, find the idea a diversion and its study, occasionally, a delight."

He tilted up his head to watch the clouds - dimnesses edged in pearl - go drifting over the road of stars. Eventually, long after Adela had ceased to hope that what he had said would make sense, he finished the thought: "I cannot make my people less strange to you. I can only ask you to find them diverting."

They paused on the rubble strewn crest of the first peak. The moon had risen now and was bathing the scattered stones with nacreous light. With a rush like the passing of huntsmen the pack of silvery wolves circled around the two of them, transmuting in a thought to wheeling bats and the spectral pale shapes of white owls.

"I feel defenseless as a newborn child," she said, trusting him with her feelings as lightly as though he was an old friend.

"But you are not bored?"

"No!" she laughed, astonished, "Certainly not bored."

"Good," he said and smiled at her. "That is worth a great deal." And then, pointing down to the narrow valley at their feet, "Look. We are going to bury Needle there."

Though the high hills where they stood were bathed in the hoar light of moon and stars the valley lay in utter darkness. The sinuous line of owls and bats swept down into it silently and disappeared. A smell came up from it - the dank, moist smell of passages under the ground.

"You mean to have the funeral now? In the middle of the night?" Adela asked, nervously. The cold smell of damp earth caught at her throat. A little-girl terror of churchyards rose up in her; the sense of all those dead things lying close by underfoot.

"Why not?" said Gennan. His words were careless, but he, even he, lowered his voice, unconsciously she thought, in reaction to the shadows. "If you can ease your heart before the morning, why spend the night sad?"

Adela picked her way carefully down into the valley's dimness, the elf-lord silent as a ghost beside her. Lights had begun to show now - seeds of cold blue light, drifting aimlessly on the air, sheets of dimly glowing vapor which twisted into strange shapes as she passed.

Gauzy, dreamlike, the veils of pale light floated about Adela as she walked. The cold from them spilled over her like a breath from a tomb. She shivered.

As though her thought had shaped them, mounds began to show, silhouetted by the gray light: A fleet of them like ships capsized, drowning endlessly beneath the faded grass.

Doorways gaped - the dank earth smell flowed out of them like another darkness. The stone lintels were all written over with deep runes, moss-grown but potent, an ancient magic guarding graves.

Some mounds had fallen in, still water lay polished like steel on their bowl-like surfaces. Some had been pillaged, leaving stained yellow bones lying scattered over the valley floor. Some were complete, doors shut tightly against prying eyes. Whatever lay in them still slept untouched. Adela hardly breathed, frightened they might wake.

They came out from among the mounds, but the dark prows brooded behind them, a silent presence at their backs. Rings and trenches of stone lay

Chapter 17

exposed under the scarves of pallid light. Scattered stones and black empty graves stretched out of sight - an unquiet necropolis silvered by the glow.

"I am quite safe," Adela told herself nervously. "I am quite safe. Gennan is here," but when she looked at him, his skin whey-colored, the tips of his wolf teeth gleaming against his lips, she felt suddenly as though one of the dead was walking beside her, and she wanted to scream.

"I will not be put to shame again," she hissed fiercely at herself, "God will make sure I come to no harm. I am quite safe." But she could not make herself believe it.

"This is where the Fell Dwellers, humans, buried their corpses," said Gennan quietly. His breath brushed her cheek - cold as the night air. "Many hundreds of summers ago. I hope Needle will rest quietly among them."

"If there's some doubt of it," Adela whispered back, knotting her free hand in the folds of her hood to keep it from trembling, "then for Heaven's sake don't bury her here."

"If she walks," Gennan said, shrugging, "she will have company."

Adela had to stop herself from pulling free of him and bolting.

By the side of one open grave a shallow mound of earth had been piled. Needle lay beside it on a pallet made of spears. A mantle of ermine had been draped over her, argent and sable like snow in shade, but her white face was uncovered to the night. Under the translucent skin the skull was already beginning to show.

Mourners stood silently about the bier and the yawning pit, their faces, icy and wan in the blue glow, twisted into masks of grief. Torch, his wood-fire hair dimmed to bone-yellow, stood at the head of the grave and sang. It seemed to Adela, painfully aware of the twisting shadows, that if he fell silent all the lights would go out.

She looked for her lord. He had stepped up to the lip of the grave and was looking down as they lined the grave with the fur mantle and then lowered the elfen into the darkness. The haunted night pressed at her back. A twinge of panic stabbed her. Hurriedly she scrambled up to his side.

In the pit, the girl's body glimmered. There was the grating sound of wood being driven through dry earth - and then someone brought a shield heaped high with dust and gravel and emptied it over her face. An elfen in the crowd tossed back her head and began to keen - a horrible wailing which seemed to coil into Adela's lungs and make her choke with panic. She could not take her eyes off the body. She was sure it was going to move.

A second shield-full of earth cascaded down. A thin layer now covered the corpse, outlining the curves of its shoulders and small breasts like a sheet of silk. It was going to move. Adela knew it.

The rest of the soil went in - making a shallow swelling of dry earth not thick enough to keep scavenging beasts away from the dead flesh. They didn't know how to do this properly. Of course the corpse would walk. It was going to move now! She held her breath.

There was a whisper of sound; coarse soil shifting. A piece of gray flint on top of the heap shuddered and went tumbling. The mound itself bulged from within. A scream began in Adela's chest, pushed itself into her throat like bile. Torch faltered in his song. The ghastly lights dimmed and fluttered.

Hands pushed out of the earth like strange growths, scrabbled at the edges of the grave. The head came up, dust scattering. It opened its mouth - soil dribbled out - and groaned in gibberish. The closed eyes scanned the crowd and found Adela. It snuffed at the air, as if it could smell her blood. Then it began to climb out of the grave.

Adela screamed, a high-pitched, hysterical shouting which she hated but could not stop.

One by one, around her, the elves doubled up howling with laughter.

Needle got to her feet, giggling, and shook the earth out of her hair. Her wounded side was completely healed. She looked radiant with health and high spirits.

A part of Adela's mind began shouting at her: 'It's just a trick! She's not dead at all! It's a trick!' but she could not stop screaming.

"Needle my sharpness!" Gennan swept the girl up and kissed her soundly, "That was superb!" and he went off into a peal of merry laughter which stopped Adela's screams like a slap across the face. Her terror and humiliation turned instantly to fury.

"What the hell is going on?!" she demanded, "What's so funny?"

Around Gennan the lights had changed to gold and green and silver, like summer sunlight. He gave her a smile of pure delight which matched them, his amber eyes sparkling with glee. But she was armored against him now, with outrage and hurt. She glared, and his smile faltered.

"Are you angry?" he asked innocently, his voice puzzled. He held out his hand to her confidently. She ignored it. "You are!" he said, astonished.

Chapter 17

The lights were dancing on the air like dragonflies, drenching the suddenly moonlit hills with a summery glow. Torch still sang, but his voice trembled with laughter. The field of empty graves had become a meadow, threaded with a silent silver brook. The 'mourners', all clad now in bright colors, had begun to dance there in a speeding, leaping circle of chaos.

"Tell me!" she insisted, refusing to be sidetracked by any of this, "What is happening?"

He came noiselessly to her side, his presence like strong wine. His voice was soft and carried still a note of honest puzzlement.

"You made us happy," he said. "My people and I. You made us forget our grief for a little while. Do you begrudge us that?"

Her anger faltered briefly - he seemed so sincere - and then boiled over as she remembered:

"What grief?!" she shouted, "She never was dead at all, was she? It was all a lie! And now you're trying to make me feel sorry for you, so I'll forget you've just humiliated me in front of your whole kingdom. What grief!"

"What grief?!" he repeated, his wolf-like eyes snapping with anger in return. The aura of his power seemed to scorch her for a moment, making her step back in fear. The anger passed with inhuman swiftness, leaving him gentled and a little sad.

He sighed, "You are cruel, my lady," and sat down in the long grass at her feet. "I have lost today a good friend, in a way which makes me sick with terror. I had hoped to forget my grief, and my fear, but you must make me talk about it? Why?"

"I want to know," she insisted, all the more strongly because already sympathy for him was washing out her anger as a wave washes out writing on the sand.

"If I know," she said tentatively, "I will know what to do if it ever happens again."

"It never will happen again!" he said, with a ferocity which made it clear he was trying to lie to himself.

Something, the little voice which had told her she was needed here, was nagging at her not to let this go. Already her anger at him was barely more than a memory, a memory she was ashamed of, but curiosity led her on, and obedience to the voice.

"Please tell me," she begged, kneeling down by his side and taking one of his hands in hers. It was neither as warm nor as solid as a human hand. It lay in her palm like a pool of sunlight given shape by a strong will. She found herself reaching up to see if his long white-gold hair felt the same.

He smiled at her. She moved away sharply, furious with herself. "Tell me who died," she demanded angrily, turning her blushing face away.

He sighed again. "No one died," he said and began, meditatively, to pick wind-frayed daisies and weave them into a wilted garland. "We are not animals like you are. We cannot die."

He tossed a stem away, frowning. "I wish we could," he said. "Life grows so heavy sometimes. We go on and on, and each day is so much like the last, and everything begins to wear out - surprise and excitement and pleasure - and even true love seems hardly worth while, because everything has already been said,"

He picked the garland apart again and scattered the dying flowers on the grass.

"Then you come to a point," he said, and turned a desolate look on the moon as if somehow it had wronged him, "when you could begin to hate it all - the empty world, your useless friends, the stupid mongrel humans who don't appreciate the gift of death, oh and especially whatever cruel force created you and put you here in the first place."

He wavered for a moment, just as Torch had, his long hands gripping the earth as if in pain. When he straightened up again his face was anguished.

"At that point," he said, "you can curse yourself, your friends, your maker, and become the hate. And such a choice is forever. Once you join the Horde you can never come back."

"The Dark One you stripped of its form..." Adela gasped, astonished and horrified,

"Was an elf called Tinder," he said. "He was my friend."

"I understand now," she whispered, shocked into near numbness by this horror. "You don't have to say any more."

He gave her a look of wretched honesty. "I hurt you, didn't I? When I laughed?"

She nodded, speechless.

"Then I owe you this pain in return," he said and frowned as though he were trying to measure out the exact amount of agony required to pay his debt.

Chapter 17

"Because you do not understand," he said, miserably. "Not fully. The choice to join the Horde - become what you call a demon - is forever. But the choice not to join sometimes lasts no longer than it takes for a leaf to fall."

His soft voice trembled under the burden of grief and fear. She wanted to beg him to stop - not to torture himself anymore - but she knew she had to hear it.

"Don't you see," he said, "We have no hope - it pulls at us. And the longer we live, the more empty our lives become, the more it pulls. It will wait for us forever. I do not believe any of us are strong enough to resist it so long. We have no hope. It will happen to us all in the end. "

He put his head in his hands as though he were trying to hide from himself or her. "It will happen to me," he said, almost inaudibly, and cringed as if the very words were sharp as knives in his throat. She moved closer to him again, kneeling on the disheveled flowers, guilt-stricken because she had done this to him.

"Are you paid?" he asked, his voice muffled, "For your hurt?"

"Three times over!" she exclaimed, vehemently, "What can I do to make it better?"

"Go away," he said. "Find Torch. Be the light he has been searching for. It would pay a great many debts."

A human man would have been crying, and hating himself for his weakness even as he did it. She understood. She rose and went away, though it felt like a betrayal, leaving him to master his grief alone.

From every quarter of the sky, clouds came up and blotted out the stars. The night wind became a breath of ice which hissed among the autumn grasses, leaving them lying brittle and gleaming with hoar frost. The dancers faltered, looking up into the darkness with startled eyes. Then, one by one, pouring into their new shapes like quicksilver into vessels of glass, they slipped into the forms of pale wolves and raised their heads to howl.

In the growing darkness Adela could only just make out the shape of Gennan kneeling on the brow of the hill and singing, very quietly, his voice whispering into the night like the icy breeze. She understood, with awe, that he was singing the ice, the clouds, the cold into being. As the first snowflake touched her cheek she remembered Torch's astonishment at her tears and realized that Gennan sang the winter because he could not weep.

Softly the snow began to fall, a weightless, featherlike drift of white which laid a hush, profound as in any church, over the wide land. Under the dark sky the Fells began to glimmer as though edged with crystal. The wolf voices floated on the night as cold and pure as the ice.

Adela hugged herself, shivering in her patched tunic, and yearned for walls, safety and sleep. Nevertheless, because she had as good as promised it, she walked in search of Torch over the whitening meadow towards the howling pack.

A golden coated wolf at the edge of the circle lowered its singing mouth and gazed at her with bright emerald eyes. When she stopped it loped up to her, wagging its tail in not-quite-perfect imitation of a friendly dog. She recognized the uncertain gestures as much as the green eyes.

"Torch?" she asked, wearily, and when it had flowed into the form of her fire-haired companion, she sighed and said "isn't it time to put me to the test? It may be your quest is ended today."

With a look of terror and hope he went silently before her - a gleam of amber light against the falling feathers of ice - up to the thorn-crowned cap of the looming tor. She followed, the worn soles of her borrowed shoes slithering on the deepening snow, icy water seeping through the thin leather. Where the slope was steepest she had to crawl, her fine-boned hands turning first red and then deadly pale from the cold.

Just below the final rise, where the boulders stood, meaningless and foreboding against the sky, curved a path, slightly hollowed, like a fosse filled in by time and neglect. Torch stopped there, looking up into the night. Adela thrust her hands into the baggy sleeves of her tunic and warmed them into stinging life on her sides while she waited for his lead.

The snow was easing, the clouds flowing away from over the ancient blackthorns like ripples in water. Above the tor stars came out, scattered gleaming among the heavens like raindrops on tilled dark soil. Against their luminosity the trees seemed as black and as still as the rocks. Wind sighed among them, left them unmoved.

Try as she might, Adela could see no sign of habitation, not even a doorway in one of the stones which might lead - she shivered at the thought - into damp earthen passages and a kingdom under the ground. Turning to Torch in puzzlement she found him singing, his face so rapt that she dared not speak, but stood, hugging herself while the notes fell around her, precise and beautiful, filling the jagged peaks with power.

The ground began to shake and stretch beneath her feet, like a giant waking. Then, with a huge shudder, with a sound like packed ice on a frozen

Chapter 17

lake breaking into a thousand pieces, the crown of the hill, trees, boulders and all, began slowly to rise up on slender pillars. Warm air smoked out, forming a fringe of icicles like a glass wall between the two great lips of soil. Through it light poured, shimmering. Adela could see battlements; a castle which flashed like crystal, banners of azure and scarlet like ice and fire, a flowering meadow under a joyous sun, and far away the edges of a forest, deep and green.

She hesitated only a second, wondering if she would ever come back, but it seemed to her she had been looking for that country all her life. Cold and weariness fell briefly away. She went forward, into the elvish mound.

Chapter Eighteen

"In here." The maid-servant, Thornberry, paused before a pale ash-wood door over which snails were tracing an elaborate network of shimmering trails. Her piercingly high voice sent little echoes running down the long lambent corridor, making the white flames shudder and dance in their silver bowls.

"Wait! Just a moment," Adela gasped, and as the creature's tiny brown hand paused on the ring, she took two or three deliberate deep breaths to calm herself.

The maid's black, apple-pip eyes lingered on her incuriously, like a horse lifting its head to look at a hind.

Adela was glad the painted lines and spirals on the elfen's tanned face made it hard to read her expression. She suspected a sneer. "I just need a moment to prepare myself," she said, while within her a frightened voice was crying 'This prophecy! - Why wasn't I nervous before? I must have been asleep on my feet! - What if Torch is wrong? What if I'm not the one?'

She pulled apprehensively at her borrowed dress - the rose-colored silk felt choking tight around her chest and throat. Her hands were clammy. She laid them flat against the door, to cool them, and her fingers brushed a tiny crawling snail. With a start of surprise she found it metal - a doorstud cunningly shaped.

'If I do fulfill it,' she thought, 'what will Torch do then? I'll be taking away the very purpose of his life. Suppose he Changes?' and a memory of him, twisted and stinking with anger, turned her spread hands cold.

'But, if I don't,' a very young voice this one, the voice of a girl crying over her first love, thinking her heart is broken forever, 'If I don't, will they send me away? Would He - would Gennan - send me away? I don't want to leave him!'

Thornberry's unblinking stare roused her.

'You're a grown woman.' she told herself with disgust, 'Act like one.' And drawing herself up she turned to face the disconcerting gaze. "I'm ready."

Chapter 18

"In here," Thornberry repeated, and pulling the heavy portal open she motioned Adela through.

Adela went in - and was suddenly outside; in a ruined amphitheatre, where the great cream blocks of the seats lay tumbled by twisted roots, and broken pillars, carved with strange, fleshy leaves, stood up jaggedly from nests of ivy.

Beneath her feet the vivid blue flowers of periwinkle sprawled over shattered pavements. Around her the tiers, a great bowl of cracked stones - grass grown, overshadowed by dark trees - swept up to a circle of dawn sky.

Milky, glimmering slightly, the wall of the elven citadel rose behind her in one long frozen leap to distant crenellations where vivid banners snapped, golden-edged against the dim sky. An oak grew beside the door, its roots folding the flagstones like linen, its spreading branches laced with the dusky stems and tattered blossoms of honeysuckle.

The Lady Silence stood there, like a shaft of sunlight caught in the fragrant cage of branches. She turned, beckoning Adela to join her.

Adela came almost timidly, like a poor knight's squire approaching a prince.

"She's wonderful!" was her first thought, and her reason seized on it eagerly as a puzzle with which to distract her from her fear. "What is it about her? She reminds me of the heroes of old tales, Arion, maybe, or Ilionika. Perhaps she's a holy woman?"

But though she studied the lady carefully for signs of piety she could see only more of the ambivalence which had intrigued her about the elves from the very start:

Silence was tall, and moved like a queen, but something about her frank emerald gaze and ready smile reminded the Holmr woman of a country maiden out a-maying. Her full gown, blue as the periwinkles, was demure as any saint's, but the waist-long braids of her bright gold hair were, Adela thought, immodestly unveiled, and plaited with bells of glass and crystal, so they chimed as she moved.

At the lady's gestured invitation Adela sat down on the springy cushion of moss which overgrew one of the larger stones, and wondered awkwardly if she should speak, or sing, or remain silent.

Thornberry came forward, reaching out a tiny hand to her mistress's grasp. Silence's long fingers closed around her wrist like a bracelet of pearl. When the girl spoke again her voice was octaves lower and almost soft.

"Child, Starlight." The maid brushed idle circles in the grass with her bare foot as Silence watched Adela's face with gentle intensity. "I am borrowing Thornberry's speech," the voice went on, "For one final time," and Silence smiled as the maid spoke, "Did you sleep well, my dear?" she said.

"I did," Adela relaxed a little at the familiar pleasantry and savored even in memory her bed of cloud-soft furs. "It was kind of you to let me rest, when it may have meant depriving you of your voice, for hours."

The lady covered a silent laugh with her hand. "I have been waiting for a thousand summers, Starlight," she said, "It was kind of you to give me a little time in which to come to terms with hope."

"There I think your son may disagree with you," Adela searched for the gleam of him through the forest gloom, "He is very concerned for you." She offered the excuse gently, remembering his anxious pacing while she ate and slept - it had set a nervous heartbeat drumming through her dreams.

"I ask you to forgive him," The maid's voice stumbled over forgive as though it was a word totally foreign to her, but her white-less eyes remained untouched by either interest or shame at her fault.

"Among our people," Silence explained, "Sleep is unknown, and eating is a pleasure which we can indulge or forbear at will. It would not have occurred to him that you might need such things."

"In which case," Adela smoothed her veil - a thing of golden gauze as fine as mist - over her shorn brown hair, "there's nothing to forgive. I keep forgetting your folk must find me almost as strange, and," she paused and turned her head away so the slight flush of color might pass unnoticed in the uncertain light.

"And wonderful," she said, "As I find them."

"Very few of us know anything about humans," Silence agreed serenely, but a gleam of motherly complicity in her eyes - wicked as a toddler's dimpled grin - made Adela blush harder. She had totally forgotten, for this moment, any ancient prophesy and grief. She found herself smiling foolishly. It was an effort to wipe it away.

"But I," Silence continued, mirroring the smile for an instant, "I know a little of them - I was married to one, many summers ago."

"Married!" Adela exclaimed, louder than she had intended. Silence's smile broadened, before fading away.

Chapter 18

"It was not a great success," she sighed apologetically. "He was so changeable! Every year he was different, and each decade he had altered so much it was as though he was another man. His life was so rapid! I simply could not keep up with it."

She sat then, on a weathered wooden stool, with her back to the castle's standing wall, and looked out sadly at the sparrows piping on the rough slopes and over the twisted pines.

Torch came through the snail-strewn doorway singing under his breath in uneasy snatches of words. The sound of the tune - merry and sad at once - floated out into the captive sky like the pale equivocal light.

When he saw Adela his singing faltered and died. "It's time," he said.

The dawn hush seemed to deepen around Adela. Thoughts of marriage and its uncertainty went down under a wave of fear. Her heart began to pound again and her mouth went dry.

"I may not be what you are waiting for," she whispered, swallowing, while the shadows of failure, disappointment, continuing tragedy came to rest on her shoulders like a gray cloak.

"You are," Silence smiled with calm certainty, "I can feel it."

She looked fondly at her son. He avoided her eyes, but sank down beside her against the nacreous wall putting his cheek to the smooth stone as if for solace.

"If it comforts you, Starlight," Silence said suddenly, "We too are afraid. This has nothing to do, really, with the restoration of my voice. I feel an ending coming. You are bringing a great light; something of terror and glory, something which will be remembered among our people for all time."

"Because of me?" Adela gasped, and stood up hurriedly.

Because of me, her mind repeated, *I can't do it! I'll fail, they'll laugh at me. All history will laugh at me!* She stared wildly at the twilight slope as if expecting to see, already, an ocean of mocking faces.

"I... I don't know if I can do it."

A clatter of wings made her look up as five white doves wheeled over the pearly battlements and came to settle on the twigs of the oak. They had bright, intelligent eyes, she knew when she saw them that an audience had begun to arrive.

Gennan stepped neatly from the final tier of steps, the wolf-pack seething behind him like a cascade of foam. He gave her a bow, hand on heart, before stretching out on his chosen seat like a Duguth Emperor contemplating the games.

She looked away from him, ashamed: She had not wanted him to see her fail.

By seconds the ruined theater began to fill with elves; courtiers, and servants, sprites whose shapes were neither human nor animal. The dim blue light of dawn picked out fine embroidery, glimmered on circlets of silver, on curving polished talons, and in hundreds of watching eyes. Adela's breathing grew even more ragged. She clenched her fists.

I can't do it, she wailed in silent panic, *I just can't do it!*

"Do not be afraid," Silence reached out to touch her knee in reassurance, and yet she felt the slender hand tremble as it withdrew. "You are like Thornberry," the lady encouraged her, gently. "You are someone else's voice."

And, as though the lady's words had shown it to her, all at once Adela felt the presence of God - like a thing of solid light, a deep golden kindness lying separately on every created thing in the courtyard, edging each blade of grass, each blossom of the honeysuckle with the radiance of love. It was a palpable, silent peace which she could breathe in, which buoyed her up like clean water, and sharpened every sense into an instrument of joy.

"God is here!" she exclaimed. Her fear fell away, she grinned from ear to ear in unladylike glee.

"The human god?" Torch glanced around wildly, searching the shadows for this frightening deity.

"Everybody's God!" she laughed.

Torch shook his head, the flame of his hair whipping across his face. "We don't want it."

He looked at Silence, inquiringly, but her eyes were fixed on Adela and she did not acknowledge his glance.

"We don't want your God," he said warily. "Just make the light. Just sing!"

Adela needed no urging. What she wanted most of all was to sing in praise.

"Sun and stars are singing of God,"

Chapter 18

She sang, and though she knew her voice was weak and untuneful when compared to the elves' music, there was no room in her for shame. She was too glad.

"Moon, Star and Sunshine proclaim him Prince
Down all the years and over all the worlds
their voices are ringing his praise.
no one is hidden from their light,
there is no island, and no sea
where their song of praise has never been heard."

The song came out, not against her will - never that - but without her conscious volition, exactly as if someone very great and very joyful were singing through her and with her. It was a greater happiness than anything she had ever known.

"The rules of God are sure," she sang,
"like a smooth path to my feet,
The ways of God are right,
those who follow them will never be ashamed,
The word of God is radiant,
making my heart rejoice,
Darkness flees from him, and though I am afraid
still I will follow him."

"Stop it! Stop it!" She became suddenly aware that Torch was yelling, she took her eyes off the paling saffron sky and looked for him, puzzled at the sound of distress in his voice. Her breath caught in her throat as she saw the panic - wolves pawing at their muzzles in pain, gaily clad courtiers running for the forest cover like peasants from the razing of a village.

Silence was pressed against the wall, head back, eyes wide in fear, like a thief held at bay by a circle of spears. Torch stood cringing a step in front of her, arm raised as if protecting her from a scorching heat. He struggled to look at Adela, his face contorted in anguish.

"It was not like this before!" he shouted, "You are doing it wrong!"

One of the doves, a desperate little missile of shimmering feathers, flung itself at him, scoring his face with its clawed feet, driving the small beak towards his eyes. He flung it away and turned to beg for understanding from the howling crowd, "I swear it! It was not like this before! Or I would not have let her start. Stop!"

She fell silent, while cries of fear buffeted her. Somewhere a wolf whined in pain. A tiny brown servant-lad, crawling up the slope opposite her, was trodden underfoot as the nobles turned to flee. Their pain and panic tore at her, making her eyes brim, and yet somehow, in the core of her soul, peace held fast like a storm anchor.

"Silence?" she asked, uncertainly, "What's happening? Do you want me to stop?"

But Silence could not speak. The maid, Thornberry, lay at her feet and keened a jarring, vile whine like an armorer sharpening a sword. Her arms were over her head, covering the bright black eyes in shadow.

"Of course she wants you to stop!" Torch shouted, "Can't you see you're hurting her? You're hurting all of us!"

Then Silence tried to stagger forward, as if she was leaning into a wind of fire. She fell back, panting, defeated, catching at Torch's hand for support. Desperately she struggled to speak. Her green eyes, full of agony and awe pleaded with him for something.

"Make her sing!" Silence mouthed, shaking with frustration, while Torch pulled her back to the shelter of the wall as though he was hauling her away from an abyss.

"What's happening?" Like stormy winds confusion and distress whistled about the tiny golden sun which was the presence of God in Adela's heart. Their tugging was harsh; without that brilliant focus she knew she would have been swept away.

"What's going on? Is it another trick?" And to Silence she whispered

"Are you sure? If it hurts so much..."

Chapter 18

Silence shook her son off - the bells in her hair ringing wild and furiously as the heavy braids lashed around her. She fell to her knees and began to crawl forward, wincing each time she moved a hand.

"No!" Torch tried to go after her, and was beaten back by unseen flames. Yet all Adela could see were cool stones, laced by periwinkle flowers, blue as summer skies in the broadening light.

There was quiet now, a hush of fear over the whole auditorium, broken only by a whimpering from Torch as he recoiled once more from the invisible threat.

Adela glanced around, and shook her head violently. The weed-grown tiers of the ancient theatre were deserted. Her audience had fled. Surely if it was a trick they would have stayed?

Were they really gone? She scanned the empty shadows under the twisted pines, and saw only Gennan, belly-down on the lowest step, squinting at her through pain-narrowed eyes, as though he was trying to look into a great light.

She looked back, and met Silence's agonized gaze. Certainty hit her; this was no trick.

Silence shook her head - the bells rang a carillon of despair. Her mouth worked with the effort of trying to speak, but still she was silent.

"Sing!" she shouted mutely.

Adela began to sing again, and screams almost drowned her clear voice. A wind arose and snapped through the gnarled branches of the trees, so they thrashed in pain. Thornberry, scrabbling at the door, wrenched it open and crept through, cowering even as she moved.

"Let me understand!" Adela prayed, "Let me see what they see. Let me share this with them, please...if it won't destroy me..."

And she saw it: It spread out from her in a vast scintillating globe whose edge just brushed the lip of the first tier with molten silver, whose dome rose above her head like a perfect crystal made from a million raging stars. Tongues of flame, white and white-gold, deep gold and silver, were dancing in it, and out-flung amber lightnings twisted there like bright silk scarves cast on a sunlit sea.

Holiness spun like drifting white roses, within a finger's breadth of her, blooming with heartbreaking purity just out of her reach. And even the sight of it burned her; every private darkness in her screamed with terror - It will kill us! It will kill us! Don't let it touch us! You must get away!

But there was nowhere to run to. She was in the center of it.

Between Adela and the cauterizing flames there was a thin membrane, a bubble, blood-red in the pristine light, protecting her. She dared not move - the bubble seemed so fragile.

Still she sang, and understood suddenly the invitation in the words:

I will scour your heart and make it clean;
I will wash you, and you will be clean.

She could wade in the flame until all the darkness was burned out of her. One moment of agony and everything she hated about herself would be gone. One moment of death and she would be really alive for the first time. She knew she should want it - She wanted to want it. But her flesh crawled from the thought of the pain. "I can't!" she sobbed in prayer, "I dare not! I'm sorry. I'm so useless! I'm sorry!"

Silence forced herself to her feet and stumbled forward, into the fire. It leaped up to meet her like eager, welcoming hands. It enfolded her in planes and prisms of dancing light. There was a roaring, like a great voice exulting.

And then Silence caught on fire, blazing up like a firebrand, hanging, screaming with agony in the flames - the first sound she had made in a thousand years.

With a choke of horror Adela fell silent. The scouring flames roared on, the elvish lady twisting in the center of them like a fleck of ash in a bonfire's heat. Lightnings glided over her, making her spasm. Her screaming became more frantic. Her fists clenched and beat at the air as she kicked like a hanging man.

Gennan hurled himself at the silver globe and fell back, howling. Torch crawled into a corner of the wall and curled up there into a ball of misery, wrapping his arms around his face, so he might not see. Adela wished she could do the same, but she dared not move.

Above the bowl of broken seats the sky flushed into a glory of rose and peach and palest blue. The sun came up, scattering beams like tossed coins into the shade beneath the trees.

Chapter 18

Silence grew still, her screams fading to a whisper. She lay limply on the air, still drifting on white pillows of flame, and gasped in relief, like a patient once the arrow-head has finally been wrenched out.

Gradually her faint whimper of pain became song, fainter at first than the distant chorus of the birds. Shimmering, like a cloud of may-blossom whirled in a warm breeze, tiny flowers of light began to bloom about her - a cloak of stars. Her voice swelled into a music of incredible sweetness, deep and rich and full of power, and the light caught the timbre of it, mellowing into honey and buttercups. There was a scent of summer and a glow brushed Adela's face like petals.

She fell to her knees, confusion and horror lifting away, leaving no stain behind them.

Silence sang on, her eyes sparkling with joy. A wind sprang up - silver edged, glittering - and streamed around her. Her hair, unraveling from its braids, lifted and floated behind her - showering crystal bells onto the earth.

"Starlight!" she exclaimed, her smile exultant, "Look what you have done for me!"

And behind her, green as every kind of leaf, each feather edged with sunshine, her great wings unfurled in a fan of splendor.

"Silence?" Gennan staggered up, shielding his eyes from the light of her. He looked vulnerable, fragile as blown glass, in the aura of her radiance, "Silence, is that you?"

The new angel had her head tilted slightly, her gaze on something out of their sight. Her face shone with delight. "I'm coming, my lord." she promised, "soon."

Then lightly she stepped down from the air, her small feet settling firmly onto the cracked pavement, and crouched down beside her huddled son.

Whispering to him she stroked back the red hair from his forehead and smiled as he looked up at her with astonished eyes.

Adela found herself beside Gennan, clutching his hand, but whether she gave, or received support, she did not know.

An angel, her mind repeated numbly, *I've seen an angel!*

"Silence?" Gennan asked again, his husky voice full of uncertainty. She turned and smiled at him, the wings like noon on a canopy of beech leaves. The newly risen sun cloaked her in citrine and saffron, but still, among the glinting strands of her hair, pale stars shone keenly.

"I was Silence," she said, "But I have made a new Choice. I'm Niniel now."

She took Gennan's right hand, Adela's left, so they formed a little circle like dancing children. Ease flowed into them at the touch.

"It was brave of you to stay and watch, Icewolf," she said, her voice like a music of harps. "And kind. It will have done you good."

His poise returned, subdued but unmistakable, "I stayed because I was too terrified to crawl away," he said, with a flash of his fanged grin.

"You should not lie to a Bright One," she laughed, while the twisted pines leaned in to listen, "It shows."

To Adela she said, gently, "Your obedience has done this for me. Never think you failed today. You did what was wanted from you. Thank you," and she raised one gleaming hand to touch Adela's forehead. It felt shocking, like the press of a hot coal onto her skin.

"When you are in deadly danger," the angel said, "Call, and if I am permitted, I will come."

She turned away, the great arch of verdant feathers sweeping out to gather Torch into its warmth.

"Goodbye."

"Wait!" Gennan strode out after her, "What does this mean?"

"Hope," she said simply, "It means there is hope, for you and all your people. Oh Icewolf, don't make me stay and explain. I so much long to go. Starlight can tell you. She knows."

The wing-tips arched upwards, sending twin zephyrs spinning through the dawn dew. Water droplets leaped and sparkled, so rainbows danced around her feet.

"Mother!" Torch ran forward to grasp one emerald pinion. He was transparent in her light, a smudge of red and sulfur, even the unruffled feathers were visible through his clutching fingers.

"Don't go!" he begged.

She enclosed him in her wings, like a mother eagle mantling over her chicks.

"Come to me soon." She smiled, and suddenly she was a pillar of light, blazing up into the sky, flowers of brilliance wheeling around her. Briefly her glory dimmed the sun, and then she was gone.

Chapter 18

Torch stood aghast, staring at his hands as if they were stained with guilty blood. Then, pouring into his animal-shape he lifted up his mouth and sang. Wolf-song, cold and desolate, floated out over the shivering trees.

"What does it mean?" Gennan turned a puzzled face to Adela, dropping her hand as if it scorched him. Her heart gave a little lurch of grief at that, even while her common sense told her it was a good thing.

"I... I'm not sure," she sank weakly down onto the mossy boulder. Her body began to tremble in reaction to what she had seen. "I need to think."

He left her alone, pacing over to stroke behind the wolf's pricked ears. Torch growled at him, half-heartedly, and then fell silent.

"I know!" Adela looked up, astonished, one of Godgifu's tales coming back to her from forgotten days in the nursery, and striking her like a revelation.

"Do you remember the Choice of Lords?" she asked, and the elf-lord's frown deepened, as though he was chasing an elusive memory across millions of years of forgetfulness.

"I do not know," he said, uncertainly, "I do not think so."

"In the earliest days," she explained gently, recasting the story to what she knew of him and his culture. "Just after the world was made, the best of the Bright Ones became swell-headed, rebellious. He made a choice, like yours, to curse God and himself. We think - humans think - it was because God created us. We think he was jealous.

However it was, he went to God and demanded the other angels be given a choice - the Choice of Lords, to choose between their maker, or himself."

Gennan's lip curled back from his teeth at this tale of treachery, leaving his fine-drawn face almost as wolfish as Torch. His white-gold hair gleamed softly in the early morning sun. Adela looked away from him quickly, with a sudden wrench of sorrow - if what she believed was true, how could she dare continue to think of him as she did?

"It's said," she glanced at him to see if he recognized any part of the tale yet. It did not seem so; he watched her too calmly. "It's said a full third of the holy angels - they became the Dark Ones - took his side, and had to be banished from Heaven, cast down into the depths of all that is made - into the Abyss."

"So?"

"It's said," she fiddled with the carved links of her girdle, avoiding his topaz gaze, "The loyal host was also one third of the original number. No one knows what happened to the final third, but some people say they dithered. They couldn't choose, or they refused to choose."

She swallowed, reluctant to utter her conclusion, to bind them both in the fetters of the truth, "And they became the elves," she said in a small voice. "You and your folk."

"No," he shook his head, "That cannot be." But his voice was unsure - perhaps the tale had stirred some deep memory he was reluctant to acknowledge. He cast a glance over the sighing pines, the bright young sun, as if seeking support.

"But it can," Adela insisted, "don't you see? The choice has never been taken away from you. You can still make it - You can become again the blessed angel you once were."

A flight of crows, solemn and glossy against the pale blue sky, came drifting out of the woods, cawing. Gennan looked up, sharply, and watched them as they set their clawed black feet on the flag-poles and battlements of his castle. His bright face became suddenly focused and taut.

"I'll think about this later," he said.

"But..." Adela protested, astonished.

Running lightly down the boulder-strewn slope, leaping over tangled tree-roots and the scree of small stones, the youth Lightning darted into the arena like his name.

"My lord!" he cried, his clear voice unmarred by any trace of breathlessness, "Weasel and Sunshock are here, as messengers. They say they must speak at once."

"I will hear them," Gennan nodded briskly, and the lad sped away, his yellow hair glimmering among the trees like a splash of primroses. Then, silently, thoughtfully, Gennan led Adela back through the maze of gleaming corridors to the rosewood door of her own chamber.

When they halted he looked at her very intently. "You have a star on your brow," he said after a time, "Like a High Queen."

His smoky amber gaze slid away from her briefly, and he frowned, as if weighing up dues and obligations, "I have treated you lightly in the past," he said softly, "I will do so no more."

Chapter 18

"Wait!" she cried, and felt again a stab of bereavement at his subdued politeness.

Maybe he never felt anything for me at all, she thought suddenly. *Maybe he was only amusing himself, like a great lord with his serving-maid. But I do wish nothing had changed between us.*

And then sanity returned, leaving her amazed at her own fickleness; she had just witnessed a miracle. She had had God sing through her, she had felt more whole and at peace than ever in her life, and now she had let it all fall away in grief over some foolish dream.

"Yes?" there was the curve of a slight smile on Gennan's lips as he waited for her to speak, a renewed readiness. She sensed him emerging from his shock like a newborn dragonfly out of the water.

"It's nothing." She twisted the brass ring of her door, pushed it ajar a little, waiting with forced composure to be dismissed.

His fingers brushed the back of her hand like silk, making her catch her breath in surprise and pleasure. His lean face, drawn out of strokes of silver in the corridor's lambent glow, was rueful, but warm.

"I was frightened," he said, without the slightest trace of embarrassment, "And I still am. It was a strange and awful thing. I need so much to think about it. "

He tossed his head, as if he was shrugging the subject away. The glow which came off him brightened into moonlight and pearl. "I will deal with these messengers as quickly as I may," he said, "And then I will find time to sit down with you and..." his smile broadened, wickedly, "Talk?"

She stood open mouthed, speechless, and his grin took on a shade of satisfied mischief. Then, changing moods like quicksilver, serious in an instant, he said,

"Put on your finest and come sit beside me when I hear the messengers. They are great nobles in Crow's kingdom. They would not have been sent for something slight. It maybe I need your council." And he strode away, leaving her astonished and dizzy with so many swings between grief and joy.

Icewolf, Prince of the elves of Shining Tor, lounged indolently on his throne. Upon his long gilded-ice hair a circlet of bone and gold was set, saw-edged as a butcher's knife. His wolfish, yellow eyes were half closed in seeming boredom, but his right hand never strayed from the hilt of a gleaming, slender blade which lay unsheathed across his knees.

Behind him Lightning stood, holding ready a red round shield and a sword which blazed even through its scabbard. All around his throne, glimmering like frost, beneath his feet, pouring over the dais and the pale stone floor, the wolves of his kingdom lay, and stared like a single being toward the great hall's open door.

Adela sat self-consciously on her councilor's seat. Noble elves leaned away from her, whispering, their faces so exquisite that she felt, for a moment, even in her cloth-of-gold gown, impossibly ugly, ridiculously out of place. She adjusted the fine net of jewels which covered her shorn locks, and forgot about herself in attention to the messengers.

They came a little uneasily into the alabaster hall, bowed and made their introductions. Weasel; a warrior with the same coloring as his sword, and Sunshock, whose gleaming black braids framed a child's innocent face, and eyes like molten steel.

It was the elfen - the female - who spoke, her voice a solid thing, a weapon of solid light; "Prince Icewolf, some time ago you aided Crow in keeping the humans from his land. We are here to offer you some part of a payment of that debt."

"I was told it was a thing of great urgency." Gennan leaned forward, holding her raging gaze nonchalantly. "There have never been any formalities between Crow and I. Tell me it all."

Among the councilors there was a murmur of surprise. The crystal pillars of the hall resonated to it, sending it back to them as a faint tinkling of bells.

"The law!" An elf by Adela's side spoke out, his narrow face sharpened by shock.

"I lay it aside for now," said Gennan firmly, and stared his councilor down, while Weasel dimmed visibly with relief.

"You are wise," Sunshock paced closer, until her feet touched white fur. "There is little time." She rubbed at her wrists, like a slave rubbing at the gall of manacles, and stared at the floor. With tight control she continued.

"He came a night ago, a human man, and demanded instant passage from one side of Crow's domains to the other. At first we laughed at him, but he commanded us - and he made us obey. It was as if he knew our true names."

Chapter 18

She paused and thought, bitterness showing in the compression of her blood-red lips. Something, a premonition perhaps, began to fill Adela's veins with ice-cold lead. Something in the woman's beaten, shamed stance, seemed horribly familiar.

Oh please, no she prayed, and knew even as she was saying it the answer to the prayer.

"He had... something." Sunshock was still speaking, her finely honed voice piercing Adela's preoccupation like lightning piercing clouds, "Something in his hand, by which he made us obey, but there was... a forbidding... about it, and we could not see what it was."

She braced herself, and finished quickly, "We took him, at his command, to the manor of Langley, on our borders, and left him there. But he threatened to return. He is hunting, he said, and he will not stop until he makes his kill."

Adela let out a shaky breath, blood roaring in her ears, and it seemed to her the whole white hall with its tapestries of azure and ruby, darkened in her sight. Langley - that was her manor! It was Adam! There was no longer any doubt about it. She turned briefly, desperately, to the thought of Gennan's protection. He would fight for her, she was sure. And then she remembered what had happened to the other men whose help she had sought. She could not stand to watch it happen to him. Dread fell on her, and not the wide landscapes beyond the bright windows, nor the fresh sunlight, could lift it.

"As soon as the human left us," Sunshock continued, still with the forced indifference which seemed more terrible than tears, "Crow sent us out, to warn you."

Passion broke through at last, an outburst which set Gennan's courtiers reeling; "Scatter your kingdom, Icewolf! If he comes you will be powerless against him. Do not let him do to you what he has done to us. He has stamped on our faces. "

I don't want to leave! Adela wailed silently, and felt duty, honor, crushing her, while inside something screamed in panic, like a badly wounded horse.

Guiltily, trembling, she bowed her head, twisting her shaking hands together in a white, tight knot, and tried to keep silence.

"I grieve for my brother, and his people." Gennan's tone was formal, calming, absolutely neutral. Both Sunshock and Weasel reacted to it like runners to a cool breeze. "But why should this human ever come to me?"

The moment stretched to an eternity of darkness, and then suddenly Adela was standing, breathless and quaking with every creature in the assembly staring at her, aghast.

"I must leave." Sparks of jeweled light chased across the upturned faces as she turned her head, belatedly, to beg permission to speak. Gennan nodded curtly to her, his lupine eyes blazing with surprise. She moistened her lips, her voice tiny in the lily-pale expanse of hall.

"His name is Adam de Limoges," she said, "and he will come because of me. Because I am the prey he is hunting."

She took several shallow breaths, loud in the astounded silence, and forced herself to say it again; "I must go away. Now."

Chapter Nineteen

The fresh herbs - pennyroyal and tansy - strewn among the straw felt deliciously cool under Oswy's bare feet as he came in out of the late August heat.

He had been practicing a technique which Sulien called Net-running - sending the bundle of fibers that was his body weaving like a shuttle through the loom of the world, pulling it together again in far-off places within minutes of leaving home.

He rubbed his aching shoulders cautiously, and hoped the bruises on his legs would be hidden under the dust and summer tan. His master had taught him this great magic as a means of swift escape. He had surely not intended it to be used to visit Edward, Leofwine's son, and play knights-on-horseback against John of Wyrmbank's Holmr squires.

Still, Oswy thought, beginning to shiver as the chill of the walls seeped through his linen tunic - the hem of it above his knees now, he had grown so much - if he didn't see someone cheerful now and again he would probably go mad in this place. And his master would never notice: If he even looked up from his scrying-bowl, or pendulum or crystal, it would be a wonder in itself.

The carved oak door of the great hall stood slightly ajar, sunlight lancing out of the crack into the dark corridor. The sound of voices, low but intent, drifted out with the light. Cautiously, Oswy pushed it fully open and looked in.

Tables had been taken down, pushed against the walls. The paved floor had been swept free of straw and strewing herbs. The great bare sweep of it lay open to the sun, gilded into cloth of gold by the flood of light from the high windows. Creamy beeswax candles were anchored there, unlit. Within their circle runes had been drawn, with slate and salt and blood. Oswy studied them eagerly at first, and then shrank away with fear. What they were, he could not tell, but he was thankful they seemed incomplete.

On the trestle-stacked dais, glowing like a scene from a church window, Hugo knelt, his red tunic newly dyed, his armor beside him sparkling.

He offered up his clasped hands to Sulien's white grip, while Father Paul, hair like floating seeds, read out of his mass-book the words and their responses.

It might have made a fine picture - a young knight taking his oath of allegiance to his Lord - only the Lord's face was drawn and haunted, the priest's black with rage and horror, and the knight himself stumbled over the ancient words while his troubled gaze kept straying from the nick on Sulien's wrist to the drying pentagram on the floor.

Oswy slipped into the room silently, eased himself into a patch of sable shade by the door, curiosity warring with his peasant cautiousness. He had meant to go up to his chamber and study for a while, in case his master came to himself enough to test him. But it could wait.

Hugo straightened up lithely, "I mean to keep this, you know," he said, "since it's plain you value me more than my father does. My loyalty to him ends here." He tore his gaze from the thing on the floor, looked into Sulien's shadowed eyes. "You can trust my oath," he insisted.

"If I did not think so," Sulien replied harshly, "I would not have troubled taking it."

He turned away, pushing up his stained sleeves, baring arms marked from palm to elbow with angry red cuts.

"Command me then, Lord," Hugo asked, and braced himself grimly for the answer.

"Go to your father," Sulien's voice was remote, as though the business of this world hardly concerned him. He stepped carefully from the dais, began to stalk up to the magic signs as though he was hunting a vicious beast.

"Go to him," he repeated with an effort. "Tell him what you have done. Tell him I no longer demand anything from him. Return when you may."

Hugo stood awhile, bemusement succeeding his determined frown, but Sulien was no longer looking at him, he had crouched down beside the line of salt and was cautiously rearranging the curved tail of one symbol.

Pleasure began to break through Hugo's puzzlement, brightening his young face. "You trust me to go there and return again?" He sounded astonished, as though he had been given an unfamiliar coin, infinitely valuable. When he received no answer he bowed himself out of the room, smiling.

"If he returns," said Sulien, shifting into his native Sceavish as if he spoke to himself, "I'll know he keeps his word. If he does not, he'll be no loss."

Chapter 19

Oswy straightened up in his pool of shadow, wondering if now was the time to leave. But Father Paul picked up his hazel cane and came shakily down the dais steps.

In the same language, his voice quaking with fury he said, "If you can be that prudent in some things, how is it you can be so stupid when it really matters?"

There was a hiss of indrawn breath. Oswy tracked the sound, recognized Gunnar gone to ground under the pile of stacked trestles. He edged, sighing, around the walls to join him.

Gunnar looked at Oswy with indignant amber eyes,

"Did you hear what that priest said?" he whispered, "How dare he?"

"Shut up!" Oswy breathed, angrily, "Haven't you learned yet?" He flicked his fingers towards the bruises on Gunnar's freckled face, his swollen, purple lips. "My lord doesn't want your sympathy," he insisted, "it makes him angry. Why don't you just leave him alone, and spare us all the pain?"

"If leaving him alone is such a good idea," Gunnar muttered back, covering the tell-tale marks with a furtive hand, "why are you here?"

"I just want to know what's going on."

Father Paul pointed at the pentagram on the floor, "What is this, Sulien?" he demanded, "What do you think you are doing?"

"I brought you here to witness Hugo's oath," Sulien looked up from his sigils blackly. "Not to preach me a sermon."

"But you will hear one nevertheless." The old man reached out gingerly with the tip of his stick, touched the edge of the salt circle. Sulien, leaping to his feet slapped the support out of Paul's hand. It went clattering into the shadows.

"Don't interfere!" he hissed, "You don't even know what I'm trying to do!"

"Summon the Darkness!" Father Paul exclaimed, and began to scuff out the markings with his foot. The witch shoved him and he reeled away, still shouting; "Your soul is in my charge. I won't let you do it."

There was a brief charged moment. Sulien caught himself on the edge of rage, clenched his scabbed fists until the split knuckles began to weep. Then he sighed and turned away.

"Not Dark Ones," he said quietly, "nothing would drive me to that. I've seen what they do to those who are indebted to them." He sighed again, sounding achingly tired, "Not demons. A god. One of the old gods."

Oswy held his breath, frightened and awed, saw beside him Gunnar open-mouthed with shock.

"I am going to summon Egesa," Sulien said softly, and rubbed a hand over his face, raising bleak eyes to the old man's suddenly gentled gaze.

"The terror-god?" said Paul in a hush.

"God of revenge," the witch-lord corrected him. "He should at least have some stake in the answer." Uncertainly he went on, "I don't know if it can even be done. Or if it can be controlled when it is done, but what choice do I have? I must know."

The priest sank down on the bottom step and smoothed down his dandelion-clock hair with an unsteady hand.

"I don't know what to say first." He looked up abruptly, "Where is Leofwine?"

"With Edith." Sulien frowned, "Why?"

"At times like these, I feel I need his protection."

The witch's back stiffened with insult, but he laughed, a harsh sound. "I will not lay a hand on you," he said, "I swear it. Now get your lecture over with. I'm listening."

"First of all," Father Paul looked up to the thin stripe of sky which showed through a high window, as though he was looking up to the throne of God, "First of all, tell me what it is you must know. Maybe I can help."

"I have to find..." Sulien hesitated over the name, "I have to find Tancred, before he is ready, before he comes for us."

"Surely there is a less perilous way than this."

"You think I haven't tried?" The witch began to pace, gesturing with restless movements, his face gone sharp with frustration. Dust eddied through the shafts of sun as he paced from dark to light and back again.

"I've tried all summer. It should be easy. I've got the boy's brooch for a link, as if I wasn't link enough myself! Damn it, I shouldn't even need magic! I know him so well I should feel his presence on the web of the world like a fly feels a spider. But I can't!"

His pacing became swifter, the gestures angrier.

Chapter 19

Gunnar fidgeted in his concealment, and Oswy held him down by the skirts of his tunic.

"Stay still!" he whispered, "He hasn't sworn not to hit you."

"I don't care!"

"You're an idiot!"

"And you're just a baby. What do you know?!"

"I must find him," Sulien muttered to himself, brown eyes sullen as ashes in his gaunt face, "I must."

"To do what, child?" Father Paul asked as he looked down. The younger man was suddenly still, staring at him astonished.

"Kill him, of course," he said simply.

In the silence the priest's sigh sounded loud as he briefly lowered his head into his hands.

"Oh, my son," he said, "what an education you've had! Don't you know vengeance is forbidden?" He looked about for his stick, leaned out to get it as if its very touch could bring him support.

"Vengeance is a terrible thing," he said firmly. "It binds you together with the object of your hatred in a bond almost as strong as love. While that exists between you you will never be free, you will never be able to put the offence behind you and begin to heal. Please, child, let it alone. It will only do you harm."

Sulien swayed back against the wall, resting briefly against the cool stone, letting the flood of light wash over him. He closed his eyes.

"I don't want vengeance," he said wearily, admitting it as if it was something shameful. "Can't you understand? I've had two years in which I could have hunted him down, if I had wanted to. But I didn't. Because all I want," he laughed again, a bitter, contemptuous sound, "all I want is to be left alone."

Wisely, Father Paul said nothing, and sat quietly, his hands laid over the stick like a benediction. A moment passed, and then another, while the silver dust circled in the sun like dancing angels, and the warm beeswax candles filled the open room with the scent of honey. Then Sulien braced his shoulders, levered himself from the wall, paced back, reluctantly, to the edge of the magic circle.

"If Tancred comes back," he said calmly, "He will kill you, and everyone in this manor, one by one. And he will make the boy and I like himself, passing the evil on from generation to generation. Do you want that?"

"I don't," Father Paul sighed again, sitting huddled in his pool of light. "No, I don't want it. But neither do I want you imperiling your soul by dealing with the old gods. If they're not Dark Ones themselves, then I don't know what they are."

"I have no choice," Sulien repeated, coming to stand over the old man, his arms folded, his face bland as if he was considering where to place the first kick. Paul was very still, but his eyes fell and he studied the patterns of the stone floor with studious interest.

"If he has become, somehow," the witch explained levelly, "strong enough to turn away my sight, then I must ask someone from whom it should not be possible to hide; a god, a fiend, or a dead man. I thought of them all this would be the most innocent."

Gunnar hissed again, a sound of satisfaction and self-importance. Then he began to prize open Oswy's fingers, bending them back painfully. Oswy released him in sudden anger.

"I was trying to help you," he whispered. "Go and get beaten then. I don't care!"

The priest drew up his knees, linked his thin arms around them, resting his chin on his bony limbs. There was something reassuring about his ugliness, like a gargoyle, a creature made to frighten away evil with its very gaze.

He frowned. "Have you even tried prayer?" he asked sternly.

"Why would God listen to me?"

"My lord!" Gunnar rose into the light like a leaping flame and stumbled over the trestles in his eagerness to be of use. Sulien's face darkened with anger at the sight of him. He strode onto the dais, grabbed the lad by his bright hair, dragged him off-balance down the steps, throwing him onto the floor almost casually.

"Don't you have work to do, that you should be spying on me?"

Gunnar scrabbled to his knees, his eyes tightly closed in fear of a blow. "I know a ghost!" he cried, "A ghost. I know her name. Everything!"

There was a silence, and then, very gently, Sulien reached down and helped Gunnar to his feet.

Chapter 19

"Tell me," he said, rapt with new hope. Father Paul opened his mouth to protest and then shut it again into a line like drawn wire. He fumbled for his prayer-beads, fingered them determinedly, but said nothing.

Gunnar, turning, gave Oswy an "I told you so!" smile before launching into zealous explanation. "She's my kin - the one the ring was given to, the founder of my family. Her name is Raegn, and her haudh is about a day's journey from here. I can take you there."

"Her haudh? She was a pagan then?"

"Yes, my lord."

Sulien returned to Paul, his movements vehement with sudden energy. "I don't have to summon her, I don't have to do anything except bind her to tell the truth," he smiled, an eager, predatory smile, "And when I've asked my questions you," he moved closer, "can do your priestly duty and lay the poor spirit to rest. Well?"

"I will do it," Paul replied grudgingly, sighing again, "And God forgive me if I am encouraging you in any way to sin."

Sulien whirled on his heel, raked the shadows with his gaze, stopped at Oswy crouching movelessly in the deep shade. Oswy felt the shock of the glance and wondered uneasily if the witch could see in the dark like a cat. Reluctantly he straightened into the light.

"You will want to see this," his master said evenly. "Be ready to leave at dawn tomorrow."

An evening breeze sighed through the treetops and hissed towards them through the stems of dusky wheat. But for the wind, and the mutter of water over the stony ford behind them, there was no sound. Even though the last wash of light lingered in the sky, and the pale moon was floating like a feather over the fields, the village of Knut's ford lay already shuttered and dark. No one stirred there as the horses went by, picking their way across the ploughed land and up to the wooded mound.

"My master and I are outcasts," thought Oswy, uneasily. "Folk lock their doors against us." All his witch-lore seemed briefly nothing more than an outlaw's brand. He looked up and saw the mound again, looming greyly over the cultivated fields like a great wave poised to crash down on them. It felt suddenly cold in the clear summer night.

Ahead of him Father Paul's mule stopped in its tracks, putting its head down stubbornly. The priest began to urge it on in a soft voice edged with impatience.

"Let it alone," said Sulien quietly, "It feels the haunt. It won't come further." His own horse was skittering nervously beneath him, the whites of its eyes showing as a silver gleam in the twilight. "We'll leave them here," he said, dismounting lightly, "Gunnar will stay with them."

Gunnar looked so disappointed at this that Oswy lingered to explain; "It's for your sake he orders it." He frowned, trying to remember the reference, picturing the nun's tiny handwriting in the margins of one of Sulien's books. "Wulfwaru of Sceaftesige," he quoted importantly, "says a ghost may take over the mind of close kin at need. Especially to avoid being banished. You could endanger us all."

"I wanted to say goodbye to her, that's all." The older lad busied himself with the pony's reins to avoid Oswy's eyes, but his voice sounded tearful.

"I'll say it for you." Oswy said brusquely, and turned to race after the others. He was ashamed to discover that he too found Gunnar's vulnerability simply annoying.

The little spark of irritation guttered like a candle and died as he came under the shadow of the trees. The night was darker there, and the hissing of the wind was like many voices.

A fosse was delved all about the smooth swell of the huge mound, and at its bottom the shade lay like midnight. Something black fluttered on its lip. Oswy's heart lurched, and his feet seemed to take flight of their own accord, bringing him close within the circle of his master's power - the aura of which gleamed in his eyes like sunset and fire against the dark.

"Look." Sulien's voice was full of wary interest as he came closer to the swirl of black, "They have left her gifts."

A seed of witch-light showed a lashed frame, brought reeling shadows to life beneath the tattered ribbons flapping there. The carcasses of small birds swung forlornly from their broken necks among garlands of withered flowers. Rotten food soiled the grass. A string of human teeth rattled against the twisted wood, glistening in the night.

"Benel forgive them!" Paul hissed, catching sight of it, but Sulien reached out and touched it curiously. It lay over his fingers like prayer-beads.

"Milk teeth," he said dismissively.

Chapter 19

At the northernmost point of the haudh they found a causeway, weed-grown and disheveled, which stretched across the deep fosse, running up onto the lightless slopes of the hill and the dark places beneath the trees. On either side of it stood a pale stone, glimmering like frost. Dragons were carved there, and runes worn now beyond meaning.

"A hero's barrow," said Sulien with interest, and went in confidently under the shivering arches of branches. But when Oswy followed dread began to settle on him as soundlessly as snow.

At first, going into the inky blackness of the trees, he called up his own witch-light and set it to float in the air above his head. But it waned and wavered with his sinking courage, and its livid light called up bruise-colored shadows which swept over him like ghostly wings. When he let the light die - frightened of the whirling shapes - the darkness seemed heavier than before. He took hold of his master's belt and stumbled behind him, afraid to close his eyes, but more afraid to see.

From the top of the mound the trees drew back, leaving it bare as a monk's crown. The darkness eased a little: Stars were coming out like sharp spear-points in the twilight sky.

On the east side of the hill's crest they sat and awaited the coming of the ghost; Sulien and Oswy together within a circle marked out with salt; Father Paul, pointedly, outside it, trusting in prayer for his protection.

The night deepened. The wind blew cold and murmured in all the hollow spaces of the wood. Dread grew in Oswy's heart, weighing him down like a cloak of lead. His back prickled with fear, but when he turned at last to look behind him he saw only the trees, leaning down over him like inquisitors.

Hoping to distract himself he gazed up at the constellations, preparing to find them, recite their names and their influences.

His heart sank, and then stopped with terror. "The stars!" he gasped. They shone bleakly, ash-gray, in strange dim groupings utterly unlike the firmament of this world. "The stars!"

He felt Sulien stir beside him, and at that moment wisps of cold fire began to rise from the slopes of the mound and twist in hissing serpents across the grass. The stars went out. It became utterly black. A chill breath touched their faces, and there was a whispering around them in the darkness. The ribbons of corpse-fire writhed, but lit nothing.

How long he sat in the darkness with terror pressing him into the ground, Oswy did not know. Very slowly a comfortless light returned. He became aware of faint shapes; the half-dissolved spirits came flocking around the circle of salt. They were formless as breath on a frosty night - every shape, and none - but here and there a ruined face looked out at them, or a mist-like hand stretched out to touch. Their stifled voices ached with hunger.

The drone of Father Paul's prayers increased in pitch.

"Ghosts!" Oswy scrambled to his feet, his breathing so ragged he felt faint with it. He staggered, and the creatures pressed in around the circle, like sharks to spilled blood.

"A hero indeed," Sulien observed and reaching up one steady hand pulled Oswy down to safety beside him. "These are her servants, whom she will have had killed at the funeral and buried around her. Fine company for so many years."

"What do we do?!"

"Wait."

All of a sudden the corpse-fire leaped and roared, blazing into a blue inferno against the dark sky. The hill was swept with fleeting shadows and lights. When they died the ghost was there; a tall woman with cobweb-pale hair who lifted her hollow eyes to Sulien and said; "It has been a long time, Sulien FitzGuimar, since I have drunk a child's blood. Send him out to me, and I will answer your question."

Oswy opened his mouth, but could not speak. Even within the protecting circle he could feel the cold of her drawing at him, leaching all the warmth from his soul.

"Is that what you truly want, Raegn Aldrethsdotar?" the witch asked mildly, and as Father Paul lurched unsteadily to his feet he motioned him to silence.

"Surely, Lord of Harrowden," the ghost's smile opened onto darkness, "you know how much the dead thirst for the living."

She drifted towards them, weightless, graceful, and passing by Father Paul as though he was invisible, she stopped at the very edge of the circle. The wraiths of her servants mewled with disappointment and fled away.

"Do you not also desire release?"

"Release!" she threw back her head as if to laugh, but no sound came out, only dust, "You cannot give me release!" she cried, "The bond holding me here is stronger than your magic."

"What holds you?"

Chapter 19

"You will give me the child! Swear it!"

"I do not swear it." Sulien stood, paced to the edge of the circle. Their faces came close, flesh and spirit, one inside and one outside of the invisible barrier.

"I will give you release," he said gently. "Or I will feed you from my veins. This I swear. What holds you?"

With her blank eyes closed she looked almost human; a fair woman in men's clothes, with a sword on her hip. Then she moved, like a wisp of smoke, and the illusion dissolved.

"I made an oath," she said softly. "An oath of vengeance. Three days I was dying, a spear through my stomach, betrayed by one of my own men. He took my enemy's coin - my shield companion, who owed me his life many times over! I swore, on every god in the nine worlds, that I would see his whole race perish from the earth, before I went to rest."

Sulien's snort of distaste brought no reaction from the ghost, her voice mumbled on, dreary as sin.

"The hatred was strong in those days, salty, warm. I held on to it, even after I died, even as my body decayed. The worms in it ate, and bred and ate again, and still I nursed my hate."

Oswy choked back a noise of disgust. The voice droned on.

"I think, for a time, I was quite mad. I remember thirst, and despair, and my kinsmen bringing me bowls of fresh blood, and asking me questions. Just like you. But now there is nothing left. Only bones; bones and dust in the darkness... and cold..." The moaning drifted away into silence, lifted again briefly, "If I could unsay the oath I would. His kindred are slaves now, serfs, just like my own. Men and women who mean nothing to me. They are not worth my hatred."

There was no sign of either condemnation or sympathy on Sulien's gaunt face, only an overmastering eagerness. He spoke rapidly, urgently, with his grazed hands clenched.

"If you swore by the pagan gods then your oath may be released - by the authority of the One True God. This exile of yours may be ended now. Just answer my question."

She laughed again - dim balls of storm-gray light came scattering from her mouth and drifted aimlessly out into the night. "Like all the others!" she said scornfully, "You could let me go freely, but you don't. Remember, Lord of

Harrowden, this act of selfishness may be held against you, when you are in my place."

"Do you want release or not?" he answered her irritably, and she shrugged.

"Very well. Ask me your question and I will answer."

"I bind you to tell me the truth," Sulien declaimed formally, and swayed on his feet as though only pride prevented him from bowing down to the ground in weariness and relief. It occurred to Oswy to wonder how much of his master's power was being drawn on to keep them both safe. Once he had begun to wonder he could not stop thinking of it.

"Where is Tancred of Harrowden?" Sulien asked at a rush, "Where is he hiding?"

The spirit wavered, her long pale hair floating out behind her like steam.

"Tell me!" Sulien demanded, gone from relief to anger in a breath. He strode forward as if to shake it from her, but balked at the line of salt, flinging up his hands in fury. "Tell me!"

"I don't know." Her smile was a cavern of malice, "I answer you honestly. I cannot see Tancred of Harrowden anywhere on earth."

"Is he dead?" eagerness and frustration made Sulien's light voice sharp as a sword. The ghost smiled again, thoroughly amused.

"Now, that's a second question," she said, "We didn't bargain on two."

"For God's sake, Raegn!" the witch burst out suddenly, "The pit of Hell is gaping beneath you. Do this for me out of charity, while you still can!"

If she had had breath in her she might have sighed. As it was she only closed her blank eyes again and drifted a little further away. A tiny thread of warmth came back to Oswy's icy skin.

"After all," she whispered, "what good would it do to drag you into despair after me? He is not dead, but I cannot see him. I'm sorry."

The moon - the dappled, imperfect moon of the real world - began to show above the trees. The ghost faded to little more than a smudge of icy vapor in its whey-pale light. There was a muffled ringing as Father Paul picked the hand-bell from his bag and set it down in front of him with ritual precision.

Chapter 19

"Priest," Sulien's voice was weighed down with dismay, although his face was utterly still. "Send her to rest," he said, "And if you could then do the same for me, I would be very glad."

Oswy stood, a dutiful page, with his back to the tapestry of the white unicorn, and strove to look unafraid. In the high windows of the hall the evening sky showed dark gold and indigo, but shadows had flocked into the corners of the great bare room as if to echo the darkness he felt descending on them all.

He wondered how much more grief it would take before his heart would break; how many more cycles of pointless violence and despair he would have to witness and avoid. Day and night he longed to run away, to get clean away, to start afresh. But he knew now how easy he would be to catch, and he had done too much running in the past to try it again.

He watched the candle-light flash, darken, and flash again from Sulien's moving hands, and it seemed hard to him that he should have to be the calm one. He had begun to realize he was the stronger of the two of them; not in power, but in sheer human resilience. He felt oppressed by the thought, and by the feeling that he should do something to bring his master out of this mood: he did not know what to do, and besides, he was afraid to go near the man.

"Everything is ready," Dame Edith hobbled into the hall, breaking the dense silence briskly. Her steps were more unsteady and her face more sunken than they had been in the summer, but competence still swathed her like a mantle and her silver-gray eyes were sharp.

She looked at Sulien, who sat, head bowed, at the top of the table turning his knife over and over in his hands. He did not return the glance.

"I can leave tomorrow," she continued. "But I would as lief die here as live in my son-in-law's house. To Gervase Croix-de-Noir I am only an embarrassment. Here I am needed."

Leofwine, sitting warily at his lord's right hand, pushed back his unruly hair and tried, seemingly with the same gesture, to wipe away his permanent frown of concern. The smile of pride and admiration which he lifted to the old woman's gaze was briefly the brightest thing in the whole room.

"You are not needed," still Sulien did not raise his eyes, his voice was dull and heavy. "Go away."

Edith raised one quizzical eyebrow at this, and looked at her son as if to say "He's worse." Leofwine shrugged apologetically.

"Best to go, mother," he said quietly, "Ailith will be glad to see you, and you haven't seen your new grandson yet."

"Huh!" the old lady snorted with disgust, "Stuck away in the women's quarters - caged up like an animal - with nothing to talk about except embroidery and babies. Ailith making me speak Holmsh all the time." She caught Leofwine's warning glance and sighed, seeming suddenly frailer than ever.

"I'll go and tell Gytha and Brand then," she said, "I'm taking them with me for servants." She hobbled to the doorway, turned back almost timidly. Her words were practical, but her tone was one of hopeless farewell. "You will remember to eat, won't you?" she said, "Even if you have to make it yourself?"

"I will." Leofwine rose as if to say something more, but he had to struggle with the words, and the old lady had gone out and shut the door behind her before he could bring himself to speak.

The repetitive slap of the knife handle against Sulien's palm halted, like a heart stopping. Without raising his head more than a finger's breadth he peered up sullenly at his knight through the fringe of his uncombed hair.

"You're leaving too," he said, and drew his gaze back to linger upon the star of light which hung on the very point of the blade. He poised the needle-tip of it over his open fingers.

"No!" The light from the long fire burnished Leofwine's outraged form, turning his dark hair bronze, calling an answering fire from the gold stitchwork on his cuffs. To Oswy he seemed the only thing in the cavernous room on which the color rested - from everything else it slithered away, leaving darkness.

"No!" Leofwine cried, "I swore to defend you! My place is here!"

"Your place is to do what I say." Sulien bent his head further, so his face was entirely hidden in shadow. "I don't want you here."

The silence became a deadly thing, full of reproach, then Leofwine took one stiff, affronted pace forward. "You shame me," he said quietly. "Sending me away like a woman. I thought I deserved better of you."

Sulien said nothing, only watched from beneath his dull hair while, unconsciously, Leofwine rubbed the aching bones of his half-healed fingers.

Chapter 19

The knight looked down, caught the gesture, clenched the painful hand angrily, but said no more, waiting for some kind of answer. Silence became a presence, like a black beast crouching over them all.

Oswy, still watching hopelessly, felt torn in two. He dared not think of what life would be like in the keep without Leofwine's calming presence, yet he wanted no more than his master for his friend to be tortured a second time. He knew, from the aftertaste Tancred had left on his mind, that the second time would be infinitely worse.

Sulien took up his knife again, and pushing back his sleeve began calmly, methodically, to cut the flesh of his arm into bleeding ribbons. His expression; blank, almost peaceful, did not change even when the blade sawed across bone.

Leofwine strode forward, grasped his knife-hand, forcing the knife away, thrusting it deep into the wood of the table. It juddered there, and a thin metallic whine came from it.

"Who taught you to do this to yourself!" he exclaimed, rhetorically, "Think! How happy he would be to see you now. You're turning back into his boy right in front of my eyes!"

"The pain helps me think," Sulien muttered, and Leofwine took in a deep breath of anger.

"Don't talk like a fool!"

A ghost of the man Oswy had come to care about, the man who had taught him how to fly, warmed the vacant brown eyes for a moment. The mouth twisted, a little, into the echo of a rueful smile. "Very well," he admitted, "the truth is it helps me not to think."

He shook the restraining hand off, and calmness came back down over his face like a mask, "Nevertheless, you will leave."

Leofwine pushed him in the chest, forcing him backwards, forcing him to look up and meet his eyes.

"Don't make me say this," he begged.

"Go away," Sulien repeated sullenly.

"If I leave," Leofwine sighed, a shuddering, exasperated sound, "how long will it be before you begin to see things, because you cannot sleep? How long before you go mad, as you were when I found you?" He paused meaningfully, went on, without mercy, "How long before you kill the boy, to 'save' him from your master?"

He caught the brief flicker of admission, stepped back hissing with shock. "I hoped I was wrong!"

He began to rub his hands again, as if washing them, striding back and forth in front of the fire. Oswy, invisible in the deepening darkness by the wall, watched him numbly while his heart seemed to freeze inside him. Then he slid to his knees, sick with an old fear.

It's not fair, his mind kept telling God. *It's not fair! Why are you doing this to me?* And he could think of nothing else; there was nothing to do, nothing he could say, nowhere he could go to make it better. He was not even wholly sure he did not want to die.

A late summer breeze whistled in the high windows of the hall, blowing the smoke back in fire-stained billows into the room. The reek began to drift out into the corridors and up the stairs, twisting like wraiths. Among the roof-beams a sparrow cheeped forlornly, but over it all the silence grew. A silence not of peace, nor even any longer a silence of despair - there was too much anger in it for either.

"I won't leave," Leofwine burst out at last, "I'll stay despite you."

"You defy me?!" suddenly Sulien was on his feet, his eyes blazing, face gone pale and cold with fury. He wrenched at the deeply embedded knife.

"No!" Leofwine quietened instantly, "Just listen to me..." but it was too late.

"Stinking traitor!" the witch kicked at the table. The knife came free. He poised it and threw in the same gesture. "I thought I could trust you! Bastard turncoat traitor! Just get out of my house! Go away!"

Leofwine side-stepped. The knife grazed his arm, struck the door and stuck there singing. He backed away, gone grim, silent, while Sulien stalked him like a man-eating lion.

"I want to kill someone," Sulien tore a bar of iron out of the fire-pit. It hissed in his hand, and the further end of it was red.

Leofwine fumbled behind him for the door-latch, never taking his eyes from his friend's face.

"That would really take my mind off things," Sulien raised the bar - it gave off a thin acrid smoke. "Shall it be you?" he said, and swung.

The door caught the blow in a long charred gouge. Leofwine had opened it and dived through quicker than seemed possible for a man of his size.

Chapter 19

The oak slammed on his retreating heels. Splinters flew as Sulien hammered it again, a two-handed blow which made it rattle on its hinges.

"And stay away!" he yelled, "Just stay away!"

In the distance the sound of footsteps grew fainter and faded away. Silence returned. Sulien's fury turned slowly to puzzlement. He looked down at his hand; dropped the iron bar as if only now had he realized it was burning him - it clanged on the stone floor like a broken bell. Then slowly, like a man with a mortal wound, he drifted back to his own seat, lowering himself down gently, and without a word.

They had been left alone; Oswy and Sulien, alone in the great empty space of the hall. Silence settled over them like a cloud of carrion wings. The knife blade still shuddered in the scarred door, a shivering point of light among the descending shadows.

Oswy's breaking heart ached within him, and there came over him a sense of fatalism and doom. He wanted to weep, but his eyes were dry.

Then Sulien put his head down on the rough board of the table, and covered it over with his bloody arms.

"Oh God!" the whisper came threading out hoarsely into the night, "Oh God, help me!"

Chapter Twenty

"How can you leave?" Gennan had asked, sounding more astonished than sad, "Don't you love me?"

The hurtful little question returned to Adela endlessly as she stumbled through the bracken and branches. With it the pain, the anger and the fear all stabbed her again - Why couldn't he understand she was doing this for him? Couldn't he see she didn't want to go? Didn't it make any difference to him?

Her mind was weary with the thoughts, turning them over and over again while her body picked its way through the shadowy paths under the trees, and dew-wet leaves brushed against her outstretched fingers.

The gleaming shape of Torch ahead of her drew away, until she could catch only fitful glimpses of him through the sable pillars of the wood, but still she could not stop the roil of distraction, the storm of distress which made her slow and falter.

"We need you," Gennan had said, with the honesty which was so alien about him. "What if another of us wishes to make Niniel's choice? Who will sing for them? I could not get those words out of my mouth, they would burn me up. How can you think of going now?"

She remembered the lupine topaz eyes - suspicious, as though he felt he was being betrayed - and again she wanted to shout at him "Why can't you understand!"

"I don't want to leave!" she had finally answered him, choking it out through her tears, "I belong here. God put me here. I know! I don't want to go! I have to go! But I'll come back!"

"You will not come back," he had dismissed her coldly. "You humans never do."

Other griefs echoed her sense of loss, as if they had been awoken from their restless sleep by the touch of this recent sorrow. A picture of Drago recurred to her - silenced, diminished by fear, facing his damnation in the parchment littered chaos of his chamber. She remembered Guy, shuddering under the touch of the spell - his closed face, as he struggled against shame and defilement.

Chapter 20

She thought of Godgifu, who had fed Adam a lie, and must surely have died for it. And she saw again the white-faced nun as she sent her away from the room where they prepared her brother's body for burial. What was it they had not let her see? She could not stop herself from wondering.

She halted. It was utterly dark around her, and utterly still.

"When will I wake from this nightmare, God?" she pleaded silently, "When?"

Nothing happened, except anger. It kindled in her, bright as a star, and fire burned up the grief and the fear together. All this evil and pain was Adam's doing. It came to her like a revelation: As long as she continued to run from him he would follow, bringing the ruin with him. It had to be stopped.

She had no idea how she was going to do it, but she vowed now she would stop him. And when she had done it she would go back and carry on the work she had begun. With God's help, she would do it.

A wind arose, soughing like a sea through the branches. Tattered clouds streamed away from the moon and all at once the cold droplets were crystal-edged as they spattered from the leaves onto her face and hands.

"Torch!" she shouted out, and his voice drifted back to her in snatches, like the dappled moonlight. Following it she came down into a hollow place bordered by yew trees, plump berries black as death in the night. The elf was there, outlined in gold, a mist of light around his feet. The colors of the trees stood out with strange intensity in his radiance.

He lifted to her the courteous smile which she thought of as his mask.

"Don't be angry with me," she began gently, "I know you explained it all to the Lord Icewolf..."

She vaguely recalled them talking over her bowed head, making plans for her safety; Gennan talking calmly, dispassionately, so she had no idea whether in the end he had felt any sort of emotion at all.

"But," she went on, "I could not listen for sorrow. Please, Torch, tell me about this woman you're taking me to."

He began to pick the berries, throwing them onto the bag he was carrying for her, arranging them in graceful spiral patterns. They blushed from gray to glossy red as his fingers touched them, faded again as he tossed them away. The poisonous slime of them trailed from his hands in long strings of saffron. His perfect face was as expressionless as Gennan's had been.

"Torch?" Adela asked, shocked out of her preoccupation by his continued silence. She had not even considered his loss. "Are you still grieving for your mother?" she asked softly, and tentatively, "Do you blame me for it?"

The leaping blaze of his true smile answered her more fully than his words; "She has what she wanted," he said, "I have no right to be sad. No. I was remembering my Seagull; how she was when I first saw her."

"Seagull?" Adela sat, thankfully, on a fallen log among pale domes and sails of fungus. There was a black scurrying by her feet, and she drew them up hurriedly, brushing the earwigs and the armored lice from her skirts.

Because she was going to a Sceafn household, and a fellow woman, she had decided to abandon her disguise and wear a borrowed dress, and an approximation of the Sceafn wimple. The wimple irritated her almost more than a grima, and though it covered all her hair and her neck she still felt more exposed than she had in her boy's clothes. She was thankful that Torch had promised to avoid all humans, except the one they sought.

"What kind of a name is Seagull?!" she asked.

"I gave it to her," he made that tentative shrug of his, and she wondered how many hundreds of years he had been practicing the gesture.

"It suits her temper," he said, the untamed smile flashing again across his face as he swung up with agile ease to sit among the needles of the yews. "She is a noblewoman, a woman with power, and best of all her mother is a witch, and strong in runemal. She should know better than many how to deal with this hunter of yours."

The breeze stroked over the leaves once more and departed, leaving the peace of the night stitched with the sound of droplets falling. Close by, a dark shape heaved its way through the undergrowth. It turned its head - a skeletal outline of white stripes gleamed briefly - and then it was gone. The scents of leaf-mould and cold water lifted into the darkness.

"Another witch?" Adela pondered, "I'm not sure. I had thought of going to the church."

But even as she spoke she realized no church would dare aid her against the will of the new king, not while the quality of his mercy was so unknown. And from Adam's possession of Langley it seemed the king's will was, as she had been warned, in Adam's keeping.

"It would be a start, I suppose," she conceded reluctantly, "Where does she live?"

Chapter 20

Torch laughed merrily, the sound like a shaft of light in the dark place. "How should I know?" he said.

Adela frowned back at him with a certain sharpness, "Do you know her real name?"

"No."

She got to her feet irritably. "Then exactly how do you propose finding her?"

He leaped down from his branch, light and sure-footed as a pine-martin; the gray wood-lice rolled themselves into little shiny spheres at his feet.

"I marked her," he said, and his eyes gleamed like green fire in pleasure at his cleverness, "She owes me a life-debt. But humans are well known for wriggling out of their debts. So with stone and silver I marked her. I hear the mark calling even now."

Adela sighed, brushing aside curiosity, concentrating on the practical; "Is it far?"

"No," he turned his back on her, began to walk. The words drifted over his shoulders; "We should be there by daybreak."

In the bitter hour before dawn they passed, warily, through a sleeping village.

"Not here," Torch whispered, standing for a moment by the well, head lifted as if he scented his quarry over the dung and smoke-drenched air, "But close."

Adela was weary now, and the little town seemed like a bad omen to her; quiet, disheveled. Many of the houses stood empty, falling in on themselves amongst a drizzle of mud and the smell of rotting hay. Their gardens were rank with weeds, and the fields she had trodden were unfruitful, lying fallow under the pale moon.

This Seagull of his doesn't know how to manage a manor, she thought, uncharitably, and then details began to rebuke her: New thatch on the occupied houses, new daub on their walls, so they slept as snug as cats by the fire. The treadmill of the well, too, was so new she could still smell the sap in the split logs.

A local uprising, maybe, she thought, *Put down harshly. Probably as much as a couple of years ago, for there to have been so much recovery since.*

She began to regret her ignorance of this part of her family's holding. But at first she had not been able to speak to her father about it because the grief of her mother's loss was too fresh, and then it had become a habit, a subject which was not discussed, and which neither of them had had the courage to raise again. She wondered briefly, if she had turned up on their doorstep unannounced, whether any of the servants would have recognized her.

A mongrel dog, nose down on the dusty earthen path, padded from the alley between two houses, flung up its head to bark hoarsely. Adela started. Rotten teeth glinted in a gray snarl, and the mangy fur on the beast's back stood up like a boar's bristle.

She held her ground. Other dogs had begun to answer with a clamor of howling. A baby cried, playing on the tension like a bard. Voices broke out, bemused, frightened and angry.

"Come!" Torch seized Adela's wrist, walked forward singing one note under his breath at the growling cur. It shook itself and fell silent suddenly. Then it yawned - a noisome gape of blackened teeth - and fell asleep at his feet. They ran past it, out into the vacant fields, just as the first door was opened and the first villager came, scythe in hand, into the night.

"They could have helped us!" Adela gasped as she loped along at Torch's side.

"Helped you maybe," the elf's melodious voice carried bitterness and a strange merriment as he answered. "Me they would help to an iron cage and a "See the ancient legend, only a farthing a look." No. That's not the fate I intend. I want to see my Seagull again."

Dawn came - a streak of pearl over the high peaks. They had climbed out of farmland and into forest. Now they stood among the silver birches on the edge of the barren hills and peered out at the world of men like wild children, raised by wolves.

Beyond the woods the moor-land swept up to the tensed shoulders of the hill. A keep loomed there, heavy, black and threatening against the delicate sky.

Something in its position; here on the very tips of the Fells, looking down on all humankind like a malevolent giant, reminded Adela of a story she had heard as a little girl. A ghost story, she thought, or some other matter of horror; something the adults fell silent about, as soon as she came into the room.

Chapter 20

"Here?" she said, "I don't like the look of it. "

But just then a limb of the sun lifted itself over the further hills and the whitewashed stones of the castle blushed first rose and then gilt, mirroring the morning in a great flame of gold. A stain of color flowed across the world, leaving it bright as a reliquary casket; bronze and beryl and silver.

Adela rubbed her tired eyes against the sting of so much glory and smiled.

"Look!" Torch's voice sounded almost eager, "That's her! The mark calls to me."

In the shadow of the blazing walls night still lingered, only the illuminated margins of the darkness showed tended plants and the polished brass heads of wheat. A figure moved there, hooded and cloaked in protection against the humors of the dawn, anonymous and sexless as a cloister-nun.

"What's she doing out here at this hour?" Adela was shocked, the more so as a breeze lifted the hem of the cloak and two brown bare ankles showed themselves to the world. "I hope this woman of yours is no wanton."

"You must take what help you can get," Torch replied, and began to lace his fingers together and apart nervously. "Let us go and speak to her."

The figure, unaware of them, had knelt down now on the dusty soil.

"Praying?" thought Adela. But no. It was digging.

They came up behind it, running across the open moor and into the deep shade of the keep like Mearh raiders, running beaten for their ship.

At the sound of Adela's footfalls it turned, leaping up, fumbling for something under the cloak. Then it saw her, and stiffened with surprise.

"Lady!" The hood came off with a clumsy flourish and a young man emerged, bowing uncouthly while his vivid red hair whipped this way and that across a bruised face.

"No!" The word screamed from Torch in a banshee's wail. Adela's bag fell from his hand. There was a roaring and a brightness - a devouring fire let loose. It knocked the youth flying, his breath coming out of him in a painful gulp. He crashed into the baked ground, opening up new furrows with his shoulders, lay like a beached fish, open mouthed, gasping. And Torch was there, kneeling on his chest, one hand pressing a long knife to his throat, while the other held, throttling-tight, a length of thong he wore as a necklace.

"Where is she?" The elf's voice was poison-sweet. He opened his hand and showed, glimmering on the end of the greasy leather thong, a ring of soft silver with a stone like a tear. "She who wore this. Where is she?"

The young man's face went slack with awe, the round eyes, a foxy yellow, gazed up at Torch with abject innocence. For long heartbeats he seemed not even to breathe. Then, gathering up his jaw with an effort, he whispered "Holy Shevaiel! I'm sorry! Tell me what I've done. I'll make it right. I promise."

Adela's heart went out to him, remembering her own shocked reaction to Torch's appearance. She knelt down by the youth's side reassuringly. "He's not an angel," she explained, "but an elf. And if you answer me honesty I won't let him harm you. Tell me; where did you get this ring?"

Torch looked down on her with a closed expression which told her he was not pleased with such restraints, but the young man began to breathe again.

"It's always been mine," he said trustingly, "And my mother's before me - every eldest child in our family, right back to..." And his jaw dropped again, his mouth and eyes rounding once more in a silent 'Oh!' of understanding.

Torch wrenched out a lock of his captive's brilliant copper hair. The lad winced, yelping like a puppy.

"Tell me, little Ember." Torch laid the strands over the exposed throat, considered the color, "Tell me the riddle's answer. I gave the ring to a woman. How does it come to be around your neck?"

"Lord," the newly named Ember drew in a shaky breath and tried to explain, "A man of the elves gave this ring to my foremother, yes." He swallowed, braced his dusty shoulders, began again, "But it was over five hundred years ago. She's dead, lord. Long dead."

Torch went still. Darkness moved beneath his golden skin, like a wasp-maggot, eating a living caterpillar from within.

"Cheat!" he exclaimed, at last, "How dare she die?! She owes me! How could she? I marked her!" His form wavered with anger. The hands at Ember's throat grew long black claws.

"Assume the debt!" Adela reached out to the peasant lad, shook him urgently, desperately, "Say you'll pay it!"

"What's happening?!"

Chapter 20

Ice had begun to form beneath Torch's sharp talons, burning dead white patches on the young man's skin.

"Just say it!" Adela hissed, "If you value your soul. Now!"

Her panic spread, filling up Ember's sulfurous eyes in a trembling flood. "I swear it!" he gasped, "I'll do whatever it was you wanted. Whatever she owed you, I'll pay."

"You? Pitiful little creature?" Torch sneered. The darkness faded slightly. The smoke of cold curled away from his flesh and was gone. "What can you do?"

"Not much, it's true." The flush of modesty showed even through the coating of sunburn and freckles, the lad's yellow eyes were veiled for a moment. "But I have a powerful lord, and a good one. He can do anything."

Torch drifted to his feet like chaff blown on the breeze, hollow now the darkness was gone.

"I saved her life." He spoke, but his spirit seemed lifetimes away, remote as the stars. "I drew her from the deep water. Barely a summertime ago, it seems to me. I was so sure she would wait for me. I never imagined she would give my mark away, alive or dead."

The illusion of solid flesh which he wore dimmed quietly, until he seemed no more than an aftershock of the sun - a burst of light reflected from a window of glass. His voice had become very soft.

"Very well. You may pay her debt. I saved her life; you will save the life of Lady Starlight here."

The golden outline of his form became briefly sword sharp, blinding. "I will count the years," he said evenly, "And if she does not come back to me within three summers, telling me you have saved her from the hunter who stalks her, then I will have your life in payment. I care not. I will be cheated no longer."

And he faded - a glimmer, a whispered "Farewell," and the shadow was empty of him. The breeze blew dust out in elfish spirals into the sunlight, but no eddy showed where he trod. The dry soil was unstirred by any foot.

"Torch?" Adela looked about wildly, startled, "Torch?" She felt like a lost child, calling out "Where are you?", "Please!" she shouted, "I don't know how to get back!"

Witch's Boy

But there was no answer. Suddenly as he had come into her life he had gone, and she stood now on farmed land, with a human serf, as if none of it had ever happened.

"My life is with them now..." Adela whispered to herself, "But I don't know how to return. What am I to do?"

"Come speak to my Lord," the young man answered her thought, "he'll know. He knows everything," and, casting one last astonished look at the darkness into which Torch had vanished, he bowed again, offering her the path with a sweeping gesture of his calloused hand. His loyalty was so welcome to Adela's taste that it briefly lifted away her sense of loss. She smiled at him and walked where he showed, out of the shade, into the breeze and brightness of the new day.

The drawbridge echoed hollowly beneath their feet and the long dappled shapes of pikes came drifting out of its shade like malicious spirits. They walked from the cold of the massive walls into silence; a hush which seemed not of peace but of desertion. The bright sunshine shone on emptiness - rubble by the gate-tower, a dispirited horse in the shafts of a heavy cart, dust.

In all of the wide enclosure no human creature stirred. A hand of fear clenched itself around Adela's hear. Had Adam been here already, done his work, left this desolation to welcome her? She turned to Ember, expecting to see shock, distress, but he was smiling, as if this was all he had ever expected.

Trying to feel reassured she straightened her shoulders, walked braced and upright into the disconsolate arena.

Silently the great door of the keep swung open until the iron nails ground into the stone wall. The unexpected crash made Adela's breath come fast. She spun to face the threat, and an old woman came hobbling out into the light on the arm of what was obviously her son.

"Fool!" Adela chided herself, while her rapid-beating heart returned to normal. "You've begun to see danger everywhere, even where there is none. They must be recovering from a rebellion, just like the village. That's all."

Yet the man was mailed for battle, and both their faces were grim.

"Sir!" Even as Ember shouted out, the man had become aware of them - the clear gray eyes narrowed with concern. He strode out to meet them, a massive man, bearing the weight of the chain-mail lightly, but burdened, Adela thought, by some other heaviness. He seemed ill-at-ease with the very frown he wore.

Chapter 20

"Lady?" his voice was dark, soft, with a roughness to it he must have got from shouting on the battlefield. There was a pause, very decorous, very brief, while he looked her up and down, and smiled his admiration, then he bowed, asking earnestly, but gently, "What has happened? Where are your retinue? What may we do to aid you?"

Now the question had been asked she felt shaky with weariness, and sudden fear. This tale of hers - witches and elves and angels - seemed incredible, even to her. What if he did not believe it? What if he went to his lord saying "There's a madwoman outside, raving. Shall I tell her you're away hunting?"

"I have to see your lord," she said, and was annoyed by the tremor in her voice.

The shadow over him lightened a little. He smiled, a flash of boyish candor strange on his harsh face. "God sent you, maybe," he said. "Whatever your trouble, if it takes my lord's mind from his own distress it will be a blessing here." He offered her his shield arm, keeping the sword arm free. She reached out to take it, and recoiled at the sight of his malformed hand.

Patiently, looking down into her face without rancor, he waited for her recovery, saying nothing, perhaps simply pretending it had not happened. She was shamed by his courtesy.

"I'm sorry," she forced herself to lay her own slight hand over the twisted fingers, tried not to cause him any more pain by her revulsion. Yet the silence and the feeling of oppression had begun to wear at her nerves, and this deformity seemed, like the desolate village, one more omen to her, one more warning to get away.

You are being stupid, she told herself firmly, *there's no threat here. You're just tired.* And she suffered herself to be led into the darkness behind the keep doors.

A carved oak portal standing ajar showed the great hall dusty in the morning light: A glimmer of white behind the high seat, the dull embers of an untended fire, a paved floor swept curiously bare, and then they were past, climbing up the dimly lit stairs.

Someone breathed behind her - the old woman, laboring up the spiral on her heels. She was grateful for the propriety of it, but still the sense of being followed made her back prickle with tension. She pressed on, picking up the pace, and the presence withdrew a little.

On the second level they turned away from the stairwell, going past a series of small rooms with heavy doors. New nails gleamed from the first, hammered into the lintel and joists, wedging the door permanently shut. A line of dirt had blown out from beneath it, and rust smudged the floor under the hinges, as if after a long time standing open it had been violently slammed shut.

"What's in there?" she asked.

"Nothing," her companion replied, uncertainly.

The solar stood open, but the faded back of a tapestry - warhorses neighing as they trampled on dying men - screened the room from view. From the chapel opposite Benel watched, dying on his own sword, as the knight raised his good hand and knocked, hesitantly, at the open door.

Without waiting for a reply, he lifted aside the heavy folds of embroidery, motioned Adela inside, and stepped in behind her like a shadow.

The lord of the keep made no reaction at their entrance. He was standing with his back to them, gazing out of the high window with the bright sun pouring past him into the room.

Little details wove themselves into Adela's imagination - the deadly stillness of his poise; the sense that, even though he stared into the morning light, still he was watching her intently. She saw blood on his cuffs, and smelled the faint odor of it on the air. Memories of Adam came crowding around her at the scent. Dread came with them, nameless dread. What she feared, she could not say, but all of a sudden her heart failed, and she could hardly bear still to stand.

Then he turned; she saw him clearly.

Vision and reality collided - the picture of him, shaped out of flames at the king's banquet, conjured up out of a child's pain, flickered in her sight over his flesh-and-blood face.

"So that's your son?" Drago had said, icily, "He doesn't look much like you."

"No, but he takes after me in other ways," Adam had replied, gloating.

A bubble of shrill, hysterical mirth arose in her belly, she felt it shatter her ribs as it forced itself out of her mouth, and even she could not tell, as it ripped open her throat, whether she was laughing or screaming.

It was so typical it was almost funny! Death and flight and terror, parting and grief, all to bring her somewhere where she might find help.

Chapter 20

And here she was, trapped! An armored man blocked the door behind her, before her, stalking her slowly, his face waking out of blankness into increasing interest, the son of Adam de Limoges. It was so funny! She could not stop sobbing with laughter. All her striving and praying, all of it, had simply brought her straight into the hands of Adam's son!

Chapter Twenty One

He came closer, threat in every graceful movement. The laughter choked itself. Adela turned and ran for the door.

But his henchman was there, blocking it, a massive shape clothed in steel. She raised a desperate fist, swung to punch at his unprotected face. He caught her hand with nonchalant ease, pushing it down, grabbing at the other with his misshapen fingers. And then, somehow, faster than she had time to think, he had both her wrists locked together, holding her away from him, while she struggled to kick and to bite.

"This is not the effect I usually have on women." They spoke over her head, the cream-colored voice of the lord vaguely amused, the knight, even while he held her still, reproachful;

"Have some pity my lord, can't you see she's terrified."

He dragged her off her feet, forcing her onto a bench, saying something she was too wild with terror and anger to understand. Kneeling before her, both her hands still locked in his grip, he repeated it, softer, more intent. "Calm yourself, lady. You are quite safe here."

Over his bent dark head she could see the lord, at bay now, motionless, watching her with grim curiosity. Unmistakable, he was: gaunter than he had seemed in the vision, the long yellow hair darkened by neglect, yet it was the same man, no doubt about it.

Recognizing it as futile, she had stopped her peasant scuffling. She sat now very straight and still. "Liar!" Icily, she hissed it at the knight, "You know what he is. Adam's son! Quite safe?! You liar!"

Yet something nagged her about this witch's boy, just as it had when she had seen his face in the flames - a sense that, long ago, in another life perhaps, she might have known him. A memory struggled to surface, sank again, leaving an aftertaste of frustration to gild her fear.

"Adam?" the lord stalked closer. He moved like a predator, Adela noticed, but there were scars on his wrists, shadows under his eyes; he was not a man who slept easy at night. "I know of no one called Adam."

Chapter 21

"You needn't deny it," she treated him with the contempt he deserved, "He owned you - in front of the king and all his court - he made a picture of you; his son."

He came crouching down beside her, challenging her with sullen brown eyes. Despite capture and fear and indignity, she found herself reacting to his haunted beauty, and self-disgust quickened her anger. She spat in his face.

As he wiped it away his gaze promised long and brooding revenge, but he said only, coldly, "You are overwrought," and, speaking over her shoulder, "Edith!" he summoned the old woman.

"This behavior is very unbecoming, my dear." That lady came rustling up, whispering the words in Adela's ear, "And I am sure, before long, you will be ashamed of yourself."

Stung in the midst of her panic Adela glanced up at her, astonished, and felt for a moment as if she looked into the face of her old nurse. This dame too wore, with the Sceafn wimple, the dignity of partial victory after total defeat. Under Edith's calm regard some of her hysterical anger began to wear away.

"I don't understand," she exclaimed weakly. "You must know what Adam is like. How can you serve his son?"

He was turning back to his window, light and darkness cleaving his face so half was outlined in gold and half drowned deep in shadow. He was frowning, she thought, as at some old pain. When he spoke his quiet voice too was full of shades she could not quite comprehend, "I know no Adam," he said, simply. "My father was Guimar Lord of Shricleah. I swear it on what is left of my soul."

And, immediately, she knew him: The memory came over her like a wave breaking. She saw a tourney, the details blurred with distance and summer brightness; herself, a tiny girl clinging to her father's leg. They had all been named for her; the heir, Odo, a brown little thing, with an invalid's ruined temper; Guimar, handsome and happy; and the half-breed son - a quick, proud, valiant boy, a leader in all the lad's games, and a name which had just begun to feature, speculatively, in the giggling debates of the older girls: Sulien FitzGuimar, a hero and a scandal in one.

What had happened to them? She chased recollection, but it led into darkness. After that long summer, it seemed, no one had seen the boy or his father again, and their names had been buried in determined silence. Suddenly the wife had been a widow, the problem of the slaves-son had been solved, and nothing more had been said.

"Guimar's Sceafn bastard!" she exclaimed with triumph, "I remember you!" and then, hearing what she had said, she covered her mouth as if, belatedly, to hold the words in. She began to stammer out apologies for the unintended insult, but he was smiling - a flash of human warmth which brought his resemblance to that bright boy so close Adela wondered it had taken her so long to see it.

"Time was," he said, with rueful pleasure, "when being called that would be the worst thing to happen to me in a whole week." Then bluntly, "I don't remember you."

"I was very young," she smiled up at the knight, and returning the gesture warmly, he released her hands sketching her a bow as he straightened up, as if to welcome her back into her right mind. "And usually with the women. But," confusion surfaced again, its prodding harder now the fear had faded. "But I don't understand. It was your face Adam conjured up. His son, he said, it was definitely you."

"Conjured!" in two swift strides he was by her side his face all sharpened into eagerness, the intensity of his gaze frightening. "What do you mean? Conjured?"

He was reaching as if to shake the answer out of her. She shrank back, and immediately the burly knight stepped between them like a shield.

"I mean, conjured," she sought swiftly for the right words, but his urgency made the pause seem to stretch on forever. Instinct convinced her that here, somehow, her story had become the answer to some terrible mystery. The moment felt numinous, she hardly dared speak.

"He... he made a circle," the bald words seemed horribly inadequate, she stumbled on, "With the blood of one of the pages. He made your image in fire. I am fleeing from him, for my life. His name is Adam de Limoges; he is a witch."

The lord was as still and tense as a mantrap, his voice very quiet, but bowstring-taut. "Describe him."

"He must be nearly fifty," she began methodically, "but still hale and strong, with graying brown hair, and very pale blue eyes."

"His beard is reddish, and his voice is deep and beautiful." He finished the description for her, spun suddenly on his heel, paced back to the high window, restlessly.

Chapter 21

"I don't understand," she said it again, the words heavy in his charged silence. It was only by force of will that she held herself back from drowning in his intensity. "I thought you said you didn't know him."

"I know no Adam," he turned back, speaking vehemently, his grazed hands beginning fierce gestures, fiercely suppressed, "The man you speak of is Tancred of Harrowden, lord of this manor and my master. All this summer I have been trying to find him."

He took a shallow labored breath, crouched down beside her again. A little trickle of blood seeped out between his fingers, where his clenched grip had opened a cut in his palm. The drop fell in silence, and then, "Do you know where he is?" he asked in a voice which trembled with dreadful gentleness.

His presence was intolerable, she felt him vicious and dangerous as a wounded bear. Cringing, she answered - only to get him away from her - "Yes."

He leaped up, took his knight by the shoulders, and shook him;

"You hear!"

"Yes!"

Both of them were smiling in triumph. For them, she could see, hope had entered the room like a shining cloud, its very brightness making her feel more at sea.

Confusion pressed on her, panic threatened to return because she could not understand what was happening. Was she safe or not? What did he mean by calling Adam his master? - Guimar would never have sold his son as a slave... unless.... Her heart sank further, freezing into a fist of ice in her chest; unless, of course, he meant the master of his craft, and FitzGuimar was himself a witch.

She felt at first relief, at something making sense, and then further oppression, for surely, exchanging a son for an apprentice made her position no better - he would still take her straight back to Adam.

"Find Oswy," FitzGuimar was saying, "he has a right to hear this."

"Where should I look?"

She watched closely - it was not spectacular; he turned his head slightly as if listening, and he said, with certainty "In the kennels, with that dog of his," - but it confirmed her suspicions. She had seen magic worked.

The knight pulled the door to as he left, she heard the iron latch fall, and knew she could not lift aside the tapestry and open the heavy door quickly enough to escape this swift-moving man, let alone sorcery. She stayed where she was, petrified as a fly in amber.

The old woman, Edith, sat down beside her comfortably, sewing at a band of fine embroidery. Her presence, like her son's, felt protective, comforting, thawing Adela's frozen heart once more into puzzlement.

FitzGuimar had returned to his window, grasping the ledge, watching the dark specks of birds circle in the luminous sky. Quietly, to himself, as though he hardly knew whether to feel touched or revolted, he said "He calls me his son now, does he? Well, so I am, in a way. The only son he's likely to get."

She could no longer bear the uncertainty, she had to know. "So," she interrupted his musing, very coldly, pride keeping her a hair's width above the lakes of despair, "You will give me to him after all."

Startled, he really looked at her then, seeing her for herself, not just as an answer to his own problems.

"Lady!" he exclaimed, the pale voice full of honest surprise, "For your sake as well as my own, I will kill him... if I can."

"But... you think of yourself as his son." She was too weary for all these subtleties, she felt the whole day must have gone in this interview - the twists of confusion and fear - but the sun's light still beat almost level on her face, turning the world outside the window into a sheet of molten gold.

"I thought you knew the man," FitzGuimar's voice was soft, but bitter; "Who would have more cause to hate him, than his son?"

The sound of feet in the corridor distracted her, but not before she touched the dark heart of the thought and flinched, trying to shut the understanding away.

The latch lifted and a boy slipped cautiously in. He halted, breathing hard, in the center of the room, and after a moment's thought, straightened himself up to stand like a noble page.

"Master?"

His head was decorously lowered, but now and again, under the curtain of his night-black hair his eyes slid her way, and beneath his coarse lashes he watched her silently.

"The next time you see Father Paul," the lord answered him, "tell him he's right. Sometimes prayer is answered."

Chapter 21

The boy struggled - vainly - not to show his ravenous curiosity. Adela watched the efforts with a certain amount of amusement. What a strange thing he was! Wary as a beast from the woods, black as a carrion bird, with his mongrel mix of noble and peasant manners, and his child's sweet voice. He must be not yet as old as Giles, she thought, and the rush of pain, when she remembered Giles was gone, nearly made her cry aloud. She bit her lip and forced herself to turn the memories away.

Brushing the tapestry aside with his great shoulders the knight returned, bearing cups and a pitcher of warmed wine. Its heat was comforting in Adela's hands, she breathed out, finally, a great sigh of relief that one danger, at least, had proved to be illusory.

The lord began; "My name at least you've guessed, and Edith's you've overheard. My knight is Leofwine, and the boy, my apprentice, is Oswy the Raven. Tell us now your tale, what you know of my master, and above all where he is. Begin with your name."

She told them all of her story, as briefly as she could, though there were infinite bleak pauses in it as she struggled to keep back her grief. When she had done there was silence for a long while - the caws of crows came floating through the open window on the fresh breeze. She sensed sympathy, from the servants, but from the master of the house only a grim, dark brooding which made her afraid.

"King Drago is dead!" Leofwine spoke softly, regretfully, breaking the tense stillness, "I knew him. I fought for him in Holm. Perhaps his choices weren't always wise, but he was a fine knight, a magnificent warrior. The country had peace in his reign."

His voice fell off into private contemplation, and a servant-woman, coming in with a tray laden with bread, meat and apples, stepped into a hollow of silence. She found a stool, balanced the tray. Adela had an impression of merry blue eyes in a poverty-aged face, and then the woman fled, the door swinging closed behind her.

"Well," FitzGuimar came out of his brooding with difficulty, she could see it like a shadow at his shoulder, waiting for him. "You will hear our story now. When they are put together, perhaps they will make a whole."

And he told her, his voice utterly calm, a tale of pain and despair almost as dark as her own. She would have thought him unmoved by the horror of it, he spoke so easily, only, at the most terrible parts, and at every mention of his master's name, his grip tightened on his belt-buckle until the tongue of it was forced through his hand like a nail.

"He is insane!" she thought, watching it - the metal coming slowly through the flesh. She felt momentarily sickened at his presence; as if she might catch his defilement.

"He is unhinged!" she thought, "I don't want this man's help. I don't want anything from him." But another inner voice, weighed down with compassion, said "He must have been hurt so badly, to be so damaged. Another admirable thing Adam has spoiled."

She studied the dark boy, Oswy, with suspicious eyes. He was watching this self-torture with a blend of nervousness and concern. There seemed to be a bond of... what? Empathy or understanding between those two, and the boy seemed cautiously fond of his master. Plainly FitzGuimar had not repeated on his apprentice what had been done to him. A relieved respect for him began to dawn on her; it rarely happened, she believed, that the sins of the father were successfully resisted in the son.

"A relic, you said?"

She shook herself into alertness to find his gaze fixed on her. He had asked her some question. "I'm sorry," she faltered, "I've had no sleep, for a day and a night. I drifted off. I'm sorry. What did you say?"

"Tancred offered Drago dominion and riches, by means of a relic from the World's center," he made his repetition insultingly simple, she heard the bite of impatience behind every word, but it made her think of Torch; the way he hated to say anything twice. She smiled.

"What was the relic?" he insisted, "Think. It is important."

"I... I don't know."

He took a step towards her, fists clenched. Edith at her side lifted a polite, inquiring face to his; there was a stir of chain-mail by the door. Balked, he turned his back and strode away to his window. There was blood on the sill where his hands had lain; he covered it. Beyond him, under the risen sun, the wheat-fields lay golden, and a dot of fire moved there - the bright head of the young man, Ember.

"My master was not born a witch," FitzGuimar began to explain, his voice deadly calm. "He has no talent, by nature, as Oswy and I have, and the power to work magic is not in him. He has either to steal it from one of the mage-born, or get it from other things - from blood, from..." he was not looking at her, his face was towards the bright world, but she saw his shoulders tighten as he said it; "From certain types of sex, and from death.

Chapter 21

"If he cannot obtain any of these, then there are... other things; devices which store power - rings and amulets and talismans. They are, almost all, exhaustible."

He turned back to her. She noticed a hint of surprise cross his face, as if he had not expected her still to be able to look him in the eye.

"In my last battle with him," he went on, quickly, "I drained the power of every amulet he possessed. They are not easy things to replace. The chances are he is powerless, except for this thing. If I knew what it was, I would know better how to counter it."

"I can't." She chased the memory down all the reluctant corridors of her past, "Something to do with the Empire. A Duguth thing?" She shrugged apologetically, "I'm sorry, I wasn't listening. I've always thought all magic was alike."

"I hope you live long enough to realize your mistake." The flat reply had a tone of dismissal in it, which she bridled at. But Edith rose, in a whisper of linen.

"Come," she said, "I'm sure there is water heated. Why don't you have a bath, while I prepare a bed for you in my chamber? You must be very tired. I'll sit and watch with you while you sleep. Tomorrow is soon enough to decide what to do."

"Decide?" FitzGuimar whirled to face them, his fine brown eyes filling with anger, "Decide! The decision is made! You and Leofwine leave tomorrow at dawn for your daughter's house. The lady Adela will go with you."

"And you?" a mirroring anger straightened Adela's back, she was not used to taking the orders of minor lords, however powerful.

"Oswy and I will go to Langley, to fight my master, for the last time."

She rose to her feet, indignant; took a threatening step towards him, without being aware of it. He watched her with a new respect which only made her angrier. "You would take a child into that man's grasp, knowing what he is?"

The boy was staring at her openly now, his plain face showing awe, and pleasure, and a tinge of resentment.

"Thinks himself too old to be called a child," she observed, trying to feel amused, but the black glitter of his eyes disconcerted her. He was not an easy child to patronize.

"It may be I need Oswy's strength," FitzGuimar answered her straightforwardly, "And if I go alone, and am defeated, then Tancred will have him anyway."

"The same applies to me," she folded her arms, lifted her chin rebelliously, "I will come with you. I am tired of running from him. I must be sure it's over, one way or another."

He returned her gaze. Something thawed between them then, as though finally they had reached a basic ground of understanding.

"Yes," he murmured. "One way or another." And then, hardening again to steel; "I have no authority over you. You must do what you wish."

"You'll take her and not me!" The cry of outrage startled her, as Leofwine strode forward. Brushing past her, knocking over the tray of bread, shouldering aside the boy, he stood, towering with rage, over his lord. "You are unjust!"

Tension drew itself out between them, thin as armorer's wire. Edith rose calmly, backed away toward the door. Adela followed willingly; a number of Friday Feasts had taught her this game - leaving the men to brawl. She held out a hand to the child, but he tugged her back into the room.

"They won't fight," he whispered, with a hint of boyish disappointment, "Leofwine will back down. Just watch."

But he was wrong, in a way; it was FitzGuimar who broke the level stare first, who turned away with lowered head, sighing.

"Why won't you understand?" he said, wearily, "You are the one thing out of this whole debacle that I know I can save. He thinks you're dead. Whether I succeed or fail, you can be rid of him."

"I swore to protect you. I didn't swear to be kept safe." It was Leofwine who sounded sullen now, like someone who has been hurt by mistake, who has no one to strike out against.

"For God's sake, Leofwine!" The anguish in the cry was so great Adela shivered, stirring out of her watchfulness.

"Come on," she pulled the boy gently towards the door. "This is some private grief. We shouldn't listen."

"If we don't listen," he said innocently, "how are we going to know what to say to him afterwards?"

"Must you make me say this?" FitzGuimar, leaning against the wall, had covered his face with his hands, as if he could not bear even to be seen.

Chapter 21

But still Leofwine stood rigid, glowering, hugging his anger to himself, refusing to be placated.

The lord's voice came out thin, as if he had had to force it out of a throat constricted with pain. "I had to watch what he did to my father - I had to help! Don't make me go through it again, with you. I... It's the only thing in the world I'm still afraid of."

"I'm sorry," the stiff, affronted anger went out of the knight suddenly. He sagged, leaning on the vine-carved reading desk like a man who has been fighting all day in the tourney and is too exhausted to care whether he has won or lost. "I'm sorry. But I have my honor too. No one has ever before asked me to do something so cowardly. To let a child and a woman go into battle for me, while I run away to safety. I can't do it. I just can't."

A silence grew about them, till Adela, still convinced she should leave, was too afraid to move lest she should break it. Then, still thin, but cold and brittle as a dagger of ice, the lord's voice came again.

"I can make you obey me." He straightened up, hiding fear and friendship behind a veil of threat, paced toward the larger man like a stalking cat. "I have never used magic to control you, but I can, and I will, if you try to thwart me in this."

"My lord!" Leofwine took an involuntary step backwards, his broad, honest face clouded over with concern and confusion. Then, the echo of some inner decision, the frown was wiped away suddenly. He sighed, lifting a twisted hand to push back his unruly hair.

"Very well," he said, passively, the very picture of obedience, "I had rather be your servant than your slave, my lord. I will leave with my mother, tomorrow morning, I swear it."

"Come," Edith plucked at Adela's arm, guided her gently toward the corridor outside. As Adela lifted the tapestry, holding it up so the older woman could go through, she saw the boy half dissolved in the shadows by the wall, still watching.

Her last glance showed her FitzGuimar's face without the mask of intimidation - fear of loss naked on it.

"Leofwine?" he asked, with a kind of uncertain dismay, as though the sudden submission had frightened him.

Quickly she turned away then, letting the door swing closed behind her. It seemed clear to her this was a bitter argument between old friends, and she had found it painful to watch.

The old lady by her side looked down into her face with a smile. "It would take a great deal more to separate allies like those two," she said, reassuringly, reading Adela's distress, maybe, in her closed face, or fists. "And my son gave in far sooner than I would have expected. I was sure it would come to blows. Your influence perhaps, my dear, or..."

She pondered for a little while, silently, and then laughed - a dry chuckle which rustled along the wooden floors like her skirts.

"However it was," she said, "And don't tell him I said this, but I'm glad Lord Sulien got him to agree. It's only an old woman's selfishness, but I would very much like to die before either of my children."

Adela reached out for her hand - dry skin loose over the sturdy bones - and squeezed it in sympathy and thanks. The Sceafn lady stopped in her tracks, startled, and then smiled like a gleam of winter sunshine, but she only said; "You must be very tired, my dear. Come, your room is up here," and led Adela gently towards the stairs.

Grey, drab, reluctant, the morning dawned. Rain blew in through the empty arrow-slits, making the stone walls dank and the polished floors treacherous. Smoke from the great hall, weighed down by the heavy air, fretted at the lower treads of the staircase, like fog over dark water.

The smells of damp wool and charred wood wove themselves into Oswy's dream; and he wandered, lashed by sea-spray, through the burnt ruins of his home, looking for something which would make everything better, but which he could no longer remember what it was.

Waking turned the dream into a walled garden of contentment. It was a long time before he could force himself to abandon it, to crawl out of his blankets and into the chill air.

Fear began to nag at him; he pushed it away - there was nothing to fear at this moment, only his room, damp clothes to pull on, the prospect of porridge for breakfast. Nothing to fear, yet. Perhaps he would let himself feel a little frightened when they rode out, but that was an hour off, maybe more. He need not be afraid yet.

Chapter 21

"Beyond this ridge," the Lady Adela said, her silver voice a little breathless from riding, but calm, "the forest ends. The land slopes up bare to the bailey walls - we will be visible to the guards."

It wasn't fair, Oswy thought, how could she, a woman, seem so unafraid, when terror dogged his every forward step. Again he tried to thrust it away, again the effort proved too great.

"I can shield us from the sight of guards." Sulien answered her, his own voice tight with exultation. He too seemed fearless - reckless to the point of joy.

Cold water drizzled from Oswy's sodden hood, seeping coldly down his cheek. Suddenly, heartbreakingly, he found himself yearning for his own people - peasants, like him, whose first instincts would be to run, or to hide. What was he doing here among the nobility? Even their women had more bravery than him. Father Paul had been right; he was not made for this.

Edith's face recurred to him, seen through the gray downpour this morning as her litter had set out for safety. She should have been glad, he thought irritably, a little guilty perhaps, but glad all the same. Instead there had been strain and sorrow behind her old eyes, as if something had happened since last night to make her duty taste like ashes to her.

And Leofwine, whom he had expected to wear that face, had been cheerful, bidding him goodbye with no more ceremony than he would have used before going out hunting.

He shook his head. He could not fathom any of them. It was as if he and they were of different species. A sense of isolation came over him, deepening his fear, making it icy, poignant. It was terrible to be thus alone with dread.

"We'll leave the horses here." Sulien interrupted his self-pity, swinging down to the ground, unbuckling his bridle even as he spoke, tucking it into the full saddlebags.

"Unfettered and unguarded?" Lady Adela's voice was perhaps sharper than she intended; her face softened after it, in mute apology.

The awe Oswy had felt for her last night stirred once more: How could she remain so unintimidated? So unaffected by his master's power? Could it be she was foolish enough to think Sulien would not strike a woman? Or, like Gunnar, did she simply not care?

Again he abandoned understanding, clambering off Amber's back. What did any of it matter? She would be dead before nightfall, and he... worse than a slave. Memory came, unbidden, of sharing body, mind and soul with the old man's spirit, the sense of being filled with something rotten, which had once been sweet.

His cold hands fumbled at the bridle. The frigid, slippery buckles and swollen leather made his fingertips ache with prying them apart. He leaned his head against the pony's warm neck, fighting nausea and despair.

"Do you forget what I am?"

It was unbelievable! Astonishment roused him a little. They were sparring again, over precedence, like two cocks fighting over the same dunghill. How could his master spare the energy? He knew what awaited them, why did he spend his strength on this?

Straightening, weary with distress, Oswy led his sorrel pony under the thick canopy of an ancient holly tree. The prickly leaf-litter was still dry underfoot, and only at the edges of the dark boughs did rain twist down like snakes.

Could it be, he wondered, that fear aroused anger in them, while for him it brought only misery? Could it be they too felt the terror? Only to hide it in petty quarrels and irritability?

"The horses will not stray." Yes! There was an undercurrent of fraying tension in Sulien's reasonable voice. "No thief, no wolf will be aware of them. Unless we are defeated. In which case it will be the least of many losses. Are you content, my lady?" The words were polite, but the intonation bitter, edgy.

"I'm sorry," Adela said, in a little voice, "I had forgotten."

"I wish others forgot as easily."

Sulien paused, the downpour turning the harvested field into a marsh beneath his feet.

"This isn't right." Stress roughened the words. Water, slicking down his long hair, made the gaunt angles of his face stand out sharply. "There should have been some defenses by now - traps, some warning we're here."

Unending rain came down, and the featureless slope rose dreary under the premature twilight. The manor-house, ahead of them, was a mass of shadows against the gray sky, its earthwork defenses dimly guessed at shapes and bulks of darkness.

Was it him, Oswy wondered, or was it blacker than it should be?

Chapter 21

"Could it be," the tremor was plain now in the lady's soft words. She was whispering, though all around bare fields stretched empty to the bleak horizon, "Could we have already sounded the warnings? Without being aware of it?"

"No."

They went on slowly, ever more slowly, every step more reluctant than the last, and still, with forced calm, the nobles talked over Oswy's head.

"At foot pace even Oswy would be able to detect such a snare, yards before we tripped it."

"Then," despair and hope mingled in the question, as though Adela knew the hope was vain even as she said it. "Perhaps he's not here any more. Maybe he moved on?"

Sulien stopped, looking at her curiously.

"I hadn't thought..." he said, standing uncertain for a heartbeat. Suddenly, his face grim with resolution, he turned his head, listening. The moment drew itself out - a torture, like the rack. Then he gasped, recoiling, a little frightened movement which from him seemed a shout of terror.

"He's here," he said faintly, and in a whisper, cold as the voices of the water, "but something else is here with him. I think it heard me."

Fear leaped howling on Oswy again. He could not fight it off. He shrank to his master's side, trying to grab on to his belt, as he had done in the glade of ghosts.

Sulien pushed him off with a kind of desperation, "Get away!"

"I'm frightened!" He clutched at an arm.

"Just don't touch me!"

Wind, sudden, bitter, screamed over the stubbled fields, tearing away the veil of rain. Oswy, looking for comfort, saw Adela's face go blank with shock. She muffled a scream behind her hand. Reluctantly, compelled, he followed her gaze to the manor house, and saw them.

Like writhing black slime they came creeping out of the arrowslits, oozing head-downward over the walls. The presences which lurk unseen in nightmares were made visible, the beings who haunt night's shadows were coming down over the battlements with heavy reptilian purpose.

He tried to tear his eyes away, but he was held. Slowly - he knew it would happen before it did - one of the things raised its head and looked at him.

Seeing its face was like being turned to stone; frozen forever into an eternity of resentment and loss. Its gaze accused him, as if it knew every wrong deed, every vileness he had ever thought. Answering its contempt, a sense of his own worthlessness crushed him with misery and despair.

Crying out, he flung his arms round his masters waist, buried his face in the soaked folds of cloak. This time Sulien did not resist - motionless as a corpse.

"My God!" he breathed, a stunned whisper, "These things are Princes of the Abyss. Lords of the Ruined Lands," a note of resignation, profound as relief, crept into the pale voice. "I'm sorry, Oswy. Against them, there's nothing I can do."

"Don't let them get me!" The shout was muffled in sodden wool. Oswy squeezed his eyes tighter shut. This was a nightmare, a nightmare, he would wake up soon. "Don't let them get me!"

"Adela?" Hope surfaced in Sulien's tone; dutiful, almost grudging hope. His voice had strengthened, as though he at least was recovering from the sight of the things. "You've fought the Dark Ones before."

The little brightness of hope made Oswy lift his head. He saw the lady, her face white as her linen veil. She was swaying on her feet, her eyes unfocused.

"I..." she said, "I..."

And a blur of blackness moving faster than sight smashed into him. Confused images, stench and heaviness, hugeness, filth and despair, wheeled around him. There were eyes, dead eyes, and membranes, and mouths full of yellow teeth.

Something pressed him into the ground - he must have fallen – when? Mud rose around him, blessedly clean in comparison with the thing on his back. Pressure mounted; his ribs and skull ached; mocking stars swam in grayness behind his eyes.

He was conscious of desperate struggle, a very long way away. Mud filled his mouth and his nose. Self-hatred suffocated him. "I didn't even fight them!" he thought.

Chapter 21

And he went down under a roaring of darkness, and saw and heard no more.

Chapter Twenty Two

One side of Oswy's face was warm. The other was cold, wet, pressed to a smooth wooden floor. Something was wrong with him, or with the very fabric of the world. He felt empty, but bruised - the phantom ache of a lost limb - and something was moving inside the cavity, like a live tapeworm in the stomach of a dead calf.

He opened one eye - a crack in the boards beneath him seemed momentarily huge as a precipice, chill draughts striking up through it from the deeps below. Even the wood seemed hollow and thin, a ghost of itself. What had happened to him? Had they cut out his soul already, and given it to the fiends?

"Though I'll say this for you," the voice seemed to have been speaking for some time, a beautiful voice, deep gold, like pouring honey, "you have kept him delightfully naive. It will be an ease and a pleasure to spoil that."

There was a smile in its gentleness, an invitation into the world of its own pleasures. "You can help me teach him," it said, "If you like."

The warmth moved against his face, resolving itself suddenly into the pressure of fingers, the texture of flesh dragging across his skin. He recoiled, and the voice chuckled a little to itself.

"Why do you talk as though you still had a future?" Sulien sounded so familiar, so comfortable in the presence of this man. A feeling of betrayal came over Oswy like the mire. All the talk about hatred seemed to vanish like vapor. It was a quite a while before he realized that the words were hardly compliant.

"How long before these creatures eat you? How long before they're wearing you like a cloak? A puppet is more convenient than a slave. I'd give you a week."

"I have the scepter of Varian!" The hand was sharply withdrawn. A garment - the fur-trimmed hem of a robe - brushed against Oswy's outstretched palm, there was a footstep and then the sharp retort of a blow.

"But not the will of Varian." Sulien's reply came a heartbeat late, as though he had had to catch his breath, "You should know the amount of will-

Chapter 22

power it takes to keep yourself separate from these things. Just looking at them is disease. You feel it already, don't you - the pressure of their desires?"

"Be silent!" The smack of another blow. Oswy risked opening his other eye, edging himself into a position from which he could see.

"Emperor Varian's will was in the keeping of God," Sulien wiped blood from his nose. Other than the red seeds of bruises his face showed nothing, but he sounded vaguely pleased with himself. "So they couldn't touch him. But you..." Still the familiar tone edged his words, very much like a son offering his aged father contempt. "Master, you never had the willpower to refuse a third dish at dinner, or walk away from a public hanging..."

Around Sulien's raised wrist something glittered sharply. As Oswy looked at it it filled his head with knives. His gaze flinched away, and then dropped unwillingly to his own arms. There too the witch-bracelets shone, their bitter light somehow alive. He knew then what was wrong with him - his powers were bound. There would be no escape by magic from this room.

He drew himself together: Maybe, while they were talking, he could make a sprint for the door. It stood half open behind Tancred, a slit of blackness in the painted wall.

Something heavy tugged at him; there was the sound of metal on wood. A pain around his ankle revealed itself to his groping fingers as a band of iron bolted tight, from which the chain stretched away to a loop newly hammered into the wall. Numbly he subsided again.

His fear, along with his magic, seemed suspended just out of his reach. He was free to notice - dully, without interest - small details; light drizzle blowing in through the lancet window; scenes of courtly love painted on the plastered walls; a slave's iron collar on the end of a rope, hanging from the enameled torch-bracket by the door.

Now and again his emptiness was filled up with shattering emotion; hatred, despair, envy, impatience, huge and implacable as the oceans. It filled him and then ebbed away, leaving him stained and weary.

Focus sharpened slowly. He began to see, on the air of the room, darknesses moving like tendrils of greasy smoke. A shadow solidified - became a swollen scaly tail which dragged itself across the floorboards with a noise like a bone-file - dissolved again as though even in the gray light of the rain-filled sky it could not support itself in being.

The dim corners of the room had become vile lairs of half-guessed claws and eyes. Drifting out from them, like locks of drowned black hair, came filaments of night, passing into the walls or through the boards into the cold drop of the empty tower.

Something slithered. A twist of darkness came floating out of the fire, nosed Oswy like a questing worm, and with a lunge passed into his face.

"Aaah!" disgust forced the scream out, "Get it off me! Get it off!" But it burrowed into him and suddenly his disgust was overwhelmed with spite - spite grown to a consuming passion, spite so choking he could not speak for it.

Muffled, a long way away, he heard Tancred chuckle again with amusement, and the room swam away from him reddened with an overwhelming desire to get back at that man.

"Oswy!" Sulien's voice too was faint, but urgent, "Deny it - the dark one - or ignore it, but don't let it get a foothold, or it'll be in there forever!"

"You shut up!" No more amusement now in Tancred's tone. He had gone from good-humor to rage in an instant. "You shut up! I've told you! You don't talk to anyone. You don't look at anyone but me. Must I tame you again?"

There was something important going on out there. Oswy was curious. Some old power-struggle, something which touched Tancred to the bone. He wanted to listen, but still spite had him in its breathless grip.

"Oh go away!" he thought at it, annoyed, "I can't be bothered with this. I want to listen." And at once it went, pushing out of his mouth like a blunted sword. He was briefly amazed by the amount of light in the world.

"Oswy?" At the furthest extent of his chain the younger witch was within touch. He crouched down there, on the end of his leash, and studied Oswy's face carefully. "Are you alright?" he asked.

It seemed to Oswy there was a little more in Sulien's display of concern than a mere show of defiance for his master. Very little, perhaps, but still, more. A tiny stir of gratitude rose up to match it.

Then Tancred slid the scepter - a delicate wand of gold, star-tipped - under his heavy bracelet, where the stone stood out like a picked knuckle-bone. He took up a weighty iron-studded staff which stood in one of those haunted corners, stepped forward to stand over them both. Gratitude became fear. Oswy bit his lip and covered his face.

Dark filaments reached out - responsive to Tancred's will - wrapped themselves tight around Sulien's wrists, ankles, waist and neck, held him still. He did not try to struggle.

Chapter 22

When their captor had finished beating him, and he lay in a red-stained huddle on the floor, Tancred whispered it again, panting between the words. "Don't speak to anyone! Only me!"

"There's..." Sulien raised his head, gingerly, coughed out blood, breaking the determined silence in which he had endured his punishment, "There's nothing you can do, to either of us, which you do not already intend. Nothing you can threaten with."

Still trembling with rage and frustration Tancred retreated from the calm voice. His grip on the staff was white; his jaw muscles worked. Backing he trod on Oswy's hand, stumbled over it, cursing the floor. At this moment, it seemed, he had totally forgotten Oswy's existence.

"You little bastard!" he hissed at Sulien, as though he spoke to the boy he had once known, "You little bastard! Gods! I hate you! I'd forgotten how much I hate you!"

Exasperation pulled his lip back, showed his yellowed teeth in a snarl. "Why can't you just do as you're told!" he yelled, turned away, breathing hard.

Patches of blackness began to creep out of the cracks of the floor, out of the shadows. The fire - or was it the fire? - began to hiss. Outside the open window the rain had ceased, but the sky darkened at the approach of night. There was a faint chittering and scratching in the silence of the room, like the voices of rats in the walls.

Tancred's head snapped round. He gazed wide-eyed into the darkness. A flash of panic and terror lit his pale eyes. "Be silent!" he shouted, "I command you!"

The sounds faded, and at their compliance - the instant obedience of demons - urbanity flowed slowly back over his broad face. He returned to crouch cautiously just outside the limit of Sulien's grasp. His breathing had steadied, but his fists still clenched and unclenched as he spoke;

"I know you," he said, a tempter's voice again, pleading a little, "I know what you desire: I made you what you are. Listen. We can hunt together, we can share the kills, the power." The note of pleading increased, became desperate - like a wife begging her husband not to leave her behind, not to enter the cloister and forsake her. "Only you must obey... a few tiny rules, that's all. You must obey me."

Sulien raised his bloody face. "The greatest desire of my life," he said painfully, "Is not to be like you. And I will never obey you again."

"Never!" Tancred recoiled and rage leaped once more into his sky blue eyes. He drove his staff – nail-heads glittering on it - two-handed at the younger man's face. Sulien twisted, the blow coming down on his raised arm. Bone snapped with a crack.

"Never?" Tancred was shaking again with fury, the beautiful voice gone shrill, "Nothing I can threaten you with? I'll show you. Did you think I'd lost all my inventiveness when I lost your power? I'll show you!"

And to the darkness, to the creatures in the darkness he shouted "Bring her in!"

There was movement; a sense of hideous excitement; impatience finally gratified; a surge of interest centered on the open door.

A blur of white showed in the unlit corridor, like the ghost of a woman. It came nearer - the Lady Adela, gagged, stripped to her shift, wrapped in writhing darkness; a smoke which lifted her unveiled brown hair, which plucked at the thin linen dress like groping hands. She moved like a sleepwalker, drifted to where the ugly metal yoke hung on its greasy rope, stopped.

"A lesson for you, my love." Behind Tancred's once more melodious tones passion still trembled; fury ebbing, fear and eagerness rising. "To teach you what will happen if you displease me again. Watch, and defy me later if you still can."

He bolted the iron collar around the woman's bare neck, stood back. They watched together as the blankness dissolved from her face, and terror, devouring terror overwhelmed it.

Drugged. She felt drugged, drunk. This couldn't be real. In this state she couldn't be walking. She was asleep. Yes, she had had this nightmare before: walking, walking somewhere terrible, unable to stop, while leering inhuman faces came out of the darkness at her, and hands pawed. There was nothing really there; it was a nightmare. It would end in the morning.

And now she had come to that terrible place. She stood, waiting to wake up, and felt something cold and hard on her throat: the texture of metal; the texture of reality.

Chapter 22

Dreams became waking. The nightmare became fact. She knew without questioning what they meant for her - the faces all around her, taunting, threatening, dirtying the fire-lit air.

Tearing frantically at the iron fetter - her hands were free - she saw Adam. He was sweating; triumphant but nervous, as though he wondered if even he had the stomach for this.

The yoke was fast, the rope short. She could not get away. She should do something. Someone should do something.

The darkness was thickening, coalescing. It began with drooling lipless mouths; bare and filthy taloned feet, tails.

She felt herself fracturing, pieces of her mind flying apart. Part of her saw, and even pitied, the boy, Oswy, hiding his face; FitzGuimar, slumped, defeated, far away in some untouchable refuge of the spirit.

Another facet of her soul - a little girl - cried out 'It isn't fair! It's my mother's room! They can't do this to me in my mother's room!' This was the place in her thoughts which had always stood for comfort and safety. This was her retreat...

A third spoke harshly - 'Do something! Get the scepter away from him somehow! Pray, if you can't do anything else!'

But there were eyes now, gloating, holding her pinned, and long poisonous tongues, and slime. She could not breathe, she could not think. God! they stank! And there were so many of them!

She would go mad - that was it! Escape them all by going mad. They were almost whole now; priapic monsters gathering for their sport.

She reached inside her mind for insanity to overwhelm her.

And then Sulien raised his head, looked past her to the gape of doorway, surprise and gladness and fear alive again on his battered face.

She had a moment to resent it before she too felt the movement at her back. Madness would have been easier, but she braced herself for hope.

He came softly out of the shadow, silent as a cat, the great bulk of him moving lightly - a stalking hunter. For a second he hesitated in the light. His face showed: Leofwine, sickened, shocked, unmanned by the vileness before him. And he was seen.

"You!" Tancred exclaimed. "You!"

It was enough. Freed from the spell of horror Leofwine turned, swinging his pattern-welded sword. It bit through the rope - Adela was choked and then suddenly free.

"No!" shouted Tancred, lifting up his right hand. He had clutched the scepter again. The tip had become a clear light in his grasp.

"Get out!" Leofwine pushed Adela behind him, shoved her toward the open door, "Run!" But the fiends still surrounded her, single minded, intent.

"Grab him!" Tancred yelled, diminished by the stone's aura, like an undusted room shown up by the sun's light. It seemed impossible for a man holding up that star to speak such platitudes. "I want him alive. And guard the door - don't let either of them get away!"

They were feeling her now. Disregarding him. The sheer uncleanness of them made the lightest touch a torture. What could she do? If she ran they would catch her.

"Leofwine! I need your knife!" That was Sulien's voice. She could not see him for the wall of naked flesh which enveloped her, but she heard the whisper and thrum of a thrown knife, the smack of a hand catching it.

"Whatever you're going to do", she thought, choking down the scream - if she let it out it would consume her - "Do it quickly!"

"Obey me!" the old man's voice was shrill with indignity and fear. He had realized perhaps that nothing now stood between him and the bright edged sword. "I command you by the rod of Varian! Leave her be and get him! Guard the door!" And in one last effort of will power, the words trembling with force.

"You WILL obey me in this."

They fell away from her reluctantly, like leeches at the touch of salt. Their resentment was palpable, unreasoning, unrestrained. Hatred of the man who commanded them, hatred of all men who dared oppose their will filled the room, until the air became heavy and dark with it, and breathing was like drowning in bile.

Adela swayed, gasping in the bitterness. Her body wanted to vomit with reaction and relief, but her mind was finally clear; clear and sharp as the head of an arrow.

Swiftly she took in the room: A clot of darkness blocking the doorway; Sulien levering the knife-blade beneath the silver bracelets on his wrist - blood strangely bright in the polluted air; Oswy - a huddle with a pair of

Chapter 22

frightened eyes; Leofwine driven back against the wall - flesh parting before his sword and closing up unharmed. She had no time for thought - she must act now, before he was overcome, before they were free to return to her.

With three steps - bold, unhesitating - she was across the polished floor in front of Tancred, her hands moving. He met her eyes; a start of surprise because she had not tried to run, and then a shrug, discounting her. What was she, after all? Only a woman; weaponless, defenseless.

Nonchalantly, his eyes already returning to Leofwine's unequal combat, he lifted his clenched hand to knock her aside.

She seized it, both of her small fists locked around his, and wrenched.

There was a snap, a smell of lightning, and the old witch yelped like a puppy. The scepter of Varian leaped out of his grasp as though it was glad to be free. It lay in her fists like a sleeping beast; living, aware.

The witch's face grayed with shock. He lunged for her. She twisted away, running to press herself against the wall behind FitzGuimar. The blond man had leaped to his feet, his face alight with ferocity and eagerness, knife in hand.

Tancred balked, afraid to come close, while behind him demons turned from their tasks, began to seep closer; watching, waiting, in dreadful suspense.

Adela opened her fingers. The stone of the scepter lay against her palm like a globe of solid light - cream colored, flecked with moving aureate sparks. Looking down on it was like seeing, from infinitely far away, a vast, glorious palace, where radiant beings danced in arabesques of light. Awe of it overcame her, and with it anger: How had this vile creature dared touch it?

"Use it!" Sulien's voice, urgent, commanding, snapped through her wonderment. "Banish them! There's not much time!"

She should. She knew it. She should accept the authority, wield the scepter; command the fiends to bind Tancred and be gone. She held deliverance in the palm of her hand - she had only to claim it.

Heavily, with a rasping, like a saw through gristle, the darkness separated from Leofwine's prostrate form, slithered away from the doorway, creeping, moment by moment, closer. She felt their minds on her - on the bearer of the rod - with an intensity of resentment which made her cower.

"What are you waiting for?" Sulien's voice was rough with fear, as he watched victory trickle out of her grasp like snatched sand.

But now she was aware - so clearly she could almost see it - of the Abyss: Of depth after depth, going down into impenetrable darkness; the congregation of the damned, before whose solid evil her very existence seemed frail as a candle-flame.

All their subtle and joyless cunning was bent on her, waiting for her command, because in making herself their master she would acknowledge them, willingly bringing them into her life, giving them power to begin slowly, artfully twisting her to their own design.

"Come on," they seemed to say, pulling at her, wheedling. "Come now. Let it begin."

"No!" The shout of denial made her mouth bleed - the gag was tight - and no sound came out, but it filled her with strength like a battle cry. Inarticulate, in a moment of blind faith, she rejected them all. She would have no dealings with them. God would protect her.

She turned, hurled the wand away from her. It flew like an arrow from the bow - a line of light in the dark room - through the lancet arch, flaming in sunset's angry light like a comet at the death of kings.

"No! No!" Tancred shook his head, trembling. His words whispered into the stunned silence.

The fiends came closer; a dark wall compressing, driving the humans together, keeping them within their circle, penning them like cattle.

"No, this can't be happening. Stupid. Stupid bloody woman. No."

Distantly, outside, came the splash as the ancient scepter plummeted into the waters of the moat.

And then everything happened.

FitzGuimar thrust the knife under his fetters again, pulling, reckless of the huge wounds. The air reeked coppery, blood-hot, but the witch-bracelets snapped. He stood up, great syllables of nonsense words coming out of his mouth like song, and every bond in the room was freed.

Adela felt the gag come loose. She spat out cloth and hard-edged wood. She too had a word to call. Why had she forgotten it until now?

The silver manacles fell away. Power came back to Oswy like sight after blindness, but sight brought terror.

Chapter 22

He felt himself seized. A slippery red hand clamped itself around his arm. Sulien dragged him - limp as a carcass - across the floor, dumped him beside Leofwine.

"Come here!" His master's light voice cracked like a whip. The lady moved - her body obeying it without thought. They were all huddled around the unconscious man now. Like an honor guard. Like a last stand.

"Niniel!" The woman put back her head and shouted it, her face radiant with defiance and hope.

Something quailed. The black wall wavered. Heaviness withdrew, a little, dismayed, shedding solidity as a man drops his shield before running. "Niniel come help us!"

And then the moment passed. Matter poured back into the nightmare shapes. Floorboards groaned and cracked under the pressure of taloned feet. They surged forward - an ugly, greedy movement. An empty, senile giggling came from them, and a spattering of scalding drool.

Tancred, only two paces from them now, cried out suddenly; a high pitched wail of fear. He spun. Stumbling, running, his face all naked with ruin, he threw himself at Sulien, caught at his waist, buried his face in the damp wolf-skin cloak.

"Sulien! Sulien, my love," he wailed, "You'll protect me. You won't let them hurt me."

There was a mixture of disgust and triumph in the younger man's brown eyes as he began, almost silently, to speak his spell, but he did not shake off the clutching hands. When the light came - a globe purer than starlight, pristine as the heavens - enveloping them all, Tancred too was within it.

Damnation paused. The fiends turned, shielding streaming eyes with filthy claws. The cacophony of their spite and frustration shook plaster from the walls. Flakes of it drifted through the bright sphere like a fall of pearls

"Look! Look!" Still sobbing with fear, the older man pulled at Sulien's arm - the arm broken by his own blow. "The dust gets through. What's to stop them? This won't stop them! Do something!"

"This is..." already pain and fatigue weakened the clear voice. Some superficial part of Oswy's master spoke, but the rest was withdrawn. Far away Oswy sensed it; an axis, a focus, balancing, controlling forces too vast to comprehend. Alone of all the onlookers in Sulien's protection he felt how precarious that balance was; the abominable strain of it.

"This is..." Sulien said, "the first created light. Before them. They won't dare touch it."

Looking down on Oswy he smiled suddenly, like the leaping of flame as a branch falls into ash, spoke, with an artist's pride in his skill. "...Didn't know this was possible - made it up."

But the flame passed. His face grayed. "It hurts me too," he said faintly, "Don't know how long I can bear it."

"Niniel." Adela spoke at Oswy's elbow, whispering her word again, this time in dismay.

"What..?" Leofwine stirred, the word whining through his broken nose. He struggled to sit and the lady drew him up, her delicate face passing from disappointment to fury as she saw his hurts. Something broke in her then. Oswy saw it in her eyes - too much pain, and the failure of her hope. Desolation spoke next, turning on Tancred like a harpy.

"What's he doing here!" she yelled at him. "This is all his fault! He killed Giles! And the king! And..."

Sulien staggered, went down on his knees, his eyes closed with exhaustion, his head back. The globe of piercing light shrank with him. Now the starry clarity ceased little more than an arms length above his head. Outside of it the sound of jeering rose in an anguished wail.

Oswy crawled closer to his master - they were all huddled together now, cramped within the frail bubble. He should offer his power, he knew it, before Sulien drained himself to death. But he had sensed, at a distance, the scorching, stripping magnitude of the summoned light. Handling it would be like slowly reaching in to the white center of a smithy fire. He could not do it.

"We came here to kill him!" Adela's complaint grated on his nerves; how could she go on talking? Couldn't she feel how close they were to disaster, how desperate and failing was his master's grip on concentration and strength?

"What are we doing protecting him?" Her voice was shrill - like his mothers when she was one step away from tears. That he understood. There was nothing he wanted more himself than to cry and be comforted. "Throw him out to them. Then maybe they'll leave us alone. It's what he deserves!"

"Don't listen to her!" Tancred, oblivious to anything but his own fear, tugged again on Sulien's broken arm.

Chapter 22

Sulien moaned, the agonized frown tightening over his face. A wash of glaring crimson sped over the globe's bright surface. Shadow followed it like a wound.

A bellow of triumph; the rattle of scaly wings; stench curling about them, the demons edged closer to the failing shield, their merciless faces gore-stained by the light.

"Leave him alone!" Fury and some emotion he did not understand - heady, valiant - drove Oswy suddenly out of fear. He shouldered Adela and Tancred aside, grabbed the knife, slashed one shallow cut along his palm and grabbed, knuckles white, at his master's bleeding wrist. "Shut up both of you and leave him alone! Master?"

The drain of power was not like light at all, but like darkness, and cold. The eviscerating pain he had feared did not come, only an ache over his whole body, like the ache of a leech sucking out life-blood.

Sagging, suddenly weak, against his master's side, light beat again on his face. The globe, focused now by his soul's strength, blazed out. And in it the pale shifting colors of his own witch-light trembled like a rainbow in mist.

But the night grew darker, and the ache grew deeper, and the demons waited, taunting.

Weakness began to overwhelm Oswy. He saw, behind his closed eyes, his body as a network of stars, and watched, one by one, as those stars went out. The drain of energy between himself and his master was like a blue pathway against ink and pitch. Far away, shielded from him by Sulien's dim presence the intolerable light burned, but where he was, in the blackness, it was utterly cold.

"We're dying, aren't we?" he asked, too tired to be afraid. The question drifted wordlessly along the link between them.

"Yes," came the answer, faint and calm, "But dying well. Leofwine will give the others clean death too."

His voice paused, came again, whispering from an infinite distance; "Oswy, I'm sorry. If I had never touched your life..."

Oswy was silent, even the ache fading away under the balm of the cold. He didn't know what he wanted to say - something too complex for this moment.

"I..." he began at last, but the link was gone, and the effort of thought exhausted him, and the darkness was now comforting.

He floated there alone for eternity.

Chapter Twenty Three

There was a light - red - and agony all over Oswy's body. Thought came back to him blearily;

'I'm in the Abyss!'

He thrashed, and the movement translated itself into a weak twitching and waves of stinging pain.

The Abyss smelled good, like a forest sleeping under summer sunshine.

"Don't be afraid!"

The voice was like Victory morning - when the altars are white, blazing with candles, the priests are in cloth of gold, the sword is like a comet burning on the snowy linen, and the choir sings like a music of bells.

Oswy's heart leaped. The pain fled out of him, leaving little more than pins and needles. He opened his eyes and saw her.

She was a glory of color in the night's darkness - a mantle of blue, fresh as new flowers; the great sweep of wings, emerald, fanning the scent of sap and honey over the dead air of the room; her hands, bare feet, and face golden, shining with light. There were stars entangled in her hair.

'I'm in Heaven!'

Joy bewildered him, so he could not understand why heaven was the shape of a tower room. If he glanced, reluctantly, away from the angel's beauty he saw splintered floorboards, Sulien, pushing himself up onto hands and knees, awe on his face and his hair all pointed with drying blood. A ring of shoots and leaf-buds quivering with new life where the globe of light had touched the dry wood.

Adela and Leofwine were supporting each other as they tottered to their feet. Tancred, crouching in Sulien's shadow, covered his head with his arms and whined in terror.

And in the darkest corners of the room, driven back, with a patience which had endured since the ruin of the world, the nightmare shapes re-formed, crept stealthily forward once more.

Not heaven then. He was still alive! The realization went through him like a sword; sharp and bitter. He had been so well prepared for the end of life's labors. But if not Heaven, then how had this happened?

"Niniel!" Adela lurched into the comfort of one encircling wing. How good it looked, Oswy thought, like warm grass spangled with buttercups. Without conscious effort he began to crawl forward himself into that refuge.

"Starlight!" The angel looked down on Adela's drawn white face with a smile of gentle reproof. "Why did you call on me, and not on my Lord?" she said, "He had hosts of angels nearer at hand than I. As it was, I almost came too late."

Creeping into the fortress of her green wings, Oswy had no desire but to be as near as he could to such goodness and such beauty. It was warm in the enclosure of feathers, with warmth like a mother's hug. Life lapped over him, and as he breathed it in he felt renewed. Niniel reached down to put her long bright hand on his head, and joy transfixed him, keen as pain.

Outside his refuge a sound began again, a sound it seemed to him he had loathed all his life - the hissing whisper of demon voices; their stealthy slither. They were coming closer, cautiously, like vultures sidling up to feast on what the lion had left unguarded.

"My lord!" he called, urgent now, seeing the danger, "Leofwine! Come here!"

But Sulien's face was wracked with indecision, yearning warring with fear, while the old man, his master, plucked at his belt, trying to pull him further into hiding in the shadows. And Leofwine was on his knees in prayer, heedless of the peril.

"No!" The angel's cry was sharp with command. She moved forward one step, Adela and Oswy moving with her like chicks with their dam. She stooped - like a line of sun's gold in a waterfall - to take Leofwine's clasped hands and make him rise. "Don't kneel to me, my brother. Come in where you belong."

The darkness stirred again. A creature came out of the clotted shades - the robe it wore not quite concealing its deformity, the flash of saw-edged talons on its bare and dirty feet. Its face was angelic, proud and cruel and

Chapter 23

beautiful, but it could not avoid cringing a little as it spoke; "You have your due," it said, "Now begone. These two belong to us."

Sulien staggered to his feet, drew the old man up with him: Dust colored Tancred was in the angel's aureate light, withered by his life. They stood together and, whether he was aware of it or not, Sulien held his master protectively in one bloodstained arm. Very weak and vulnerable they both looked in the circle of predatory shapes, their faces finally alike in the resignation of despair.

"That decision is neither yours nor mine to make," Niniel replied. Her voice was calm, but her eyes were full of mingled pity and disgust. The maimed thing could not meet her gaze. It looked away, licking its pointed teeth.

"It is their decision," she finished, "I will not take it away from them."

"Then they're ours," The demon grinned, its smile wiping out the last shreds of its decaying beauty. "We don't share your stupid scruples. If you won't make a move, you can just stand there and watch us take them."

Even in his rescued bliss Oswy's heart lurched with horror. He leaped to his feet.

"No!" he shouted, and dared to pull on the angel's wrist, "You can't just let him die!"

Feelings, loyalties, clear in his mind, would not come out in sensible words. "So he's not a good man! It's not his fault!"

Light stabbed out from the angel's face into every corner of the room. It stopped Oswy's mouth like a hot coal, burning the horror away. Demons went reeling from it.

"Sulien FitzGuimar," she said, her voice the same; pure, ungentle, "You have only seconds in which to choose. Will you come to me?"

Layer after layer of mask seemed to fall away from the young witch's face,

"I still have the chance?" he asked, uncertainly.

"Yes," she said, "but you know the price."

Sulien shuddered. He looked from the angel to his master, and back, in boyish supplication. "My magic? It's all I've lived for."

"What are you talking about!" Tancred revived, in self-defense, his fine voice frayed with anxiety, "You're not leaving me!"

Uncompromising, harsh as cauterizing flame upon a wound, the angel's voice sounded out, her fierce eyes holding Sulien at bay. "Your magic has God's place in your heart. Pluck it out, and come to me now."

Sulien looked round him, the movements panicked, his gaunt face hideously unsure. The nightmare shapes of the fiends swam reflected in his wide brown eyes.

Tancred, trembling with rage or fear - his own eyes pale as if with cataracts in the fierce light - took him by the collar, pulled; "After all I've done for you. You can't leave me!' he panted. 'I forbid it! Do you hear? I forbid it!"

And Oswy, unable to bear it any longer, tugged on Leofwine's sleeve, whispering, "Can't we go and get him?"

"No, Oswy," the knight answered, firmly, "You'll leave well alone. It's about time you learned to trust him, as I do."

One more moment Sulien hesitated, his master growing frantic beside him.

"Don't you dare! Don't you dare!"

Then, with a face as desperate, as full of pain, as a wolf gnawing through its trapped leg, he took a step towards the angel.

"Twelve years! I raised you, clothed you, fed you, taught you everything you know!" Both of Tancred's fists were tight now around Sulien's broken arm. Old he might be, but still hale; heavy enough to hold the younger man back for the few seconds left. "This is your gratitude?" he whined, "You think you can just abandon me? Abandon me to death? Well I won't have it. I won't let you go."

Swift as light, Niniel opened one wing, touched the clenched fists with the tips of her feathers. Tancred screamed, recoiling, great blisters of burns standing up white on his skin. A gloating, anticipatory laughter filled the room.

Sulien reeled into shelter like a man dazed, and there seemed no ease for him in the angel's presence. He stood and shuddered, like a notched rope unwinding before it snaps.

"What's wrong with him?" Oswy tugged at Leofwine's sleeve, frightened by the strangeness, "What's wrong?"

Chapter 23

The circle of horror began to tighten now on Tancred. He stood alone, one frail human figure in the center of a swarm of evil. Terror swept again over his broad face, and devoured itself, leaving an insane calm.

"There's still time," the angel spoke again, like trumpets, "Tancred FitzJohn, you too can be saved. Come."

"Come to you?" the old witch held up his blistered hands and laughed, a bitter sound, high-pitched with new madness. "What, so you can burn me entire?"

She opened her mouth to reply, and he interrupted her angrily; "No! Even if your mere touch didn't kill me, you've stolen my son. I want nothing from you. Especially your bloody charity!"

The rope snapped; Sulien moved, grabbing at the leaf-green pinions, pulling at handfuls of feathers. The face he raised to the angel's compassionate gaze was full of desperation. "Make him come in! You're stronger than him. You can make him be safe!"

"No," she said, smiling down on him with pity and resignation, her voice sad, "No, I can't do that. God is no rapist, Sulien. He forces no one. "

"But he's going to die!"

Oswy could hardly believe it - it was the voice of the boy he had met in the tower room; anger barely covering the tears. Disbelief overwhelmed him suddenly: "You came here to kill him yourself!" he shouted, and Adela hushed him, taking his shoulders gently, while she exchanged a weighted, adult look with Leofwine over his head.

They might all have been invisible to the young witch: He turned, his movements sharp with brittle energy, lunged forward. And Leofwine caught him just before he passed out into the darkness of the haunted room.

"No, my lord."

"Master!"

The Dark Ones were a hand's breadth away from Tancred now; more than a wall - an arch, a closing globe of vileness. Even the membranes of their wings were lined with blunted teeth, and a giggling came from them, demented with hunger.

"Master please! Before it's too late! Nothing can be worth this!" Leaning out, as far into danger as they would let him, Sulien pleaded with the doomed man.

"Oh," Tancred replied, with childish meanness, "You want me to do something for you now? Well I won't."

There was a rustle, an oozing scrape, the trap of darkness around the witch began to throb, as though it had become one creature, with one purpose. A tic of uncertainty briefly jumped in Tancred's eyes.

"Master! Please! I beg you!"

Satisfaction spread slowly over Tancred's face like decay. "I knew I would make you beg in the end," he said, and smiled.

Something in the charnel-yard of shapes began to laugh. Something reached out; brushed across the old man's forehead, leaving an acid-track of blood and dissolving gray hair. The kindly madness was swept away. He was screaming before the next talon touched him.

Niniel closed her wings. Oswy could see nothing but gentle green and gold; her robe like the sky, and her fists, clenched, bright as burning silver. Only the sounds came to him - laughter and agonized, unstoppable screaming; the damp rip of flesh; the crack of gristle and bone.

Lapped in the angel's other wing Sulien and Leofwine were invisible, but the knight's voice, with a terrible self-control of calm murmured in the spaces between horror, meeting silence. He yearned for its comfort, but he could not hear the words.

Adela stood behind him, her hands tightening painfully on his shoulders. He heard her breath coming in sobs, but he could not look at her. To turn to her would mean sharing his horror, making it real. It would mean showing her his face, appalled and guilty as it must be, and seeing hers, the same. They had both wanted this to happen. How could either look the other in the eye, knowing that?

The sounds stopped, eventually, tailing off into the rattle of death - blood choked - and a satisfied, slick withdrawal. Even within Niniel's protection Oswy could feel the demons go, by a lessening of his self-hatred, a lift of the heart.

The angel bent her head over them. "Leave this room and its horrors behind you," she said, whether in blessing or command he could not tell, "And I will give you sleep, if you desire it, and healing dreams."

Chapter 23

As though she read his mind, she smiled down at Oswy like a tree full of singing linnets. "Be comforted. It wasn't your choice which led to this - it was his. Now go. Go out into the clean air and don't look back."

She shepherded them to the open door, and at her glance, torches sprang into burning light down the long chill stairwell, making the bright colors of the painted walls glow.

"Go on," she said, like a mother pushing forward a tardy child. And when Adela took the first shaky step forward the angel raised her hand in blessing and suddenly was gone.

At once Sulien turned, drawn into the slaughter-house. In the flickering firelight he was alternately crimson and dark, like the walls. There was no sound at all but his footsteps, and the liquid drip and patter from the once white ceiling.

Reluctantly, Oswy watched him, and reluctantly the details of carnage printed themselves on his mind. The stench came out to him in drifts; bile and blood and ordure, making him retch miserably. Of the body there was very little left - only a limbless and open torso, and the head, peeled, the sky-blue eyes left lidless to stare out at an infinity of pain.

"You bastard!" Sulien spoke to it very softly, looking down, while the tension seemed to spread from him, locking up the night in one terrible overwrought stillness.

He will turn now, thought Oswy dizzily, in a flash of insight which made him afraid, with whatever madness this is still inside him. He'll force it down, and come back, and take out the memory on himself with a knife.

But then a drop of the dark rain fell stickily onto Sulien's cheek, and another onto his hand. He shuddered, and the brittle bloodstained calm shattered around him. Shouting - strings of curses - his face under the dirt and bruises gone berserker-pale, he kicked and stamped on the corpse until it was shapeless under his feet.

Suddenly, as it had begun, the fit passed. He fell to his knees beside the mess and clutched it. "I hate you," he said, very softly, very gently. Then with the bitter, racking ineptness of a man who has never cried in his life, he began to weep, hugging the dead thing to himself and rocking it as though it were a child he rocked to sleep.

Leofwine stirred, "Lady," he said, the dark voice a compound of pity and practical concern, "Are you in command of yourself enough to take the boy somewhere safe?"

"I think so," she replied, hushed and shaken, and stole one delicate arm around Oswy's waist, pulling him away from the red room and its smell. "We'll go to the guard-house. Nowhere in the keep seems fit somehow."

"Good," he said soberly. "Go now then, I'll deal with this." And as Oswy stumbled willingly away down the long bright staircase, he heard the knight's footfalls in the room above, wary and quiet.

It's over, he thought with surprise, *really over*! And exhaustion settled on him suddenly, like a weight of warm blankets, so he was hardly aware of reaching the shelter, or of lying down on a guard's pallet beside the empty hearth.

Chapter 24

Chapter Twenty four

Adela awoke from a dream of water and lay, feeling clean and content. Her blanket was a green cloak, lined with bear-skin, thick and tawny in the fire's amber glow. As she lay, touching the memories of last night with wincing caution, finding herself pleased, and surprised and guilty at how little they hurt her, the dawn light washed in through the arrow-slits white as sea-foam.

She brought her recollection up to covering the boy with the guard's blankets, sinking onto a pallet herself, thinking it was far too cold to sleep, and then nothing.

The boy, Oswy, was still asleep. Swinging up, putting her bare feet down on the stone floor with an icy jolt which was almost pleasant - it said so loudly 'You are still alive' - she saw him, curled up improbably, one arm flung wide, his face full of a child's proper innocence.

What a blessing, she thought, Niniel had given them with her gift of sleep. Now all that blood and darkness seemed past, dealt with, unable to reach out and sully this silver dawn; this new day.

Quietly, pulling the borrowed cloak more closely about her, she rose and looked around. On the hearth, over the newly made fire, a cauldron of tepid water hung heating, and four or five smooth stones nestled like phoenix eggs in the red heart of the blaze. There was a mess of cold water and oatmeal soaking in a leather bucket by the wall, the fire-irons stacked beside them, so she, or whoever woke first, could add the glowing stones and make porridge almost instantly.

The sight of it all made her smile. Someone was caring for them well, and the evidence of this little decency heartened her.

A wash of gold had entered the dawn light as she looked around. The scent of lifting mist curled briefly through the smoke, bringing hints of wet leaves and a wild, clean sky. It would be good, she thought, to walk on the palisade and let the freshness of a new morning fill her while she welcomed the sun.

Opening the guard-room's iron-bound door she found, Leofwine, fast asleep on a bed of straw which smelled strongly of the stables. He was guarding them even while he slept; like a favored retainer of the days of heroes - or a mastiff-dog.

His delicacy - in refusing to enter the room of a lady even to collapse in sleep on the floor - amused and touched her, and she looked down on him with tenderness.

How filthy he was! The thought came unbidden. His hands and face were brown with dried blood, purple with bruises, the shoulders of his tunic were torn and stained, and the wine-colored cloak in which he was wrapped - too short for him - was in places almost as brown as the mud in which his left hand lay.

Did she look that bad, she wondered, and lifting her palms into the light she saw she did. But the washing water was not yet warm, and the pale fathoms of blue and citrine sky still beckoned. So, careful not to disturb his well-earned rest, she edged past the sleeping knight and climbed the wide stairs up to the walkway, the slight warmth of wood welcome under her bare feet.

Sulien was there before her, standing, looking out as she had wished to, while the heaving shapes of the peaks began to show fallow and pale green, and in the forest the leaves kindled into an amber and ochre glow. She saw him as she stepped out onto the platform, and balked, remembering last night. Fear and embarrassment held her still for a moment, and she watched him warily, trying to judge whether it was safe to approach.

In the level rays of clear light he seemed almost to shine - his tunic blue as polished lapis, his drying hair like fired gold against the pale sky. At first, against all reason, she felt he had been transformed somehow; illumined. Then she laughed at herself - he had had time to wash and put on clean clothes, that was all.

The laugh, hushed though it was, turned him to look at her, and something in his face - a perilous calm, like dark water lying under ice - changed her mind again. A difference nagged at her, but she could not say what it was. She saw that he had washed, with the dirt, every bruise and injury off his face, and the strangeness of such sudden healing robbed her of speech.

With an effort she came forward and stood quietly near him, looking out on an achingly familiar landscape. The recognized shapes of her manor made grim bulks of responsibility and duty emerge from her peace like the harsh bones of the Fells pushing through the thinning mist, but still over it all pale sunlight shone.

Chapter 24

She became aware of Sulien's hand on the parapet beside her own - the white skin unblemished, the wrist unscarred. He was leaning too, with no apparent pain, on the arm she had seen broken last night. A question surfaced, but she had no idea how to ask it, and at the same time he said, pointing; "There's soapwort growing by the wall there, and your horse is in the stables with a clean dress in her saddlebags. The water should be hot by now."

"You did it all?" She didn't mean her tone to be incredulous, but she had not imagined he could be so thoughtful.

Still he did not look at her, and, repentant, she said, sympathetically, "You must have walked all night to get the horses."

"No. I called them." His glance touched her briefly, slid back to the blue, far hills. "I called your servants too, but they had run further, they'll be a little longer returning."

It was inescapable now, the question. "But your magic?" she asked tentatively, "I thought."

"So did I."

Mist smoked up from the forest in gilded elvish spirals which made Adela's chest tighten with remembered desires. The sun flashed from the puddles in the muddy bailey below like scattered coins, valuable but prosaic. She knew she had a choice to make, but just at this moment she could not bear to make it. Thrusting it aside, she answered the puzzlement in Sulien's voice, reached out to reassure. "Do you know the story of Marcellus and Fortunata?"

His glance was longer this time, curious.

"Only what Tancred taught me: God made him give up his wife to the fires. As a test."

"But he didn't!" In her earnestness she actually touched his hand. He drew it away, but without loathing, and looked at her steadily, with a frown.

"When the Empire turned from magic to the Church," she explained, cautiously, "They said it was God's will that all the witches be burned. But Marcellus fled with his mage-wife, refusing to give her up. She escaped him and came back - she said if it was God's will she die, then she didn't want to live."

"What happened to her?"

"They had her in witch-bracelets - like the ones on you - but they still couldn't light the fire. And while they were pouring more oil on the kindling the Archbishop pelted into the square in his bedclothes - woken from a dream -

shouting 'Stop! This woman is justified! She has sacrificed her life and her talent to God. Now he gives it back!' She went into a nunnery, and used her magic for healing, and defending the holy places. But Marcellus never saw her again."

"What you let go of you may keep. What you try to keep will be taken away." The witch-lord drew the moral out easily as a court bard. A slight, regretful smile saddened his face. He turned back to his contemplation of the unstained land. "I think I understand that."

His voice was very gentle. It made her wonder if she had dismissed him too easily; perhaps there was more to him than power, passion and violence.

"My master told me," he said, "'If you want a thing, take it. Grasp it and never let go. The more it struggles the more you tighten your grip.'"

He laughed, ruefully. "And at the end," he said, "My master had nothing. Nothing at all. But he couldn't even let go of that."

Adela shivered, wiped dew and dirt from her face - her skin cold and slick as stone. "You loved him, didn't you?" she said impulsively, and did not know if she felt disgust or pity. He looked at her with surprise, and away again quickly. One hand strayed to twist the crystal ring on his finger.

After a little while he answered, quietly, "For twelve years he was my life."

A fleeting smile and a shrug, as though none of this mattered very much, "He was Mother, Father, Teacher... everything. And he was not always only what you've seen. There used to be more."

"How do you feel? Now he's gone?"

"I don't know." He shook his head, again with a rueful laugh, and fell silent. Finally, with a shiver of sympathy, she placed the difference she had sensed in him - it was peace, the peace of an empty place.

Below, sharp in the deserted silence, came the creak and thump of the door; voices speaking comfortably, still muffled by sleep.

"Finally!" With a quicksilver speed which reminded her painfully of Prince Gennan, the witch's mood shifted at once, seeming now all action and humor. Adela shook her head at him, tired of pondering how little she knew him and, yearning for warmth, she led the way down the echoing wooden steps.

"I have a job for that boy, before he thinks of getting clean. Oswy!"

Chapter 24

The child looked up, quick and nervous, like any peasant hailed by his lord, or any son by his father. It was good, Adela thought, to see him look so normal.

"You can swim, can't you?" Sulien delivered his orders briskly, as though no horror had ever touched him, but the subject of his words gave Adela pause. "I want the scepter of Varian brought out of the moat," he was saying, "If you've been attending to all those spells of Fetching and Finding I've taught you, you should have no trouble in locating it."

Adela had a vision of them all stooping, bracing their backs against the burdens of the world and, after a little reprieve, taking them up again. She sighed and went into the warmth of the little room. It was time she faced her own life again. Time to choose.

The gown she pulled from the sweet, musty-scented depths of her saddle-bags, almost made the choice for her - it had come from Shining Tor. Dusk-pink, heavy and soft, with a texture like mixed silk and fur, and embroidery in thread the exact color of the dawn sunlight. When she ran it through her fingers the scent of snowdrops and long grass under dew lifted from it, driving the smoke and tallow of the guard-house even out of memory.

Washing away blood and filth, and putting on that gown was like climbing out of a dungeon pit into the light of a spring morning. It filled her with yearning for the land from which it came; the endless surprise, and delight and confusion of it. And for Gennan, for the Icewolf, of course. She tried to pretend she didn't want to fly back to him like a linnet to its cage, but she was too honest. He tempted her, there was no denying it.

Perhaps it would be better then, she thought heavily, to stay here; make it plain to the king that she was not dead; she still owned these lands, these people, and he could not just dispose of them as he wished. What was to stop him from giving them to some other tyrant, some baron almost as bad as the cruel old man who had them last? Nothing, but her, and she had a duty to protect them.

Yet... She stood suddenly, strode to the fire and picked out the red-hot stones with frowning concentration. The hiss and snap as they hit the cold water was like the frustrated protest of her heart.

Yet what could she do? The king would marry her where he wished, giving her away like a prize to whomever he chose. How could she protect anyone by staying? And she also had a duty to the elves.

The food was warm. She dug in the battered oak chest and brought out two mismatched bowls and a platter, then she opened the door and called the men in.

"I have been thinking." Sulien sat beside her on the steep shelving bank of the moat watching, with vague amusement, his apprentice's ungainly attempts at diving in the muddy water. The sun had strengthened into autumnal gold and it was pleasant to be sitting in its warmth. In this gentled mood Adela found the witch's company almost calming. His silence, up until now, had certainly been welcome while she wrestled with her dilemma.

"I thought," he said, and bowed his golden head to stare at the grass in front of his feet. The bright tail of his hair slid over one shoulder, baring the cream-colored skin of his neck. In a flash of amusement she wondered how many ladies of the court would kill to have his complexion, and it was a moment before she could listen seriously to what he said.

When she did, it staggered her.

"So I thought we should get married." He looked up just in time to catch her recoil, her gasp of shock, and turned away as quickly as if she had slapped him. "You should think about it," he said, doggedly.

"I... I'm sorry? I..." Marry him? Her mind reeled at the thought while she tried to school her face into politeness. It was something she had never imagined having to contemplate.

"I don't think you have understood me," he went on, coolly. There was no sign to show he was greatly insulted by her shock, no apparent hurt in his voice, and she was comforted. "I'm proposing this as a solution to some of our problems."

He looked up, at Oswy, who was for the fourth or fifth time washing away a handful of weeds and sludge. She was thankful he did not look at her.

"You want to go back to the Icewolf," Sulien said quietly, his tone one of practicality. She let herself glance at him, and again saw nothing to trouble her. "And I have no use for a wife."

He met her gaze then, challenging her reaction. She could not help letting him see it was relief.

"But you need a good steward for your land." He smiled with a bitter twist which somehow suited him - "And I need villeins to work mine."

Chapter 24

Some persuasive urgency broke the indifference now. "I would be a good landlord," he said. "If you've seen my manor you know that."

Her heartbeat steadied, though her thoughts raced: It was, she supposed, a solution. "You'd really let me go? Go and live in Elfland?"

There was a certain mischief in his brown eyes when he answered, as though he welcomed this chance to avenge his wounded pride. "The sooner the better."

Present the king with a fait accompli, she wondered. It had its attractions. With faint discomfort she acknowledged them all: It provided her with freedom, her people with protection. It might even be pleasant to have someone to talk to in this world, someone who would not scoff at or disbelieve her tales of elves. It would leave her a refuge, somewhere human to come back to.

Only - it seemed her heart shriveled within her - if she married him there would be no marrying Gennan. *Just as well*, said a ruthless voice within her. *He is an angel! Now I know it, I know marriage with him is sacrilege!*

"But," she wriggled with embarrassment on the long grass, picked at the bright stitches of her hem, "Children? Heirs?"

"Over there." Following the turn of his head she saw the peasant boy, Oswy, grimed from head to toe, dripping, huddled over a gleam in his hands like a beggar over his bowl.

"Him? But..."

"There will be no others." She had thought before how terrible his honesty was; how he drew it out of himself like a chipped stone blade. She found herself unable to meet his eyes. "Knowing what I am," he was saying, with measured bleakness, "what I like, I couldn't inflict that on anyone. I made a vow. I don't propose to break it."

The child was standing now, looking over at them with uncertainty in his crow-black gaze. Reluctantly she acknowledged his intelligence; a certain grace, now he was out of the water; his bravery, and the pleasing loyalty he showed. It was, after all, not bad material.

"Let me think," she said eventually, and rising gave him a smile of hard-won kindness. "Give me a fortnight; to speak to your tenants and mine; to think."

She turned away, and conscience stabbed her. She owed him at least the same honesty as he had given. "Forgive me," she said, "For reacting so badly. It's just..."

But when she tried to pin down the distaste she felt for him, to explain it, the words would not come. "That man killed my brother," she said, at last. "And you loved him, and love him still. He was your master. It is very hard for me to trust you, knowing that."

"You are wise," he said, without rancor, and beckoned to his boy.

She slipped away thankfully and wandered for a long time through the empty rooms and deserted gardens of her childhood home, thinking.

* * *

The rod in Oswy's hand was cold, colder than the water or the faint breeze against his soaked skin. He did not like the touch of it - it was as though it was watching him. But the stone! So beautiful! So full of light and distance; a window into a cleaner world. It was like the light in the angel's eyes when she had looked at him; pure, untouchable, healing. He could drown in it.

"Oswy!"

The summons brought him back from crystal halls, palaces built of light. The smell of the earth - pondweed, and apples from the orchard - was flung to him like an anchor. He ran to his master in relief. Beautiful, this thing was and sinister, and powerful. More than he could deal with. Let Sulien take care of it. He would know what to do.

He held it out, and it blazed in the morning light like a captured sun.

"Here!" he exclaimed, and grinned up at the blond man. How nice it was, he thought suddenly, to be back to normal - with nothing more to be frightened about than a hasty temper and the occasional slap. Maybe they would even be able to get back to lessons? The Fetching spell had certainly not gone as well as he intended.

"Put it in this," Sulien drew a square of cloth-of-gold out of his pouch; a square embroidered with the symbols of his manor church, the decoration sparse but flowing, in the Sceafn style. "I don't want to touch it," he said.

One or two threads of dead hair clung to the cloth-of-gold, and there were ancient creases in it, where it had been folded around a face. Oswy

Chapter 24

dropped the scepter into the center of it gingerly, recognizing with shocked glee the grave-wrapping of an embalmed saint. It seemed appropriate, somehow. But what on earth had Father Paul said!

"What are we going to do with it?" he asked boldly.

"God knows!" Sulien shook his head and sighed, tucking the thing away as though it scorched him even through the cloth.

"Find some way of putting it out of harm's reach," he said, with an almost inaudible touch of reluctance. "Maybe take it back to where Tancred found it."

He smiled suddenly, that rare, genuine smile of his, and shoved Oswy, not ungently, toward the keep. "I'll think about it. Go get washed. We're going home."

"It's really all over, isn't it," said Oswy, sharing the gladness, looking forward to food, his own room, the cramped writing of some learned palimpsest. "Everything's back to normal?"

"Everything's..." Sulien's head snapped up suddenly, the reassurance dying on his lips. Oswy was aware of it an instant later; the flying thunder of a horse in wild gallop. A presence was coming. Something familiar, in panic and haste.

He recognized the aura just as the young man came riding breakneck out of the trees.

"Hugo!" Sulien called out in surprise.

"My lord!" There were rope galls about the Holmr's swarthy wrists, he was unshaven, wild as his horse. "I had to escape them! I rode as soon as I could! My lord! Father thinks you have bewitched me! He's raised an army! He's besieging your house even now!"

Sulien laughed, loud and joyously. "Yes!" he said, with satisfaction, "Now everything's back to normal!"